# HOMBRECITO'S
# WAR

W. Michael Farmer

Llumina Press

Requests for permission to make copies of any part of this work should be mailed to Permissions Department, Llumina Press, PO Box 772246, Coral Springs, FL 33077-2246

ISBN:   PB  1-59526-082-X
        HC  1-59526-083-8

Printed in the United States of America by Llumina Press

Library of Congress Cataloging-in-Publication Data

Farmer, W. Michael, 1944-
 Hombrecito's war / W. Michael Farmer.
    p. cm.
 ISBN 1-59526-082-X (pbk. : alk. paper) -- ISBN 1-59526-083-8 (hardcover : alk. paper)
  I. Title.
PS3606.A725H66 2005
813'.6--dc22                                                    2005006744

To Corky,

My Wife and Best Friend

# PREFATORY NOTE

"The pursuit of truth, not facts, is the business of fiction."
— Oakley Hall, Prefatory Note to *Warlock*

This book is a novel. The characters Yellow Boy, Rufus Pike, Henry Fountain after age eight, Jack Stone, Red Tally, Charlie Bentene, Roberta Gonzalez, and Sarah Darcy are fabrications. The Fountain family members, Oliver Lee, Pat Garrett, and most of the characters and events leading up to the disappearance of Albert and Henry Fountain in the desert near White Sands, New Mexico Territory are real.

Who was responsible and what actually happened to Albert and Henry Fountain have been fiercely debated for over a hundred years. Those who knew the true facts went to their graves without telling their story, or if they did, historians have not believed them. Logic dictates that eight-year-old Henry Fountain died with his father. However, life, filled with unexpected events and inconsistencies, is not logical. What if Henry survived...This story of Henry's survival is constructed from actual events and fictional ones to create a myth for what might have been, and, for what devotees of western legends wish had been.

— W. Michael Farmer
Smithfield, Virginia
31 December 2004

# Acknowledgements

Bruce Kennedy provided many helpful comments on the manuscript and enlightening information from his historical research on the time and place of this story. Robin Smith provided an excellent review and edit of the manuscript. Original cover art is by Sara Fisher. I thank them all for much help and support in the writing of Hombrecito's War.

# PROLOGUE

It is a historical fact that Henry Fountain and his father, Albert, vanished one cold, dreary afternoon in the Tularosa Basin near White Sands, New Mexico Territory, 1 February 1896. Experienced lawmen, Mescalero Apache trackers, and ranch hands who rode the basin range every day searched weeks for some sign of them. They found nothing. Local ranchers and townspeople did not doubt that eight-year-old Henry and tough, aggressive Albert had been murdered. Speculation had it that their bones were hidden away in some deep crevice in the Sacramento or the San Andres Mountains, buried under a cairn on the top of a lonesome ridge, or consumed by fire or lye.

Albert Fountain, an attorney, politician, and newspaper publisher had many enemies. Near the top of the list was a widely respected rancher, Oliver Lee, who battled with Fountain often over range justice and politics. Lee lived by an unwritten Texas range code that often clashed with the New Mexico Territorial law Fountain vigorously enforced. Lee was a Democrat. Fountain was a Republican. Dirty tricks were common on both sides in rough and tumble New Mexico politics. On the day he and Henry disappeared, Albert was returning from Lincoln, New Mexico Territory, with thirty-two indictments of small ranchers, itinerant cowboys, and known bandits for cattle rustling. One of those indictments was for Oliver Lee. In 1899 Sheriff Pat Garrett, the man famous for killing Billy the Kid in 1881 and who was brought out of retirement in Texas to solve the case, testified against Oliver Lee and two of his friends for the murders.

A trial was held in the picturesque little mining town of Hillsboro, New Mexico Territory, at the base of the Black Range, and over fifty miles north of Las Cruces where the Fountain family and their supporters lived. Lee was supported by a large group of his family and friends who came to Hillsboro from all over the territory. He was defended by another Fountain enemy, Albert Fall, who became Secretary of the Interior under Warren Harding. After eighteen days, including several nights of testimony from a long list of witnesses, the case was given to the jury. The jury deliberated eight minutes, and found Lee not guilty. Thereafter, the countryside was divided into two factions that have never stopped arguing and literally fighting over the guilt or innocence of Oliver Lee in the Fountain murders. By 1951, only two men knew the true story of the murders and the hard, bloody retribution that followed. They weren't talking.

# HOMBRECITO'S
# WAR

# 1951

## Las Cruces, New Mexico

# THE REVELATION

H enry Grace had a Jesus glow. His charisma radiated from him like the golden light around Jesus in medieval paintings. As a physician, his shy and respectful manner, gregarious stories and jokes, and prince-of-the-desert face with the kind eyes made him loved by women, enjoyed by men, and instant friends with children. He was admired and respected by the entire spectrum of El Paso and Las Cruces society, which included wealthy Latino patróns, Mexican laborers, businessmen, politicians, professional colleagues, ranchers, cowboys, and Mescalero Apaches. Men of all bents crossed the street to shake his hand and speak to him, sought his quiet joviality in bars and restaurants, and copied his style. Women saw the warmth in his eyes, knew the strength and gentleness of his hands, imagined they heard passionate intimacy in his voice and passed on the latest gossip about his affairs. His quiet manners bespoke an easy-going gentleman. It was well known, however, that in any dispute, he never backed down.

Exposed to the bright New Mexico sun for nearly sixty-four years, his warm, black marble eyes were etched at the corners by dry washes of crow's feet. Short salt-and-pepper hair and a brilliant white mustache framed his Latino or perhaps Indian face, which was the color of old tanned gun leather. A thin, long-healed, but evil-looking scar left a track from below his right eye to his chin. It passed through his mustache clearly dividing it into two pieces that his vanity hid with the clever use of a comb. Just missing his lips, it was the source of much speculation from dance partners or patients at his medical clinic. When they asked about the scar, he winked and said, "I got it playing cowboy when I was a kid." Henry was not a good liar. They didn't believe him for an instant, but they weren't foolish enough to push for more details. They saw a fire smoldering behind his eyes and the dry wash wrinkles deepening to form a hard, unyielding squint as he stared back at them unblinking.

In better physical condition than most men forty years younger, Henry ran seven or eight miles a day, five days a week, thirty years before jogging became a national obsession. With his smooth steady gait, his head appeared to be gyro-stabilized as it glided effortlessly in seven-minute miles above the creosote bushes and yuccas lining his running trails. Friends just marked it off as one of his eccentricities when they saw him running in the desert heat between Las Cruces and the Organ Mountains. Those same friends would have considered him far beyond eccentric had they known he made his runs with a mouthful of water he never swallowed until he crossed his finish line.

Henry was the bachelor married men envied. The gossips claimed nearly any unmarried woman in Doña Ana County was his for the taking, and he had taken quite a few. On Friday nights, cowboys and townies, eager to prove their manhood with the ladies, knew that at the Bar F Bar they had a true woman-pleasing model in Henry. Henry sat with them around bare wood tables covered with long-necked beer bottles, baskets of crunchy tortilla chips, and little bowls of flaming red tomato salsa. He slowly sipped Jack Daniel's bourbon straight-up from an octagonal lead crystal glass tumbler he kept stashed at the bar, smoked smooth dark-leaf Cuban cigars, told tales of the wild and wooly old days, and flirted with all the girls. Henry delighted in tilting his chair back, hooking a boot on the crosspiece, and watching young men work hard to wheedle women out of a trip home after closing time. Like birds in a mating dance, the women flitted from one prospect to the next, leaving first one supplicant then another disappointed.

Henry ruled the dance floor. Even when his partners were women less than half his age, he was a confident master envied by the younger men. Holding his lady at her waist, he effortlessly floated with her in a smooth western two-step as the band played "San Antonio Rose" or "Hey, Good Lookin'." During the three-four time of a slow waltz, he swung his partner in a close, dreamily intimate rhythm that kept their bodies in perfect harmony. After the band played the last song of the last set, Henry, receiving grins, light applause, and outright envy from his younger comrades, usually went home with the lady of his choice. Having known his virility, relaxed poise, and perfect manners in their bedrooms, those same ladies came back the next Friday hoping for another dance with Henry. Invariably, they preferred Henry's ancient trim body to that of the most muscular testosterone-filled cowboy or the most suave fraternity man or tweedy professor from New Mexico A&M.

On Saturday evenings, Henry closed his office early and headed to the Hacienda del Sol. Unlike the Bar F Bar, the atmosphere in the Hacienda, a restaurant and nightclub, was cool and calm. The ambiance was soft candlelight, a smooth murmur of quiet voices, the occasional tinkle of sparkling glasses, and quiet well-mannered Mexican waiters who instantly appeared at the first sign of a request. The Hacienda was filled with middle-aged men wearing two-hundred-dollar suits, Arrow shirts, straight neckties, and smoking Chesterfield cigarettes. Their women wore expensive perfumes and bright dresses with modest hemlines. These were the men and their wives who guided the university, owned the stores, ran the government, and fired the rockets at White Sands Proving Grounds. Although the crowd was much more dignified than the one at the Bar F Bar, it often pursued Henry to enliven its banal conversations with his unlimited supply of jokes and tales about the old days.

At the Hacienda, he played trumpet in an amateur swing band made up of local attorneys, physicians, and professors from New Mexico A&M. The band filled many evenings with arrangements from Glen Miller, Tommy Dorsey, and Les Brown. Henry had the lungpower of Louis Armstrong, even if he didn't have the lip. With his cheeks puffed out and the veins standing out at his temples, he could hold a note longer than any horn player in Las Cruces or El Paso. Often invited to play the opening horn at the bullfights in Ciudad Juarez, across the river from El Paso, he rarely turned down the invitation. The drama and action of a life-and-death struggle, in which the larger, stronger, deadlier animal was defeated by the smaller, faster, smarter one made his heart thump and race.

On Sundays Henry went to shooting matches in a large arroyo northeast of town. Every marksman in the southwest knew Henry Grace. He rarely lost in long-gun contests using targets at ranges exceeding three hundred yards. Men, young and old, stared in disbelief at the tight two-inch diameter circles full of half-inch holes he consistently put in targets with his thundering seventy-five-year old Model 1874 Sharps rifle. It shot .45-70 cartridges that were nearly two inches long and projected about an ounce of lead capable of passing through a half-ton buffalo at a thousand yards. The weapon had a thirty-two-inch barrel mounted on a fine-grained walnut stock waxed to high polish and trimmed in German silver. It had double set triggers that allowed Henry to set the firing trigger to such sensitivity that the cocked hammer fell when Henry just imagined he wanted the ten-pound weapon to fire. Holding cartridges between his long fingers for fast reloading,

3

Henry loaded and fired the old single-shot breechloader faster than most men could lever a Winchester. Even when telescopic sights were allowed, he often won five-hundred-yard matches using iron sights. Some speculated the competitors wouldn't even shoot against him if he had used a telescope on the old rifle.

Henry spent weekdays as a skilled general practitioner setting broken bones, delivering babies, identifying and fighting common diseases, easing elderly people into their last years, and counseling alcoholics. He refused to send his poor patients a bill when times were hard. Even in good times, when the chile and the vegetable crops were plentiful and the wages were good, Henry billed them only enough to salve their pride. Schoolteachers from every grade in every school knew that if they had a poor student in need - for anything - Henry never said no. There was an unspoken understanding that his clients never asked for more than they needed and he always gave more than they required.

The Mescalero Apache people living on their reservation at the foot of the majestic mountain, Sierra Blanca, eighty miles northeast of Las Cruces, knew Henry always came when they asked for his help. He was the only doctor they trusted and their needs often were a major drain on his time. When the calls came from Mescalero, appointments in his Las Cruces clinic were delayed and waiting rooms filled with patients were sent home. They were told to come back later, or to expect a visit at their homes when he got back. Henry never complained and neither did his patients. Friends of the tribe even claimed the Apaches loved him like a relative, but they had to confess they had no idea why. Others said it was probably because Father Braun, the Catholic priest who had lived with them nearly forty years, told Henry that purgatory wouldn't hold his womanizing and carousing against him if he helped the Apaches.

Therefore, Roberta Gonzales, Henry's nurse, receptionist, and bookkeeper for over twenty years, was not surprised to receive a telephone call one morning from Mescalero tribal headquarters. A smooth feminine voice said rhythmically in precise English with a Spanish cadence and accent, "I'm Maria Estrada? At tribal headquarters in Mescalero New Mexico? Is this Nurse Gonzales?"

"Yes?" Roberta answered in exasperation. The office was a beehive filled with patients. The adults were continually getting up to get a *Life* magazine from a big rack Henry kept under the front of her receptionist's desk. They sat down to flip through the pictures, then, just ten minutes later, would get up for another issue. Children were banging wooden blocks and toys on the floor or yelling at each other and generally being ignored or undisciplined by their parents. And, she was trying to pry a medical history out of an old Mexican man who didn't speak good English and whose brain worked slowly, very slowly.

The voice floated out of the telephone: "I'm calling for John Burning Tree? John asked that I tell Dr. Grace his friend Yellow Boy is very sick? John thinks maybe Señor Yellow Boy is dying? He says Dr. Grace should come quick!"

Roberta quickly glanced about but couldn't find the notepad she usually used for telephone messages. It was buried under the papers strewn all over her reception desk. She grabbed a prescription pad and jotted down the note. Frowning in concern as she scribbled the note and tore it off the pad, she spoke into the heavy black receiver clamped between her shoulder and ear. "Okay! Muchas gracias, Señorita. He's with a patient right now. Please let John know that I'll give Dr. Grace the message just as soon as he's free."

"That will be fine," said the smooth rhythmic voice. "I'll tell John. Buenos dias, Señora Gonzales."

Within seconds after Roberta hung up, the clinic door burst open, a Mexican child in his father's arms. The boy was screaming and kicking a bloody foot up and down. As the man, almost black from years of work in the chili fields, walked self-consciously toward her desk, she jumped up to guide him to an examining room. Her quick start scattered her papers all over the floor. She motioned for him to follow her as she hurried down the softly lighted, surgical-green, hallway to an examining room. The waiting room behind them got very still. Patients sitting in their chrome and black leather chairs leaned forward and stared after the intruders disappearing down the hallway. Children stopped playing and scampered on all fours across the black-and-white checkerboard tile floor to sit between the feet of their parents. Cowed by the wailing of one of their own and the trail of blood drops he left in the hallway, they forgot about their blocks, toys, and arguments.

Roberta took the child from the father who winced as if struck in the face at his child's wails of pain. She said in her most professional soothing voice, "Let's just sit him on the edge of this table." The burden of concern showing in the man's eyes prompted her to comfort him too. "He'll be fine, *senor*. Don't worry, *por favor*. Wait here. I'll be right back with the doctor *pronto*."

She stepped across the hallway, knocked on Henry's office door, cracked it open, and quickly stuck her head around the edge. A very pregnant young woman was listening attentively as Henry explained what to expect in her last trimester. Roberta didn't hesitate to butt in. "*Pardona me, señora*. Dr. Grace, we have an emergency with a child. He has a puncture wound, I think from a nail, in the ball of his left foot. Please come as soon as you can." Henry nodded and quickly finished the interview.

Roberta returned to the examining room and tried to soothe the youngster. Giving him a quick once-over, she saw the wound was deep but bled slowly. She filled a basin with warm water and began to tenderly wash his foot. The child's loud wails slowly turned to snuffles as she worked. They turned to wails again as she poured stinging alcohol on the puncture. Henry passed through the door and spoke calmly to the wide-eyed father, examined the wound, soothed the child back to snuffles, and gently felt for broken bones. He felt none, but he picked the child up, and, whispering comforting words in his ear, carried him two doors down the hallway to the x-ray machine just to be sure he had not missed any damage. X-rays soon verified the wound was a simple puncture and that no bones or major blood vessels were affected.

As Roberta dressed the wound, Henry put his hand on the father's shoulder and gave it a reassuring squeeze. "So *Chico* has a rough time at play, eh, *señor*? When I was a *muchacho* I hurt myself many times. *Que paso*?"

The sunburned field laborer would not look in Henry's eyes and stared at the floor. It was improper to look directly at the face of a patrón. When he answered, he spoke in a mixture of Spanish and English, common for bilingual Mexicans struggling to establish their place in the land of the Americans. "*Mi muchacho es en* the yard. He plays *con* his *hermanos* … his brothers. They play *bueno* together *patrón*. I build a shed *en* the yard por *mi señora's pollos* … her chickens, from scrap lumber I save from building a big tool shed *por Señor* Montoya. *Chico*, he steps on a long nail in a scrap of board I used on the shed. He knows not what bites him on the bottom of his foot. He thinks perhaps it is a snake. The sting, it scares him and he runs all over the yard on his heel to get away from it. He screams and cries. I am *muy* scared, *patrón*. I run after him, and I finally catch him. I see the board and pull it from his foot. I drive him here in my truck *pronto*! He cries all the way here. There is much fear *en mi* old Ford, *patrón*."

Henry nodded understandingly. "*Como se llamo, señor*?"

"*Me llamo, Jose Salazar, patrón*."

Henry shook his head. "*Señor* Salazar, I am your doctor, not your *patrón*." He pointed at his eyes with the index and forefinger of his right hand. "Look in *mi ojos, por favor*, when you speak with me, eh?" Lifting his head, Jose Salazar managed a smile of relief and nodded.

After a tetanus shot to the hip that made the child whine and a clean gauze bandage to protect the wound, Henry rubbed the boy's back as Roberta tided up from their work. "Stay off that wound and keep the bandage clean. Eh, *muchacho*?" The child snuffled back further tears and nodded. Jose, smiling with relief, swooped his boy up in his arms and carried him as if he weighed ten pounds, not sixty. Walking down the hall with Henry to the waiting room, he felt Henry slip some folded cash into his shirt pocket. Jose tried to give it back but Henry wouldn't take it.

"*Señor* Salazar, as a favor to me and my patients, buy the *muchacho* some shoes with strong soles. Make him wear them when the foot is well again in two or three weeks. *Por favor*, have your other sons pick up the old lumber scraps so they do not find a nail with their feet."

Jose Salazar's eyes lit up in gratitude, but he said, "Oh no, *patrón*...Uh, Dr. Grace. I'll buy the shoes *por mi muchacho*. I cannot pay you back for many months. I have no extra *dinero* until after the chilies are picked."

Henry shook his head and smiled. "No, it's okay if you wait many months, *señor*. Just pay me when you can, what you can. *Es importanté* to me that the *muchacho* have warm protected feet. *Comprendé*?"

Jose Salazar, his hands covered with calluses and scars, the father of nine children, respected by field bosses from El Paso to Albuquerque, and a king in his home, whispered with tears in his eyes, "*Gracias*, Dr. Grace, *gracias*."

The office soon returned to normal as Roberta reappeared at her desk, picked up the scattered papers, signed in new patients, and ushered an unending stream of them in to see the doctor.

It wasn't until the end of the day that she found the message from John Burning Tree, a corner of it peeping out from under the base of the big black telephone. When she saw it, her eyes grew wide. *Oh hell!* flashed in her mind. Fighting back tears, she grabbed the note and rushed from her desk down the hall to Henry's office. She practically ran through the open door, her smooth brown skin almost white with panic, despair filling her eyes.

"Oh! I'm such an idiot." In frustration she groaned, grit her teeth and stamped her foot. "I deserve to be fired. Please forgive me." She thrust the note toward him with a trembling hand, rubbing her throbbing temples with the other.

Henry sitting with his feet up on his desk, sipping a late-afternoon bourbon, the latest issue of *JAMA* on his lap, gazed calmly at her through the haze of smoke coming from an ancient briarwood pipe clamped under his brilliant white mustache. "Why? What's the matter? It can't be as bad as all that. Settle down now Bertie and tell me what's going on."

He stretched across the desk with a low groan telegraphed from his stiff joints. He took the note from her trembling hand and read it through the glasses perched crookedly at the end of his nose. *Yellow Boy very ill. Come quick. John Burning Tree.*

Without a word, Henry swung his stocking-covered feet to the floor and reached for the telephone. He tapped his fingers waiting for the rotor to click through the numbers to the tribal center office in Mescalero. He motioned Roberta to sit down in the chair next to his desk with an open palm waving toward the floor for her to calm down. He said in an easy rumble, "It's okay. It's okay! Now just calm down. The world's not going to stop turning because a telephone call is returned a few hours late. Nobody's perfect. It's gonna be all right. Just relax now."

Soon he said with restrained urgency, "Hello! This is Dr. Henry Grace. Is John Burning Tree nearby? Yes! Thank you! I can wait. Okay. Hurry please."

Henry put his hand over the mouthpiece to speak to Roberta while he held the receiver to his ear, "John's been there all day. She's gone to get him. It'll be okay, don't worry now."

Roberta sat in a chair in front of his desk chewing her lip. Henry reached for his glass of bourbon with his free hand and threw down the remaining Jack Daniel's in one gulp. He ran his fingers through his hair and squeezed the back of his neck to relieve the tension building in his shoulders.

They seemed to wait hours, but in five minutes John Burning Tree, breathless, spoke into the receiver at Mescalero. "Dr. Grace! Where are you, man?"

"I'm in Cruces, just got your message," he nearly shouted into the receiver. Calming himself, he said in a low apologetic rumble, "It's been real busy here today. I'm sorry I'm so late in calling. How's Yellow Boy?"

"I don't think he's so good. He said he was okay earlier today, but, I saw him spit blood this morning while he was splitting firewood then sit down like he was dizzy. He said he was tired and wanted to nap after we ate breakfast. Usually he goes for his walk up the canyon. I could tell he wasn't feeling so good. As soon as I got him in bed, I got Sara to come stay with him. I drove down here and had them call your office. Dr. Grace, he's nearly ninety years old and hasn't moved much since he went to bed. His breathing, it has bad wheezes and gurgles in it and he coughs so hard sometimes he gags trying to get his wind. He hasn't sounded right all day. I'm no doctor, but I think he's real sick and maybe close to dying. Can...can...you come quick?" John said in a wavering voice that needed immediate emotional support.

"I'll be there in less than three hours. I'm leaving right now. Give him hot tea if he's awake or a little whiskey with honey if he'll take it. Check his sputum for blood when he coughs. If he's feverish, keep him lightly covered by the fire and give him lots of water so he can sweat it out. I'll be there as soon as I can. Don't worry now. We'll get him fixed up."

"Okay Dr. Grace. *Muchas gracias*. We'll see you in a little while. *Adios*."

Henry put down the telephone, swung around in his wooden low-backed banker's chair, and grabbed his shiny black boots. As he pulled them on, he said over his shoulder, "Yellow Boy sounds in bad shape. I've got to get up there right away."

Roberta, the sorrow of the world in her face and its weight on her shoulders, said with tears streaming from her eyes, "I'm so sorry. I just don't know how I forgot and overlooked that message."

Henry waved his hand as though swatting away a fly. "Hush now. Everybody makes mistakes! With all the commotion from that child this morning it's a wonder you ever remembered it. Yellow Boy is a tougher than whip leather. I'll get up there and he'll proba- bly be sitting by the fire in that old slat-back chair of his, smoking a cigar. Call my patients for the next couple of days and reschedule. You go on home and get some rest. I should be back no later than day after tomorrow. If it looks like I might have to stay longer, I'll call you."

He stood up, thumped the floor as he stomped down on his boots, put on his Stetson with one hand and began buttoning his vest with the other. The Stetson was one of his prized possessions. It was black with a big flat brim. Like most cowboys, he wore his hat everywhere, even in his car, and sometimes at dinner. He pushed a big gold pocket watch into a vest pocket and its fob through a buttonhole. The watch chain held an exquisitely carved blue turquoise eagle mounted in silver de- scending with claws and wings extended. He was never without that eagle. He pulled on a heavily fringed buckskin jacket with fancy bead- work down the front. When the weather was chilly with calm winds in Las Cruces, as it was that day, it was often cold and windy at Mesca- lero. He checked his black bag, and after rummaging in the clinic refrigerator, threw in some vials of his most potent penicillin and some other bronchial infection medicines. Yellow Boy had been coughing for nearly a month. Henry was fearful the old man was tottering on the edge of pneumonia. Even with all the medicine Henry had prescribed over the past three weeks, Yellow Boy was only a little better.

Roberta watched Henry rush around his office for a moment before she raced to the front closet in the waiting room. She began pulling on her long wool coat and pulling out the bobbie pins that held her nurse's hat in place. Yellow Boy had been Henry's close friend for many years. The idea that she might be the reason Yellow Boy died without his best friend there to tell him good-by made her heartsick. Ready to travel, she came back to Henry's office, shaking her head. "No, sir! I won't let you go up there alone! I can get Juanita to call the patients. Please let me come with you. At least let me help make up for my negligence." She begged with her eyes floating on edge of tears and fists held tightly at her sides, "Please take me with you! Please?"

Henry smiled at his nurse of over twenty years. She was a very good one. Never married – too independent for local Mexican men – she was always on call anywhere, anytime Henry needed her. It didn't make any difference whether it was for patients or just for the comfort of intimate conversation. She had helped him at the reservation many times. The Apaches knew her by name and understood she was a significant part of Henry Grace's most potent medicine. They were always grateful for her help.

Roberta rarely made mistakes; Henry understood her compelling need for atonement. He wasn't at all reluctant for her to come with him if that's what she wanted. He would enjoy her company on the long drive to Mescalero and her medical support was always superb.

Henry grinned. "Okay, if that's what you want. Call Juanita while I get a couple more things, then let's get out of here!"

In five minutes, they were down the office steps and slamming the doors of his shiny, sky-blue Plymouth. It roared down the hard, washboard caliche road toward Route 70, bouncing them about in the front seat as it threw a rooster tail of dust into the still air and fading light. It was clear and getting colder in Las Cruces. With the sun fading behind the Florida Mountains on the horizon near Deming, the ground was rapidly giving up its heat and a diffuse patina of oranges, reds, and violets was glowing on the Organ Mountains above the shadow-filled desert. By the time they reached Route 70 and turned east toward San Augustin Pass, the car's heater had made it warm enough for Roberta to pull off her coat and help Henry off with his jacket.

Half an hour later, they stopped and filled up with gas at a Texaco station next to a brightly lighted restaurant in the little village of Organ, half way up the mountain to San Augustin Pass. Roberta took Henry's thermos to the restaurant filled with technicians and engineers from the Proving Grounds and had it filled with black, steaming coffee while he pumped gas. As she came out the restaurant door, she saw Henry standing by the car, one hand on the door handle. He appeared to be in a trance as he looked toward the glow of lights down in the Mesilla valley. Slowly turning his head, he stared for a long moment down the side of the dark mountains sweeping toward El Paso. As if awakening from a dream, he gave his head a quick little shake and turned to the gas pumps.

She hurried back to the car, practically running, desperate to arrive in Mescalero before Yellow Boy went to the grandfathers. Jerking open the door she practically jumped into her seat then slid the Aladdin Thermos under it for safekeeping. She knew how Henry drove when he was in a hurry.

A teenager with long greasy hair combed straight back and a face covered with pimples came out to pump gas. Henry, in a hurry, filled the car himself and then paid the boy who had stood shivering in the cold dark with his hands in his pockets. After hooking the hose back on the pump, Henry swung the Plymouth's door open and slid shivering under the steering wheel. Blowing on his hands, he glanced with a smile at Roberta as he asked, "Are you ready?"

She nodded and murmured, "Yes sir," as he cranked the engine and pulled the column-mounted gearshift into first gear. The Plymouth roared out of the service station with a vengeance up on to the steep, two-lane asphalt road leading to the Pass.

The car was warm and comfortable. As they topped the pass and saw range lights twinkling in the distance, Henry pulled his pipe and tobacco pouch from his vest pockets. Handing them to Roberta, he grinned. "Would you light my fire, Nurse Gonzalez?" It had taken her numerous trips across the Tularosa basin with Henry to see Apache patients in Mescalero before she learned to pack the bowl just right and light a good coal. She filled and tamped the fine, long-cut strands of Flying Dutchman into the ancient briar bowl, clamped it in her teeth, found matches in her purse, and lighted it for him. Tiny sparks fell from the bowl. She didn't own a nurse's uniform that close inspection wouldn't reveal tiny burn holes in the fabric across her lap. The smooth smoke scratched at the back of her throat as she puffed to make the pipe's bowl glow from a steadily growing, dull-red coal. Satisfied the tobacco was well lighted, she handed the pipe back to Henry, who took it smiling in gratitude.

She dug around in her purse, and found herself a smooth straight cigarette in a crushed pack of Lucky Strikes. Lighting up, she took a deep
draw, and, blowing it out the whistling vent window on her side, began to
relax. The drone of the engine made her drowsy; it would take at least
three hours to reach Mescalero. She fidgeted around in her seat for a few
minutes trying to stay awake, afraid she might doze off and let the old man
go to sleep too. She searched her mind for some topic of conversation that
might keep them occupied for the trip. As a moth drawn to a bright candle,
her long-held curiosity about his origins with old Yellow Boy floated in
through the smoke and the rush of whistling air.

"Do you want some hot coffee and a little conversation?"

Henry smiled. There was a knowing look in his eyes and questioning wrinkle on his brow. Roberta always started long early-morning
conversations at the office with that line. They were always fun. She
usually wanted his counsel on how to deal with a presumptuous boyfriend or an ornery family member.

"Sure. What's on your mind?" He cracked his vent window wider
to let in a little more fresh air and to vent out the accumulating smoke
that made his eyes water.

Roberta reached under the seat, feeling for the smooth warm surface of the thermos. Henry kept a couple of cups in the glove box she
found just as the Plymouth reached the pass ridgeline. After straining a
few seconds to get the stopper loose from a tightening applied by an
overly zealous waitress, Roberta carefully poured half a cup for Henry,
then one for herself. They first blew then sipped boiling hot brew and
stared off into the dark space at the end of the headlights.

From the top of the pass a velvety black universe stretched out before them. The gusting wind blowing through the Organs made Henry
work to keep the car tacking in the right hand lane down the backside
of the pass. Lights from late traffic leaving the proving grounds were a
moving constellation along Route 70 stretching back toward Alamogordo. Proving Ground facility lights twinkled unmoving on the
black desert floor below them. With stars appearing above them and the
star-like range lights below them, Roberta imagined they were flying
through the universe in one of the spaceships she heard the government
tested on that very range.

As Henry took another sip of his coffee, she said, "You and Yellow
Boy have been friends a long time. How did you come to know him?"

Henry swallowed a couple more noisy slurps. He took, she thought,
an extra long time to answer a simple question. He pushed on the gas
pedal a little harder, making the Plymouth go five miles an hour faster

as it hummed smoothly into the black night. Not speaking, he was, for all appearances, a thoughtful college professor contemplating a lecture question as he finished his coffee and handed his cup back to her.

Taking a long draw from the old briar pipe, he blew the smoke toward the vent window before he said, "Well, fact of the matter is I've known Yellow Boy since I was a small boy."

"Oh?" Arched eyebrows framed her growing curiosity. "You know, I've never heard you talk about your boyhood in the twenty years I've worked for you. Did you grow-up on a ranch near here or somewhere else?" Now that she thought about it, it was very curious that he never mentioned relatives or childhood memories. For most men, they were a favorite topic of conversation – next to women or baseball.

Henry sighed and snapped his teeth against the rush of the cool window air. There was a little argumentative shake of his head as he hunched his shoulders and cocked his ear to one side as though listening to some inner voice. He took a deep breath, started to say something, thought better of it, and just cleared his throat. For a while he stared straight ahead. Roberta watched him with narrowed eyes, a cat eager for a mouse of information about to scamper out of its hole. *It must be good*, she thought. She had never seen Henry hesitate to tell her anything.

Finally, he glanced at her, his eyes glittering in the light from the dashboard instruments, his hands locked in a white-knuckle death grip on the steering wheel. He said in a low voice she strained to hear, "Without getting into a long story, I'll tell you that Yellow Boy saved my life when I was a little boy. He helped me find justice when justice was missing, and he adopted me when I was almost alone in the world. I can never forget how much I owe him."

Suddenly, Roberta wasn't sleepy anymore. Her cat waiting for the little mouse of information to scamper out, tensed to pounce on a much bigger rat. "I never knew that! Tell me how it happened! Please? Come on now don't leave me twisting in the wind. You can tell me." She smiled coyly at him, knowing Henry liked to tell a good story, and he rarely turned down anything she asked.

Henry stared straight ahead, lost in his thoughts. A big tumbleweed, a six-foot ball of dry, brittle weeds and twigs appeared in the headlights startling him out of his reverie. He had no time to swerve as they passed through it with a crash of small sticks flying against the windshield and a large piece sailing over the car intact. "Damn!" he said in disgust. "I hate to hit those things. You never know if an animal or somebody might be behind them."

Roberta was not to be ignored. "Don't ignore the question now. Come on. Let's hear it. Tell me about you and Yellow Boy," she coaxed, flirting and coquettish. "Surely he's not called Yellow Boy because of some act of cowardice? Is he..."

Henry laughed and shook his head. "Oh no, not hardly. Yellow Boy is a true warrior. He's no coward by any standard anywhere. He's a real, honest-to-God, eye-for-an-eye Indian. He even scouted a while for General Crook when Crook was chasing Geronimo all over hell and half of Arizona." He paused, stepping up to the edge of his revelation, and then backing away. "All right. I'll tell you the story. You probably won't believe it. It's okay if you don't. I won't blame you if you don't, but it's true. If I tell you, you have to give me your solemn oath not to repeat it – ever. If you do, I'll say you're lying and swear I never told you any such thing. Promise?"

Roberta's cat waiting for the mouse was now a tiger pacing up and down in a cage, wanting red meat. What could the beloved Dr. Henry Grace possibly have to hide? Everyone knew Dr. Grace; there were no secrets about Dr. Grace. This had be something extraordinary. *Maybe*, she thought, *he's had an affair with a politician's wife or murdered somebody and Yellow Boy got him out of it*! She knew she might have an ethical dilemma to keep from spreading the story, but she could and would keep quiet about it.

"Yes, sir, I promise." She said with her most earnest and serious face. "You know I keep my promises. Unless you release me from my vow, your words will go no further than this Plymouth."

Henry nodded, biting his lower lip. He gazed off into the darkness toward the low glow in the sky above Alamogordo and the inky blackness of the Sacramento Mountains just behind it. Roberta turned in the seat so she could watch the side of his face in the glow from the dashboard. She pulled her left foot up under her right leg so she was comfortable and modestly pulled her hemline down over her knees.

Roberta saw Henry's jaw muscles ripple then stiffen as he forced himself to speak. "Well...the name I was born with...is not Henry Grace. It's Henry Fountain. The same Henry Fountain presumed murdered for fifty-five years. I'm sure you know the Fountain murder story."

She nodded slowly, her eyes wide, staring without blinking, her mouth forming an Oh! "Oh yes," she said breathlessly. "I know it very well. My grandfather rode with the Fountain family and the sheriff to look for Henry and his father. My father nearly got in a fight one time with a man in a bar when the man said Albert Fountain only got what he deserved."

She stopped and frowned at him. "Oh, stop it! You're not Henry Fountain!" she said as she folded her arms and arched her eyebrows wrinkling her normally smooth brow in disbelief. "You're just teasing! Why haven't you made yourself known if you are? Why haven't you told the law who murdered you...uh, your father and why weren't the murderers brought to justice? What are..."

Henry waved a flat horizontal palm at her as he smiled and said, "Easy now, *Señorita*. Patience. Please, just listen to my story. I'll answer all your questions. I promise. But, you have to promise never to repeat what I'm telling you."

Roberta gazed earnestly at his face, every strong feature etched in the light and shadows cast by the dash lights. She nodded rapidly and said, "I promise to keep my mouth shut. You know I can and I will. I'll die before I'll ever speak a word." She reached over and patted him on the shoulder. "I'm sorry, Dr. Grace, but I just can't believe you're Henry Fountain. Everyone knows that child's been dead over fifty years. But, please...please ignore my bad manners. Tell me your story. It's a great mystery that's haunted this country for years. I want to hear your version of it too."

# 2

# Stranded On San Augustin Pass

Henry took a deep breath, puffed out his cheeks, and blowing out the air made a sound like a surfacing whale. Pulling on the smooth smoke offered by his pipe, he leaned forward over the steering wheel. He wiggled his shoulders and stretched his back, rocking his neck side to side. There was a far-away look, deep and thoughtful, floating in his eyes as he stared down the road into the darkness beyond the reach of the headlights. Roberta knew that look. She saw it often when he sat at his desk late in the afternoons, puffing his pipe, sipping his bourbon, an unread JAMA on his lap, and his stocking feet resting on the corner of his desk. He stared at his bookshelves on the far wall, his face framing his concentration on ethereal images. He never shared those images with her, even when he caught her studying him with a questioning look from his doorway.

Finally, his attention focused back on his quiet audience awaiting his revelations. He glanced at her, then winked as he swapped the pipe stem from one side of his mouth to the other and clamped it solid with a full set of teeth in a Teddy Roosevelt smile.

Speaking casually, off-handedly, as if he were telling her about problems with Mrs. Oliva's surgery or the latest political scandal, he said, "Remember now, you promised you'll never share what I tell you."

Roberta nodded, biting the inside of her cheek. She stared at him trying to think of something convincing to say that would assure him of her future silence. She felt an odd sense of relief that it was dark outside. The air in the Plymouth tingled with a sense of intimacy. It reminded her of how she felt years ago when her best friend offered to tell her what a man did to his wife behind the door of their bedroom and where babies came from. She had to promise then never to tell her mother what she learned or from whom.

Her friend's secret sent her mind reeling in disbelief. How nasty! How tantalizingly exciting! Questions flew through her mind like confused arrows seeking a target in the darkest night. What did it feel like to make love? How could a man fit inside a woman? How could a huge baby pop out of her belly and pass between a mother's legs? That revelation had changed her life. It drew waters deep from her well of curiosity, making her crave to learn all she could about the human body. Constantly rummaging through the stacks at New Mexico A&M library, she breathlessly looked at nude pictures and detailed diagrams in medical books. The more she learned, the more she had to know. That day of revelation led her to attend nursing school.

She sensed forbidden knowledge awaiting her again. Hidden in the dark, hidden for years by men who had died rather than tell the truth, it crouched like a big cat waiting to spring into her life and change her forever. Her hand trembled as she reached for her purse to find another cigarette. Staring at him as she lighted it, she drew the smoke deep in her lungs and felt it calm her as she slowly released it toward the Plymouth's ceiling. As she steadied, she knew she had to know Henry's story. Whatever price he demanded for the telling, she would gladly pay. She needed to hear this story. Roberta tilted her head back and smoothed flying tendrils that had escaped from the French twist of her long black hair.

"Yes, sir, I promised! I did!" Holding up her right hand as though testifying in court, but with the cigarette between her middle and index fingers, she said irritably, "I promise I'll never repeat what I hear tonight unless you say I can." She pointed her left index finger at him as if it were the barrel of a gun. "Now, you tell the truth. No yarns! No teasing! Don't you tell me a lie, Dr. Henry Grace! Don't you tell me you're Henry Fountain when I know you're not!"

Out of the shadows, Henry cleared his throat. He said in a voice just loud enough to hear above the whistle of the wind in the window vents, "Roberta, I...am...Henry Fountain. Believe it!"

His jaw muscles rippled as his teeth ground into the pipe stem. He relaxed again, wagging his head from side to side, grabbed the pipe with his right hand, and blew a long stream of smoke out the vent window. "Do you know much about the Fountain family and what went on after my father was murdered only a few miles from where we are right now?"

Propping her head again on her hand, Roberta stared over the steering wheel out into the dark. She rubbed the back of a thumbnail over her front teeth as she tried to remember tidbits she had learned about the Fountain family.

Most of what she knew fell from the lips of old men who came to visit her father for Saturday night conversation, tequila, and cigars when she was a young girl. Stoop-shouldered, faces and arms darkened by years in the sun, hands scarred and gnarled from years of work in the chile fields, they were men her father, a small grocery owner, admired and respected. Invariably, after a couple of shots of the golden fire going down smooth and easy, they got around to talking about the old days. The good days etched in their memories, the days long gone, the days they longed for, but knew they would never see again. They sat on overturned buckets or cross-legged on the grass in the backyard under the willow trees as the acrid cigar smoke filled their lungs and the liquid fire warmed their bellies.

The night air was soft and warm after a day filled with fiery sunlight. She often sneaked out of her room to sit in the shadows and listen to their stories as she watched the moon, huge and brilliant, float up over the Organs. The smell of cigars or honeysuckle always brought back her memory of those nights filled with the smell of pungent cigar smoke mixed with the fine perfume from honeysuckle blossoms in her mother's little garden. Ah, the stories those old men told. She had only to close her eyes to see their shadowy forms in the moonlight and remember every word they spoke.

Reluctant to give away too much of what she thought she knew, so she could test Henry's story against her own knowledge, she lied a little. "Well...not much...really. I know my father's friends, to a man, believed you, if you're truly Henry Fountain, and your father were murdered. Most of them believed Oliver Lee was behind it, even if he didn't pull the trigger. But, a few believed Lee was innocent and unjustly accused of the murders. There were always arguments about his guilt or innocence. Everybody had a theory about what happened to you.

"As for the rest of your family, uhmmm...Let's see...I believe your mother was Mexican. I know my father loved and respected your three brothers. I vaguely remember my father and mother taking me with them one time when they went to visit your brothers and one or two of your sisters one Sunday afternoon. I was a little kid and they were old middle-aged people, like my parents. The most outgoing, the one most outspoken about anything they discussed, and who was kind of their leader was, uh...I think Maggie was her name.

"I remember when I misbehaved at home, my father scared me to death by saying, *Roberta! Henry's killers - they come for you too if you don't straighten up!* Every time Papa told us the story about how evil men killed you and your father, I wanted to hide, to pull the covers over my head. I had to get away from the thought that anybody could murder a little kid my age. It was too terrible to even think about.

"I guess I truly don't know very much about the Fountains or the murders at all. All I know are just childhood imaginings and old men's speculations over a cigar and a couple of shots of tequila."

Henry slowly shook his head. "You know more than most folks. Although I was too young, at the time it happened, to know all I'm going to tell you, I've since learned quite a bit about my daddy and the family he and Mama raised. Let me give you some background on Daddy so you'll understand the magnitude of what happened.

"Daddy published a paper in Mesilla and wrote political editorials and grand columns about his adventures. He was an attorney and a retired Army officer. He often led posses that went after some bad, bad men, red, brown, and white. It was rare that he didn't come back with anyone he went after. He was fearless, and one of the bravest, toughest men I've known in a lifetime of knowing brave, tough men.

"Daddy joined the Army in California as a corporal during the Civil War. His troop marched across the desert to New Mexico from California. Their objective was to take New Mexico Territory back from the Confederacy. When they finally got here, there weren't any more Confederates, just tribes of angry Indians defending their land. By 1863 Daddy had been commissioned a second lieutenant. At the end of the war, General Carleton made him a captain. He led volunteer scouts against the Apaches and Navahos. He and the Indians neither gave nor accepted any mercy, but the Indians respected him for being very brave and very smart. They were never able to ambush any of the scouting parties or posses he led."

Henry finished his pipe, tapped it in the ashtray hanging under the radio, and pulled the vent window closed so he didn't have to speak over the wind whistling through it.

"On the march from California his troop fought the great Apache chief Cochise. It was in a big battle at Apache Pass near the Arizona-New Mexico border – 200 soldiers against 1200 Indians. The only things that saved his troop's hide were their artillery with exploding shells, and, some say, Daddy's courage leading a foot-charge straight up a hill against Apaches who were shooting down on them. It was a bloody, bitter battle. Cochise and his warriors had never seen artillery with exploding shells. They just couldn't cope with the big gun's range and devastation, and the unyielding courage of the troopers they were fighting. So, they broke off fighting and disappeared back into the mountains. The Apaches still tell tales about that battle. I've heard their stories. They talk about the courage of *Fonntoon* and what a great victory it might have been if they had been able to kill him. Unfortunately, for them, he led a charmed life as an Army officer.

"In late '65 or early '66, Daddy was badly wounded in an Indian fight in Arizona. His scouts managed to get him back to El Paso where there was an Army surgeon who could get the bullet out of him without killing him. After he recovered, he stayed on in El Paso, and, for a while, worked as the chief assistant for W.W. Mills, the customs collector. Old Mills and his associates, leading citizens who wouldn't hesitate to shoot you if you got in their way, were trying to take over the big salt deposits about a hundred miles east of El Paso. The Mexicans considered those deposits public property, so Mills had to maneuver quietly to get his hands on them. He knew that if the Mexicans raised too much hell when he got the property, the government might get involved. If that happened he could lose his customs job or even get tossed in jail. There was a real possibility that when government accountants started looking at the records of custom fees they'd find he took bribes and became wealthy from them.

"Although Daddy was very ethical, he didn't hesitate to play rough in politics. When he found out the salt ring's plans, he double-crossed Mills, and ran against Mills's man for state senator. To top it all off, he won the election. Mills and his partners hated him for the double cross. Mills tried to lay all kinds of lies and legal dirt on him. There was a big trial in El Paso on Mills' charges around 1872. I've read some of the old newspaper accounts of what happened. It was really something. There's even an article written up in the San Antonio *Express* about it on microfilm over in the A&M Library.

"At the trial, Daddy got off clean as a fresh shirt at Ortega's laundry. Of course, Mills and his friends weren't happy with the verdict. There was an attorney on Mills's side named Williams. He got drunk shortly after the trial and shot Daddy twice with a derringer while Daddy tried to defend himself with a cane. After the derringer was empty, Williams ran and hid out in a room he was renting. Daddy managed to limp back home, get a rifle, and come back after Williams.

"On the way back, he met Judge Clarke who told him to stay back, that he would take care of Mr. Williams. Judge Clarke found Captain French of the State Police to accompany him. With Daddy trailing along behind, they found Williams room. Clark banged on the door, trying to get Williams to come out and settle things peaceably. After a lot of yelling through the door, Williams came out blazing away with a shotgun and killed Clarke. French shot Williams with his pistol, and Daddy put a couple of rounds in him with his rifle. Williams died with the shotgun still smoking in his hands. That's when Daddy decided it wasn't safe for him or his family in El Paso, so he moved up the Rio Grande to Mesilla in New Mexico Territory.

"The newspaper in Mesilla and his law practice were successful. He often took cases nobody else would take, mainly ones for poor Mexicans who were getting kicked around or cheated by Anglos. Those cases didn't pay him a lot of money, but they made him a powerful politician who the poor knew was their friend."

Roberta smiled at him fondly. "That sounds like a family tradition."

He glanced up from the road at the end of the bright headlights and grinned. "Yeah, I guess it is."

"Your father was quite an *hombre*, eh?"

"*Si! Un hombre, magnifico!*

"Daddy was also friends with several of the Mescalero. He often got them out of trouble with the Army. He protected their interests from crummy business deals ranchers tried to pull when cattle or horses were bought or sold or when big developers tried to steal their reservation land by changing government policy."

Roberta arched her brows in surprise. "Why? I'd have thought the Mescalero hated him for killing so many of their people. Even my Papa remembers Grandfather talking about some of the bloody Indian fights with posses Albert Fountain led in the late 1870s, early 1880s. Is that why you do so much for the Mescalero? Because he was a friend to them?"

Henry shook his head. "No, not directly. They're my friends for what they did for me, especially Yellow Boy, and for what I do to support them. The Apaches loved Daddy because he wasn't afraid to be their attorney. He was their advocate to a hostile government whenever they needed him. There just wasn't anyone else who would plead cases for them.

"I remember a tale I overheard Daddy telling my oldest brother Albert. The Army wanted to disarm all the men in the tribe around 1879. Several of the Mescalero men took off to hide out in the mountains in order to keep their rifles. They figured they'd starve or be killed if they couldn't hunt or defend themselves against the Texas cattlemen drifting into the Tularosa basin. They were right too. In Texas the solution to the Comanche problem was to wipe them out or run them off. Why those Texans would just as soon shoot an Indian as spit. In any case, the Army finally rounded up most of the Mescaleros who'd run off and put them in a stockade. The local commander wanted to send them off to Florida just as General Miles did with Geronimo and his followers eight or nine years later. Daddy found out that several men in the stockade had actually gone out to try to talk the others into coming back. He wrote letters, banged on politicians' desks, and jawed with the Army until they let those men go back to their families. None of the others were sent to Florida either.

"One of the Mescaleros Daddy got out of the stockade was named Yellow Boy. He was young, but very skilled at tracking and using weapons. Daddy pushed the Army to let Yellow Boy become a tribal law officer. They gave him a horse, a sergeant's coat, an old Calvary hat, and they let him keep his rifle. It was an old 44-40 caliber Henry Rifle with a brass receiver. The Indians often called guns with brass receivers Yellow Boy. Yellow Boy got his name because he was a dead shot with his Yellow Boy. You never saw him without it in his younger days. It's a beautiful weapon. Maybe you remember seeing it hanging on those pegs over his fireplace?"

"Yes, I remember. It's beautiful." The first time Roberta saw the old rifle, she couldn't resist running her fingers over the smooth patina of the walnut stock and the gleaming brass behind its long barrel. She watched Yellow Boy lovingly take it off its pegs, gently, easily, like a man caressing a woman. He handed it to her to feel its heft as if it were his most treasured possession. It was heavy, but the balance was good and she found she could hold a steady aim without too much strain or wiggle on the sight point.

"Yellow Boy was so grateful to have his life back, and for the pay he got as a tribal peace officer, he offered to give Daddy five or six good horses. Daddy told him he didn't need them and not to worry. There was no debt to pay. Yellow Boy told Daddy that some day he'd make things right with him, and he did too.

"You know, I loved my Daddy, but I have to confess I was afraid of him. You didn't cross him. Didn't make any difference whether you were his son or his worst enemy – you didn't cross Daddy. People either hated him or loved him. There just weren't any in-between feelings about him. Sometimes I think it's a miracle he lived as long as he did because he stood up to so many people and never backed down."

The straight road and steady hum of the engine made Henry yawn. He quickly rolled his window all the way down, then back up to get some wholesale fresh air in the cabin. Roberta shivered at the icy blast, but kept a steady gaze on his face as if afraid lies would creep into his mouth when she wasn't looking.

"My mother was Mariana Perez de Ovante. She was about fourteen when she married daddy in 1862. She loved him passionately. Daddy was so much older than she I think he was both a husband and father to her. From the pictures I've seen, taken when she was about twenty, she was a genuine beauty, even after having four or five kids. I was her twelfth and last child, one of four sons. With few exceptions, Mama did exactly as Daddy told her. One of those exceptions is probably what got him killed and, very nearly, me. Even so, I still think she did the right thing."

He grinned mischievously. "See there, women were already out-numbering the men and beginning to run things even then. Daddy taught her to read and write and to do sums. She was shy and didn't mix much socially. He used to send wagons out to the house loaded with dresses for her to pick through. That way she didn't have to go shopping in Las Cruces – twelve kids are a lot to look after even when you have a housekeeper or two to help with the chores. Her shyness didn't buy him many political points with the local social set, but their marriage made him part of the local Mexican community. Theirs was a good marriage in a highly respected Mexican family, and lots of work at reduced fees was enough to get him elected or reelected, sometimes with big majorities, to any political office he wanted. Her inability to be a social climber didn't seem to hamper his political career at all.

"Early one January evening, Mama called to me from the parlor. *Enrique? Muchacho, come down and sit for a while in the parlor with your father and me.* It was after supper and they had a warm piñon fire crackling in the fireplace. The way the wind whipped and whistled around the corners of the house made me glad I was inside. I can still remember the cedar-like smell of that burning piñon wood mixed with the sharp tingling smoke from daddy's big Cuban cigar. When I walked up to the parlor door Mama was dabbing her eyes. She had been crying a little. Daddy stood looking out the window, his back to the door, as though trying to ignore her.

"I knew something was going on. During the past week, my sister Maggie had a couple of long whispered conversations with Daddy while they played together at the piano. After their first talk, she started crying and moped around the house for two or three days with red eyes. You'd have thought it was the end of the world to look at her. Having seen her act that way before about boys Daddy had forbidden her to court, I first thought maybe her latest beau was in hot water with Daddy. But I also knew Maggie was courting a friend of the family, so it didn't make sense to think all the gloom and doom around the house had much to do with that possibility. Another thing out of the ordinary was that Daddy, a very busy man, spent time with my brother Jack shooting targets with a Winchester every day out behind the corral. He even asked Jack to keep the rifle clean and well oiled for him in case he needed it quick. What was even stranger was that I was the only one who had been asked to a sit-down with Mama and Daddy in the parlor. Usually, everyone was called to the parlor when they announced some big family event.

"I was a spindly little kid, some even said I looked sickly, but I was just tall and thin for my age. My brothers often played rough, adolescent games with me. Trying to survive around them, I was a lot tougher than I looked, and I had to be tough because Mama sometimes made me wear sissy suits with fancy lace collars that got me in fights at school. I was more than a little concerned that this visit to the parlor was about my most recent fight. I'd whacked a kid in the head with a stick just like my brother Jack said to do. The kid was a bully and bigger than me to boot. The kid left me alone after I whacked him too. In fact, when he did come back to school, his ear was still bruised yellow and blue from where I struck him. Our teacher wanted to know what had happened to him. Fortunately, for me, he didn't say.

"I stood at the doorway until Mama saw me standing there. She smiled and motioned me to come sit down beside her. She said, *Enrique, your father and I have been talking.*

"I immediately understood from the tone of her voice that this was to be a serious conversation about more than fights at school. I knew they'd been *talking*, I could hear 'em *talking* all the way upstairs where I'd been doing my school lessons and reading *Huckleberry Finn*. Although I was just a sprout, my parents treated me the same way they treated my grown or nearly grown brothers and sisters, as an adult who was told the unvarnished truth.

*Your father has to go to Lincoln.* She sniffed and dabbed her eyes again. Her hand shook a little as she raised the handkerchief to her eyes and she looked from me to daddy's back. *He has to make a presentation to the grand jury for indictments of men he believes have been stealing cattle from some of the ranchers he represents. He's found evidence that can put the thieves in prison. Some of them are well-known, prominent men. When word gets out about what Daddy knows, there's likely to be a lot of trouble. His life will be in danger. I don't want him to go to Lincoln. I've begged him not to go. He insists he must go if he is to do his duty to his clients and keep his honor. He's stubborn and full of pride. I know he'll go, regardless of what I say.*

"She looked me straight in the eye. *Enrique, I want you to go with him. Maggie thinks, and I agree with her, that nobody would attack a man traveling with a little boy. Your father has insisted that he go alone and not expose you to any harm. Maggie and I have been equally insistent that you go, because with you along, no harm will come to anyone. I know you won't be an extra burden for him. You can look after your personal needs by yourself very well. Tonight, he agreed that you could go with him – if you want. What do you say?* She smiled and squeezed my shoulder, a drowning woman grabbing at a last straw.

"Her long shiny black hair was twisted in a bun behind her head, kind of the way you fix your hair, and her teeth were pearls of bright white against her coffee-colored skin. She was very soft spoken, almost hard to hear, and her deep brown eyes were pools of kindness and understanding in which the whole family was often lost. She wore perfumes that smelled wonderful and left the nicest trace of her in any room through which she passed. She was wearing some kind of cactus flower perfume that night. Your perfume often reminds me of it. She was always kind and gentle with her husband and all her children. I loved her so much. If she had asked me to jump in the parlor fire, I wouldn't have hesitated. She didn't have to ask me to help protect Daddy.

"I swelled up bigger than the bullfrogs I caught playing down by the Rio Grande when they puffed up for a croak that could be heard in El Paso. Mama wanted me to protect my daddy! Aye God, me! Little Henry was being asked to help the family protect his daddy. There wasn't any doubt what I'd say. So I sat up as straight as I could and said, Yes'm! I'd sure like to go. I turned from her, looked up at the back of Daddy's head, and begged, Can I, Daddy? Can I please go?

"He turned, casting a baleful squinting eye on me, half-serious, half-humorous. His mouth was drawn in a tight straight line. The fire and the golden lamplight cast shadows on his face that made it look hard and stone-like as though it was chiseled from granite.

"Looking from mama to me a couple of times, he scratched his chin, slowly ran a finger over his big mustache in contemplation, and finally nodded. *It's true, Henry. Mama and Maggie have begged and pleaded with me until I've agreed to take you on this trip if you want to go.* He sighed in surrender to their unrelenting pleas. *I guess you can go if it'll please your mother,* he said in a low voice. He wasn't a bit happy about it. Taking me with him made it look like he was hiding behind his eight-year-old son. Everybody in the southwest knew Daddy was no coward, and, Mama most of all. Taking me wasn't a question about his honor. I learned years later, Mama and Maggie, convinced I was his safe ticket to Lincoln and back, kept the pressure on him to take me for over a week. He just finally gave up trying to change their minds.

"Daddy, since I'm gonna be ridin' shotgun –

"Before I could finish the sentence he held up the palm of his hand to stop me. *Whoa! Stop right there, little man! You're not doing this to protect me! You're just along for the ride. You're just going to visit for a while in Lincoln, understand? It's bad enough folks are liable to think I'm hiding behind a little boy. It's downright idiotic to have that child think he can protect me with a damn gun! Do you understand?* Angrily, he spat out the words, straining to maintain his self-control. His anger and frustration with the iron will of my mother made him even more direct and uncompromising than usual. It was very rare that she didn't go along with what he wanted. He didn't have much practice dealing with her when she insisted on getting her own way.

"Yes, sir, I mumbled looking at the floor nearly in tears. But, I wasn't about to let this opportunity get away from me. No sir, not this one!

"I was just gonna ask if we could do some target shooting on the way. Maybe we'll see a bear or mountain lion when we cross the mountains and we can get us a hide for Mama's floor. Can't we do that?

"I knew how to handle the old '73 Winchester carbine standing in his gun rack. He and my brothers taught me to shoot cans and bottles when they went out for target practice in the desert or in the big arroyo east of town. He even let me shoot his Schofield pistol a few times too. I liked the rifle best; I couldn't hit anything with that pistol. It was heavy and hard to cock. I couldn't shoot it accurately, even holding it with two hands and resting it on something for support.

"*Well...*daddy said with a grin starting to grow under his mustache, *Yeah, we can do that, but you'll be responsible for that rifle if we shoot it so don't get it dirty or lose it. We'll keep it in a scabbard under the seat. Now, I've got some business to take care of first thing in the morning. We'll leave at noon and camp in San Augustin Pass before rolling on to Tularosa the next day. I'll carry your clothes in my valise and we'll use the wagon with Sergeant and Buck rather than saddle horses. I've got to carry a trunk full of grand jury papers too.*

"Sergeant and Buck were big, black high-stepping horses Daddy bought from some farm in Tennessee. They could really cover ground, and had more endurance than any horses I've seen before or since that trip. With the light wagon we had, they could go like the wind for miles. Daddy thought those horses could do just about anything.

"Next day, after breakfast, Mama had the cook, Marta, fix us a big basket supper and a bag lunch for the following day. Daddy was always on time, never late, said if you were late to a meeting it was an insult. We were ready to go promptly at noon.

"The sky was bright blue with lots of puffy white clouds sailing across it, and, down at ground level, the wind was cold and gusty. I shivered as I climbed up on a buggy wheel to hug and kiss Mama good-by.

"Don't worry Mama, I said, I'll take real good care of Daddy. Nobody is gonna get us. She managed to smile and nodded she understood without a word. Then daddy held her close and whispered something in her ear. She smiled but her eyes were sad and near tears as she and Marta stuffed a big heavy blanket with a dog-head pattern over our laps. I was wrapped up in a big red wool Mackinaw that had been one of my brothers when he was ten or twelve and it was about three sizes too big for me. We carried a buffalo robe too, in case the blanket wasn't warm enough.

"Daddy wore his big Army overcoat with the collar pulled up high around his neck, and his campaign hat pulled down tight on his head. He looked over at me and said, *Warm enough, son?* I grinned and nodded. Just before we left he said, *Mother, my ears are about to freeze off. Do you have anything I can wear to keep 'em warm?*

"She thought a second, then held up her wait-a-minute finger. Without a word, she ran into the house. Returning in a couple of minutes she brought him her favorite head shawl, a rebozo, to tie around his head. *Now don't you lose that rebozo, Albert, it's my favorite*, she said, her teeth chattering through an I'll-be-brave smile, her lower lip trembling to keep the flood of tears back, at least until we were out of sight.

"Daddy smiled and hugged her good-by once more. *Don't worry, Mama, I won't lose it. We ought to be back around the first week in February. If you need anything, call on the boys to get it for you or to help you. If there's an emergency, send me a telegram. We'll be staying at Mrs. Darcy's rooming house in Lincoln.* She nodded, crossing her arms and shivering in wind that couldn't make up its mind whether to go or stay.

"I leaned out of the wagon and gave her a final good-by kiss and a comforting couple of pats on the back. She smiled and hugged me. *Adios, Enrique. Mama loves you and we'll miss you. Have a good time. Make Daddy come back home as soon as he can, and you two stay warm or you'll catch pneumonia!*

"Yes'm! We'll be back soon. My teeth were chattering from that cold wind and excitement. Daddy gave Buck and Sergeant a little slap with the reins and we were off, around the house, into the wind and down the street at a fast trot. Most of the trip we were as warm as a couple of bear cubs sleeping with their mama.

"I don't know if you realize it or not, Bertie, but Route 70, that we're on now, pretty well follows the old dirt road we took. Next time we're out here in the daylight, I can even show you some of the wagon wheel ruts that are still here. I remember the road as if I had traveled down it yesterday. The bare sandy spots, the reds, browns, and whites of the dirt, the thickets of creosote bushes and mesquite, and the way the land sweeps up to the mountains on a long gentle rise are all still there.

"Have you noticed how the road seems to suddenly start rising straight up as you near Organ? Most of the rise is so gentle you can't feel you're climbing, even in a horse and buggy, until you get to Organ, then the horses start pulling hard and the going is slow up that grade. I can still remember the first sensation I had of those things that day. It was cold. The wind made us huddle up close and hunker down under the blanket. Daddy kept the horses stepping along and cracked little jokes about how cold it was. You know, things like, *Son it's colder than a well digger's rear on Halloween night in the Yukon.* They made me laugh out loud in the pure joy of getting to take a trip with him, and he laughed with me.

"We stopped in San Augustin Pass about five o'clock. The shadows were just getting long from the setting sun. It was much colder and windier up there than down in the valley. We had to camp behind some boulders close to a little spring to get out of the wind and keep the fire from blowing in every direction. It was like having a nest on top of the world. The view of the valley and road back toward Las Cruces stretched forever in the last light from the sun falling behind the Floridas. You could see a few lights down in Organ, and, later, when it was pitch black, we could see a dim glow out of the valley from the streetlights in Las Cruces and Mesilla.

"Daddy fed and watered the horses right after we got there and put me to work gathering up brush for our fire. He was as particular as any cowboy about his animals. They were skittish, I think now they probably smelled a big cat or a bear, and hard to handle getting them out of their harness and rubbing them down. Daddy led them to water at a little pool fed by a slow spring leaking out of the boulders below us. Then he tied them to picket stakes out of the wind and fed them. Finally, we got to eat that nice basket supper Marta fixed for us. I was starved. Let me tell you, you haven't lived until you taste hot coffee and steak between slices of fresh-baked bread in San Augustin Pass, especially after bouncing around in the wind on a cold wagon seat half the day.

"While we ate, I got Daddy to tell me a story or two about his Indian fights. When we finished, it was fully dark and the stars were out.

We built up the fire and rolled up together in the buffalo robe right next to it. Daddy kept the Winchester within easy reach. He checked the load in his Schofield pistol before putting it under the blanket he used for a pillow. It was the first time I had spent an evening with Daddy sleeping on the trail. Of course, I had camped out with my brothers Tom, Jack, and Albert on some of their minor forays over to ranches or hunting. I knew what to expect. Still, here I was, sleeping with Daddy, who kept a rifle within easy reach and a revolver under his pillow. I had a hard time getting to sleep and wiggled around some. Daddy just patted me on the shoulder every time, saying, *It's all right son, go on to sleep now.* Soon the warmth of his body and the hot glow from the fire had me sleeping as well as I did in my own bed at home.

"The next morning, Daddy was up before dawn. He broke up some kindling and in short order built up the fire from the coals that survived the night. He let me stay wrapped in the buffalo robe watching him in the weak light of the coming dawn. After he had a nice fire going, he told me to roll out and get ready to go. He filled the grain buckets for the horses and walked around the boulders where they were staked. He came stomping back much quicker than I expected. He was cursing under his breath and he looked mad enough to bite the head off a grizzly bear!

"The horses were gone! Somehow they had pulled out their picket stakes and taken off. Daddy took a slow walk around the camp trying to figure out where they went. Their tracks led back down the trail toward Las Cruces. Although he couldn't find any other tracks, he was certain some varmint had scared them off. Daddy didn't say much as he dug in the supplies to fix us up a little breakfast.

"I was just about in tears. The only options I thought we had were to walk back home or hope somebody would come along and help us. Daddy and I looked down the road from both sides of the pass. We didn't see a soul or any animals moving for miles. Daddy knew I wasn't strong enough to walk all the way back to Las Cruces in the cold and I was too heavy for him to carry. I knew it too. It was a long, long walk back to Las Cruces.

"I sniffled over the hot bread and coffee, trying not to cry. I asked, Daddy, what are we gonna do?

"He flashed one of the most confident grins I've ever seen and said, *Nothing!* I thought he was planning to just sit up there until the animal that ran Sergeant and Buck off came back for us. I was about ready to cry when he said, without a flicker of concern, *There's not much we can do Henry. It's too cold and too far to just walk out. I can tell the horses are headed back to town. I figure they'll wander into the stable sometime this afternoon, at the latest, for feed. Somebody at home will find them and figure out something happened for them to get away from us like that. They'll bring 'em back here within a day or two. If they don't, why we'll just catch the mail wagon back in four or five days.* That shut up my whining. I realized I had at least a day or two to play way up high in the mountains. What a stroke of luck! I thought Daddy might let me shoot the rifle too. It wasn't so bad being stranded after all.

"I scouted around camp and found a long straight stick and spent most of the day playing hunter or hiding behind rocks around camp as an Indian fighter. I'll bet I killed a thousand of them and they got me a few times with arrows made of yucca stalks. Daddy got out his legal papers from the old red trunk, and sitting on a rock next to the fire, spent most of the day reviewing evidence and making final preparations for presentations to the grand jury.

"We bundled up again after supper and slept well until about midnight when the scream of a mountain lion woke us up. I tell you that lion scream made every hair on my head stand straight out. Daddy opened one eye, gave a big yawn, and said, *Go back to sleep little man. Don't be afraid. It's just an animal. Men are ten times worse than some hungry cat. Why if that cat comes around, we'll give him a new eye in his backside with the Winchester. Just like you said, we'll skin him up and have us a new rug for your mama. Go on now, go back to sleep.* I yawned and forced myself to be still. I finally got off to sleep, but it took a while.

"Next day was more of the same, except at mid-afternoon, Daddy walked out to the road and looked down the pass toward Organ and Las Cruces. He was gone so long I walked out to the road looking for him. He was there, sitting on a boulder in the sunshine looking towards Las Cruces. He didn't say a word. He just pointed to a tiny figure on a horse plodding up the road leading two horses. I turned to look at him with the question written on my face. He said, with a little sigh of relief, *Albert! He'll be here in about an hour and he has Sergeant and Buck with him. Let's go get the Dutch oven and cook us up a good supper.*

"Sure enough, Albert showed up in about an hour. Boy was I glad to see him and so was Daddy. He rode up to the fire with a big grin on his face and gave a smart military salute that Daddy returned. He said, *Pa, you and Henry had us all worried to death when Sergeant and Buck showed up at the barn. Mama and Maggie thought somebody had attacked you. I figured, at least I hoped, that somehow they just ran away and you needed them back, and, as you see, here they are.*

"Daddy, showing nothing but teeth in a big grin under his moustache said, *Albert, I raised you right, son! You figured it out exactly right. Climb down and tie those horses to the wagon wheel. I'll feed them. Henry, you and Albert get the plates and we'll eat in a little bit! I can feel my backbone rubbing my navel.* We were hungry and very relieved that the little episode of being stranded hadn't been more serious than it was. Albert bringing the horses back would get us back on the road again early the next morning.

"After we ate Daddy leaned back against a boulder. *Albert, it's clear to me that it was foolish, no, it was stupid for me to bring Henry along. I want you to take him back home with you and I'll go on alone.*

"Albert just stared at Daddy, his mouth half full of beans and biscuits. He stopped chewing, swallowed, looked at the ground, and shook his head. It was forbidden for us to argue with our parents. My older siblings could get away with arguing a little with Mama, but when Daddy told us to do something, it had better be *Yes, sir!* or expect a quick trip to the woodshed. Nevertheless, Albert was a full-grown man and I could tell he'd try to rebut daddy's order.

"*Pa, why would you want to do that? Henry seems to be doing just fine. I thought you agreed with Mama and Maggie that you would be safer if he came along.*

"Daddy pulled out a cigar, lighted it, and said, *Jack, you're not to argue with me again. Do you understand? This had best be the last time it happens. I'll let you off this time because you were so prescient in understanding we needed Sergeant and Buck back and in bringing them to us as quick as you did. Now, Henry is a good traveling companion. None better. Oh he whistles and sings a lot, but that's all right with me. However, this is a trail, not some eastern highway. If something happens to the horses or buggy out in the desert, or we get attacked, he's just not strong or mature enough yet to survive. I don't want him hurt!*

"I blurted out, Daddy, please don't send me away. Let me come with you. Please! I won't get in your way, I promise, and I can survive in the desert – Albert and Jack's told me all about what to do. Please, Daddy ...

"Then Albert joined in. *Henry's right, Pa. He does fine when we play Hideout in the desert.* Hideout is the same as playing hide-and-seek except you use horses and can hide over much larger areas than hiding on foot. Then Albert says, *Henry nearly always finds me after*

31

*I've ridden off and hidden from him. He's a good shot with the '73 too, even if he is just a little kid. Mama and Maggie want him with you, Pa, and I think you owe it to the women to keep Henry with you so their minds will be at ease. Now I've said all I'm going to say before you get set to go a round with me.*

"Well, Daddy just threw his arms up in the air and said disgustedly, *Oh, all right, all right. Henry you stay. But this sure as hell is against my better judgment. Henry, you and Jack clean up the kitchen here and I'll look after the horses. They're not getting out of here tonight!*

"We had a good time sitting around the fire that evening, Daddy telling us stories about his days down in Texas and joking with us. It got late and Albert laid his bedroll out across the fire from us as we crawled under that buffalo robe again. We all slept peacefully, but it was cold up there, even out of the wind.

"Daddy was up before dawn, hustling around building up the fire, making coffee, packing up the buggy, and harnessing the horses. Unlike the night before, he said, *Get out of that robe, Henry. We've got to get ready to roll down this mountain. There's a long day's ride in front of us. Pickup your stuff now and get it ready for packing.*

"After some hot coffee and hard bread left over from supper, Albert hugged me and said, *So long, little man, I know you're going to have fun. Bring Daddy back safe.*

"I stood up as tall and straight as I could and said, Don't worry Albert. I'll bring daddy back home safe and sound.

"He shook hands with Daddy. Shivering in the cold, he said, *Just be careful, Pa. There are some bad hombres down in that basin. I'll tell Mama that you and Henry are getting along just fine.* Daddy nodded and hugged him, slapping him on the back a couple of times.

"Albert saddled his horse and started back down the pass toward Las Cruces. Daddy and I packed up the buggy and were rolling down the other side just as the sun cracked the sky and lighted up the desert in orange and red light and purple shadows. It was beautiful to see the shadows run off to hide chased by the coming light."

# 3

# El Tigré And The Wolf

In the distant twinkling black, the sky glow over Alamogordo grew steadily brighter. Light creeping from the moon still hidden behind the Sacramentos was unsettling the dark southeastern horizon. Soon the big golden disk would float into view, its brilliant mellow light casting the desert in stark contrasts of soft white light and deep black shadows. The Plymouth hummed along, its wake through the cold dark desert shaking the creosote bushes and mesquites scattered here and there along Route 70.

Without moving her arm off the back of the seat, Roberta glanced over her shoulder into the darkness toward the southeast. Her memories from many years past fluttered awake. There she was, on her knees at the edge of the seat, in her father's old Ford pickup. She held to the door window, cracked just enough to let in a whistle of the freezing predawn air. Staring toward the coming light, her teeth chattered in anticipation. The air blowing in through the window whipped her hair, caused her eyes to water, and made her little fingers feel icy cold. Her father always woke her up after they started down San Augustin Pass toward the desert. He pointed her attention toward the coming dawn and spoke with reverence for the new day coming. He taught her to feel its joy and to savor their bond with the sun that stretched back through centuries to their Aztec ancestors. Always, as she watched, the sun came slowly, setting fire to the dawn, a blaze of oranges, golds, purples, and softly textured turquoises against a gossamer sky that made her feel warm and happy inside.

"I know exactly what you saw that morning, Dr. Grace. I've seen the sunrise over this desert many times while riding to the market in Alamogordo with my father. The images from those days are burned in my memory forever."

Henry nodded absentmindedly. He cocked his head to one side, listening to long forgotten voices murmuring softly in his mind. Roberta sensed he had dropped the thread of his story and gently prodded him to continue.

"That must have been a very long day to get from the top of San Augustin Pass to Tularosa. Didn't you freeze riding out in the cold and wind all day? I know I would have!"

Henry jerked as if awakening, surprised to realize his mind had been drifting, dreaming of days long gone. He snapped his head back and forth to drive away the ancient whispered voices as he reached to bring back the memory of that long day's ride, a memory still as vivid as any he had of yesterday's patients.

"I tell you," he said as he twisted one side of his mouth into a rueful grin and made a clicking sound, "it's cold and windy up there in that pass in January. I was glad to get down the Tularosa side of the pass and watch Daddy let the horses strut their stuff. It was so cold, that as the morning came on, I began to wish that Albert and I hadn't talked Daddy out of sending me home. My lips and cheeks were chapped, my eyes watered from the cold, and my feet and hands were so numb I kept a steady rhythm tapping them on the wagon floor just to be sure they were still attached. I didn't dare complain after begging Daddy to keep me with him. The sun finally warmed things up a little. It wasn't so bad when the winds weren't blowing down off the San Andres Mountains over there to the west. When it did blow, it came carrying dust and tumble weeds in every direction – sideways, up, down, round about – and, it was frosty! Whew! You'd better believe it was cold! I still shiver when I think about it.

"After we rode for a while, Daddy decided I needed to learn to drive the wagon. He showed me how to hold the reins and coached me on the kind of commanding voice to use when telling the team gee, haw, or whoa! He put the reins in my hands, then wrapped his arms around me and covered my hands with his. He guided me along that way for a little while as he continued to let Buck and Sergeant step along in a good, solid fast walk that ate up the miles. When we got to a long straight stretch of ruts down in the flats, he gradually released my hands and sat back, relaxing in the wagon with his arms crossed while he kept a close eye on me.

"He kept telling me *Sit up straight now Henry*, and *Just relax, son, let the horses do the work*. About every five minutes, he'd ask, *Are you tired yet, Henry? Want me to take the reins?* I'd shake my head and say No, sir! As long as I had the strength to hold them, I kept the reins. It was a matter of honor and proof of manhood for me to drive that team. I managed to hold the reins and drive the wagon for nearly an hour before my shoulders started to cramp so bad I was afraid I'd drop the reins. So I told Daddy, I'm ready for you to drive now, but can I do it some more later on – please? Daddy roared a big strong laugh. I barely heard him because the wind was gusting so hard it was stolen away. He took the reins with his right hand and gave me a hug and a shake with his left as he said, *Henry, you're going to be a first-class wagon driver! I'll let you practice some more after lunch. Now just sit back and enjoy the day while I drive for a while.*

"We rode along making jokes again about how cold the wind was. Figuring he was in a good mood and wouldn't turn me down, I begged him to tell me his El Tigré story. El Tigré was a mean outlaw who swore to kill Daddy after Daddy's posse broke up the Kinney gang and killed one of Kinney's amigos in Rincon. I'd overheard snatches of the tale when Daddy told Maggie what happened one evening while they sat and played at the piano together a few days before our trip. I think he told Maggie the story to reassure her he could take care of himself, and to tell her not to worry about him."

As she lighted another cigarette, Roberta wearily rested her head against her arm propped against the seatback, and, smoothing her hair with her long slender fingers, said with a frown of uncertainty, "Humph. I don't think I've ever heard of the Kinney gang or El Tigré."

"Few people have heard of them. It's a shame because they made outlaws like the Younger and James Gang look like choirboys; now days, folks have forgotten the bravery and skill it took to wipe out those gangs.

"Daddy was a master storyteller. First, he whetted my appetite by telling me I was too young to hear about all the fighting that went on. Then he said he was worried mama might think he was teaching me too much about fighting when she just wanted her little boy to get along with everybody. But I had to hear this story. I kept pushing what was acceptable behavior, begging him to tell it. Please, Daddy! I promise I'll never tell Mama you told me. Finally, he reluctantly gave in with a wink not to tell. He sat up straight, and, throwing his chest out, began in his best lawyer's voice that he used most often for pleading difficult jury cases. I was quite familiar with that voice. I'd heard it used several times when I had sneaked into court to watch him work.

*Well Henry,* he boomed, *when the posse and I caught up with the Kinney Gang in Rincon, there was big shoot-out. Lots of bullets were fired on both sides. However, the boys and I caught 'em with their britches down. We managed to kill most of the gang, and only one of our men was even wounded. Element of surprise I guess. They just didn't believe we could travel that far that fast to catch 'em by surprise when they rode into Rincon. Just like old J.E.B. Stuart used to say in the Civil War, 'Git thar fustest with the mostest,' and we did too. Why, they were planning to ambush us in Rincon themselves. Hard work to surprise your enemy always pays, Henry. Don't forget that. I was lucky. I shot and killed Kinney's right hand man, Doroteo Saenz, just as he was about to shoot Israel Santos. But, one of the meaner bastards, El Tigré, got away.*

Henry looked at Roberta with twisted grin. "That's what he called him, bastard. Daddy didn't use profanity often. I understood right then that this was one man for whom my Daddy had absolutely no use. But, forgive my digression. The power of those days is kinda flooding back in on me. Anyway, as Daddy told it ..."

*Nobody had any idea how El Tigré got away from us at Rincon or where he went after he got by us. I figured he must have slipped off and hid in the Bosque along the Rio Grande until he got close to El Paso. From there, he just rode across the river into Mexico. I decided I'd be patient and wait for him to come back, then I'd nail his tail and that would be the last of the Kinney gang.*

*One day, a couple of months later, I was working in my office. It was late in the afternoon, but it was after fall harvest, and the weather was perfect – the air cool and calm, the late afternoon light soft and easy on the eyes as it slowly slipped away. I had the windows to my office open to the street, enjoying that nice air and light and the sounds of nighttime coming. I heard a wagon stop outside my door and the voice of old José Padilla croaking 'Gracias, Señor.' You remember old José don't you, Henry? His voice kinda cracked like Jack's did when he was twelve, and José had this nervous habit of clearing his throat a lot.*

*There was a knock and I yelled, 'Come on in José, it's open.' José and I went back a long way. He rode with me in the early days. He was one of the best trackers I knew. The trouble with him was that he liked whiskey too much. He'd go on binges for days at time and drink up all the pesos he'd earned after we got back from posse rides. Then he'd stagger home to his poor wife, Maria, who must have loved him the way she put up with him. When he came in the office that day, he was dead sober, but he smelled to high heaven of whiskey, you know like he might have spilled it all over himself. I wasn't even paying any attention when he walked through the door, but when I looked up from my paperwork, I realized he was in bad shape. I jumped up to help him. He looked like he was about die right there in the office, but he waved to me to stay where I was. He kinda staggered toward me until he could steady himself against a chair so he could fall into a seat in front of my desk. He looked terrible. His nose was broke and pushed to one side. His face was covered with bruises. His right eye had a cut just above the eyebrow and it was swollen shut. There were bloodstains all over the front of his shirt. His left arm was broken and had been wrapped up in professional-looking splints. Shocked, I said, Good God, man! What's happened to you?*

*Well, Sir, his mouth was just about swollen shut. There was a big bruise that made a straight line that went up one side of his face, but he still managed to clear his throat a couple of times and croak, 'El Tigré...He's staying with a whore in Concordia down in El Paso.'*

*I almost grinned in spite of how much I knew José must be suffering and how bad I felt for him. I knew El Tigré would come back, and, he did. Every word José spoke was causing him pain. I tried to hush him up so I could go get the doctor; he just shook his head and kept on talking.*

*'I saw him in an El Paso cantina last night. I was minding my own business just having a little tequila, when he recognized me about the same time I saw him. He walked over, and just stared at me. I stared back. I was ready to trade shots with him or use my hands to defend myself, when he drew his pistola. Ayeeeee, Alberto, he was a lot faster than me. My pistola never got out of the holster. He just stood staring at me and pointing that cocked pistola at my guts. He started to grin as I stood there with the sweat running down my face waiting to die. He never fired the pistola, Señor Fountain. He let the hammer down quickly, and, before I could move, he swung the pistola hard sideways and broke my arm. Then on the upswing he smashed it across my face while the good-for-nothing Mexican crowd just stood there and watched him! Everyone, they are afraid to cross him. It was quiet as a grave in that place. I remember the silence. It roared in my ears as I heard him grunt to use his strength to swing that pistola through the air. I tried to cover up against other swings but he beat me good.*

*'Finally, he got tired. He say loud enough for everybody to hear, "You sorry old dog, you tell that bastard Fountain I'm looking for him. When I find him, I'll rip his guts out and string them across El Paso like the tiger I am. Your whipping is just the beginning, you old son-of-a-bitch. When I'm through, even my woman can whip you if I tell her. You tell Fountain. You tell him. I'm here waiting to kill him good."*

'*He spit a stream of nasty tobacco juice on me, took a bottle of whiskey and poured it on my face and shirt, it burned like the fires of hell Señor Fountain. Then he stuck out his elbow for his woman to grab, and he and the whore walked out into the night like nothing happened. He was laughing loud too. The bartender sent old Cardenas to get Dr. Bright and he put splints on my broke arm. He said there wasn't anything else broke and that there wasn't a lot he could do for the bruises and swelling. He gave me a bottle of laudanum for when the pain gets bad. It works pretty good too. I used a little of the laudanum to kill the pain, and the swelling in my face is down some, I think. It don't hurt too bad now.*'

*He grinned at me like a drunk who's been given another bottle. I felt so sorry for him. I was in a fury. Nobody was going to treat my men like that or make threats against me. Other men had and I'd whipped 'em or killed 'em all.*

Henry looked over at Roberta, who was listening intently and slowly shaking her head. "Daddy's face got blood red as he told the story. I could see it even under the chaffing from the wind as he told me what El Tigré had done to José. I'd never seen him so angry, and he was just remembering how José looked and what El Tigré had said. Then he said ...

*I left José sitting in my office and ran down to the livery to get the buggy. I brought old man Adams back with me from the livery to help load José. Then I drove him to his place just down river from Mesilla. I made those horses trot then too. José wasn't feeling any pain, but I had to hold him in the buggy with one hand and drive with the other – he'd been hitting the laudanum more often than he first let on and kept dozing off. It was dark when we got to his little adobe house that sat right by the side of the El Paso road. When Maria saw me with him at the door, her eyes got big and round. She started to cry and begged God not to let José die. After I promised her he'd be all right in a few weeks, she got control of herself and helped me get him into the house. After I helped her stretch him out on their bed, I left because I was late for supper and knew your mama would be worried about me. I gave Maria some money as I was going out the door and told her to get whatever medicine she needed for José and to come see me if she needed more.*

*I made those buggy wheels turn as I headed straight back to Las Cruces. I stopped in front of Lohman's hardware store in a cloud of dust with the horses all lathered up. I found Israel Santos putting up stock for Lohman. You might remember him, Henry; he's a second or third cousin of your mother's. He's kinda short, but very strong and fearless. I've seen Israel maneuver two one-hundred-pound kegs of nails around at the same time in Lohman's store. He's a dead shot with a pistol in either hand. He drinks like a fish too, but liquor didn't control his life like it did José's. I'd saved him from a bullet in the back at the shoot-out in Rincon, so he knew and understood the kind of murderous trash El Tigré was.*

*I stepped just inside the door and motioned him outside into the shadows on the street where we'd have a little privacy. We spoke in whispers so any passerby wouldn't hear us and spread around town what I was telling him. I said, José Padilla was beat up pretty bad by El Tigré in a cantina down in El Paso last night. I'm catching the five o'clock train down to El Paso tomorrow morning and I'm going to bring El Tigré back here for trial before we hang him. Do you want to come with me? He grinned a big toothy grin and nodded. I said, Well, bring your shotgun, pistols, and lots of cartridges. His grin got bigger.*

*We were in El Paso by six-thirty the next morning. We got off the train and didn't even go for breakfast and coffee or stop for some casual conversation with a couple of ranchers we knew. We didn't want word to leak out that we were in town before we got the bastard. The ranchers caught on quick that we were in a hurry and armed to the teeth. They nodded and tipped their hats to us then left us alone as we went striding down to the livery stables. We made the horses do a fast trot as we rode over to Concordia. Neither one of us spoke a word the entire ride. Both of us were getting angrier by the minute just thinking about the beating that no-good gave José and the threats he made toward me.*

*Just outside of Concordia we met a toothless old woman with vegetables in a big willow basket on her head. She was trudging toward the El Paso market. For some reason women always seemed to trust Israel. When he asked her if she knew where El Tigré was, she didn't hesitate to point, with a grin, toward the adobe house where the whore lived. We walked the horses down the street that ran behind the adobe and casually checked out the house's windows and doors. The windows were too small for El Tigré to crawl through, but there was a front and a back door. Neither one of them looked to be locked; in fact, the front door was cracked open like someone had forgotten to close it, and it wasn't even latched.*

*I put Israel at the front door; I went around to the back. I told him when he heard me bust through the back door to come in the front ready to shoot and not to hesitate to shoot the whore if she got in the way. Those women carry pistols or knives too. They can kill you just as* dead as any man can. Don't ask me how I know that, son, I just do. So I got my pistol out at the back door and made sure it was loaded. Always be sure your gun is loaded, son. An empty one will get you killed in a hurry. I stood facing the back door with my revolver cocked and ready. Taking a deep breath, I was just reaching for the door handle when it turned and the door swung open.

There stood El Tigré in his long johns, boots, gun belt, and a big yawn, heading for the privy out back. As soon as he saw me, he tried to slam the door shut but it hung on a rug and wouldn't close. He saw my old Walker Colt was cocked and ready, pointing straight at his chest, and he knew I wouldn't hesitate to kill him if he tried for his pistol. So he put his hands up while the ash got longer on the cigarro he was smoking for breakfast. That day was my lucky day, boy! If we hadn't caught him with his pants down, there'd have been a hell of a fight. A man doesn't have many days where everything works just right. I guess that day was just our turn.

I called out, Israel! Come round to the back and see the skunk I've caught. I yelled in the door. Lady, you stay inside and stay quiet or my man will make you wish you had. Israel came running around the corner of the house with his shotgun in one hand, both hammers cocked, and a revolver in the other. I said, Israel, disarm El Pussy Gato and put the shackles on him.

He holstered the revolver walked over to him and said in a low voice, 'José Padilla es mi amigo you son-of-a-bitch!' He smashed El Tigré in the middle of his face with the butt of his shotgun – yeah, son, he broke his nose. Kind of a nose for a nose, eh? El Pussy Gato deserved it! Blood flew everywhere as he stumbled back inside, screaming in pain. I thought about shooting him in a knee so he couldn't run – it cripples a man for life and it hurts so bad you want to scream for days – but I didn't do it. Later on I wished I had. Israel pulled off Pussy Gato's gun belt and put the hand shackles on him. We dragged him outside. He was moaning, and his eyes were full of blood. The whore just stood in a corner with a blanket wrapped around her, saying over and over, 'El Tigré will keel you, Fountain, he'll keel you.' I just grinned and said to her, El Tigré isn't going to do anything except go to hell.

We washed up El Pussy Gato and got his shirt and pants on. We found a brace of the new Smith and Wesson pistols in his saddlebags, but most of the money he'd stolen was gone. I was certain the whore had most of it, probably stashed somewhere in the house, but I didn't want to stir up the village trying to find it since we didn't have any le-

*gal authority in Texas. I told Israel to keep the pistols for helping me; they were fine ones. He didn't argue about keeping them either.*

*Israel saddled El Pussy Gato's horse while I kept an eye on him and the whore. We threw him over the saddle and tied him on, then headed for the train depot rapidamenté. We sold his horse and saddle at the livery where we'd gotten our horses. He had a fancy Mexican saddle with a lot of silver trim. It fetched a good price of about fifty dollars.*

*By the time we got back to the station, it was only eight thirty. The train to Las Cruces wasn't leaving until ten-thirty so we went across the street, shackled El Tigré to a building column, and went inside to get breakfast. I bought a burrito for El Tigré's breakfast. He had a hard time putting his mouth around it cause his eyes were nearly swollen shut. Word got out that we had him in chains and a good-sized crowd gathered at the restaurant to stare at him all shackled up and looking like a whipped dog. Nobody said or did anything bad about or to him. They fully expected he'd kill us and come back for them before we could hang him.*

*After breakfast, I sent a telegram to the sheriff in Las Cruces asking him to meet us at the station to pick up El Tigré and put him in jail. The ride back to Cruces was quiet, just mesquite and creosotes sliding by. However, as we got close to the depot in Cruces, El Tigré seemed to revive and started growling about how he'd get free and shoot us in the head and cut our* cajones *off. He made Israel so mad that Israel drew his pistol to cold-cock him again, but I wouldn't let him. I said, Israel, he's going to be like this until the rope breaks his neck. Just let him be. Israel nodded, but I could tell he was hoping for an excuse to bust him another one.*

*"We were getting close to Cruces when a Texas Ranger sitting across the aisle from me told me I ought to fix my pistol like his. It had a lanyard around the handle with the other end tied to his belt. He said it had saved his bacon several times when he had scuffled with prisoners and had his weapons knocked out of his hand. I said I thought that was pretty smart thinking, so he gave me a string of rawhide and showed me how to rig my pistol up that way.*

*There was a big crowd waiting with the sheriff on the station platform when we got to Cruces. I guess they wanted to see how shot up we were and how tough the bad outlaw, El Tigré, actually was. Albert Fall was there too. I reckoned the whore had wired him and promised money if he'd defend El Tigré. I had to grin. I knew this was going to be another case where I'd beat him in court. Israel and I got off the* train with *El Tigré* between us. I had a hold of the shackles chain between his wrists. As soon as we stepped off the train and on to the platform, the sheriff, a big grin on his face, ran up to us, stuck out his hand, and said, 'Well done, Fountain! Well done!'

Like an idiot, I relaxed my grip on the chain as I shook his hand. *El Tigré* instantly jerked free and tried to jerk my pistol out of the holster, but my new lanyard jerked it out of his hands. Without an instant's pause he jumped off the platform and ran toward the desert. Israel had unloaded his shotgun for the ride back and was cursing and yelling that he couldn't fire. The sheriff and his deputy froze and just stared at *El Tigré's* fast disappearing backsides running for cover across the tracks. I used the lanyard to jerk my pistol back as I yelled at him two or three times to stop.

I still used my big old Walker Colt cap and ball revolver back in those days. There was nothing that could touch it for stopping power, although loading it was a lot slower than a revolver that used cartridges. I always figured I was a good enough shot that five good shots out of that old gun were better than ten out of a smaller caliber cartridge gun. I dropped to one knee to steady myself. I knew I had one shot, and a long one at that, to stop him. By then he was over twenty-five yards away and moving fast. I held that old Colt steady with both hands, took careful aim, yelled for him to stop one more time, and, just as he was about to disappear into the mesquite, I fired. The 44-caliber ball from that six-pound revolver struck him square in the back. It hit him so hard he did a somersault forward and landed face up. He didn't move. I tell you, son, if a ball from that old Walker Colt hits you, you're not going to be doing anything except bleed. You could hear the crowd sucking in their wind as the smoke cleared. They saw *El Tigré's* body lying face up to the sun with a big bloodstain in the middle of his shirt. It didn't take them long to realize that a long pistol shot from an old weapon had killed him. Men scratched their chins in disbelief and shook their heads, and women covered their mouths, afraid they might scream or throwup.

I tell you, boy, it really was my lucky day. Everything I tried, worked. Most days aren't like that. I stood up and was holstering the Walker when Albert Fall ran up and yelled in my face, 'You murdered him! You son-of-a-bitch! You murdered him!'

I was ready to pull the Walker again, but the sheriff grabbed him by the arm and says, 'No, he didn't, Fall. That bastard was trying to escape and Mr. Fountain told him to stop. He wouldn't. Nobody in this town wanted him to escape and start murdering and stealing again. Not *even you. So just shut up!' Fall turned around and stomped off. He was mad. He wouldn't get the whore's money after all, although he knew he was sure to lose the case. Son, I felt bad I had to shoot the man. But, Henry, I wasn't about to let him get away after the beating he gave José and the threats he'd made about killing me.*

The car was quiet again. Roberta drew deeply on her cigarette. It had never fully registered with her just how violent the old days were. She blew the smoke over her shoulder to exit directly out the cracked vent window with the wind whistling by and slowly shook her head again. "What else do you remember about the trip that day?"

He handed her his pipe and the tin of Flying Dutchman again, saying only, "Please?" She smiled, stubbed out her cigarette, and began filling the pipe. Before she finished loading the long fine strands of tobacco, he started again.

"I remember that when we stopped to eat a little lunch and rest the horses, I was warm enough from sitting under the dog-head quilt that I foolishly played around without my coat and got chilled. I stayed cold the rest of the day too, and didn't have much to say to my Daddy until we sat for supper by a big snapping fire in Tularosa that evening. I was so quiet he hadn't even offered to let me drive again after lunch.

"On the road to Tularosa, Daddy stopped about a mile from the first road cut leading through White Sands and checked the loads in his Schofield revolver and the Winchester. He kept the rifle on his knees during the ride through the Sands. In those days outlaws who had been run out of Texas liked to make hideouts around there. Daddy was supposed to meet a man in Tularosa but wasn't sure he'd be there because we were two days late. So, we rode on past the turn-off to La Luz where he had friends. He said we'd see them on the way back.

"We stopped for dinner that night at Pat Coghlan's store and cantina in Tularosa. Charlie Esparza ran it back then. It was a clean well-lighted place with a small bar at one end and Mexican waiters who didn't keep you waiting for your supper. That night the special of the house was caldillo. I don't think anybody has ever made caldillo any better than Charlie Esparza's wife, Blanca. She used the best beef, potatoes, onions, and fiery chiles and cooked it just right. Believe me, that chile was hot coming and going! It was fine! My mouth still waters when I think about her stew. We sat at a table over close to a fireplace so big I could have walked into it if there had been no fire. I was a little short for the chair, but sitting on one leg made up the difference.

"While we were eating, a cowboy walked through the door. He looked around, and then came over to our table. He was wearing a soft buckskin coat with lots of fringe, a rough wool vest buttoned top-to-bottom, and shotgun chaps that had brushed against many a mesquite and showed thousands of thorn scratches. He held up his pants with red suspenders and he had a big blue bandana tied around his neck that hung outside his jacket. He carried a big long-barreled Colt revolver backwards on his left hip in a beautifully tooled Mexican double-loop holster. His hat was pushed up in front and he smelled of sweat and tobacco. It was the first time I had seen a cowboy up close and I couldn't help staring at him and taking in every detail. I was a townie and Daddy didn't let me play where cowboys liked to congregate in Mesilla or Las Cruces.

Daddy instantly recognized him, stood up, and they shook hands. Daddy introduced him to me as Mr. Roy Tibbets. I especially remember his hands. When he shook my hand, his hand, rough and powerful, with short stubby fingers, was big and strong and covered with calluses and scars. His hands were so different from Daddy's hands, which were powerful too, but Daddy's hands had long, well-manicured fingers and they were smooth, like my mother's. Roy's hair curled out from under his hat and he'd not shaved the scraggly beard around his big swooping mustache in quite a while. His perpetual-squint eyes took in every detail about us. When he saw me staring at him he grinned and winked. I winked back and immediately liked him. I grinned as far as my mouth would stretch and then some. Roy Tibbets was a real cowboy. Here I was eating dinner with him, although I was so excited I choked on a couple of mouthfuls of that fiery caldillo. I just couldn't believe my luck as I watched him with my mouth hung open while he talked to my daddy.

"Roy said he worked for a rancher named Fremont. Even I knew who Mr. Fremont was. He owned one of the biggest ranches on the east side of the Black Range and Daddy did a lot of legal work for him. Roy said Mr. Fremont told him to ride over to Tularosa and give Daddy some pieces of cowhide he had. Daddy, not saying a word, just nodded and smiled. Daddy said he'd been expecting Roy and asked him to sit down and have dinner with us. I don't think Roy had eaten for a while. He pulled up a chair and went through two bowls of caldillo as fast as he could pitch it down, his spoon swooping through that bowl like a steam shovel. He was done with two bowls before I'd finished the one I had started when he walked up. Then he wiped the bowl clean with a tortilla. He ate that in three bites, and, sighing with contentment, wiped the outside of his mouth and mustache with the back of his hand, smacking and licking his lips all the while. He leaned back, patted his lean belly and belched so loud everybody in the cantina must have heard him, but didn't pay it any mind 'cause gas is a common occurrence in a good cantina. He reached in his vest and pulled out a sack of tobacco and some cigarette papers. Rolling himself a smoke with one hand, he pulled the sack closed by pulling its drawstring with his teeth. Daddy finishing his meal too, pulled a cigar out of his coat, thrown over the chair to his right where he had also laid his pistol belt out of sight but within quick easy reach. He struck a sulfur match and used it to light up for both of them.

"Roy said, *Sorry about eating like a wolf, Mr. Fountain, but I've been sitting on ole Claude since 'fore daylight and the wind off them mountains is down right cold. I'd expected to meet up with you in Lincoln tomorrow, but when I saw you in here, I figured I was just lucky and decided I'd gotten my days confused – which ain't that hard for me to do.*

"Daddy nodded his head appreciatively. *I'm glad you showed up when you did, Roy. We were delayed a couple of days in San Augustin Pass ourselves. Horses ran off and left us stranded. Fortunately, they went back home, and my son Albert brought them back to us. So being a little late actually saved a little time in the long run.* He looked over at me and winked like we were fellow conspirators.

"Roy nodded and grinned. *Yes, sir, horses – they's just like women – can't live with 'em, can't live without 'em.* We had a good chuckle at that bit of wisdom, although it was years later before I had any idea what he was talking about.

"Roy glanced over at me and grinned again. He said, *You got a good lookin' son there, Mr. Fountain. You ever done any ranching, boy?* I answered No, sir. But, I got kinda puffed up then and figured I must look older than my age if he was asking me those kinds of questions. Daddy just grinned, stuck his lower lip out, and slowly shook his head. My big head deflated a little. Roy nodded toward me while he took a draw on his cigarette and said, *You wanna wait 'til later to discuss business?* Daddy shook his head and said, *No, sir. Henry knows to keep his mouth shut and he does. I'm an attorney and he's my assistant. Now then, Roy, tell us about what you have.*

"Roy and Daddy talked in low voices for nearly an hour. I had to sit up on the edge of my chair and lean forward over the table on my elbows to hear what they were talking about. Roy told Daddy about what he had discovered on the hides he'd taken while butchering a couple of cows for a fiesta back before Christmas.

"Like many things in life, it was just pure accident that he happened to compare brands from two different hides. Mr. Fremont's brand was the Bar F. He had just bought some stock from Charlie Bentene who was trying to start a little ranch, the Circle Eight, over in Black Canyon. Bentene's brand was a fancy straight-sided eight with a circle around it. Roy slaughtered a couple of head for meat just before Christmas. One steer happened to be one they had just bought from Bentene and one was from Fremont's original herd. Guess what Roy saw when he happened to look at the circle eight hide next to the one from the Bar F? It was a good job, so good you couldn't tell it had been changed if you were sitting on a horse ten feet away from the branded end of the cow. However, an up close comparison of the Circle Eight with the Bar F brand made it was easy to see that the Bar F brand had been changed to make a Circle Eight! Bentene had used a running iron on stock from Fremont's ranch and then sold the stock back to him. Mr. Fremont was being tricked into paying for a cow twice! Fremont and some of the other big ranchers were hopping mad about tricks like that and wanted blood. Daddy told me the next day some of those ranchers were ready to start a war with several of the small ranchers they believed were stealing their cattle and changing the brands to start their herds or survive the drought. Fortunately, cooler heads prevailed. Nobody wanted anything even close to another Lincoln County War, the range war that made Billy the Kid famous, so they hired Daddy to have the men who were stealing from them legally convicted, then hung or thrown in jail.

"As we sat there in Pat Coghlan's place Daddy pumped Roy for all the information he had. He took out a little notebook he carried in his coat pocket, and he wrote down everything that he thought he might use in Lincoln at the grand jury presentations. Daddy had just reached over and dropped his notebook back in his coat pocket when the cantina door swung open and was slammed shut by the pull of the wind. Two well-dressed men walked in. They might have been cowboys but their clothes weren't covered with dust like nearly everyone else's. They were younger than Roy, wore stockman dress coats, and carried big heavy revolvers. One was tall and skinny with a big hooked nose and crooked teeth that stuck out even under his big walrus mustache. The other was short but walked with a cocky strut. His face was smooth and clean-shaven. He was grinning and nodding hello to everyone. His hat, a big brim white Stetson, was pushed back on his head letting his straw colored hair hang almost all the way down to his hard and piercing turquoise blue eyes. When he looked at me, I felt like a wolf was sizing me up for a meal. I was instinctively afraid of him as soon as he walked through the door, but I felt safe with Roy and Daddy. Both of the men were red-faced like they had been out in the wind most of the day too.

They pulled chairs out and slowly sat down at a table across the room close to the bar. They were laughing and joking with the men at the table next to them. They said in loud voices intended to bring a waiter on the run that they were ready to put some firewater and caldillo in their empty feed bags. I watched as a waiter came around and they ordered their supper. They sipped the short glasses of tequila the waiter brought them and looked around the room, sizing everyone up. When he saw Roy talking to Daddy, Wolf's eyes narrowed as he nodded toward us to catch Hook Nose's attention. Grinning, as they stood up from their table, they started twisting between tables as they walked over toward us. Wolf Eyes was in front. Hook Nose followed grinning like a school bully ready to pick on some little kid. Roy saw me staring at 'em across the cantina; he glanced in that direction. His jaw muscles rippled as he grew silent. His hand moved off his knee and slide back to ease the tie off the hammer of his revolver. Daddy saw 'em too. He moved his right hand down under the red and white checked tablecloth and let it rest on the handle of his holstered Schofield. I heard the hammer on the Schofield click back as he watched the men approach. He whispered just loud enough for me to hear. *Henry, if any trouble starts, you move away from Roy and me as fast you can.* I just nodded.

"Wolf Eyes came up to the table, a toothpick hanging out of the side of this mouth, and stuck his hand out toward Daddy. He said with a grin, *Howdy, Mr. Fountain, I'm Jack Stone and this here is Charlie Bentene.* Daddy's gun hand didn't move, obviously and deliberately not making a motion to take Stone's outstretched hand as he hooked his left thumb into his vest pocket, and, for a few seconds that felt like they stretched into tomorrow, didn't speak. I'd never seen him refuse to shake hands with anyone. Stones eyes narrowed as his smile changed to lips drawn tightly over a set of bright white teeth. Daddy leaned forward in his chair a little with his right hand still under the tablecloth as he continued to stare with narrowed eyes at Stone. I was scared. I felt like I was about to fight some mean kid in school who wanted to beat me up. I could tell by how quiet he was that Daddy was angry. He nodded at them and said, *Gentlemen? Mr. Tibbets here and I were discussing some personal business. If you want to wait, I'll be glad to talk to you after we're done.*

"Daddy not shaking hands seemed like an insult to me, but then what did I know? It sure looked like there was gonna be a fight and I started looking around the cantina for shelter if trouble started.

"Stone looked angry and taken aback as he said, *Well, Mr. Fountain, I just hope you ain't believing anything this old son-of-a-bitch has told you.* He spat the words out like he'd bitten into bitter weed as he stared straight at Roy. Roy, silent and poker-faced, not blinking an eye, stared right back at Stone and Bentene. His hand rested unmoving and relaxed on his revolver. I'll never forget the look on Daddy's face. His eyes became slits and his voice was a hard, flat, threatening monotone that you had to concentrate to hear and understand and it made the hair on the back of my neck stand straight out. He was furious; Stone's eyes showed surprise.

"There was a little twitch in Stone's cheek at how Daddy was angry over what, to me, was just an attempt at a friendly handshake. Daddy's eyes never left Stone's. *Watch your foul mouth, Stone. I don't want this young boy hearing rough language like that. I don't want to hear any more threats, implied or otherwise, toward us now or later. Understand me?* The way Daddy said the words, precisely and slowly with deadly calm, was enough to give any man pause. Daddy continued looking Stone straight in the eye. It made me want to be just like him when I grew up, fearless and a man to be feared. I was about to burst with pride over how cool and collected Daddy looked and sounded.

"Stone suddenly seemed to relax. He grinned and gave a little nod, but Bentene's eyes were wide and his mouth open in shock. Stone looked like a wolf showing his fangs, trying to keep a grizzly bear off him. He shook his head, held up both hands with his palms out and waved Daddy off. *Sorry...Sorry, Mr. Fountain, I didn't mean no harm, just teasing old Roy here...He's the da – I mean he's the durndest wild storyteller a feller can listen to here in Tularosa. I just don't think you want to take anything he told you too seriously.*

"Daddy nodded, saying, *I'll take it anyway I think best, Stone. I'll use it too, understand me?*

"Stone with a smirk, shrugged and nodded. *That's fine – see ya later, Tibbets!* He turned from our table and led Bentene back to theirs; their caldillo was already sitting there with steam rising off the top. Daddy never moved until they sat down. I'd never seen Daddy stare somebody down like that. In fact I'd never seen two grown men seem so ready to fight, and my heart pounded for a while just thinking about it. I have to tell you I sure was proud and glad Daddy was on my side. He finally relaxed and I heard the hammer ease down on the Schofield. Roy took his hand off his revolver but left the hammer tie loose.

"Daddy pitched some coins on the table for dinner, stood and said, *Roy let's go over to our room at Señora Esparza's boarding house and you show us those hides.* Roy just nodded and followed us out the door. They never looked back toward Stone, but I did. Stone was watching every move we made as he blew slowly on a spoonful of caldillo. Roy disappeared into the cold darkness while we walked over to our room. He showed up with a roll of hides under his arm just as we were opening the door at Señora Esparza's boarding house.

"We walked single file down the narrow hallway to our room, Roy's spurs making a pleasant jangle as he followed Daddy and me. When we got in the room he unrolled the two hides and spread 'em out on the floor. Even I could tell the Bar F brand was changed to the Circle Eight. Daddy looked at them and grinned. *Now we have enough evidence to arrest those thieves! Two of 'em are sitting down the street in the cantina right now! Roy, you've earned your pay for this one, my friend. I'm sure Mr. Fremont will be grateful.* Roy just squatted by the hides nodding and grinning all the while like he had struck the mother lode.

*Roy, I'll keep these hides and show them with the ones Les Dow is bringing. If you find out about any more anywhere in the next week or two, let me know – I'll be in Lincoln for the next two or three weeks. For your safety, I think you need to get on to Lincoln. Ride along with us. Two guns are better than one anytime. We're leaving about an hour before sun-up. I'll call you before the grand jury in the next two or three days, then you can get on back to Fremont's.*

"Roy took out his tobacco sack from a vest pocket and started rolling another cigarette. *I was just thinking the same thing, Mr. Fountain. I'll ride on over to Lincoln with Y'all and tell my story – the sooner the better. I'll be glad to hang around Lincoln and ride back to Cruces with you if you want. Y'all are gonna have to be real careful coming back cause the cat's gonna be out of the bag.*

*No, that's all right. You get on back to the ranch. I have a first class bodyguard right here,* Daddy said squeezing my shoulder.

*Then, I'll go on back to the ranch as soon as you're done with me. If I find any more of these hides I'll let you know. Wisht I had a bodyguard like you do, I'd feel a sight more safe.* Roy looked in my direction and winked. I wished mightily I was a cowboy then so I could ride with Roy. I was ready to go anywhere with that man.

"As Roy was clinking out the door Daddy said, *We'll all be fine on the ride up to Lincoln with our friends Mr. Schofield and Mr. Winchester. I expect to have my work done soon. You're a great help. Good night, see you in the morning.*

"As he was disappearing down the hall, Roy touched his hat and nodded to acknowledge what Daddy said. I didn't sleep well that night. I kept seeing Jack Stone's eyes boring into mine and feeling he was about to do something bad to us. Daddy appeared to sleep easy. But I wasn't sure he was asleep. I usually heard him snoring at home when he was sleeping in bed with Mama. He was mighty quiet in bed with me that night.

"Way before sun up, Señora Esparza served us up a big breakfast of *huevos rancheros*. Charlie Esparza harnessed Sergeant and Buck and brought the wagon around for us. When we finished breakfast, Roy was waiting outside sitting on Claude and had his Winchester laid across his saddle pommel. Daddy loaded up our Winchester, lunches, trunk of papers, the valise, and Roy's hides. In the freezing morning air, we said *Adios* to the Esparzas and headed down the dark road to Lincoln with Roy's horse trotting along beside us. It was over an hour before sun up. I was sitting next to Daddy wishing it would get light soon so Stone couldn't jump out of the bushes and start shooting without us seeing him first."

# 4

# LINCOLN

The Plymouth glided by the gypsum sand of White Sands National Monument gleaming eerily in the moonlight. Roberta finished filling Henry's pipe, and packed it off even. "Ready for a light?"

"Yes ma'am, that'd be mighty fine. Look at that sand! It looks like billowing clouds or rolling ocean waves, doesn't it? Folks ought to come out here more often when the moon is out. Beautiful! But, I can tell you on that last ride by here in the daylight with my daddy, it was like a white monster rising out of the desert, ominous and scary. I was afraid some gang of outlaws and murderers was going to ride out of those sand dunes shooting and yelling as they filled us full of holes. It didn't relieve my fright any when Daddy kept that loaded Winchester across his knees."

"Who was Jack Stone? I don't think I've ever heard my father or grandfather ever mentioned him."

"He was one mean, no-good, greedy son-of-a-bitch, that's who he was. Pardon my lack of euphemism, but my blood still gets hot when I think about him. He owned a small spread in a canyon over on the San Andreas side of the basin. He had a few cattle. I'd bet nearly all of them were stolen. He was a slick greasy thief, murderer, and con man who talked a great line about how all the small ranchers in the Tularosa basin had to stick together if they wanted to survive. He claimed unwritten open-range law said that if you found a stray unbranded calf on your property, then it was yours regardless of the mother's brand. Naturally, if you kept the calf and its mother was there, then you ought to keep the cow too. He'd say, *That's the way it is in Texas, ain't it?* Folks would think, *Well, if that's the way Texans do it then we should too.* Most of the little ranchers and farmers were desperate people in those years. The drought that started in 1890 was savaging everyone. It dried up the water supply and wiped out the gra'ma grass. No water, no grass; no cattle, no ranchers. Ranchers about to go under were eager to listen to anybody who said it was right to fight any fight, to keep cattle that weren't their own, to even kill in order to keep what little they had. Why it was worse than the Depression in the thirties for those folks, except it was about forty years earlier. Stone got several of the small ranchers to form an association. It was never formally organized on paper as nearly as I've been able to determine. The old-timers who were in it, that I've talked to, said they all agreed to put money in a pot to help Stone fight what they felt were illegal and unwarranted attacks against them by the big ranchers and their attorneys.

"Stone, despite his high-minded talk, just wanted carte blanche to steal cattle in order to build his ranch into a major operation. He was accused several times of killing or running off range detectives that were nosing around small ranchers' herds. When the sheriff tried to develop evidence to bring Stone to trial, the association ranchers all kept quiet and made sure their ranch hands kept their mouths shut. For all I know, association members might even have helped him with the killings. The law, as we know it today, almost certainly was on the side of the big ranchers, but in those days every man pretty much made his own justice. Communications were too slow and distances too great for law enforcement like there is today, and we both know it isn't so good. So, when the little operations started taking a few stray cows from the big ranches, the big-time ranchers felt like they were battling the drought and thieves. They couldn't do anything about the drought except hold on, but thievery was an opportunity for action. They weren't hesitant to play rough. Daddy knew that if he didn't put a quick stop to the rustling there would be a major shooting war between the big and small operations, just like there had been in Lincoln County during the days of Billy the Kid. If shooting started, a lot of blood was going to be spilled, and statehood was sure to be delayed. It was a bad time in a high-stakes game of blind man's bluff. Whoever got the upper hand won, regardless of how they did it."

"Hmmph," Roberta grunted, but said no more as she handed him his lighted pipe. Steering with one hand, he stared up the road, his mind drifting back in time. "Bitterly cold days always remind me of that trip to Lincoln." He yawned to shake the cobwebs from his memory. "Where was I? Oh, yeah...on the road to Lincoln.

"We made good time traveling after we left the Esparzas, and we reached Lincoln a little before dark. The lunch Mrs. Esparza fixed for us was long gone. I was ready to start chewing on cactus I was so hungry, and I shivered most of the afternoon from the cold. Daddy, too cold for casual conversation, was hunched down in his Army coat with its big collar turned up as high as it would go. Roy loped along beside us, casually rolling an occasional cigarette when we stopped to let Buck and Sergeant rest. At our mid-day stop, I kept rubbing my hands and slapping myself to keep warm. Roy looked over at me grinning and asked, *You cold, little man?* All I could do was nod. He says, *Aw, it ain't so bad. Why you'd get used to it quick if you was a cowboyin' out here for a month or two.* I tell you, Bertie, that was the first time I thought maybe I didn't want to be a cowboy after all.

"In Lincoln, Daddy rented us a room at Mrs. Darcy's boarding house on Main Street, almost right across from the two-story building that served as the courthouse where the grand jury met. Roy helped us unload our gear and carry it to our room upstairs. Then we drove over to the livery stable. Roy stabled Claude, his mustang, and headed for a saloon after Daddy told him to be careful not to drink too much. Daddy said he needed him to testify in a day or two, and he had to be clear-eyed and sober. Roy raised one hand like he was bein' sworn in at a jury trial. He says, *Mr. Fountain, I ain't no drunk. Just want to warm my innards with a meal and a little shot of good whiskey. You can count on me when you need me.* Daddy smiled and said, *I know I can Roy. Take care of yourself. I'll see you in a day or two.* Roy turned to me and said, *Get on down there and get big on Mrs. Darcy's good cookin', little man. I'll see ya 'fore I leave.* He slapped me on the back, and we all shook hands all around again before he took off down the street toward a saloon.

"Mrs. Darcy was a widow lady. She was generously broad across her backside and big in the bosom. Her blonde, gray-streaked hair rode in a big twist up on the top of her head and she was as gracious and kind a person as I've ever met. She might have been plump, but she could move faster than a cat. One morning I saw her coming through the door with a big plate of biscuits and one slid off. Her hand was nothing but a blur as she caught it before it had fallen a foot from the plate and put it right back where it belonged in one smooth motion. She saw me watching her and giggled as she winked at me. I wouldn't have believed a woman, and especially a plump one like her, could be that fast, if I hadn't seen it myself. I'm convinced that if she had been a man, she was quick enough to have been a deadly gunfighter.

"She took a shine to me right off. When Daddy and I got back from the livery, she said, *Now you gentlemen just go right up to your room and get comfortable. I'll be serving dinner in about an hour, promptly at six o'clock, so come hungry. There'll be plenty for everybody, especially Mr. Henry.* After hanging our clothes up nice and neat just the

53

way Daddy liked them, we washed up, combed down our hair, and slapped the dust out of our clothes. We walked down stairs to stand by the fire in the dining room just as the other boarders were coming in.

"Mrs. Darcy had a full house and every place at the dinner table was taken. There was a rancher from over near Roswell who never took his hat off, inside or out. He and Daddy talked quietly over in a corner for a while after dinner, but I never heard what they were saying. There was an old-timer with bright dancing eyes behind silver rimmed glasses that looked like the kind grannies wear. His name was Rufus Pike. He and Mrs. Darcy were the only ones in the room who actually paid any attention to me. Rufus talked to me all through dinner. I learned that he had a small ranch somewhere up a canyon in the Organs behind Tortugas Mountain. He and Mrs. Darcy's husband rode in the same company of dragoons in the days before the Civil War, when the militias were fighting Apaches all over the southwest. Two or three times a year Rufus rode his big gray mule, Sally, over to Lincoln where he made repairs on Mrs. Darcy's house and did general handyman chores. I understand now that he was sweet on her too, but they were so discreet that if anyone had any idea he was tiptoeing down the hall to her room in the late night hours, nothing was ever said. I liked him right away, but his chores were nearly done, and he was planning to stay only a few more days.

"There was a Methodist preacher who rode a circuit between Roswell and Las Cruces. I remembered seeing him walking around Mesilla square the previous fall. He was tall and angular with arms that were about two inches too long for his dusty black coat and legs so long that his pants rode too high on his boots. Daddy remembered him too, and reminded me as we were getting ready for bed that Methodist preachers liked to pound the lectern and bring down the wrath of God on unrepentant sinners. I thought the minister might bring the wrath of God down on me if he ever learned I wasn't real good. So, when he was around, I stayed on my best behavior. There was also an Army lieutenant with wavy black hair and a droopy little mustache from Ft. Stanton buying supplies. He looked younger than my brother Jack, but his youthful face was deceiving because he told everyone who mentioned how young he looked that he had been graduated from West Point for two years.

"Most of the folks staying with Mrs. Darcy were gone in a day or two. The preacher was there until Sunday, when he held a church service somewhere in town, and then he moved on. The rancher was gone the next day and so was the lieutenant. However, it was rare that

Mrs. Darcy didn't have every room filled. Her comfortable house and good meals were known all the way from Albuquerque to Roswell to El Paso.

"Rufus had an unlimited supply of stories, and he was a great story-teller. He'd work a while, then to relax get a cup of coffee to slurp before refreshing the wad of tobacco he kept in his cheek. While he was resting and drinking coffee he'd tell more tales about his adventures fighting Indians.

"He spent hours with a whetstone he carried in his pants pocket slowly drawing his Kissing Cranes pocketknife blades back and forth on its gritty black surface where he spat a dollop of tobacco juice. He'd stop every few minutes to see if it was sharp enough to shave a little hair off his leathery forearm. Not satisfied, he'd spit on the stone once more and keep on sharpening while he rattled off first one tale, then another about the old days. I'd sit out on the back porch with him, listening bug-eyed to his stories about all the mayhem and cruelty he'd seen from the Apaches and Navahos. After he got his blade sharp enough to shave, he wouldn't shave. He'd turn right around and use it for whittling while his scraggly gray beard continued to grow. However, to give the devil his due – I guess because he was sweet on Mrs. Darcy – he kept his long thin hair and gray-streaked beard well groomed with a nice little ivory comb he carried in a vest pocket.

"I remember that the only clothes he ever wore were old worn-out canvas pants, red suspenders, tie-up miner's boots, and a white cotton shirt with a red bandana around his neck. Brown tobacco juice stains were up and down the front of his shirt even when the shirt was fresh out of the washtub. His gray hair was thin on top and needed cutting over big ears that stuck out conspicuously under an ancient campaign hat that still had a carefully maintained shape with the brim pushed up in front. It carried a sweat stain that went half up the crown and nearly to the edge of the brim. When he took his hat off, like a gentleman should at dinner, there was a well-defined boundary etched on his forehead. The skin below the boundary line was ruddy and wrinkled, scorched to a deep brown by years in the desert sun. Above the hat line though, his skin was white as the lace on Mrs. Darcy's dresses.

"Many of his ways were just plain crude. I guess maybe it was because he had been a bachelor for so many years and had no training in manners. He blew his nose at the table, wiped his mouth with the back of his sleeve, and chewed with his mouth open. He ate things with his fingers that should have been eaten with a knife and fork, and made it a point to belch if the food was particularly good. Still, he often surprised us all with a well-developed sense of taste and style. His elegant silver-framed reading glasses had circularly shaped lenses that rode low on his nose and made him look wise when he looked over the top of them as he spoke to you. He chewed tobacco, but always spit in a little spittoon he carried with him wherever he went, and he never chewed or spat in front of a lady unless he asked first. He never used rough language around Mrs. Darcy either, and he always did a good job washing up for dinner, using just a dash of lilac water to smell good.

"Since I didn't know anyone my own age in town, I offered to help Rufus with his work while Daddy was making his presentations to the grand jury. Rufus allowed that he could use all the help he could get, especially from a strong young buck like me. It wasn't long before we were great friends. I followed him around like a pup listening to his stories and helping him with his chores. He bragged to Mrs. Darcy about how much help I was. His bragging made me want to help him even more. Apparently, he was well read. He could tell tales from *The Iliad* as easily as he could about his days of being an Army scout and fighting Indians.

"Rufus commented on how fine a weapon our Winchester was when we were unloading at Mrs. Darcy's our first day there. Daddy told him that we'd be going out to shoot Sunday afternoon and he would be glad to let him try it out if he wanted to come with us. Rufus thought that was fine idea and said so several times. On Sunday morning, we hitched up Buck and Sergeant and drove a couple of miles outside of Lincoln for target practice in a little canyon that fronted the river. Rufus watched closely as Daddy cranked a couple of cartridge loads through the Winchester, never missing anything at which he pointed. Daddy let me shoot a load while he and Rufus encouraged and coached me. After I managed to hit three or four targets out of twelve shots, I was beginning to feel like hot stuff as Rufus nodded and winked at me and Daddy stood behind me with his arms crossed, looking serious. When it was Rufus's turn to shoot, he hit every target at every distance he tried. He was a better shot than Daddy, and Daddy said so. Rufus had one round left in his load after turning a rock the size of his fist to dust twenty or thirty yards down river. In one smooth motion, never pausing to aim, he whipped the Winchester up and with the last bullet killed a grackle sitting on a bush cussin' at us. That black bird was at least a hundred yards away; after the shot, there wasn't anything left except a few black feathers floating to the ground. It was a remarkable shot. Daddy was impressed and so was I. Daddy said, *Where did you learn to shoot like that, Rufus?* Rufus just grinned and said, *Why in the old days a feller learned to do that or died in Indian country.* Daddy just nodded. He understood perfectly what Rufus meant.

"After shooting we rode down the river looking for some good fishing pools, but most of the water was gone. It was just too dry. When we got back to Mrs. Darcy's, it was the middle of the afternoon. The house was filled with the aroma of baked apple and cinnamon pies. She invited us to come sit around her kitchen table next to her cooking stove, warm up, and keep her company while she cooked for the evening meal. We didn't hesitate to accept that invitation. As we sat at the table, Daddy and Rufus told stories while we drank coffee and ate pieces of pie right out of her oven. That pie was so fresh it scalded your mouth if you didn't blow on it first. We put butter and some hard sauce on it. Ummm, ummm it was sweet and fruity all the way down. It was wonderful. I've never had any pie any better. I finished a glass of milk with my pie and Daddy and Rufus polished off a couple of cups of coffee that they loaded up with sugar.

"Rufus said with a chuckle, *Ye know, havin' sugar in coffee's a rare treat fer me. If'n I tried keeping sugar out'n a fancy sugar bowl sitting in the middle of the table at my place like Mrs. Darcy does here, why the ants and waspers would come fight me fer it. They'd probably win too! I wouldn't fight no wasper fer no sugar. No, Siree! I wouldn't do that!*

"Mrs. Darcy got the *chile rellenos* she was preparing ready for the skillet and peeled some potatoes, then sat down with us at the table for a while. She saw Daddy and Rufus had finished their pie, and offering more, which they politely refused, said, Mr. *Fountain, it's quite all right with me if you want to smoke here in the kitchen, I know you like cigars. My good departed husband enjoyed cigars too, but only smoked them on special occasions. I think a nice Sunday afternoon is a special occasion. If Mr. Pike wants to get his spittoon, he can have a chew too while we enjoy each other's company.* She looked over at me and said with a laugh, *No smoking or chewing for you, young man! It'll stunt your growth!* The men nodded and laughed. I giggled at the image I had of little me with one of Daddy's big cigars stuck out of my mouth or a chew of tobacco in one cheek.

"Rufus excused himself to get his spittoon. He was back in two ticks of the clock and already had a chew started. He plopped back down in his seat and said, *This here is mighty kind of you Mrs. Darcy, feeding us some of yore deeelicious pie, then letting us indulge in our nasty habits.*

"She tilted her head down and looked up at him with a flirt's smile. *Your company is worth it all, gentlemen, especially young Henry's. Now he's a real gentleman.* I sat up a little straighter – a man among men. Daddy wet his cigar and, grinning with a wink at me, lit up.

"Mrs. Darcy teased Rufus about carrying a spittoon during his scouting days and that set him to telling us a story about a close scrape he had with an Apache named Caballo Negro – Black Horse."

Roberta smiled. "Ah, at last we get to the Apaches!"

Henry nodded. " Yeah, we're getting closer.

"Rufus told us, *Back in '55 I was a scouting fer Cap'n Ewell and his 60th Dragoons. We was a chasin' and a fightin' Apaches down in Texas on the El Paso to San Antonio road. In those days, the Mescaleros was a wipin' out any freight outfits that warn't protected by soldiers.*

*Cap'n Ewell was determined to have some satisfaction fer all the murderin' and robbin' they'd done. We chased those damned Apaches all over hell and half of Texas. They was a few running battles with them, but they never stood and fought till they was cornered. Then they was the devil to pay. We musta lost ten or fifteen men in those fights. Lord help ye if they ever caught ye alive. They knowed how to torture a feller so's he stayed alive fer days so's they'd git more power from the sufferin'. Ewell always told us to always save one bullet fer our own use in any Indian fight. We did too. I knowed a few fellers that had to pull the trigger on they own heads. Stuck the business end of those old Walker Colts right up against an eyeball and pulled the trigger they did.*

*Well, sir, it got on into late fall and we'd just about rode our horses to death a chasing those red niggers. I found us a nice little spot to rest on the Rio Grande up in the Bosque 'bout twenty miles north of El Paso. Ewell, he decided to hole up there to escape bein' attacked by bandidos and Indians and to rest the animals and men fer a while. I tell ya, I was mighty glad not to be in the saddle fer twelve hours a day in wind and dust that cut ye just as bad as any Mescalero blade.*

*After we'd been camped fer four or five days, I reckin those Apache devils got lonesome fer us 'cause we woke up one morning with half the stock gone and the sentry with a second mouth cut across his windpipe. Nobody had heard a sound, that's how tired we all was. I s'pect the sentry just dozed off and that there was the end of him. He was my friend, but he made a big mistake and paid fer it. I didn't have a whole lot of sympathy fer him. Ye just didn't make those kinds of mistakes and expect to live in those days. Ye know what I mean don't ye, Mr. Fountain?*

"Daddy took a pull on his cigar and blowing a long stream of of smoke toward the ceiling nodded slowly. *Yes sir, Rufus, I'm afraid I know very well from long, hard experience.*

"Rufus winked at us. *Yes sir, Mr. Fountain, yore reputation as an Indian fighter runs a far piece in front of ye. Anyways, Ole Ewell just stood on the edge of the river and stared off in the distance toward the Organs and Franklins fer a long time. The rest of us just sat around the fire tryin' to get warm and a cursing those red niggers fer their damned slick trick. Finally, Ewell says, 'Rufus Pike!' I come a running with a salute and says Yes, Sir! 'Rufus,' he says, 'go find where those Mescalero are. Then come back and get me if they ain't killed all the stock they stole first by running 'em to death.' So I saddled up with the best horse that was left, cause they'd taken mine, and I started after 'em.*

*Them there devils was smart. They rode about ten mile up river then started across the desert toward Baylor Pass as a group, then a rider with three or four horses would peel off the main group and head out alone.* Rufus started using his hands and gesturing first to the right, then to the left. *Some went over the Organs by Baylor Pass, some over San Augustin Pass, a few went through Bear Canyon, and some through Soledad Canyon. Another few miles and another rider, he split off from that bunch. Before long the only thing left was four animals and a couple of riders who finally split up.*

"*I knowed what was gonna happen when the first group split out, so I stopped and sat a spell trying to figure out where they'd rendezvous. I guessed it had to be near a spring over close to the Jarilla Mountains. It was on their way home and they was water there fer the horses. Only a few old gringo desert rats like me knowed about that there spring, but all the Mescalero knowed right where it was. I figured I'd ride over there and set myself up a little ambush fer the early birds. Maybe get 'em all if they come in slow. At least I could keep 'em from water so's the horses would move real slow. I knowed I'd get there first 'cause they's riding 'round the desert in all different directions tryin' to confuse anybody that followed 'em from Ewell's camp. I wasn't shore enough about their meeting spot to go back and get Cap'n Ewell though. Ewell's animals needed rest bad, so I went Apache huntin' on my own. That there was a big mistake.*

Daddy was puffing his cigar and nodding as he listened with an ear cocked to catch all of Rufus' story.

"*I got over to the Jarillas about dark and found me a good place to make camp up a little draw and behind a mesquite thicket where I could watch the spring and not be seen. I was plum wore out and didn't* want to risk no fire, so I hid my horse and just rolled up in my blankets and went to sleep. 'Bout daylight I felt this here sharp prick on my neck and thought some sticker had blowed on to me during the night. I opened one eye and looked into the narrow slanty eyes of an Apache face that had the ugliest scar I'd ever seen on a man. Rufus took a finger and drew its pattern down his face while I sat there watching his every move with my mouth open. Daddy watched me with a big grin he tried to hide behind the hand holding his cigar. Mrs. Darcy fanned herself and listened politely while she too watched me with a smile. She'd heard the story several times.

"Rufus let his finger drop off the edge of his jaw and says, Yes, sir! That there scar, it run from his scalp line across his forehead, down by his left eye, across his cheek, and just kinda fell off the edge of his jaw. He had this big Bowie knife ready to cut my throat and he was grinning like a cat with a cornered mouse. I found out a few years later his name was Fast Hand and he had fought and killed two men in his own clan who'd objected to him taking a couple of Mexican women fer wives. That's how he'd got that there scar, but nobody objected to the Mexican women being around after the fight! No, sir! They shore didn't.

I knowed I was gonna die. In fact, I couldn't quite figure out why I was still a living. He had me dead to rights. I did a to-die-fer stupid thing when Apaches is around – I went to sleep – and I knowed I deserved to die. They's nothin' I could do about it 'cept die quick or if I couldn't pull that off not scream loud while he tortured me. He was a grittin' his teeth to keep from killin' me as he held that blade against my wind pipe and motioned to the boy with him to come over beside him. The boy had already found and saddled my horse and was ready to ride off.

That boy wasn't much older than ye are now, Henry, maybe twelve or fourteen. He didn't have no shirt and he had streaks of black running the full length of his arms and on one side of his face like the man's scar. It musta been his first raid as warrior. That there Indian who had me on the edge of his Bowie was a wantin' to teach him what to do with a prisoner. Why, it was just like I'd seen a lion teaching a cub to hunt, 'cept I was the rabbit. Lordy, lordy, I knowed I was a gonna suffer and I decided when the cuttin' was about to start I'd try to kill myself by pushing my throat against that big Bowie knife blade he had against my windpipe. When the young 'un walked over to us, Fast Hand motioned fer him to pull out the skinning knife he was packin'. He started making signs about where the boy should cut me so's I'd suffer but not die quick. The cutting wasn't gonna be just around by face and neck either, if ye get my meaning.

"I saw Mrs. Darcy blush but I didn't have a clue why.

*The kid just looked at me fer a while and ole Fast Hand nodded his head toward me a couple times, signing again and again where to cut me. Finally the boy turned to Fast Hand and said something in Apache I couldn't understand. Fast Hand nodded, and, without a word, slowly pulls the blanket off me. He takes my big hawg leg Walker Colt and skinning knife, feels me up fer other weapons, and motions fer me to take off my boots, shirt, and pants. Now it was cold, let me tell ye, and I figured they was gonna watch me die naked a freezin' to death. He kept watching me holding that big knife on me not six inches from my throat and his other hand grabbed on to my hair so fer sure I wasn't going nowheres. It was just a game fer him. He needn't have worried. I had expected to be dead by then but was still livin'. I wasn't about to do anything rash to get myself killed.*

*Fast Hand says in pretty good Spanish, 'Habla Espanol?'*

*Si, un poco, a little, says I.*

*Ole Fast Hand says in Spanish, 'El muchacho, he say it is too easy to kill ye this way. He wants strong enemies to defeat. Ye look weak as a woman. Go, get strong, and come again if ye can survive in the cold. We'll kill ye when it is worth our trouble.'*

*I said, 'Gracias hombre. I'll come again in the spring to get yer hair.' Fast Hand nodded and grinned. 'Bueno! Ye come. It is good to kill ye then. Tell Ewell we look fer him too. Now go!' I got up real slow and started a shiverin'. I was curious about the boy who didn't seem to be cold at all, but already had on my shirt. I said,* Como se llamo el muchacho, Señor? *The boy heard me and he said,* 'Me llamo El Caballo Negro – *I am called The Black Horse!' Well sir, I'm here to tell ye he might be called Black Horse, but he shore as blue blazes stood in my book as White Horse fer not killin' me. I was mighty grateful he'd decided not to practice a cutting me. Why, he'd made a friend fer life after the fool stunt I'd pulled. Didn't matter none though 'cause we'd probably try to kill each other the next time we met.*

*They took everything I had 'cept my long johns and the boy rode off on my horse. There was a little ranch about twenty miles away over toward El Paso. I figured that if I trotted the whole way I could keep warm enough to keep from freezing and I'd probably make it in four or five hours if I didn't run into any more Indians. If I couldn't run that far, I was gonna die anyway, and I knowed it. Well sir, I got to that ranch before midday. I reckon it must have taken me 'bout five hours. I could barely walk and I'd run by or through so many sticker plants there warn't a part of my body that warn't bleedin' a little and hurtin' like hell, but, aye God, I was alive! The Morales family took me in, pulled the stickers, washed me up, fed me, and put me to bed. I got strong enough to head back to Ewell after resting fer the rest of that day and the next. The third morning I paid 'em fer a horse, a serapé, and some sandals, then lit out to Ewell's camp.*

*I found Ewell and the troops late the next day. Ewell was glad to see me. He didn't look too disappointed when I told him I hadn't been able to find the stock. Said he'd decided we needed to rest up the rest of the winter anyway so he was gonna ease on up to Mesilla now that I was back and rest the company till after the spring winds. I was glad to hear that. I'd already decided I was done scoutin' fer the Army. It was too hard and risky. So I quit after we got to Mesilla. Ewell said he hated to lose me but understood why I wanted to leave.*

*I found me a spot in a canyon up in the Organs behind Tortugas Mountain. It had good water and there was enough grass so I could do a little ranching – ye know just enough to get by, didn't want a big spread. I stocked it with some wild cattle rounded up outa Mexico. In a couple of year I had a poke big enough to live on, and built myself a comfortable little shack outta timber I hauled up from Las Cruces. One of these here days I'm a gonna make one outta rocks and a little lumber like old Frenchy Rochas made over to Dog Canyon. I still live over behind Tortugas Mountain most of the year, but come over here onct in a while to help out Mrs. Darcy. Her husband rode with Ewell too. He carried an arrowhead in his back from a Mescalero ambush. He did fine fer a few years 'fore it finally shifted around too close to his spine and killed him. Good man. I shore hated to see him go.*

"I cheered and clapped my hands at Rufus's story. I had heard quite a few tales about the Apaches already. The ranchers that worked with Daddy still told stories about near scrapes with Geronimo and of outrages he was supposed to have done. You couldn't walk in a store in Mesilla or Las Cruces more than five minutes before you'd hear somebody start talking about a relative they'd lost in Apache raids. This was the first time, though, I'd ever heard a tale about the Apache wars from somebody who'd actually fought the Indians. Daddy just wouldn't talk about his soldiering days. I said, *Mr. Pike, do you ever hear any more about Fast Hand or Caballo Negro? I mean, do you think they're still on the reservation now or rode with Geronimo and got shipped off to Florida?* Daddy took a swallow of coffee and nodded; he was thinking the same thing.

"Rufus said, *Naw, they didn't ride with Geronimo. Ole Fast Hand wasn't so fast after all. A Mexican Army patrol run into him by acci-*

dent when he was leadin' a raidin' party tryin' to steal some more women from a little village, Aqua Blanco, he'd terrorized fer years. The Mexicans shot him and his raiders so full a holes all they had left to bury was air. Caballo Negro and his son, Muchacho Amarillo, Yellow Boy, who must be close to thirty now, stop by my place fer water two or three times a year. Black Horse still sneaks off the Mescalero reservation to hunt. Yellow Boy eases down into Mexico to visit a woman he's a courtin'. She's a hidin' in the Sierra Madre with Apaches left from those that run off with Geronimo in one of his breaks from San Carlos and others that decided they'd jest stay in Mexico rather than have peace with the Americanos. They's still there cause they played it safe and didn't come back across the border with Geronimo on his raids. Ain't many folks knows about 'em. Yellow Boy has this old lever-action Henry rifle with a brass receiver. You know the gun I'm talking about, don't you, Colonel Fountain? It loads by dropping cartridges down a tube under the barrel.

"Daddy nodded, his eyes twinkling. He said, You know I do, Rufus, but I hadn't heard this tale about Yellow Boy before.

"Rufus spat, wiped the dribble from his beard and nodded back. Yes, sir, I do that. Anyways, Black Horse took it off some pore pilgrim that was wiped out a tryin' to get to California. The Indians call those rifles with brass receivers Yellow Boys, and they call him 'Muchacho Amarillo' 'cause they's no difference 'tween him and that old rifle. Wherever he points it, that's where the bullet goes dead center ever time. Let me tell ye fellers somethin', that there Yellow Boy's a deadly shot. I ain't never seen him miss in over fifteen years, since I taught him how to shoot. But that there is another story. Never seen anybody shoot as good as him. He even scouted fer the Army against Geronimo when he was still a pup, but he quit 'fore Geronimo was captured. He lives with a woman on the reservation just over the mountains there. The other woman he visits down in the Sierra Madre is his first wife's sister. That there is the woman he goes to see. I remember the first time I found him gettin' water at my spring. I had him dead to rights and was ready to put some holes in his hide when I saw he was with Caballo Negro. Ole Caballo, he remembered me too. So we had us a talkin' instead of a shootin'. We ain't exactly friends, ye understand, but we ain't enemies neither. I told him I was glad fer 'em to use my water and to stop any time. He gave me a haunch of deer he'd killed and told me in pretty good English there was nobody he knew that'd bother me. And they ain't been neither.

"I said, Mr. Pike is Yellow Boy a better shot than you? Old Rufus said, nodding, He shore as hell is Henry. It's about like comparing ye

63

*to me, as to compare me to him. He could be a big-time pistolero if he warn't no Indian. But he just shoots when he needs food or to defend his self. Army lets him keep the rifle 'cause he's a tribal policeman. Ye know all about that too, don't ye, Mr Fountain?*

"Daddy grinned and slowly nodded his head. *Yes, I guess I do, Rufus. You're right, Yellow Boy is the best shot I ever saw.*

"Rufus took the opportunity to spit, then he said, *Yes, sir, he carries that there Henry everwhere. He's like a ghost when he travels too. Has this black and white Pinto he rides, but once he slides out of sight into the mesquite and creosotes he just disappears. It's a scarifying the way he becomes invisible like he does. He's still got his Army coat with sergeant's strips and a hat like mine. The soldiers pretty much leave him alone cause they respect him and they know how well he can shoot. They ain't stupid.*

"Daddy said, *Rufus, how'd you say you got your first cattle – from Mexico?* I knew Daddy was gonna ask that question because of his business with the grand jury in Lincoln. Maybe he thought Rufus was stealing stock for his herd too.

"Rufus nodded and spat again, making a little *ping* sound in the spittoon. *Yes, sir, I did say Mexico. Durin' the forty-nine gold rush and the war, stock got free from wagon trains passing through El Paso. Then they was some from the free ranges north of the Rio Grande that just wandered across the river and started breeding wild and free down there in the Bosque along the river. I had a few cows and was just barely getting by when Mr. Fremont, he come by my shack and told me about the strays south of the river in Mexico. Said he was a getting' a crew together to git stock fer their ranches, and wanted to know if I wanted to come along. He said he'd give us a quarter of all the stock we caught to split between us, plus some wages if'n we helped him out. I said, Shore, I'll come. We spent about a month running and branding cattle out of the Bosque along the river on both sides. I managed to wind up with about fifty head and they's a real bull with 'em. I ain't needed to buy stock since.*

"Daddy laughed and said, *You're right there Rufus. Keep that bull busy and you won't need to find stock in the Bosque anymore.* Rufus grinned and spat again in his little spittoon. Tobacco juice etched the corners of his mouth and his Sunday-best white shirt showed a few more brown spots and streaks. He said, *Well, sir, I'll tell you, that old bull is about as run-down as I am, but I ain't heard the cows complaining yet, and none of this old bull's herd is either.* Daddy laughed again. I have to admit, it was several years before I finally figured out what they were talking about.

"That evening Mrs. Darcy had a special meal of steaks, fried pota-toes, *chile rellenos*, and southern style cornbread with butter. I'd never eaten southern-style cornbread. Let me tell you it was fine, especially with butter melted into a piece. You know the texture of the bread is so coarse the butter just flows right into it. It doesn't just sit on the top like it does on a tortilla."

Henry smacked his lips just remembering that delicious bread. Roberta giggled trying to imagine how it must taste if Henry liked it that well. Pulling a pencil from her purse, she wrote on a scrap of paper that she needed a recipe for southern-style cornbread.

"Mrs. Darcy had more hot apple pie for dessert at dinner too. I thought I'd died and gone to heaven. At the end of the meal everybody just leaned back in their chairs, dropped their hands down by their sides and sighed. I wasn't even sure I could get out of my chair. I felt like a fat pup after a meal and my belly was about as swollen too. Daddy and I were in Lincoln for nearly two weeks after that meal and let me tell you our pants were getting tighter every day from eating at Mrs. Darcy's table.

"It took Rufus and me another couple of days to finish the fence around the backyard. Tuesday night Mrs. Darcy and Rufus sat in the kitchen talking by themselves for a long time. Daddy sat reading some notes from the grand jury meetings. I was trying to read *Huck Finn*. After a while Mrs. Darcy came out of the kitchen and brought me a glass of buttermilk and Daddy some coffee. Her eyes were red and she didn't look too happy, but she spoke kindly to both of us before she returned to the kitchen.

"The next day Rufus loaded up his pack mule with his supplies, saddled his riding mule Sally, and told Mrs. Darcy good-by. She laughed and joked with him about his trip, but her eyes begged him to stay. I watched him swing into Sally's saddle with a grunt and a groan. When he was aboard he leaned over the saddle and stuck out his hand for mine. We shook hands like equals. He said, *Henry, my place is over on the Mesilla Valley side of the Organs. It's up a little canyon that lies almost on a straight line from the center of Mesilla through Tortugas Mountain. It's about ten miles from Las Cruces. Ye and yore daddy come fer a visit. Ye're good folks and I'd enjoy visiting with ya. I might even show you some real shooting when you come.*

"I said, Mr. Pike, you can count on us to come calling. I think Daddy knows just about exactly where your ranch is. Be careful going through the white sands. Daddy says there's some new bushwackers from Texas roosting in there.

"He spat a dark brown stream of tobacco juice several feet and said, *Thanks fer the warning, son, I'd heard that too. Reckin I'll cut around by the big mesquite thicket on the south side and miss it all together. Ya'll be careful too. I'll see ye after the winds stop and 'fore it gits too hot. Take care now.* He touched the brim of his hat with a one-finger salute toward Mrs. Darcy, saying almost in a whisper, *I'll see you in a few months, Sarah.* Then he headed down the road toward Ruidoso while Mrs. Darcy and I waved him out of sight. She rubbed her apron against her eyes, sighed a deep sigh, and said softly to herself as she walked back inside with her hand on my shoulder, *You come back to me, Rufus Pike.*"

# 5

# RED BEARD

Roberta and Henry passed the entrance to Hollomon Air Force Base and soon saw Alamogordo's streetlights standing at attention to welcome them down the long straight highway.

Roberta said, "I'd give ten dollars to have known Rufus Pike. He must have been a pistol! So how long were you in Lincoln before you left for home?"

Henry ran his fingers through his thick damp hair and squared his shoulders in a stretch as they slowed to stop at a red light.

"Yeah, there was no one better than Rufus with a rifle or a story. You could depend on him with your life. After he left Lincoln for his ranch, I guess Daddy and I were in Lincoln another eight to ten days. We left a day before the end of January. With Rufus and his stories gone, I'd play for a while in Mrs. Darcy's backyard or try to read some more of *Huck Finn* while Daddy was with the grand jury. I liked the story, but the colloquialisms Twain put in Huck's mouth made it hard to follow. After a while I'd get tired of reading and sneak over to watch Daddy presenting evidence to the grand jury. They were a grim bunch of passive townie businessmen and a few big ranchers who didn't ask questions and always voted the same way on the evidence – indict. The evidence Daddy had collected was direct and impressive. The grand jurors knew what the evidence meant. Any indictments they returned were likely to get men killed on both sides.

"On the morning of our last day in Lincoln, Daddy had about thirty indictments from the grand jury. There was going to be war. Several of the big ranchers in the association Daddy worked for had come to Lincoln to watch his progress and to do a little dickering on beef contracts with the Army at Fort Stanton. Up on the second floor of the courthouse where the grand jury had returned the indictments, the big ranchers were standing around talking, all jovial grins, slaps on the back, and cigars. Daddy wasn't grinning; he knew men were about to

67

die over a few cows. To Daddy, stealing was stealing and it had to be stopped. Each side thought they were in the right. The big ranchers and Daddy believed they had the law on their side, and, by today's standards, they probably did. They were bound and determined to set things right. It didn't matter that the association was spending more for Daddy's legal fees and range detectives than the value of all the stolen stock put together. Principles were codes not to be broken, especially when money was involved. I didn't know what it was all about then, I was just too young to understand. But, even at my tender age, I sensed that Daddy was calmly holding a lighted match as he stood on a keg of gunpowder.

"After the grand jury completed its business, I helped Daddy collect his papers, which were stacked up all over the table he used for his evidence presentations, as he packed them in his trunk. Mrs. Darcy rushed up the backstairs and swept through the door to the grand jury room. I saw her staring around the room for a moment before she spied us and rushed over to hand Daddy a small white envelope.

"Breathless, she said, *Mr. Fountain, a man I've never seen before stopped by my house and asked me to give you this. I told him you were just across the street, but he said he knew you were busy and he was in a hurry to get on the road.*

"Daddy thanked Mrs. Darcy for her kindness in making a special effort to bring the envelope over to him. She gave this funny little curtsy. It looked kind of like a semi-bow and one-step jig. She said, *Won't you and Henry have lunch with us before you leave? I've plenty and you've been such wonderful boarders, it's my treat.*

"Daddy nodded his head and said, *Why, thank you, Mrs. Darcy. That's very kind of you. We'll be right over as soon as I get my papers packed in this old trunk. Tell me, just out of curiosity, what did this gentleman look like?*

"She said, *Well, he was dressed like a rancher going to church. It looked like he'd been out in the sun too long because any of his face you could see was almost as red as his beard. He had a long red beard with gray streaks that reached to the middle of his chest. Why, Lordy! That beard stuck out everywhere. He wore his hat pulled way down close to his eyes, and it was creased and rolled like a Texan's. Oh, and either he had only one eye or he squinted out of the other so much it looked gone! I'm not so sure he was a rancher, though, because his hands were smooth and he wore a big 44 on his hip and had another pistol holstered under his coat.*

"Daddy nodded and said, *Hmmmph. I don't believe I know the gentleman. We'll be right over for lunch, Mrs. Darcy.* She grinned and curtsied again and swept back down the backstairs.

"Daddy opened the envelope and took out a single folded sheet of paper. I was picking up his papers and saw it as he read. It said, *If you drop this we'll be your friends. If you go on with it, you will never reach home alive.* Daddy just snorted, gritted his teeth when he read it, and said under his breath, *Sorry cowards!* He saw me staring at the paper and realized I'd seen it. He folded it back up, put it back in the envelope, and stuffed it in his coat with one hand while he tousled my hair with the other. He said, *Henry you're white as a sheet. Don't let that note bother you. Cowards who were afraid to give it to me personally wrote it. Those cowards aren't going to have the nerve to face us. Everything will be fine.* I just said, Yes, sir. I knew Daddy never let anybody scare him. I was wishing I had a gun to help protect him.

"We finished packing the papers, slid the trunk down the steps to where we'd pick it up as we left town and crossed the street to Mrs. Darcy's. That meal was a lot more than just lunch. It was more like Sunday dinner. There was a pot roast and dried or canned vegetables out of her garden, and a big slice of her apple pie. Daddy drank several cups of her strong coffee and I had a couple of glasses of buttermilk.

"As we were leaving, Mrs. Darcy became teary-eyed. She shook hands with Daddy using both of hers. She leaned down to give me a tight hug against her big soft bosom. She shook her finger at Daddy, saying, *Now you men have a real safe trip and be sure to stay with me whenever you're in Lincoln.* I nodded and said, We will, Mrs. Darcy. You sure make good pies! She even managed a smile when Daddy said, *Henry's right on that one, Mrs. Darcy! Thanks for the great lunch and all your many kindnesses. We'll be sure to stay with you the next time we're here.*

"Right on time, a stable boy brought Buck and Sergeant prancing up the street from the livery, all hitched to the wagon and ready to go. Daddy sauntered across the street and got the trunk with his indictments and other papers. He loaded up the rest of our gear while I scrambled up on the seat. Daddy, not far behind me, climbed aboard, and taking the reins, clicked to the horses and said, *Hey Buck!* We were off at a fast trot. For those horses, a fast trot was a good ten to twelve miles an hour. Mrs. Darcy stood in her doorway and waved good-by as they high-stepped it out of town.

"It was one of those cold, clear days where you almost have to squint your eyes shut to see, it was so bright. The sky was deep blue;

there were no clouds; there was no wind; and there was no sound except the steady rhythm of Buck and Sergeant strutting along and the jangle of the harness. The stillness that had settled in the air relaxed us all for a time. Daddy drove lost in thought. I watched the sides of the trail for birds, jackrabbits, and other varmints to shoot with my finger pistol. We headed up the west road toward the Mescalero turn-off with Buck and Sergeant's trot eating up the miles. They snorted and pranced along, glad to be out and moving again.

"A few miles up the road, Daddy stopped, pulled the rifle out of its scabbard, filled the magazine, levered a cartridge into the chamber, set the hammer to safety, and put it across his knees. He checked the load in his Schofield revolver too. *Just being careful,* he said.

"After that, it wasn't long before we turned off toward Mescalero. He wanted to visit and stay the evening with Doc Blazer, former dentist, keeper of the peace between Apaches and whites, and sometime innkeeper over on the reservation. Doc had a sawmill he and the Apaches operated, and he and his wife made a little money on a few rooms he rented out to travelers in his big old adobe house. Daddy had been friends with him for years. Doc and his Indians knew more about what was going on in the Tularosa Basin cattle country than any reporter or politician in El Paso, Mesilla, or Las Cruces. Daddy wanted and needed that news, and he wanted Doc's advice in tracking down some of the names on the grand jury indictments.

"The ride to Doc's place was through tall pines growing along a road that wound back and forth up ridges and down passes through the mountains. There were patches of snow on the ground, and we occasionally saw Sierra Blanca, white and majestic, rising through breakouts in the trees. It was colder going up to Mescalero than down in the valley on the road from Lincoln. The shade from the big trees holding court along the road cast sleepy shadows where the sun managed to break through. Even up high in the mountains, there wasn't any wind that day. The horses were fresh and it was an easy ride.

"We got to Doc's place well before dark, but the shadows from the mountains were making it hard to see much in the distance. I remember Doc Blazer as a big heavyset man, and although he must have been close to seventy then and rounded in the shoulders, he didn't have a single gray hair and he still had all his teeth. We tied the buggy up under the porch that wound around the second floor and provided shade for the first. Daddy asked the housekeeper who met us at the doorway where he could find Doc. She smiled and pointed to the stairs that ran up to his second-floor office.

"Doc gave a little whoop when he saw Daddy and me walk in his office. He hopped up from his desk beaming, shook hands with me and said, *I'll declare, Albert, who's this new law partner of yours?*

"There was a concerned squint around his wide-set eyes when he shook hands with Daddy and squeezed him on the shoulder with the other. *I heard about the indictments from some stay-overs that had supper here with us last night. Albert, they were saying people around here won't put up with harassment from you and the big ranchers and that there's big trouble coming.*

"Daddy said, *Let me guess. One of them had a long red beard, one eye, and he carried a gun in a shoulder holster.*

"Doc's mouth dropped open and he raised his eyebrows in surprise. *How in the hell did you know that?*

"Daddy just smiled, *Nothing special. I just got a note from him earlier today. I didn't have the opportunity to visit with the gentleman face-to-face. I reckon I won't have a chance to hear his views. Doc, Henry and I were hoping we could visit and stay the evening with you.*

"Doc bowed from the waist and made a big sweeping gesture toward the porch stairs. *We'd be delighted to have you. Dinner ought to be just about ready. Let me get somebody to stable your horses and bring your gear in. We've got plenty of room and I know our Apache friends here will be glad to see you. In fact, old Man Who Sees Far was asking me about you just the other day. Said he wanted to pay you for settling his business with that shopkeeper over in Tularosa.*

"Daddy grinned, *I told Man Who Sees Far that I didn't want any pay. It didn't take me any time at all to convince the judge that the shopkeeper had cheated the old boy when he tried to pay for those horses he bought from him. That shopkeeper was lucky Man Who Sees Far didn't stake him out in the desert somewhere and cut him from his crotch to his nose so his guts spilled out and the ants ate him. Besides, where in the world would Man Who Sees Far get any money to pay me?*

"Doc just shrugged his sloping shoulders and said, *I can't tell you that, but you'd be surprised what these Indians can get. It's no matter now. Come on, let's get washed up and let Tikila know she needs to set a couple of extra places. By the time you fellows clean up, supper will be on the table.*

"Doc gave us one of his bedrooms and some hot water for washing up. As I was washing my face I got real homesick and thought how nice it would be to be getting ready for supper in our own house on Water Street. Just two more nights and we'd be home. I'd learned a lot

71

traveling with Daddy, but I was ready to see Mama, Maggie and my brothers and sisters. I missed them all, especially Mama. I remembered how good Mama and Maggie always smelled and how soft and warm they were when they hugged you.

"Doc Blazer laid us out a feast fit for a chief and even broke out a bottle of his best Madeira wine. Of course, all they gave me was just a little taste. I made a face that made them all laugh – it just tasted nasty to me. I couldn't imagine why anyone wanted to drink that stuff, but Daddy and Doc smacked their lips and sipped it like it was nectar from the gods. Tikila laid out a venison roast, fry bread, boiled potatoes, and peaches out of a can. There wasn't much said at dinner, we were all too busy wolfing it down. Tikila was an old Apache woman, fat and covered with wrinkles, and she sure knew how to make great fry bread. I think it was about the best I ever ate.

"A couple of Apache men, No Foot and Quick Knife, who worked with Doc at the mill and who were friends of Daddy's, had supper with us. They didn't say much, but obviously felt at home eating with Doc and Daddy. No Foot was an old man, still strong, nothing but sinew in his arms and legs. He had survived many battles with the whites in his younger days. He and Daddy became friends after Daddy got him out of the Army's lock-up for being off the reservation. He had two normal feet, but Daddy told me next day, that the Apaches called him No Foot because of his uncanny ability to avoid leaving tracks, even in snow. No Foot understood and spoke English very well and laughed out loud at the stories Daddy and Doc told as they reminisced about the old days. Quick Knife must have been about forty. He was short and muscular. You could see his shirt sleeves bulge when he flexed his arms. He was called Quick Knife because he was deadlier and faster throwing a knife than most men were with a revolver. He had scouted for the Army tracking Geronimo in the early days. Daddy had managed to keep him from being shipped to Florida along with Geronimo's band after they surrendered to General Miles. Quick Knife spoke good English too, although not as well as No Foot.

"After I realized that they could speak English, I spoke up during a lull in the conversation and asked the Apaches, Do you know Yellow Boy? Their smiles disappeared as they cut their eyes to Doc Blazer for guidance. Doc looked over at me and smiled. He laid his fork on his plate, wiped his chin, and waved his hand. *It's good. You can speak. Henry and Albert have silent tongues.* They relaxed a little and No Foot said, almost in a whisper, *Yes, Yellow Boy we know. He is our friend. He hunts far now. He is not here.*

"Doc Blazer saw me frown trying to interpret what No Foot told me. He said with a sly grin, *What No Foot means is that Yellow Boy is off the reservation hunting somewhere or maybe he's slipped back down into Mexico to see a woman he has down there. In any case, according to the Army, he's not supposed to leave the reservation. He's not breaking any rule because I gave him a pass letter. But that damned commander over at Ft. Stanton thinks he makes the rules. I take the position that if the Army doesn't ask, I don't tell. So you'll see the best hunters often quietly leave the reservation and come back. I don't know when they go; but they always come back, and I know that too. Of course they always come back because their families are here.*

"I nodded I understood and said, Does he still have his Yellow Boy rifle?

"No Foot spoke up quickly and said, *Yes, he still has the Yellow Boy. He shoots best among us. He never comes home without meat.*

"Doc Blazer leaned back in his chair and sucked through his teeth as he said, *Henry, I've seen Yellow Boy drive a ten-penny nail through a board at two hundred yards with a bullet from that rifle. It was so far that the only way I could see the nail at all was an occasional glint from the sun off its head. His shooting skill is impossible to believe until you've seen it. He might even top Oliver Lee, who I heard hit a plank five shots out of six at nearly a mile with a rifle one Fourth of July a few years back.* My mouth dropped open and my eyes went wide at that story.

"Daddy spoke up and said, *Come on, Doc. I've heard that story too, and I don't believe it. A man can't even see a plank at a mile using iron sights.*

"Doc raised his brows and looked at us over the top of his glasses. *He sure as hell can if you tie some ribbon to it.* Daddy nodded and let the subject drop.

"After dinner, Doc poured some brandy for himself and Daddy, gave No Foot and Quick Knife cigars, and he gave me a sarsaparilla out of the spring where he kept the bottles cool. We sat around the big fireplace relaxing, telling stories, and letting the dancing fire warm us through to our bones. Sleep was filling my eyes when I heard Doc ask Daddy about the Lincoln indictments. I snapped awake. Even No Foot and Quick Knife leaned forward holding hands to their ears to catch every word.

"Daddy took a swallow of brandy, *Well, I got thirty-two indictments, nearly all of which will send men, in a few cases prominent men* such as Oliver Lee, to jail. There're many people not happy about those indictments. If they don't do away with me or my witnesses, they're gone.

"Doc's eyes narrowed in concern. *Do you mean someone will try to murder you?*

"Daddy pulled the envelope with the note out of his pocket and handed it to Doc. He read the note, then stared at the fire for a couple of minutes. When he handed it back he said, *Damn, Albert, that's a murder threat if I ever saw one! Are you going to back down?*

*No!*

"Doc nodded slowly. *I was afraid you'd say that. Now, listen to me. The Army is sending an escort in here day after tomorrow for Quick Knife to haul a load of lumber to Las Cruces. You wait here a couple of days and ride across White Sands with that escort. At least you'll get back to Las Cruces alive.*

"Daddy shook his head. *Thanks for the offer, but we have a wife and mother, sons, daughters, and brothers and sisters we haven't seen in nearly three weeks. I've been all over this country since I married. I've fought outlaws, Apaches, and Mexican bandits. I've been wounded five or six times, and once I thought I'd probably die. I've killed bad hombres who made the mistake of threatening me. I've come close to shootouts with Albert Fall and Oliver Lee over this and other business, and I've always come out on top. There's a crowd in Las Cruces and Mesilla who think I'm protecting myself by hiding behind Henry here – nobody would deliberately hurt an eight-year old boy. Well, I intend to prove that I'm not afraid of any coward making a threat. No, I can take care of us without any help from the Army.*

"Doc slumped further down in his chair and silently gazed at the fire. There was no sound except the crackle of burning piñon. He knew how stubborn Daddy was when he got his dander up. I sat back in my big chair, there in the warm glow of that room, and listened to them argue about our safety. I thought, Nobody can beat my Daddy.

"Then No Foot spoke up. *Fountain, you are our friend. You are a good friend. All of us here, we owe you much.* He waved a hand between himself and Quick Knife. *Quick Knife and No Foot will ride with you tomorrow. Some other man can drive the lumber wagon for Doctor Blazer. Doctor Blazer will give us a paper to go with you. We will go. You will be safe. Young Henry will be safe. Your woman and children will be happy you come home. We are strong, good fighters. Men will not attack you when we are there. You know this is true. We will go with you.*

"Daddy stared into the fire after No Foot spoke. I could tell he was giving No Foot's offer serious consideration. A long time passed as they waited for him to make up his mind. Finally, he shook his head, and, looking directly at No Foot and Quick Knife with watery eyes, he said, *You are true friends. Any debts to me you have paid many times over. Friends have no debts with each other and that is as it should be. I am honored that you want to travel with us to protect Henry and me. I have lived in this country a long time, fought many battles in the desert and in the courts. I know these men who threaten us. If I show the first sign of fear, they will be like wolves that smell blood early in the hunt. I must show them I am not afraid, and that I can defend my family and myself. I must never show them I need help when I am threatened. If you ride with me tomorrow, then they will know they have given me fear and the threats and attempts at intimidation will only get worse. I cannot and will not live like that. I know my young son here does not want to live like that either. Do you, Henry?*

"Of course, I said, No, sir! I was ready to leave right then if it meant facing and beating those men who were trying to scare us. I thought Doc had the saddest face I'd ever seen, but Daddy grinned real big and said, *See, gentlemen, I'm raising a fighting man!*

"No Foot grunted and stood up. *Yo comprendo, Señor Fountain. A man must go where his spirit leads him. Tomorrow travel safe. You are in our hearts. We go to the warmth of our wives' beds.* After they left Doc tried once more to get Daddy to travel with them, but he wouldn't have it. They were quiet for a while and then started talking about reservation business.

"I was warm and comfortable sitting in that big chair by the fire and dozed off. The next thing I knew Daddy was shaking me awake in our bedroom and telling me to get dressed, it was time to get on the road. I smelled fresh bread being baked down the hall as I rolled out of bed, splashed some water on my face, and got dressed. Daddy said, *Hurry up, Henry. We have to eat and get on down the road. We'll be home in one more night, and you can finally sleep all you want in your own bed.*

"Doc and Tikila were up fixing us a hot meal of freshly baked bread, bacon, fried potatoes and strong black coffee. It was good eating. The sun was just starting to give good light at the top of the canyon when Quick Knife brought the horses and wagon around and we loaded up. Doves were calling, and everyone's breath made it look like we were a collection of steam engines. I pulled the buffalo robe over our seat while Daddy checked the loads on his guns. Once more he levered a round into the rifle's chamber, put the hammer on safety, and laid it under the seat where it was in easy reach. Smiling through her mass of wrinkles, Tikila gave us a sack lunch and said, *Adios, señors.*

"Daddy grinned through the cloud made by his breath, *Gracias, Señora.* He and I shook hands with Doc. Daddy shook his head, *Don't look so worried, we'll be fine.* Doc said with a nod and little hand salute, *I sure hope so my good friend, I sure hope so. I wish you'd wait. Be real careful on the White Sands road. See you in Mesilla in a couple of weeks. Adios.*

"We said *Adios* and took off in the deep dawn shadows along the road. The way the cold air caught our breath and that from the horses, you would have thought we were a small train rolling down that rocky road lined with streamers of light shining in the mists through the trees. Daddy and I were in good spirits. We were headed home.

"After two or three miles, we rounded a turn and there sat an Indian sitting on his horse, one leg crooked around the horn of an old McClellan cavalry saddle, its warm bronze patina scarred and scratched from years of use and abuse. He was holding a beautiful little brown and white pinto on a lead line. Daddy handed me the reins and reached for the rifle, but, as we rolled slowly toward the Mescalero, he relaxed, put the rifle back where it was and took the reins back from me. We stopped within ten feet of the old man.

"It was Man Who Sees Far. He sat straight on his pony. His long gray hair was tied back with a red bandana and his face in the early light was covered with streaks of dark shadows from deep wrinkles. They could have been part of a relief map of the Tularosa watershed. Without speaking, he waved his hand out from his chest and flicked his palm up in a hello.

"Daddy said, *I know Man Who Sees Far! You are on the road with the coming light. Why do you wait here?*

"Man Who Sees Far said, *Fountain, you helped me with the man who cheated me in Tularosa. I have a debt. This pony is part of what I owe to you.*

"I thought it was about the prettiest paint pony I'd ever seen and hoped maybe Daddy would let me ride it when we got home. Daddy shook his head and said, *No, no, Man Who Sees Far, I don't have any need for your pony. I told you when we settled with that shopkeeper that you didn't owe me anything.*

"Man Who Sees Far was just as stubborn as Daddy. He didn't move and said, *I owe you Fountain. You take pony now.*

"Daddy shook his head again, much to my disappointment, and said, *Look, I don't need that horse. You keep it!*

"Man Who Sees Far still didn't move. Looking over at me, he said, *If you not take it for yourself, then take it for your son. Take it for your children. You take!*

"I could see Daddy's jaw muscles rippling in impatience. He wanted to get on down the road to Tularosa and not sit there arguing with an immovable Mescalero. Finally, he gave a little snort and said, *All right, Man Who Sees Far, all right. Just tie the pony on to the back of the wagon, and Henry here will have it. Then we must be on our way, we have far to go.*

"Man Who Sees Far gave a little grunt of satisfaction and rode around to the back of the buggy and tied the pony on to the back rail. As we watched him tie a good tight knot, I wondered how many whites he had tied that tight. Then he held up his right palm and said, *Adios, Fountain. Ride in peace.*

"I chirped up, *Muchas gracias, señor*, and Daddy said, *Muchas, gracias Man Who Sees Far, it is a good pony. Adios.* Without another word Man Who Sees Far turned and rode back up the road toward Mescalero. I studied every inch of that pinto as we rode along to Tularosa. It was hard to believe that such good fortune appeared for me right out of nowhere. I smiled. I knew it was going to be a fine day.

"We went another two or three miles before we went around another bend in the road and saw a breathtaking sight. Spread out before us was the Tularosa Basin, and, off in the distance, was the big sweep of White Sands reaching right up to the edge of the San Andres Mountains. I had never seen it from up high before, and although Daddy had seen this view many times he still stopped the wagon to marvel at its majesty. The sand was blazing white, the sky a gossamer blue and the San Andreas a fuzzy gray with streaks of light brown. I still get a thrill when I see that view and I must have seen it a thousand times. We stopped long enough to have a couple of good swallows from the canteen and to give the horses the last of our oats. Then we rolled off again toward Tularosa.

"Along the road down to Tularosa I kept studying that paint pony and imaging how I would ride and play with it when I got home. About an hour before we reached Tularosa, I noticed two men were trailing along behind us, one on each side of the road. They had beards, long beards, and they stayed far enough behind that I couldn't make out their features. I saw that one of them had a red beard – it stood out well from the shadow of the man's hat – and that they wore long duster overcoats. I told Daddy that there were two men following a ways behind us.

"He nodded and said, *I know, son, they've been on the road for the last mile or two. It's a free country. They're probably just going into Tularosa to have a good time. The saloons in that place can get rowdy.*

"We finally reached Tularosa and stopped at Adam Dieter's store. I was rubbing the paint pony while Daddy gave Sergeant and Buck a long drink at the trough in front of the store. He kept his coat open with that .45 caliber Schofield revolver easy to reach and see as our two distant companions slowly rode down the street toward us. Both of them had red faces as if they'd been out in the sun too long without a hat, which I remember thinking at the time was not very smart for men who worked outside. I stared at Red Beard. As he passed, I saw that he was missing an eye! He smiled with a twisted little grin, touched his hat with a flick of his fingers in a kind of wave and said *Howdy* as he and his partner, who looked straight ahead, rode by. Daddy seemed to be paying attention to the horses drinking. But I saw his eyes following their every move while his head nodded to our gear on the buggy. He told me to get the feed sack as Red Beard's and his partner's horses casually wandered out of sight down the street.

"We went inside Mr. Dieter's store. I tell you after being out in that cold air for the morning, the warm air off the big pot-bellied cast-iron stove he had sitting in the middle of his store was like a gift from heaven. The stove was surrounded by a couple of local farmers and several old timers who were smoking or chewing tobacco, whittling, and talking about politics and Daddy's success with the grand jury in Lincoln. Mr. Dieter had been part of the conversation, leaning in over his counter a little distance from the stove. When he saw me and Daddy come in the store, he said, *Well look who's here, gentlemen! It's Colonel Fountain and his new law partner!* The stove crew all turned their heads toward the door and the room got quiet as they watched Daddy and me walk over to the counter.

"Mr. Dieter said, *Let me get you gentlemen some lunch. We just ate about an hour ago and I think there're still some frijoles in a pot there on the stove. We'd all be mighty interested to hear your views on what the Lincoln indictments mean for this part of the country, wouldn't we, boys?* The heads on the stove crew nodded like they were all attached to the same string.

"Daddy shook his head. *We just had a sack lunch a little while ago. Thanks just the same. I do need forty pounds of oats for the horses though. Henry has the sack. We're anxious to get home and need to get on down the road. However, the next time any of you gentlemen are in*

*Mesilla, I'd be happy to have a smoke with you and talk about what the indictments from the Lincoln grand jury might mean.*

"The heads nodded again and the men turned back to their arguments about New Mexico politics, smoking and chewing all the while. I gave the sack to Mr. Dieter. He told me to take a peppermint stick out of the jar on his counter while he sent his clerk to fill up the sack from the grain supply in the back. Mr. Dieter and Daddy talked quietly while the clerk was gone. I only heard snippets of their conversation, but I remember Daddy asking Mr. Dieter if he knew who Red Beard was and Mr. Dieter, wrinkling his forehead in concentration then shaking his head, said something about Texas.

"The clerk soon reappeared with the sack of oats thrown over his shoulder and we followed him out the door to show him where to put the sack on the wagon. We climbed aboard the buggy after the clerk went back into the store. Mr. Dieter, shading his eyes with his hand as he looked up at Daddy, said, *Albert, you and that partner of yours be careful. Those strangers with the beards sound like trouble. Watch out for 'em.*

"Daddy nodded. *We will. See you next trip, maybe in the late spring.* Mr. Dieter waved and said *Adios, you two.* Vaya con Dios. *See you when you come back through.* I saw him shaking his head as the store door closed behind him.

"From Tularosa we drove over to La Luz to have supper and stay the evening with Dave Sutherland, another old friend and political ally of Daddy's. La Luz had been a prosperous little village before the drought came in eighty-nine. There wasn't much left when Daddy and I stayed that night with Mr. Sutherland. It was an easy wagon ride from Tularosa and we watched the southern end of White Sands grow in the distance, off on the right, as we trotted along. Mr. Sutherland owned a store in La Luz and had his home, an adobe hacienda, next door. We tied the buggy up and watered the horses before we stepped inside. With the sun falling behind the San Andres Mountains, it was already starting to get colder.

"Mr. Sutherland was leaning over the counter, talking to a short Mexican man nodding with his hat in his hands, when we walked through the door. When he saw us he yelled with delight. *Well, I'll be damned! They haven't killed you yet, have they? Come on in here out of the cold and let's have a hot toddy and some hot cocoa for your partner there.* Then he said to the Mexican, *Luis, tell Mrs. Stevenson I'll ask Señor Fountain, then send José over with an answer before dinner.* The Mexican nodded and said, *Si, Patrón. Muchas gracias,* and, nodding to us, quickly backed out the door.

"Sutherland was a tall gangly man with a big bulbous nose and a hunched back caused by years of being bent over account books. When I first saw him, I immediately thought of Ichabod Crane. I'd read about tall skinny Ichabod in the *Legend of Sleepy Hollow* just before school let out for Christmas. Yet Sutherland had a kind of gracious patrician air about him that commanded instant respect and made you forget how he could pass for a scarecrow with that hatchet thin face and long black coat draped over his angular frame. Daddy reached out and pumped Sutherland's extended hand and said, *We almost froze our cajones off getting here, Dave. A hot toddy and cocoa will be lifesavers.*

"Dave laughed and said, *Serves you right for riding up and down the road in the winter time. How are you doin' there Señor Henry? You cold too?*

"I was glad to be inside in the warm cozy store. It had a big potbellied iron stove and all those good store smells of ground coffee, pipe and cigar smoke, new cloth on the bolt, saddle and gun leather, gun oil, lavender soap, even the musty smell of oats for horses kept in the back room. I stuck out my hand and said, I'm fine, Mr. Sutherland, just cold is all and that hot cocoa sure sounds good. I turned to Daddy and said, Daddy, what're cajones? I knew it must be something a little vulgar the way they grinned at the word, and Dave haw-hawed at Daddy who just shook his head and didn't say a thing.

"Dave, still laughing, said, *Boys, just settle in there by the stove and warm yourselves up while I get the refreshments.* He disappeared behind the backroom curtain. I could hear him talking to some clerk who was working in the back storeroom. *José, run next door and have Glorietta make a couple of rum toddies and a hot cocoa, and bring them back when they're ready. In the meantime, take Mr. Fountain's things on the wagon and put them in the back bedroom, and then take his rig over to the stable and have Riggs put the horses up. Tell him they'll want to leave shortly after first light in the morning.*

"By the time Sutherland came back through the backroom curtain, Daddy and I had our backsides well-roasted. He said in high good humor, *Gentlemen, refreshments are on the way!* He pulled up a tall straight-back chair with a cane bottom that must have come from somewhere east of the Mississippi and south of the Ohio River. Dropping his long lanky body on the creaking weave and slumping back as he crossed his arms, he said, *I was just talking to Mrs. Fannie Stevenson's man, Luis. I mentioned to her, a couple of days ago, you were gonna stay the night with me. She sent Luis over to ask if she could ride into Las Cruces with you tomorrow.*

"Daddy gave half a nod, stuck out his lower lip, and said, *Why, I reckon so if she can stand to be out in the cold that long. Guess she could keep the other side of Henry warm if he sits between us. Tell her we'll leave about seven o'clock.* Sutherland nodded and said, *All right, I'll see she gets the word she has a ride. I really don't think she'll go. She wheezes and coughs all the time and says the cold air is bad for her lungs.* He paused, and clearing his throat, looked sideways, with a sly grin, at Daddy. *So, Albert, did you manage to get a grand jury indictment against Oliver Lee?*

"Daddy turned around, holding his hands out and flexing his fingers to catch the stove's warmth and nodded, *Yes, sir. I sure did!*

"*Hmmmph*, Dave grunted. Reflecting for a moment he said, *Good...work...Albert! I guess when you convict him, Albert Fall will lose his chief enforcer. We oughta have free rein in the next election and not have to worry about being hustled for weapons by the sheriff's deputies every time we go to town.* He glanced over at me, winked and nodded his head, *That'll be real fine Señor Henry, real fine. Your papa there is doin' the civilized people around here a real service goin' after Oliver Lee.* I didn't have the foggiest idea what he was talking about so I just stayed as close to the stove as I could and nodded like I understood what he meant.

"They talked about the impact of those indictments on local politics through the toddies and cocoa, through supper, and well after I dozed off in Sutherland's parlor. Daddy finally shook me awake to walk down the hall and climb into bed under a down comforter. It was a little cool getting under, but warmed up quick. It felt good to drift back to sleep in that comforter knowing I'd be out of the cold and sleeping in my own bed the next night. It felt like years since I'd seen Mama, Maggie, and my brothers.

"Next morning we were up early for breakfast. Glorietta cooked some fine *huevos rancheros* and a big pot of hot coffee. She had spiced 'em up good with dried red chiles. I was sitting there next to the kitchen stove, sweating as much from the *huevos rancheros* as from the stove's heat, when there was a soft knock on the kitchen door. As Glorietta cracked the door, there was a puff of wind and the whole room got cold. I saw through the crack that Luis was standing there mumbling something to her as she cocked her head and turned her ear to him. Gloomy light showed through the door. It was evident the day was going to be cold and overcast, not sunny like the day before. She finally nodded she understood him, and, waving him off, she closed the door. She turned to Sutherland and said, *Señora Stevenson thanks Señor*

*Fountain, but she doesn't think her lungs will stand up to the cold air on the trip today, so she's staying at home.* Sutherland nodded and Daddy said, after a big swallow of black coffee, *Just as well. It's going to be cold out there today. Still, we'd have enjoyed her company, wouldn't we, Henry?* I just nodded as I continued to stuff my face with that delicious breakfast.

"Mr. Riggs brought the buggy and horses around; we loaded up and were ready to go. Daddy made sure the rifle was loaded and easy to reach under the seat, and he slid his holstered revolver up his side a notch. Sutherland said, *Wish you'd wait another day or two until you had some company on the way Albert.*

"Daddy squared his jaw and said, *No, it's time to get on home. We're lonesome for the family and we'll be there tonight. You know I can take care of business if there's trouble, and I've got a good man with a gun right here with me too, so we'll be fine.*

"Sutherland was somber as the wind whipped his long black coat around making him shout into the wind, *All right, you know best. I'm sure you'll be fine. It's just so damn windy and cold, it's not gonna be a pleasant trip.* Vaya con Dios.

We waved good-by and headed down the road toward White Sands. The sky was mottled in black and gray clouds that swirled along at a good clip and it looked like it might rain. I didn't care. We were headed home and nothing was going to stop us."

# 6

# FRIENDS

The Plymouth was approaching the last traffic light in Alamogordo. Henry had started telling his story as if it were a fond memory. As it developed he became more earnest, his breathing noticeably faster, and he was forcing himself to speak slowly as he groped for words. Little rivulets of sweat rolled down the sides of his face. The car wasn't that hot.

Roberta listened carefully, wanting to hear every word. She was worried he might be in some kind of physical distress, near a stroke or a heart attack, but she hesitated to ask him if he felt well.

The traffic light changed to yellow. Although Henry could have driven through it easily before it changed to red, he slowed down and pulled into an Esso gas station sitting on their corner of the intersection. He reached for the door handle and said, "Too much coffee for an old man. I need to visit the facilities. Do you need to go?" Roberta shook her head and noticed with concern that his usually steady hand had a slight tremor. "Okay, I'll be right back. Can I get you anything?" Again she shook her head and cranked the window down a little to let in some of the cold night air and take out remnants of the smoke left hanging in the car. Henry tried the men's room door, found it locked and walked around to the front to get the key.

Roberta had a sad feeling in the pit of her stomach that Henry was telling her the truth. She slowly rubbed her temples thinking about that possibility, and cringed at the thought of what he might tell her next.

Everything he told her was consistent with stories her grandfather had told about the times and what the papers reported Pinkerton investigators had learned about what happened to Albert and Henry on their way home. The typical citizen of Las Cruces now barely knew anything about Albert and Henry in the first place, much less the details that Henry had been giving her. Still, a good historian could find out those details. However, Henry was showing signs of stress associated with a dark memory. So what in the world did this have to do with Yellow Boy? Perhaps, when she knew, Yellow Boy might still be around to help answer the myriad of questions filling her head. It was all so strange.

Roberta got out of the car and paced about in the cold air trying to clear her mind. It had been a long day. She told herself she was getting too old to work twenty-four hours a day without rest. Henry came out of the men's room and gave her a little salute and grin as he quickly walked the key back around to the front of the station. She looked up the cross street. It ran toward the Sacramento Mountains and turned into a hazy dirt road lined with creosote bushes a couple of blocks from their gas station. It seemed to her that every town in New Mexico was built half on rough paved roads and half on dirt roads. Dust kicked up by passing cars on the dirt roads hung curtain-like in the still night air. Henry came back around the corner and hurriedly opened the car door for her before opening his and sliding under the steering wheel. His cheeks were rosy from the night air and water he had slapped on his face. He looked refreshed. He cranked the Plymouth, backed up a little and pulled into the street facing the traffic light, now red again, and stopped.

Turning to face him and again bringing her left foot up under herself for support, Roberta said, "Your story sounds so believable. Isn't it hard for you to drive near the places you and your father were on that last day? Why, you must have passed near this very point on your way home."

Henry was staring at the light, waiting for it to change, tensed like a runner for the starting gun. He winced and nodded. "I do think about it every time I travel this road. Of course, Alamogordo wasn't here then, but this light isn't far from the road we traveled from La Luz to the road that ran between Tularosa and Las Cruces. I've told an imaginary interlocutor this story for years. Now I'm telling it to you and it's not at all like I'd imagined. I thought I'd be telling it to a man. I thought I'd tell a historian, probably a stranger, just to clear the air before I died. Instead, I'm telling a woman and one of my closest friends. I hope I'm not close to death either, and I don't want you telling it to other people. I guess life rarely turns out quite the way we expect it to, does it?"

She smiled as the light changed and he charged through it. She said softly, "No, sir, it doesn't. But I'm glad to be a woman, and proud to be your friend. This night has been a revelation! When did you first realize that you might be in trouble on your way home that day?"

"Well, we were just a mile or so outside of La Luz when three men from the direction of White Sands rode up on to the road in front of us. I didn't see them at first; I was too busy watching my pony tied on the back of the wagon. But as soon as they appeared, Daddy said *hmmph.* I looked around and he pointed down the road without taking his hands off the reins. Two stayed on the left side, one on the right. They were too far away to recognize any of their features, and as we rode along they stayed just far enough in front so we couldn't recognize them. But it was obvious they weren't letting us out of their sight.

"When we stopped to let the horses rest, they stopped too, but kept their distance. When we started again, Daddy had the rifle up from under the seat and on his lap. I knew there was a cartridge levered into the chamber and the hammer was pulled back to safety. He had also pulled the stay strap off his Schofield in its holster and checked its load. Usually he kept an empty chamber under the hammer, but I saw him drop a cartridge into it so he had a full load. I grinned. We were finally going to have it out with those men who had threatened us. Maybe it would be a fight like he had with El Tigre and I'd get to see it. It never occurred to me that with all the lead flying I might get killed or wounded. I wondered when he would give me the rifle so he could use the Schofield. I was grinning and burning for action, thinking this was just like a game with my school friends, but Daddy was deadly serious. I noticed him glancing over at me once in while. I guess he wanted to see if I was scared; he seemed satisfied that I wasn't.

"In a little while a rider passed the other three and came toward us. Daddy said, *It's Judge Hill. I wonder why he's out on a cold day like this?* Judge Hill was a justice of the peace; he and Daddy had known each other for years. He was a big jolly man whose vest buttons strained to hold the blue floral print vest closed over a big belly that hung over his pants. His white shirt showed between every button on his vest. His pork pie hat was pulled down close to his eyes and his big duster overcoat flapped in the wind. He rode a big bay mare he had for years. She was stepping down the road smartly making him kinda jiggle all over. We stopped and waited as he rode up to us, a big crooked pipe jammed in his mouth. Daddy affectionately called him Hump. The judge stopped and said through clinched teeth holding the pipe, *Morning, boys. Kinda cold for a ride, ain't it? Guess you fellows are headin' home. It's 'bout time. I know Marianna is anxious to see you two. Lookin' for varmits with that rifle?*

"Daddy said, *Morning, Judge. Yes, sir, we're heading home. We're as anxious to see Mother as she is us. It's been a long three weeks. Hump, did you notice if any of those men you just passed had a red beard and one eye?*

"Judge Hill's brow wrinkled in concern as he took the pipe out of his mouth and looked back up the road toward the men he had just passed who were moving slowly out of sight. When he turned back to Daddy and me he said slowly, *Why...no, none of them looked like that. I didn't recognize them. They just nodded howdy to me as they passed. I thought they were just regular cowboys headed back to Texas. They all had Texas rigs. Why?*

"Daddy hesitated, then said, *Oh, as you might guess, I've been threatened since I got all those indictments in Lincoln. Got a note from a red beard with one eye, who with another fellow followed us down from Doc Blazer's to Tularosa yesterday. He was riding a gray and one of those cowboys up yonder is too. I have a Winchester and a Schofield revolver. I can take care of myself, but now I'm worried about Henry here catching a stray bullet if there's a fight.* I was indignant, but afraid to say so. I could take care of myself! Daddy didn't need to worry about me. No, sir, not me!

"Judge Hill looked back up the road again; the riders had disappeared in the distance. Turning back to us, he said, *They looked all right to me, but you never know about killers, do you? Why don't you stop at Luna's Well and wait there to ride back with the mail wagon from Las Cruces? I'd ride back with you now, but I've got to be in La Luz for some business with Dave Sutherland Monday.*

"Daddy shook his head and said, *Thanks, Hump. Wouldn't dream of having you escort us. We'll be fine. I'm just being extra cautious with Henry along. Tell Sutherland you saw us and we said hello. We stayed with him last night and Glorietta packed us up a big lunch. Well, gotta get on down the road before it gets too late. Adios.*

"The judge tipped his hat, grinned around his pipe and said, *Adios, gentlemen,* and we passed on.

"It couldn't have been more than another mile before we saw the three riders again. They seemed to have paused in the road, then they were riding again in the same formation, still too far for us to see who they were and what they looked like. Daddy kept the rifle on his knees. In a couple of hours we got to Pellman's Well on the northern edge of White Sands. We hadn't seen another soul except the men in front of us. It was nearly noon, so Daddy pulled into the corral, watered the horses, and put on their feedbags. My little paint pony was a good traveler; we hadn't had a bit of trouble with him following us. The wind came off the mountains in puffs and rolls, and, with no sun showing through that somber gray sky pockmarked with dark clouds wanting to rain, we ate the lunch Glorietta fixed for us. We took a full hour to eat and let the horses rest. It would be a long pull up San Augustin Pass later in the afternoon. Daddy stayed on the wagon but I got out and ran around in the corral, using my finger pistol to shoot at bad guys through the corral bars. Our escort had disappeared up the road again, but Daddy kept the Winchester on his lap or in the crook of his arm while he ate and rested.

"We got back on the road and were almost to Luna's Well when we met the La Luz mail wagon. Santos Alvarado was driving and had just left the mail bags from Tularosa off at Luna's Well for pick up by the mail wagon from Las Cruces. He was all wrapped up in a big wool serape and had a quilt over his knees and another thrown over his shoulders. About all you could see under his hat were his black squinting eyes, big bushy eyebrows and big mustache under a wide flat nose. Daddy stopped the team as Santos pulled up and stopped almost axle to axle with us.

"Daddy said, *Buenos tardes, Santos! Como esta?*

"Santos grinned, honored that Daddy would speak to him in his own tongue. But Santos answered him in English, proud that he knew the language of the local patróns. *I am fine, but it's a cold day for a ride, Colonel Fountain. And yourselves? I guess you're on your way home from Lincoln, eh?* He nodded toward the rifle and furrowed his brow questioningly.

"Daddy grinned, *Si, Santos. We're going home, finally. Expect to be in Mesilla tonight. It's been a long trip. Old Henry here has been a big help to me though. There've been some threats made against us and we just want to be prepared if they're more than threats. Did you pass three men on the road before you got to us?*

"Santos nodded. *Si, señor. One on a big gray and two others on bays. When they saw me they turned off the road and galloped toward the Sacramentos. They were too far for me to tell too much about them, but they looked and rode like cowboys. Why do you ask, Colonel Fountain?*

*Well, they've stayed out in front of us most of the day. We were followed by a couple of men from Doc Blazer's yesterday. I've got a feeling that some ranch hands are being used to keep an eye on us for some reason. It's probably nothing. Keep the mail rolling there, Santos! We've got to get on home. Adios.* Santos nodded with a light smile. *Adios, señores. Hace un paseo bueno a su casa...Have a good ride home!*

"The horses, rested after our short stop to chat with Santos, loped right along in that half-walk, half-canter of theirs that ate up the miles. Daddy seemed to relax after Santos had told him that the three riders had ridden off toward the Sacramentos.

"We passed Luna's Well and were two or three miles from the Black Mountain cut just before you get to Chalk Hill when we met Saturnino Barela driving the Las Cruces mail wagon to make the pickup at Luna's Well. He was another friend of Daddy's. He looked like a wild man, but he loved Daddy. He didn't wear a hat like most people, and his hair was long and whipped into twists and snarls. Most of his face was covered by a big wooly beard that reached half way down to his belly, and peering out from this brush pile were two of the brightest eyes I've ever seen. He was a big man. Sitting on his wagon seat, he blocked my view of a wide span of the Organs behind him. He had big gnarly hands and didn't wear gloves, and sitting out in that cold wind all he had on was a wool shirt and a big leather vest. He left the shirt open for two buttons down from the collar just so he'd have room to swallow when he drank. You could see what looked like bear hair all over his chest and the backs of his hands. Between the hair and those piercing eyes, he looked like a man a body wouldn't want to ever cross, a troll straight out of a Hans Christian Andersen fairy tale.

"Saturnino usually drove alone. That day there was a crowd riding along with him. He met a wagon just leaving Chalk Hill after stopping for lunch. It was driven by an old man who had two women with him and there was a teen-aged boy, maybe eighteen or nineteen, riding along with them. When Saturnino saw us, we saw every crooked tooth in his grin hidden in that brush pile on his face. Daddy immediately knew who it was and I could see the tension on his face relax as he pulled up, stopped, and nodded hello.

*Buenos tardes, Saturnino! Como esta hombre? Aren't you freezing out in this wind without a coat?*

*Buenos tardes, Señor Fountain y Enrique, mi muchacho. Es muy bueno to see you. No, No. This little breeze, it is nothing for a man who grows his own bear coat, eh? Ha...ha...ha. But what are you doing with that big gun on your knees, trying to find a bear to make a coat? Ha, ha, ha, ha.* His laugh came rolling up from his belly in a deep guttural roar. It even sounded like a bear might laugh.

"Daddy and I laughed with him, then Daddy, eyeing the people with Saturnino, said, *No, no bears for the gun. It's just a little extra comfort. Quien estas sus amigos Saturnino?*

"Saturnino looked back over his shoulder at the old man and two women in the wagon. As he turned back to us again, the young man walked his horse up beside the mail wagon and gave us a little salute. Saturnino said, *Oh, Señor Fountain, I met them at Chalk Hill. They were just getting back on the road for Tularosa. It is Señor Ruiz and his two daughters on their way back from visiting family in Las Cruces.* Señor Ruiz nodded his brown weathered face toward us with dignity, but didn't say a word. The women had quilts in gay Mexican patterns wrapped around them and they smiled and nodded hello but said nothing.

"Saturnino turned his right hand toward the boy on the horse, but before he could say anything, the boy said, *Con mucho gusto, Señor Fountain y Enrique. Me llamo Fajardo. I work for Señor Ruiz and his family. He has un ranchito near the norte end of the Jarillas. I speak Americano muy bien, si?* Saturnino scowled at him for his impertinence and interrupting his introduction to Daddy, who they all considered an important man in the territory.

"Daddy laughed and said, *Con mucho gusto Señor Fajardo. Si, su English es muy bien. Your Americano is well-spoken. Where did you learn to speak English? From Señor Ruiz and his family?*

"*Oh no, Señor Fountain. When I was a muchacho like Señor Enrique I work in Señor Dieter's store in Tularosa por mucho años. I learn nuevo words each day and practice with all who will listen to mi mal English. I want to speak with tres hombres about a mile in front of your wagon when we saw them but they rode off the road and keeping their distance did not even wave at us. I have never seen them before and they didn't wear their sombreros like any vaqueros...uh...cowboys I know. I ask Señor Barela who see them also, but he think they are cowboys. You see them, señor? They are cowboys, si?*

"I looked up to see Daddy slowly shaking his head and gritting his teeth. He looked like he had that night in Tularosa when we were having dinner with Roy Tibbets, and Jack Stone and Charlie Bentene walked over to our table to call Roy a liar. Daddy was furious then and he looked the same now. Pure blazing fury, that's what it was.

"Saturnino stared at the cloud over Daddy's face and frowned. *Que pasa, Señor Fountain?*

"*Those hombres have been staying just in front of us, far enough that we couldn't recognize them for miles, Saturnino. I received a death threat after the grand jury recessed in Lincoln. There were even threats before I left Mesilla. We were followed out of Mescalero to Tularosa. Powerful people want me gone, and I'm just afraid these are the men they've hired to do it. I'm not a bit concerned about myself. I have a couple of good guns and know how to use them. But I have Henry here with me and I don't want him to be around when the bullets start flying because I'll kill those bastards. They know Henry is riding with me and it doesn't seem to make a bit of difference!*

"Fajardo stared at Daddy, his jaw hung open in surprise. Señor Ruiz understood very little of what was said, and neither did the women. They just sat there and surveyed the mountains while they waited for the roadside chat with the important gringo to end. Saturnino's eyes glowed from his shaggy head as he looked at Daddy and then over his shoulder toward where they had seen the men. He said, *Señor Fountain, why don't you drive back to Luna's Well with us and stay the night? It's not far. Then we can travel back to Las Cruces together in the morning. It would be my pleasure for you and Enrique to accompany me. Por favor, señor, do this thing por Barela.*

"Daddy must have set there four or five minutes looking at the mountains, thinking. I could see his jaw muscles working trying to swallow his fury and to think rationally. His fingers nervously tapped on the rifle stock. We all waited for his answer. I hoped he'd say no. I was tired of traveling and I wanted to see my mama. I was thinking those men were just trying to scare him off. I hoped we'd have a chance to get them.

"Finally, Daddy said, *Muchas gracias, Saturnino. You are a good friend. But, I just can't let them scare me off. If I back down once, I'm done for as a prosecutor in this country. I know it's a gamble, maybe I'll be remembered as a fool for putting us at risk, but we have to go on. I know Henry's tired, and I am too. We want to be sitting by the home fire tonight. If they try anything, I won't hesitate to put a slug in every one of them, and they know it. They'll leave us alone. Perhaps another time we'll travel with you to Las Cruces.*

"Saturnino shrugged his shoulders and said, *Yo comprehendo, Señor Fountain. Do you need water or food for the caballos?*

"Daddy shook his head, *No, gracias. We have plenty. We'll see you in Las Cruces tomorrow evening. Come by for a hot toddy, eh?*

"Saturnino smacked his lips together in a pucker of delight, and, grinning broadly said, *Oh, si, señor! That will be very fine.* Vaya con Dios. Hasta mañana. With that he waved adios as he and his little group passed, leaving us on the road pointing toward the Organs and the climb over San Augustin Pass.

"We sat there for a minute. Daddy looked over the countryside, trying to think where we might have to confront the riders in front of us.

He checked the rifle's load again, pulled out the Schofield, cocked it, and let the hammer back down slowly as he took a deep breath and relaxed.

"He offered me the canteen. I took a couple of big gulps and handed it back to him. He had a swallow before screwing its top back on and tossing it down by our feet where it would be easy to reach.

"He said, *Henry, if those men come after us, I need for you to take the reins and make those horses move while I use the guns. Hold on to the reins tight and get down on the floor under the seat. If anything happens to me, you get as far as you can with the wagon and try to hide in the desert. When it gets dark make your way back toward the road and hide so you can see the people that pass by. Don't let strangers see you. If we don't show by tomorrow night there'll be a big uproar and Albert and Jack will come running with friends and posses. You'll get cold, tired, and thirsty. If you have to hide, take that quilt with you and the canteen. Don't lose your courage and you'll be fine. Do you understand, boy?*

"I nodded slowly, beginning to understand that this was serious business and not a game like I'd play with my friends or brothers. Daddy hugged me and playfully gave me a gentle punch on the shoulder, *We'll be fine. We just need to be ready for the worst and we'll expect the best. You can handle it. I know you can. You've done a lot of growing this trip, son. I'm real proud of you.* All I could say was, Yes sir, I can take care of myself. Don't worry none about me.

"He whipped up Buck and Sergeant and we headed for the cut leading to Chalk Hill. It felt like it was getting colder, although the wind was dying down a little. Daddy flipped open his watch. *It's nearly two-thirty.* He sighed. *We ought to be home in time for one of your mother's good dinners. It sure will be good to get home won't it?* I could only nod as I sat there shivering in the cold wind."

# 7

# YELLOW BOY

**H**enry and Roberta were well out of Alamogordo, rolling down Route 70 toward Tularosa. The wind whistling in the window vents made a cold, comforting sound. Off to their left White Sands glowed in the moonlight. Henry glanced at Roberta and saw a look of concern. The color had drained from his face and he was sweating as if the sun was shining rather than the moon.

She said, "Are you okay?" He nodded but squeezed the steering wheel with a white-knuckled death grip. "Are you sure? You don't look well."

"I'm all right. My mind is in powerful times. The memories sometimes roar in my ears and shake my day-to-day thoughts into the reality of what I lived through. It's hard to call up those times. Still, I'm glad you nudged me into remembering them."

Roberta continued to eye him closely. She saw the large luminous hand on her watch pass two, then five minutes while she waited. Finally, he sighed and relaxed a little. She continued to watch him, perplexed by the questions his story raised.

"How could your father, a good, honest man, who proved his bravery many times, who was supposed to be wise and mature, risk the life of his son like that? I just don't understand it!"

Henry nodded and looked at her with a grim face. "I don't know. There are a thousand answers, all of them a real possibility. The bones of the only one who knew for sure are lying in a crack in the walls of some deep canyon or under a stone cairn no one will ever discover. I've thought on your question for years and still don't have a good answer. For some reason Daddy felt he had to get back to Mama that day. He'd promised her to come back as fast as he could and he had already stayed two nights with friends on the way home. I guess maybe part of it was a feeling of guilt for not going home right away. He was always fearless in fights and had always come out on top. Why, even if protecting me was something of a handicap, should he have been afraid? He was right too, I think, in believing that if he backed down – just once – the threats and attempts at intimidation would be ten times worse than anything he had experienced during the previous couple of months. He was in a box. Damned if he backed down to protect me, damned if he didn't. He wouldn't be able to live and work as an attorney in southern New Mexico anymore if he showed the least fear. You know, though, after studying human nature and reading Freud's and Jung's theories for over forty years, I think it was mostly that he couldn't break his pattern."

"Pattern?"

Henry nodded slowly and winced as if holding his hand over a flame. "Yeah, pattern. During the early years of our lives we develop patterns – you know, approaches to the way we do things. We learn these patterns through trial and error. We find what works for us and we stay with it. You know what I mean. Most politicians are always trying to find a deal that works. They want to compromise. They'd rather compromise, win a little, lose a little, than stand up for their principles and perhaps win or lose it all. Or, and you know this, there are people who found out early in life that they could lie and make their problems get easier, so they'll lie to you, even if there's no reward or incentive to lie. They just can't seem to tell the truth. That's their pattern.

"Daddy's personal code, his patterns, required that he be fearless, even in the face of great danger. They required that he always do what he believed was right, and that he must never back down from anybody or any threat, regardless of the consequences. I think he honestly believed that if he faced those men trailing in front of us, regardless of who they were or how many there were, he'd come out on top. I guess he never learned that living to fight another day was better than being dead. It just wasn't part of his pattern to retreat or to lose. Those patterns had stood him in good stead for a long time. The day he died, I think he was just following his pattern. He was in automatic and not really thinking of the consequences if those patterns didn't apply that one time. It just wasn't possible for his brain to factor me into the risk he was taking."

Roberta raised her forearm off the back of the seat and rested her forehead in her palm. She said softly, "So what happened? I know it's painful to remember. You don't have to talk about it if you don't want to."

A minute passed, then two. The Plymouth bounced through a couple of rough spots in the rutted asphalt and made them momentarily sway back and forth. At last he said, "The road toward San Augustin Pass cut through a Black Mountain spur that was about a mile long. The banks on either side were about ten feet high and when you pulled up out of the cut there was a little chalky outcropping everybody called Chalk Hill. Not far from Chalk Hill was a big green bush.

"We were less than fifty yards from that bush when the one-eyed man with the red beard stepped out from behind it with a rifle up to his shoulder. Daddy had the reins in both hands. He dropped them as soon has he saw Red Beard and reached for the rifle on his lap. I heard Daddy say, *Oh, no you don't you son-of-a-bitch!* Red Beard didn't hesitate. He fired before Daddy had his rifle half way to his shoulder.

"It was like a bad dream, but worse than any nightmare because I knew it was real. Everything happened like time had slowed down to minutes between clicks of the big clock at home. I heard Red Beard's rifle boom and felt Daddy fall back against the seat. He managed to hold on to the rifle with one hand and throw the other up to his chest. The roar from Red Beard's rifle and the loose reins made the horses rear up, neighing in surprise, then plunge forward. Red Beard stood where he was, coolly levering another cartridge into his rifle still braced against his shoulder.

"I heard Daddy in a barely audible, gurgling whisper say, *Henry, grab those reins and get us out of here!* I was only eight years old, but I knew how to drive the wagon with those horses. Jack and Albert had been showing me how to drive a rig since I was six or seven. Daddy had even given me a driving lesson with the team on our way to Tularosa. I knew I could handle the rig and grabbed the reins as soon as the horses came back down on their front feet. I slapped the reins down on their backs and yelled, *Get up, Buck! Get up! Hi ya!* As I grabbed the reins to make the horse move faster, I saw the end of Red Beard's rifle following us. He had another aim point on Daddy. Buck and Sergeant took off as if a mountain cat was after them and ran a little off the road to get past Red Beard. I could hear the air gurgling in Daddy's throat. The wagon was bouncing around across the ruts so hard I nearly fell out and I was desperately afraid Daddy would, but somehow he managed to hold on. Remembering what he'd told me I dropped down in the floor under the seat and managed the horses as they charged up the road. All I knew was we had to get out of there and get away from the man with the rifle.

"The wagon swept past Red Beard on the far side of the road. He was gritting his teeth in a carnivorous grin that showed snarling yellow teeth against that big red beard. It made my heart freeze in fear. I saw his rifle smoothly following us, poised to strike. He was steady and cool. It was an eternity before I heard the pounding roar from his next shot. The second bullet made a low *whump* sound when it hit Daddy in the back. He grunted like someone had smashed him with a heavy club, and the impact pitched him out the right side of the wagon. He did a complete roll coming out of the wagon and landed face up on the side of the road. The riders who had followed us all day were flying back down the road toward us. I jerked back on the reins yelling "Whoa, Whoa Buck!" trying to stop the team, but they wanted to keep running. I wasn't about to leave Daddy. The rider's lead man brought his horse to a skid, and, coming up beside us, caught the team within a few yards of where Daddy fell out of the wagon. Red Beard turned and pulled his horse out from behind the big green bush. He levered another cartridge into the rifle, put the hammer on safety, and casually walked over to Daddy, the rifle on his shoulder and a big grin on his face, enjoying every moment of the murder he had just committed.

"I jumped out of the wagon and ran over to Daddy. The front of his shirt had a big spreading bloodstain over his right lung where he'd been shot from behind, and a stain from a smaller hole to the left of his heart. Blood was practically pumping out of his mouth, his eyes were open, and he was fighting for every breath. I wanted to cry, to hug him, to beg him not to die, but I couldn't. I just kneeled down by him and took his hand. I felt him feebly squeeze mine. He was able to turn his head and look at me as the light faded from his eyes. All he whispered was *Henry! Go!*

"Red Beard walked up and squatted down by Daddy's head, looked him in the face and said, *Reckin I've killed you, Fountain. You was easy. I've seen meskins that was harder to kill than you.* He spat on the ground and wiped his mouth on the back of his sleeve. *Guess you won't be puttin' no more small operators in prison or helpin' no more red-skins and greasers, now will ye? I bet ole Oliver Lee will be happy to know I got rid of his problem fer him. Hell, he might even pay a little extry for the good job I done. You was easy money, Fountain. Easy money!*

"He turned toward me and said, *Howdy, kid. Guess you remember me, don't you?* He nodded toward the wagon. *You just go on over there and sit in that there wagin nice and easy whiles we see to yore old man. Ain't nuthin you can do fer him, and he ain't gonna live but a bit more. Go on now!* When I didn't move, he grabbed my coat collar in a power-ful grip that jerked me off my knees and shoved me toward the wagon. I stumbled back up on the wagon and sat down to watch them gloat while Daddy drowned in his own blood. I didn't doubt they were going to kill me too and I wished they would. I wanted to die. I had let my Daddy die. It was my fault. I was in the way and I hadn't protected him like I had promised Mama and Maggie.

"I just sat there shivering in the cold wind. It felt like some wild animal was tearing at the inside of my throat and to keep back the tears, I looked up at the sky, and watched the puffy black and gray clouds sail by. Those murderers weren't going to see me cry before they killed me. I looked back over at Red Beard grinning as he talked squatting by Daddy. All I could see was Daddy's shirt covered with blood, and as the blood oozed out of the wounds it had bubbles in it. Every gurgling breath I heard was weaker than the last.

"Jack Stone was one of the riders who had come racing back down the road at the first shot. As he reined in his horse, he said to Red Beard, *By God you did it! If you ain't the damnedest son-of-a-bitch I ever saw. You're worth every penny we're paying you. Shoulda brought you up here two years ago.* I remember he had a piece of grass dangling from his lips that he used for a toothpick as he talked. He pushed his hat back on his head as if he was attending a church social. He was laughing, swearing, and slapping his knee. He and his riders walked their horses over to where Daddy was lying and just sat there looking at him. One of the other riders was the hook-nosed man with the big mustache and bad teeth I'd seen with Stone in Tularosa, Charlie Bentene.

"Stone studied Daddy with his wolfish blue eyes and said, *Look at that high and mighty bastard now. Drowning in his own damn blood, sucking wind through a couple of holes in his chest. Damn if that ain't a purty sight, by God! I know a bunch of people that'd pay money to see old Fountain sucking his last wind. Too bad Oliver ain't here. Why I bet he'd pay a thousand dollars just to see this.* He looked over at me with that snarling grin, moved his straw to the other side of his mouth, and then gazed back down at Daddy. He said in a loud voice, *I hope, by God, you suffer awhile before you die, you son-of-bitch. We're just gonna sit here, and have us a little smoke while you do. You're sure as hell not gonna put any more of us outta business.* Red Beard didn't say anything. He just looked over at me with his one seeing eye that had no more life in it than the blind one. Stone continued to run his mouth as Daddy died.

"The cold wind woke me up from a dreamlike state. I wanted to cry for Daddy so bad, and I could feel the mucus starting to drip off the end of my nose. I felt helpless knowing I couldn't help him and it was me that got him killed. I even wished they'd just go ahead and put him out of his suffering. I remembered his last words to me were *Henry! Go!* and what he'd said about getting away.

"I couldn't hear the gurgles in Daddy's breathing anymore. Stone flipped the last of the cigarette he'd rolled off into the bushes, *Sounds like he's done. If he ain't, it don't make no never mind. Charlie, you and Jake come on over here and take that piece of canvas you brought and wrap Mr. High and Mighty here up in it and throw him over a horse.*

"Bentene and the cowboy they called Jake had been sitting on their horses in front of the team. They walked their horses over to where Daddy lay. I watched them slowly and deliberately dismount and take a roll of canvas off the back of Benetene's saddle to wrap around Daddy. Daddy stared at the sky, no light in his eyes. I knew he was gone.

"A voice in the back of my head told me if I was going to get away, it had to be now. I slid down on the floor in front of the wagon seat, grabbed the reins, slapped the horses and yelled, Get up, Buck! Get up! Hi ya, Hi ya! The team jumped in the harness and took off straight up the road, as if ghosts from hell were after them. They started so fast they almost threw me under the wagon seat, but I managed to hang on. I looked back as we charged up the road in a flat-out run. Stone and Red Beard were laughing and Charlie and Jake were just standing there with their mouths open. I thought, Yeah, you'll be laughing when my brothers and I get you! We'll hang you in front of everybody. They'll know you murdered my Daddy.

"They didn't chase after me! I thought I might get away after all and get help after I got to Organ. I was too young and ignorant to figure out that they had a man up the road as a lookout. They knew he'd catch the team before I got too far. The horses charged up the slight grade just before the hard pull up toward the pass. They had been trotting all day and were already starting to tire. I saw the lookout waiting for me on his horse a mile or so up the road. I managed to turn the team off the road and headed straight out into the desert. I climbed back up on the seat and looked back. I didn't see the lookout following me. It didn't matter. In those days there was still enough gra'ma grass to raise a few cattle and the creosote and mesquite bushes weren't nearly as thick as they are now. I was leaving a trail my sisters could follow.

"It wasn't long before the wagon sailed over a shallow little wash, took a tremendous bounce and threw me out. Buck and Sergeant kept on running. I landed hard on my arm and face in some sharp scattered rocks. My right forearm hit a stone and snapped and I felt something warm running down my face. The wind was knocked out of me. I laid there for a minute, heaving to catch my breath. I knew I had to get off my back and hide. I was a goner if they found me. Finally, my breath came wheezing back. I rolled over on my left side and pushed myself to a sitting position, then got to my knees. As I staggered up, I was shaking all over. My arm was hurting and throbbing so badly I gagged as the bushes in front of me spun out of focus. When I got steady and could see straight, I felt a big knot on my right forearm halfway between my wrist and elbow. When I touched my face the fingers of my mittens came back bloody.

"Yeah, that's where I got this scar down the side of my face. It wasn't all that deep, but I thought I was about to bleed to death. I took a deep breath, surprised I was still alive. I didn't have the canteen or quilt, but I wasn't dead yet either. Daddy would have been proud that I, at least, managed to get away and make them work to find me.

"As banged up as I was after I landed, where I landed is the reason I'm alive today. It was on a path cattle followed moving around through the mesquite and creosotes. Their tracks churned up the dirt everywhere. The men who searched for me never saw my tracks in that chewed-up dirt. I saw a big stand of mesquite up the wash and decided I'd run up there and hide. I thought maybe my arm would stop hurting and my face would stop bleeding with a little rest. I ran for my life, holding my arm and getting blood all over the front of my coat. I was already thirsty, and the wind, sharp and full of water as it swept down off the Organs, was bitter cold. It was getting colder! My face felt like it was freezing, but I didn't dare touch or cover it for fear it would start bleeding again.

"I made it to the mesquite thicket, got off the cattle path, laid down on my back, and slid up under one of the bigger bushes that had caught some tumbleweeds close to the ground. I managed to get positioned behind the bush and under a big tumbleweed ball so I could peep out through a fork in the mesquite's trunk. I had a line of sight not more than a foot or two wide, through the grass and overlapping bushes down the path to where I was thrown out of the wagon. I just hoped Buck and Sergeant had run for a long time so it took the murderers a while to find them; I'd have more time to hide and get back to the road.

"After a few minutes my arm settled into a steady dull throb. I knew from stories my brothers told it must be broken and that it had to be set and bound in a splint if I was ever going to use it again. I remembered their tales about pioneers alone in the wilderness who set their own broken arms, but I didn't have the strength or knowledge to try setting it and then wrapping it in a splint myself.

"The ground was damp under the mesquite bush and my pants were starting to soak up the moisture and get damp and cold. My hat was still on the wagon along with the canteen and quilt. I was getting the shakes from the cold and my face was throbbing and burning. It started to sink in that I was probably going to die. If those murderers didn't catch and kill me, the desert and weather would do it for them. I couldn't move my arm and I was shaking from fright, cold, and fatigue.

"I decided I had to get moving and get back to the road. Just before I started sliding back out of my hiding spot I saw the four riders pass through my line of sight down the wash. One of them was leading a horse with a big roll of canvas tied over the saddle. I knew that bundle had to be Daddy. I chewed my lip until it bled to keep from crying out for him. The riders didn't seem to be in any hurry to catch me. I realized later they were sure they'd find me with the wagon, or, if not, close by. I was going to be easy pickings, easier to find than a stray calf.

"I tried to think. It's amazing how clearly you can think, even as young as I was, when your survival is on the line. I had to figure out whether to run or to stay where I was until dark. I had learned a lot about hiding from playing hide-and-seek with my brothers in the desert. The best strategy in hide-and-seek was to stay still and not move around. I knew the murderers were sure to come looking for me. I saw them commit the murder. They had to be rid of me too. I figured they'd be looking for me on the cattle paths because that was where walking was easiest. If that was true, I might as well be sitting in the middle of the road waiting for a mail wagon to run over me. On the other hand, if I struck out off those paths, I'd leave a trail any granny could find.

"I had to hide under the mesquite until dark, then strike out down a cow path that led back toward the road. I thought that maybe a little rest would give me enough strength to get back to the road by morning even as cold and shaky as I was. If I didn't make it, then I'd just hide out again until I got to the road or one of Daddy's friends or my brothers found me – maybe in a day or two. I burrowed further down under the tumbleweeds, sticks, and leaves as much as I could without disturbing them enough to draw a rider's attention. Fortunately, my coat was colored about like the tumbleweed I'd wedged myself under and with a few leaves and sticks over me I knew I'd be hard to see. I was still cold, but out of most of that icy wind. I warmed up a little and felt some better.

"When the wind passed through the mesquite it made a low rumble, like a flag being whipped about that said Hey! He's right here! I wished it would stop. Lying on my back I could look up at the overcast sky and see occasional small patches of blue beginning to gallop past. I wanted to sleep but my arm and face were hurting, and the images of Red Beard coolly murdering Daddy played over and over in my head. I thought I'd never sleep again. The stillness in the desert was my only comfort, and it was powerful. It opened my soul. In soundless whispers I started praying. I prayed that Daddy was with Jesus and that Mama would be all right. I prayed that I might be saved, and if I were saved, I would do whatever Jesus wanted of me. Mostly I prayed for revenge. I prayed that God's justice would be delivered to my Daddy's murderers, especially Red Beard and Jack Stone and that His power would burn their ashes to nothing. I prayed I'd see Oliver Lee get his reward too. I believed he was in on the murder after I'd heard Red Beard wonder what Oliver might pay to see Daddy die. Most of all I prayed that I'd be the instrument of God's justice. With gun or knife I wanted justice and I wanted to be the one who made those murderers pay for killing Daddy.

"The patches of blue sky I could see were getting that rich deep blue you see just before dark when I heard horses walking in the wash, and, very faintly, men's voices. My first impulse was to get up and run, but I didn't rise more than two or three inches before the mesquite's thorns grabbed my coat and held me fast. I could have jerked from them, but that would have raised enough ruckus for the riders to have found me for sure. Nighttime was coming on fast. I could only hope that if I were very still the riders wouldn't see me. I twisted my body just enough to look down the wash. Charlie Bentene and Jake were riding up the path through the wash and leaning over their saddles to scan the dirt, grass, and bushes for some sign of me. Bentene got to my mesquite thicket first and stopped. My heart was beating so hard I thought it was going to pop out of my chest as I waited for him to dismount and drag me out. But he stayed on his horse, looked all around, and then threw a leg around his saddle horn while he rolled a cigarette. Jake came up, stopped, stood up in his stirrups and looked around the tops of the sea of creosotes and mesquites that surrounded them. A cow bellowed in the distance. Jake settled back in his saddle and started rolling his own smoke.

"Charlie cupped his hands and snapped a sulfur match with his thumbnail to light up. He gave Jake a light then flipped the hot match over in the mesquite almost right on top of me. He said, *Cold, ain't it, Jake? Seen any signs of the little bastard?*

"Jake shook his head, hunched his shoulders up, pulled his coat collar up tighter and said, *Hell no! Kid that age is small enough to hide in a rabbit hole. Why, hell he could be hiding in that there mesquite bush and we wouldn't know it.* He took a long drag on his smoke, then blew it into the wind whipping around them. *Charlie, it's gonna be colder'n hell tonight. If he ain't by a fire he'll die and we ain't got nothin' to worry about. If he don't die we'll catch him in the mornin' and Red Tally will take care of him. I...ain't...killin'...no...kid. Ain't Tally one cold son-of-a-bitch though? Shore took care of the kid's old man easy enough, didn't he? Let's go get some bacon. I'm starvin'.*

"Charlie took a last puff of his cigarette, flipped it in my direction too, and said, *It's colder than hell Jake, but if that kid survives and tells his tale, we'll be in hell a lot faster'n we're expectin, by God! We gotta get out here in the morning before Barela gets to where that wagon run off the road. He'll know something's wrong and high tail it to Las Cruces and have half the town back here looking for Fountain and his kid. Let's git. That kid ain't gonna make it through the night, and I want to eat before Jack heads for Lee's place. Jack said he knew just where to hide the body so nobody will ever find it. Come on. We ain't gonna find that little bastard half-breed in the dark. He ain't gonna survive without no fire, that's for damn sure.*

"They rode off down the wash, still leaning over their saddles looking for signs of me in the fading light. I decided the best thing for me to do was stay under that bush, maybe until midday the next day, then walk down the wash and back toward the road. I figured they'd be long gone by then and somebody from Las Cruces would find me maybe by late that night, but surely the next day. When it finally got dark, the ground started getting colder fast.

"I drifted off to sleep. I dreamed I'd been caught and was sleeping between Charlie and Jake when Charlie decided to go ahead and kill me. That woke me up for a bit, then I drifted off again. I was shivering after a couple of hours and couldn't stop. I started having a hard time distinguishing between what was real and what were dreams. One of the times when I was lucid, I knew Jake was right. I was dying. I thought I wouldn't mind dying if I could just have a good drink of water. I was so thirsty. I hadn't known a person could ever be that thirsty.

"I thought I was going out of my mind or dreaming again when I saw the big tumbleweed I was under start to rise right off the mesquite bush like a balloon and sail off toward other bushes. There was no wind. My eyes followed the black outline of the tumbleweed sail up and away in the air, then my stupefied gaze rolled down out of the night sky to fall on the shadowy grim face of an Apache with dark penetrating eyes staring directly at me. His hair fell over his shoulders and it was held out of his face with a cavalry campaign hat folded up in front. Short and thinly built, he wore a blue army coat with a set of yellow sergeant's strips. He was carrying an old lever-action rifle. I'd never seen one like it before – it didn't even have a forestock. I could see its brass receiver even in the dim light. A big long-barreled Colt and a long skinning knife hung from a cartridge belt around his waist. He looked me over slowly, then glanced up and looked over toward the east, seeming to sniff the wind. I couldn't see much of his face. It didn't matter. He seemed friendly, and right then, I needed a friend more than anything in the world. I started to speak but he held out his hand, palm forward, and shook his head to be quiet. He looked around again, then reached down and grabbed the hand of my broken arm to help me out from under the bush. When I groaned and gritted my teeth in pain, he nodded, took the other hand and gently helped me up and brushed the dirt off my coat as I stood there swaying. The ground seemed to be spinning on its own again. I was so cold, I was shaking all over. He placed a rough hand around my neck to feel how cold I was and shook his head. He squatted down, and, gently bending me over his left shoulder, picked me up. He walked about a hundred yards down a cow path to a black-and-white paint pony that snorted in recognition as we appeared out of the darkness.

"He sat me down on my feet in front of the horse. I was shaking hard and couldn't stop. He pulled a heavy Mexican blanket off the saddle and wrapped it around my shoulders, then eased me down to sit on it. He pulled a canteen off the saddle horn and offered me water. I was very thirsty and the cold water sliding down my throat was a gift from heaven, but, after a couple of swallows, I started shaking more and he snatched it out of my hand and whispered, *No much now! Usted mucho frio! Usted drink slow or usted die!*

"Gently he slid the coat sleeve off my right arm and felt it up and down. Up close, I saw he had a broad flat nose and thin lips. His black penetrating eyes looked like they came from a hunting hawk. His rough hands gently felt the knot in my forearm while I gritted my teeth and whimpered. He looked in my eyes and whispered, *Arm break. I fix. We ride before men come. Comprendé?* I nodded. He disappeared into the dark. I pulled the blanket up close and just sat there, still shaking but not as bad as when he pulled me from the mesquite bush.

"He reappeared so quietly I jumped when I saw his boots appear at my feet. He had four short sticks of mesquite the same length, sliced clean of thorns and bark, and some long strips of some kind of gourd vine. He squatted next to me and put a short piece of stick between his teeth and bit down showing his bright white teeth. He nodded his head to see if I understood, then gave the stick to me. I had no idea what he was doing but bit down on the stick anyway. He slid the sleeve up on my broken arm and took my elbow in a firm grip, grasped my wrist, looked in my eyes and nodded ready. I bit on the stick and nodded. He pulled hard. I nearly bit the stick in two as I passed out from the pain, but I didn't even groan. I was so afraid of bringing Charlie Bentene and Jake down on us.

"I woke up sitting in the paint's saddle with my face buried in the front of the sergeant's jacket and the Apache's arm under my shoulder blades clamping me tightly to his chest. I wasn't shaking anymore. Between the Apache's body heat and the heavy wool blanket he had around me I felt warmer than I had a lifetime ago that morning when I got out of bed in La Luz. All I can remember about that ride is the feeling of the left and right sway in the saddle as the paint tacked back and forth along a trail through creosote bushes, seeing a boulder or two passing in the deep shadowy darkness, and the moaning wind ripping at my torn face before I drifted into sleep, exhausted, with my face against the Apache's warm chest."

# 8

# RUFUS

Henry glanced at Roberta's face in the glow of the Plymouth's gauges. Tears rolled down her cheeks and a large drop of mucus hung on the tip of her nose. She sat staring straight down the highway. His normally smooth brow bunched with regret that his story brought her tears. She turned in the seat and leaned forward to rummage through her purse. Finding a fresh handkerchief, she dabbed at her eyes, blew her nose, cleared the tightness in her throat, and, turning her head from him, stared out her window into the darkness.

A swirling wind made the creosote bushes wave in the Plymouth's lights as she whispered, "My God, your father didn't have a chance! You might as well have been dead too. There's no doubt Stone and Tally were going to murder you! You must have survived only by God's holy grace. That miracle has touched me all these years. I cry just to think, that if they had taken you, all the people you've helped and all the time we've shared looking after patients and ..." She struggled to get the words out, feeling them now more than ever. She often felt them, but never uttered them for reasons she admitted to no one, least of all herself. "And...and each other." She blew her nose again as she tried to swallow the sharp lump in her throat.

Henry's ear caught her oblique reference to their shared lives and held it gently in his mind like a small bird fluttering in his hand stirring into hope the little fantasies he carried in his soul.

"You know, I met Oliver Lee at a get-together of old-timers about fifteen years ago. He seemed such a nice old man. Everybody there loved him, and I even gave him a hug. Now, I hate him. I hate him. I can't believe I held that snake next to my heart. I hope he's burning in hell!"

Her passionate condemnation of Oliver Lee made Henry flinch. Although he understood her anger, it felt more vehement than what he imagined his other friends might say if they had heard his story. He glanced again at her and softly said, "Now just calm down. There's no need to get yourself in an uproar."

Roberta blew her nose again and looked at him with red eyes. "Who was the awful one-eyed killer with the red beard anyway?"

Henry rubbed his stubble-covered jaw as the shadows from the desert moonlight on the creosote bushes raced over his face. "You're right. Daddy didn't have a chance. It was just like throwing a light switch. Daddy's life ended just like that!" He snapped his fingers. The sound cracked for an instant against the low rumble and whistling air in the Plymouth's cozy cabin. "I've practiced medicine for forty years and I've never seen such an abrupt, unexpected end to so vibrant a life. It took me years to get over it. Years of bad dreams and wishing I had done something, just anything, to save him, anything to get us away from those men. All I did was get lucky and survive, which I finally realized was all I could have done."

He rubbed his free hand over his still sweating face and dried it in a pass through his hair. "Yeah, I think they planned from the beginning to kill me too. They wore no masks, nothing at all to hide who they were. They might as well have been rounding up strays or going to church. Red Tally was the one-eyed man. I learned years later that he had owned a ranch down in the Big Bend country, but he ran just a few cattle on it, like it was some kind of hobby or something – I don't know. Ranching really wasn't his trade. He learned to be a sharp-shooter in the Civil War. I've heard tales that the only man in this part of the country who could out-shoot him at distance was Oliver Lee. There's that tale that Lee hit a plank five shots out of six at nearly a mile one Fourth of July. The old timers say that Tally might hit two shots out six. Lee almost never missed anything for which he aimed. Tally hired out to cattleman's associations in Texas, Colorado, and Wyoming, and went through free rangers and squatters like a reaper through a wheat field. Farmers all over the west claiming free-range land feared the sight of that red beard and one cold blue-green eye. He was Jack Stone's cousin. Stone had tried to get him to come kill Daddy in 1894, but Tally had other fish to fry."

Roberta slumped back in the seat and took a deep breath, blowing it back out in a long low whistle. She had no doubt now who she worked for and that she was friends with a legend everybody knew had been dead over fifty years. An idea suddenly lit her mind. "It was Yellow Boy who found you wasn't it?"

"Yes'm, it was Yellow Boy. When I woke up hours later, I was lying on a cot staring up into rafters supporting a tin roof that was creaking from the wind. Beams of sunlight burning through a dirty window in a wall opposite my bed made the dust floating in the air look like flakes of gold. I could hear the crackling of a fire and a spoon rattling against the side of a bubbling iron pot. Looking around, I saw that there was only one room in the place. The walls were two-by-fours sheeted over with planks about a foot wide and nailed in place at about a forty-five-degree angle. The same planks and two-by-fours had been used to make a rough door that rattled and creaked in the same wall as the window. A rifle with the longest barrel I'd ever seen and a fine walnut stock hung upside down on pegs above the door. Nails stuck in every two-by-four had some piece of clothing, a towel, a pot, a tool of some kind, or a cartridge belt hung on it. There were a couple of stacks of books packed several feet high in the corner closest to my feet. I turned my head and could see a couple of bed rolls laid out between a big old iron cooking stove and some stools around a rough table. My face was swollen so bad I could only see out of one eye and there was some kind of poultice that stunk like wet cow manure on the cuts on my face and arms. The mesquite stick and vine splint the Indian had put on my arm had been replaced by some nice saw-cut smoothed boards tied neatly in place with dingy, but clean, white cloth. I tried to sit up, but was too weak to make it and fell back.

"The Indian was squatting on his heels next to the door. He was resting with his back leaning against the wall and he fit nicely between a set of the wall's two-by-four studs. His rifle butt was on the floor. Its stock passed between his knees so the barrel rested on his shoulder. His piercing dark eyes followed me silently like a hawk watching a rabbit.

"The door was pushed opened by an old miner's boot, then flung wide open by a gust of wind as a dark silhouette filled it. The outline of a water bucket and a washbasin were there too. The silhouette closed the door, looked over at me, and said, *Well, sir, Yellow Boy, looks like our young friend's a finally awake! It ain't been but a couple of days has it? Glad ye decided to drop in today Henry!* I knew that voice! I jerked my good eye up from staring at the Indian and into silver wire-frame glasses sitting on the end of Rufus Pike's nose! He looked at me over the glasses and smiled. He wasn't as close to being shaved as I remembered him at Mrs. Darcy's. His shirtsleeves were rolled up over his long-john sleeves and there was a big bulge of chewing tobacco in his left cheek.

*Howdy, Henry. I didn't expect to see ye again quite so soon. Ain't been home but a few days myself.* He put the bucket down on the rough-cut table made of the same sheeting and two-by-fours as the house. Dipping some water into the basin, he sat it on a stand beside the cot. He brought a dipperful over to me. Sitting on the edge of the cot, he held my head up while I drank. I tell you I was dry and I gulped that good cold water down. The drink tasted almost as good as the one from the canteen Yellow Boy had given me two nights before. Rufus patted my shoulder and gave it a gentle squeeze of affection as he said, *We're mighty sorry about yore pa, son. He's a great man and shore didn't deserve to die like that there. Mostly though, we was worried about ye. Didn't know if old Yellow Boy had found ye in time or not. Ye've been sleeping sound fer two days 'cept fer when ye'd yell yore self awake.*

"Pulling over on an ancient, dark-stained, three-legged stool that looked as if it had been whittled and chopped on for centuries, Rufus sat down. Reaching in his back pocket, he pulled out the cleanest dirty rag in the shack, dipped it in the wash pan of water he sat by the cot and carefully dabbed at the poultice.

*"This here poultice, it's a made out of some weeds the Mescalero women use and recommend fer wounds of ever kind. Stinks, don't it?* Grinning, he wrinkled his nose and stuck out his tongue in disgust while the firelight from the open door in the old cast iron kitchen stove danced, reflected in the glasses resting at the end of his nose. There was the barest hint of a smile on the thin line that formed Yellow Boy's mouth, and I smiled too in spite of all the hurt I was feeling inside and out.

"Rufus tenderly took my good hand and rubbed it in disbelief. *It's a miracle ye're a livin' Henry. Another couple of hours under that mes-quite bush and ye'd be on the wrong side of the dirt.*

"But I didn't feel like I was all that hurt, Rufus. The cold just gave me a little case of the shakes.

*Well,* when Yellow Boy got here with ye he told me that when he found ye, ye were too cold to stay alive much longer. He had to keep ye wrapped in a blanket and held up next to his belly and chest while he brought ye here. Ya don't remember ridin' backwards over Baylor Pass do ye? He looked over at Yellow Boy with the question wrinkled on his brow. Yellow Boy gave a slight nod of assent and cocked his head to listen outside.

"Rufus said, *See there, I told ye.* He sniffed over toward a big black Dutch oven sitting on the stove. The room had a pungent dry wood smell that mixed with the mouth-watering smell of cooked meat, on-ions, and baked bread and made me glad I was alive. *Stew's 'bout done. Are ye ready to eat yet, Henry?*

"I'm about to starve, but I can't get food in my mouth 'cause my face feels so swollen up. I can't see out of one eye. Is it gone?

*"Naw, it ain't gone! Ye'll see fine when the swelling goes down. Never ye mind about the swelling, boy. We'll get ye fed.* He grunted with the weight of his years as he got up and shuffled over to the Dutch oven. Yellow Boy was still listening with his ear cocked toward the door, when he suddenly turned toward Rufus and said in a low urgent voice, *Caballos!* Without a word, Rufus motioned him with spread fingers, waving toward the floor, to stay still as he stepped over and squinted into the sunlight pouring through the dirty window.

*Cowboys from over to Dripping Springs! Y'all be still and I'll see what they's a wantin'*, he said calmly in a low voice.

"He didn't waste any time flinging the door open and closing it just as quickly behind him. We held our breath inside and listened to him speaking with the horsemen that rode up to the porch.

*Howdy, boys. How's ever'thang over to Dripping Springs? Looks like ye're goin' on a long huntin' trip with that there pack mule a loaded up like that.*

"I twisted my head so I could turn my good eye and peek through a crack in the door at what was going on outside. Yellow Boy's thin lips were drawn even tighter as he waited, tense and listening, with his back to the wall, ready to move if the men came inside. I saw his rifle was cocked and his finger was curled around its trigger. It didn't occur to me, until Rufus explained later, that Yellow Boy wasn't supposed to be there and what might have happened had those men found me, banged up and missing like I was, with an Apache right there to blame.

"The horsemen stopped about five feet from Rufus who, with his hands in his pockets, was leaning against a porch post. He was grinning jovially and squinting up at them in the bright afternoon sunlight. Buck Greer was in the lead. His gray hair was cropped close up to the edge of his hat except for some curly hedge that stuck out from under the front. His hat hid most of his forehead, which was lined with deep rambling wrinkles that stacked up against his big bushy eyebrows.

"He nodded toward Rufus. *Howdy, Rufus. Don't reckon you heard. Barela, the mail wagon driver over to Luna's Well, got back into Cruces night 'fore last, tore all to pieces. He said that it looked like Colonel Fountain and his boy had come to harm somewhere around Chalk Hill over to the Sands. Seems Fountain told Barela he was worried about some men dogging his trail. Barela said he saw the men and that they wouldn't stay on the road so he could see who they was when he passed 'em. Next day on the way back he found where Fountain's wagon seemed to run off the road and he got real worried. When he got to Fountain's place last night all worried, and Fountain and the kid hadn't got home, all hell broke loose. Fountain's oldest son, ain't his name Albert? He jumped on his horse and just took off for the pass without no supplies. Then another bunch supplied up and took off too. A rider come over to the ranch where Fountain's daughter Maggie was spending some time with that beau of hers to tell her what happened and she fainted. Pete here, who drove 'em back to town said she fainted two or three times on the way back. They're a saying Fountain's wife is in a bad way too, almost crazy with grief. The whole damn town's in an uproar.*

"Greer saw Rufus had a chew, so he paused, reached inside his big canvas duster, found a twist of dark tobacco for himself, and bit off a chew. The wind swirled the dust up around the horses and mule as they stood there stamping their feet, ready to go. Rufus leaned against the porch post like it was the middle of summer and shook his head in surprise before spitting a long brown stream of tobacco juice into the wind away from the riders. Greer let the chaw soften up under his cheek and curiously looked around the place. *Mr. Van Patten said José, Pete 'n me, could ride over the pass and join the search parties. He said we oughta get back soon as Colonel Fountain and the kid were found, and for shore not to be gone more 'n a couple a weeks. We thought we'd tell you the news and see if you wanted to come with us. We shore as hell got enough supplies on that mule so you ain't a gonna get hungry. You was a tracker back in the old days, wasn't cha?*

"Rufus nodded and said in his best good ole boy voice as he squinted up at them, *Yeah, I's a tracker for Cap'n Ewell. That was back 'fore the war. We's after Apaches on the El Paso to San Antonio road in them days.*

"He paused, appearing to be considering their offer, then spat a long brown stream of tobacco juice again and said, *Boys, I'm mighty sorry to hear about the Colonel and little Henry. Why I was a talkin' with them 'bout a week ago in Lincoln. I shore hate to hear this, but this here cold and wind has give me a major dose of the gout. I'n hardly walk much less ride my toes hurt so bad. So I guess I'll leave the trackin' to you fellas. Shore sorry about the Colonel and Henry though.*

"Greer winced and nodded. *Know what you mean. I get a touch of that gout myself onct in a while. It do hurt. We'd be glad to have you, but if you got the gout, you'd just slow us down. Mind if we water the horses an' the plants fore we head on over to the pass?*

"Rufus nodded toward the corral. *Naw, boys. Ya'll be my guests. Water trough's over by the corral. Help yourself. I'm about to freeze out in this here wind. Done got too old. I'm going inside now. Good huntin'!* Greer and the other two nodded farewell to Rufus and headed toward the corral.

"It seemed forever but couldn't have been more than ten minutes that we stayed nearly motionless in that shack, waiting for the Dripping Springs hands to water their animals and leave. The animals took their time drinking, then their cinches were checked and tightened, and Pete and José took turns visiting the privy while Buck peed on a bush by the corral. Finally, they left, picking their way down the trail, and, turning, waved good-by toward Rufus's shack. Yellow Boy stood up and watched them out the window, finally easing the rifle hammer off full cock when the men were gone.

"Rufus watched with him until they were out of sight, then said, *Gentlemen, that there green chile trail stew smell is a makin' my mouth water and ready to put on the feed bag. Let's eat! Yellow Boy's always ready to eat. Ye ready to eat Henry? I know I am.*

"I just grinned and nodded my head. Rufus took three big, deep pans like the cook at home used for pies and ladled out big portions of the stew from his big bubbling pot into each one. He raised the top on the Dutch oven, got a toasty brown biscuit the size of a fist and tossed it on top of the stew in each pan. He got a couple of spoons out of a box on a shelf over the stove and put one in each of the two pans. He walked over and handed the one without a spoon to Yellow Boy sitting cross-legged on the floor near the door. He grunted as he pulled out his big knife with one hand and took the pan with the other. *Ummph, gracias, Rufus! You cook muy bueno. I take you a mi casa someday. You cook all the time there. I look after you. Not need women then!* He grinned, showing his bright white teeth, speared a chunk of meat, and bit off a mouthful, noisily smacking his lips and grinning as a little of the gravy ran down his chin.

"Rufus said, *I don't think ye'd do without a woman, Yellow Boy. Hell! Ye just rode over two hundred miles to visit one, didn't ye?* He walked over to the cot and sat a steaming pan down on his ancient stool. *Henry, I know it's a gonna be hard fer ye to sit up, but rest yore broke arm in that there sling I got around yore neck. Ye need to do fer yoreself as much as ye can as soon as ye can to get yore strenth back. Sit up now and cross ye legs. I'm a gonna put this here stool up on the cot so's ye can eat off it and not have far to go to get the spoon from the pan to yore mouth.*

"He helped me sit up. I was a little dizzy and sore at first, but eating off that stool was pretty easy. The stew was scalding hot and burned the inside of my mouth. I didn't care; it was the best-tasting food I could remember. My swollen face made me dribble the stew down my chin as I got the spoon up to my mouth, but the pan was close enough to catch the drippings. Handling the spoon with my left hand was awkward but I learned fast. Rufus took the other panful for himself and creakily sat down on an old slat-bottomed chair, making a triangle seating arrangement with Yellow Boy and me.

"I felt safer and better protected in that old shack with Rufus and Yellow Boy than in a castle surrounded by knights. We smacked, chewed, and slurped on those biscuits, meat, potatoes, onions, chiles, and brown gravy without saying a word. I studied Yellow Boy while we ate. He looked about the age of my brother Albert who was about thirty. His shiny black hair stopped at his shoulders. His face reminded me of a pie pan. It was flat and round with a big broad nose, broken at least once and pushed a little to one side. It was centered between two knife slits for eyes and above a mouth framed by very thin lips. He was short, and I was surprised at how thin he was. Somehow, I'd always imagined Apache scouts to be big and strong, but he looked almost emaciated. We were all sweating a little from the chilies. He unbuttoned his cavalry jacket to cool off a little. There was a clean white shirt underneath the dusty jacket.

"Before Rufus and I were even half-finished, Yellow Boy finished sticking the last piece of stew in his mouth with his knife. Holding the pan up, he greedily drank all the remaining gravy and belched loudly. He said, *Good, Rufus! Usted cook bueno. We hunt together sometime, you cook then, huh?* Rufus had a mouthful and just grinned and nodded. Yellow Boy wiped the grease from around his mouth with his fingers and rubbed them on his well-oiled boots. He eased back against the wall under the window once more bracing the heels of his boots so his knees were about a foot off the floor. He felt around inside his unbuttoned coat, found a black, ball-bat-shaped, Mexican cigar in an inside pocket. He lighted himself a smoke after flicking a sulfur match against his thumbnail, like any cowboy lighting a cigarette. The way he smoked, blowing big blue clouds up toward the rafters as he sat relaxed and contented, reminded me of how Daddy looked many times after a good dinner at home.

"I stared at my plate of stew while I ate, thoughts racing through my mind, roadrunners chasing snakes, juking and jumping here and there but never making a catch. The last three days were a lifetime ago.

I knew I had jumped from being a child with no cares in the world, to a midget adult who was weak and knew nothing about the world he carried on his shoulders. I felt a thousand years old and knew in my soul I could never be a kid again. I remembered Buck Greer's story about Maggie. She had practically raised me. I felt so bad for her I wanted to cry. She had first suggested that I go with Daddy to stop the very thing that had happened to us. Now she must believe we were dead. I knew she'd think it was all her fault. Lord only knew what Mama must be thinking and going through. I yearned to go home and comfort them and then to make those men who killed Daddy suffer before I tore them to pieces. Shoot'em, stick'em with a knife, anything to make them sorry beyond anything words might express. I remembered tales Jack and Albert told me sitting around a campfire about Apache torture tricks. Maybe I could bury Jack Stone, Red Tally, and Oliver Lee up to their necks in sand and smash their heads with rocks, but not kill them, so they knew when the rats and ants were chewing on them before they died. I wanted to pour kerosene on their heads and set them on fire. I wanted to cut their guts out. I wanted their blood. I heard a roaring voice in my head and soul that said no matter what, somehow, someday, I'd make them pay for what they'd done.

"I looked over at Yellow Boy; smoke caught in the streaming beam of sunlight passing over him made a blue haze as he contentedly puffed on his cigar. So many questions littered my mind I had a hard time focusing on anything. I said, Rufus how did Yellow Boy find me? Why did he save me? Rufus shrugged his shoulders said between mouthfuls, *Why don't ye ask him yerself? He's a sittin' right there.*

"I...I...I thought it was a custom for Apaches not to speak about dead people."

*Well you ain't dead! Go on and ask him! I'd like to know more about what happened myself. He didn't tell me much in the way of detail 'cept yore Daddy was dead and that he found ye on the other side of Baylor Pass nearly that way.*

"So, I looked toward the center of the blue haze, through the golden flecks of dust passing through the sunbeams falling through the window. Yellow Boy's eyes were shut like he was sleeping. Smoke slowly poured through his nose, his thin lips curved slightly in an encouraging smile. I said, Yellow Boy, I thank you. I know I owe you for my life. Why did you help a white boy whose Daddy was once your people's enemy? Why didn't you just let me die?

"Yellow Boy's eyes blinked open and he squinted at me through the smoke boiling through the sunbeam. He held his cigar carefully, gracefully, rolling it on the fingers of his left hand, his right hand never leaving the barrel of his well-oiled rifle. He took another long pull on the cigar and blew the smoke in a long swirling stream toward the rough underside of the shack's roof as he tilted his head back. He looked at the roof, thinking as he sucked some meat from between his teeth with a snapping sound. Looking directly at me with unblinking eyes, he began to speak. He spoke Spanish pretty well then, but not much English, and what came out was a jumble of mixed languages and odd metaphors."

Henry saw Roberta frown. "Oh no! He speaks English much better now than he did then." He said with a laugh. "It was hard for me to understand him at first, so I had to listen carefully and didn't dare interrupt him. Even now I couldn't repeat the mishmash of exactly how he spoke, only give you a flavor of it. He was the first real Apache that spoke directly to me. You know, man to man, not like a man to a boy. I've thought about what he said many times since then and don't think I'll ever forget it.

"He said, *Many winters have passed since my father let Rufus live. It was in the days of the Cochise Wars with the gringos. My father, se llamo, he is called Caballo Negro – usted say, I think, Black Horse, si?* I nodded. *Caballo Negro has un tio, an uncle, to teach him the way of a warrior. His uncle wants him to learn ways to make round-eye hombres they catch suffer mucho and to use a knife to do this. He wants to teach how to cut after catching Rufus sleeping. Rufus's life, es claimed by my father. He let Rufus live. But he say if Rufus fight Mescalero, he will find Rufus, cut many times before he die. He make Rufus suffer many days before he die. When Caballo Negro goes to the land of the grandfathers he give me Rufus life. Say keep promise, make Rufus keep promise. I not keep Rufus. I give life back. He free of me. Live here. Good friend to Mescalero. Good friend to Muchacho Amarillo.* He added with a long smooth wave of his flat hand toward the south, *I stop en Rufus's rancho por rest y agua when I go a Mexico and come back many time.* Rufus was grinning and nodding his head that it was so.

*I have un woman en the sierras, the mountains, sud, south, of the Rio Grande. Her people they are last left living from last Geronimo band hiding from soldiers en Mexico. They hide for many winters in Sierra Madre after Geronimo go away on big iron wagon when he quit war. My woman, she no come with me to reservation. She afraid of soldiers there. She see many of her people die at hands of soldiers. See many starve in winter at San Carlos. See many get sick. She does not come. Now she heavy with my child. I go many times a Sierra Madre no can stay, must come back for other wife on reservation. Soldiers look for me if I stay too long. My woman en Mexico y the one on reservation, they hermanas, sisters. I take one in Mexico to please wife on reservation. Someday woman in Mexico and child they come to reservation and live in my tipi with me and sister. She not afraid of soldier no more. Someday this is true. I come back from Sierra Madre y rest with Rufus four suns ago. Three suns ago, I leave. Ride to reservation through Baylor Pass. No use San Augustin Pass. Other riders no ride through Baylor Pass. They will no see Muchacho Amarillo if I ride Baylor Pass. Ranchos on other side of pass have many cows and many vaqueros on other side. They move herds to more grass. Hard to hide from vaqueros as I ride. I ride slow, hide many times. They not see Muchacho Amarillo. Use long eye to watch road, watch herds, watch riders.*

"I must have had a questioning look because Yellow Boy reached in the saddle bag sitting next to his knee and held up a big barreled collapsible telescope. It was trimmed in brass and very beautiful. It must have had a two-inch objective. He repeated, *Long eye!* I nodded I understood and he continued.

*Watch road with long eye. Wait to ride when vaqueros cannot see. I see with long eye tres vaqueros ride up road, and one more that ride out from range on to road toward San Augustin Pass after Barela go by with his wagon carrying paper that travels. With him another wagon with old man y dos womans and a man on horse. Three hombres they stay away from Barela. Barela he not see other hombre, he too far. I think, No good come! I watch. Lead rider, has red beard. He leave others and stay behind gross verde bush. He pull his rifle. He wait. I wait. Rider from range, he wait at San Augustin Pass. Tres riders walk caballos slow toward San Augustin Pass. Wagon come. Barba Rosa, Red Beard, step from behind bush, shoot quick. Horses rear up, run. Barba Rosa shoot again pronto. Hombre falls off wagon. Wagon stop quick. Muchacho jump from wagon. Run to hombre on ground. Barba Rosa come, watch hombre on ground. Laugh. Make joke I think. Make muchacho go sit in wagon. Three riders come back quick. Give big war whoop. Riders sit, talk, smoke, watch hombre on ground. Muchacho make wagon run. Riders no chase. Wagon turns off road when muchacho see other man on road. Wagon, it go like the wind. Riders no chase. They laugh. It is hard to see wagon good. The bushes mucho grande.*

*Muchacho es a mouse. Riders esta gato. Yo no like. Muchacho brave, but soon riders will kill or carry him off. I get horse. I go find muchacho. Not let gato find mouse. Brave muchacho give Muchacho Amarillo warm heart. Find muchacho's wagon trail. Hide horse. Wait until dark. Track wagon on foot. Es muy difícil. Rider come, rider go. Look mucho for muchacho. They no find. I find where muchacho fall out of wagon. Blood sign on rocks. Not good sign. Follow his trail toward big mesquite. Find muchacho under mesquite. Muchacho hide good. Muchacho very cold. Shake mucho. Arm break, no work. I fix. Muchacho hace mucho pain when arm fixed. Muchacho no cry out. Pain make muchacho sleep. Muchacho brave little man. Not cry like muchachito. Muchacho sleep next to my belly, stay warm while we ride. He wake up, then sleep, wake up, then sleep again. We ride to Rufus. He sabé muchacho's casa. He take to casa. I hide with Rufus until I go reservation but I help Rufus with muchacho. Muchacho brave hombre. No muchachito, el is hombrecito, little man!* Yellow Boy finished his smoke, got up and tossed the butt through the doorway on the iron stove. He looked at us and just shrugged his shoulders like the things he described happened every day.

"Rufus finished his plate, sat it on the floor, wiped his mouth with the back of his sleeve, and tilted his chair back on two legs while he cut himself an after dinner chew. He looked over at Yellow Boy with a raised eyebrow and said, *When ole Yellow Boy rode up to the door with ye 'fore daylight, my old hound Cody started raisin' hell.* Rufus winked and said, *I named him after Buffalo Bill 'cause he can make more noise and pass more gas than a bugle band.* I couldn't help giggling.

"Then Rufus said, *I grabbed my shotgun and run outside in my long-johns and socks. It was colder hell and I's 'bout to freeze my cajones off a lookin' to see if there was a damn cat after my stock. 'Bout made me mess my drawers when that there Indian just floated in outta the dark with somebody ridin' backards on the front of his saddle. Soon as he showed me who it was I 'bout puked and thanked God at the same time. It didn't take no lawyer to fig're out ye and yore Daddy had come to no good and that somehow ye, at least, got away. Yore face was a mess and Yellow Boy had this makeshift splint on yore arm. He said it was broke and ye had the cold shakes when he found ye, but ye had gotten better a ridin' next to him coming over Baylor Pass. He carried ye inside, and we fixed this here warm spot fer ye. We put my cot over close to the stove fire door so's ye'd git warm and stay thawed out. Worked too, didn't it?*

*Yellow Boy hid his horse up the canyon whilst I doctored yore arm with a splint that'll last fer a while. He come back with weeds he'd found fer the poultice I got on yore face. That there is gonna be a nice* scar, Henry, but it ain't deep and they warn't no need to do no sewin'. Since then we been a waitin' fer ye to get yore sleepin' done. I told him to go on back home, that I'd get ye home soon as ye were strong enough to sit a horse, but he wouldn't leave till he knew ye were a gonna make it. I ain't got a wagon, son. Can't get up that there trail in front of the shack with one too easy, so I usually just use pack animals. Yellow Boy needs to lie low here until the other side of the mountains settles down from posses riding ever which a way so's he can get through without being seen or caught. Them posses though, they ain't a gonna find nothin'. Bastards that killed yore Daddy, they's long gone. I 'spect Yellow Boy can get through in three or four days. So maybe in a few days he can take off fer the reservation and we can ease on down to Mesilla and take away a little of the grief your family's a feelin'.

"I finished my plate. Rufus took it and set it inside his on the floor. I looked first at Yellow Boy sitting between two wall studs listening to Rufus with his eyes closed, then at Rufus, who had that earnest look I remembered from talking to him in Lincoln, then back at Yellow Boy. I hung my head thinking about the miracle of salvation that had been visited on me by those two good men. I remembered seeing the glazed look in Daddy's eyes and the bubbles in the blood coming from his chest, and those murderers just sitting and laughing, while they smoked and waited for him to die.

"The dam finally broke and I hung my head and cried. I cried like I'd never cried before. I couldn't stop. Rufus just reached over and patted me on the shoulder and said, Go on and grieve, Henry. Ye're due. It don't make ye less a man that ye loved yore Daddy that much. Yellow Boy just sat and watched. Then he said softly, Show eye water now, muchacho. When you man, you no make sound of woman with a heavy heart for one vaya con grandfathers.

"I finally stopped crying and wiped at my eyes. I sighed. It had been cathartic and I felt better. Rufus said, Did ye hear anything, boy? Did ye hear anything at all that'd tell us who those men were who killed yore pa? I nodded, still snuffling up the snot and tears. I forgot about how tore up my face was and wiped my nose with my sleeve. It hurt like the devil. It felt like my face had been slapped and I felt the poultice crack and shift a little, but somehow it hung on.

"I said, Jack Stone, Charlie Bentene, and a cowboy they called Jake were up the road before the shooting started. I remember Stone and Bentene from when we stopped in Tularosa on the way to Lincoln. I think Red Beard is named Red Tally. He did the shooting. Said he was going over to Oliver Lee's to see if he could get more money. Said Lee oughta be real grateful cause he made life easier for him by killing Daddy. Tally and a couple of others followed us down from Mescalero after we stayed with Doc Blazer. I heard Stone say he wished he had Tally come in '94 when they had wanted to kill Daddy then. I hate their guts, Rufus, I hate 'em! I'm gonna kill 'em all. I started crying again. I couldn't help it.

"Yellow Boy crossed his arms and stared at me. Rufus's face had a frown of anger and concern as he spit in the old coffee can he used for a spittoon. He shook his head slowly and just said, *God a'mighty damn!* A gust of wind shook the creosote bushes outside the door and made the window and door rattle. It was like a tomb inside that shack as we sat and stared at each other while Rufus chewed and spat for a while.

"Finally, he spat a big stream into the spittoon can and said, *We gotta be real kerful here, boys. I hear tell Red Tally is one brutal, mean son-of-a-bitch killer. Hires out to stock associations to bushwhack squatters, so's they'n run the rest off. He's deadly at long distances with a Winchester. Most people he's bushwhacked never knowed what hit 'em. Up in Colorado they say he even shot a preacher standing in the middle of the street whilst he's a talking to a sheriff. Couple years back he burned down a house with a woman and two little 'uns still in it when she wouldn't leave after he killed her man. He don't hold back from killing nobody if they's money to be made.* He stared at me, his eyes narrowed and filled with anger. *They was gonna kill ye too. You know that, don't ye, boy?*

"I just nodded. I knew it was true. Rufus said, *Stone couldn't afford to pay Tally by his self. They's a group who's anted up to the pot to pay Tally. They's most likely little ranchers cause yore Daddy was working fer the big ranchers. Oliver Lee is the biggest little rancher. He proba-bly put some money in that pot his self. He's smart, that one is. If'n he thinks the law is a gonna come after him he turns his self in and lets Albert Fall get him off. You seen 'em all 'cept Lee murderin' your daddy. Your word could send 'em all to hell at the end of a rope a lot sooner than they's expectin' t'go. They's got to be rid of you, Henry. If'n you show up again...*he said slowly, shaking his head. *I 'spect right now they's thinkin' ye're froze to death out there on the range or vict-uals in the belly of wolves or coyotes. God only knows what they's done with yore Daddy's body. If I take ye back to your family now, it's likely ye'll be dead in less than a week and yore family too. What do ye sup-pose we oughter do?*

"I want to kill 'em all! I said with fire burning in my belly. If the law doesn't get 'em first, I have to. It's all my fault Daddy's dead. I have to stay alive to do that. I've got to hide until it's done. It's not right for me to go home until Daddy's murderers are dead too. I began sobbing again. Rufus just stared off into space, chewing and spitting occasional long brown streams of tobacco juice into his can spittoon and wiping his chin with the back of his hand.

"He said, with a wrinkled brow, trying to get his mind around the outrageous claims I'd just made, *Let me get this straight. Are ye telling me ye don't wanna go home? Ye really don't wanna go home? Ye ain't a gonna go comfort yore family? Even fer a few days? Ye believe yore Daddy would be alive now if ye hadn't been there? Ye plan to make war on them there killers?* I just nodded.

"He said, *Dang, son. Ye sound like ye need to be twenty or thirty years old! It's smart not to give anybody anywhere a hint ye're alive, 'cause when word gets out, they'll fer a fact come after ye. Specially Stone and Tally cause they muffed it letting ye get away. They's a hoping ye're dead. If ye ain't, they'll be shore to shut ye up at the first opportunity. Hell fire! How in the world do ye plan on wipin' out those killers and ye not more than ten or eleven year old?*

"All I could answer was, I'm eight Rufus, and I don't know how I'll do it, but I will. Will you help me? Please? He slowly shook his head as he rolled my plea around in his head and a little trickle of tobacco juice ran down the side of his mouth before he could spit. He chewed a couple more times and spit the whole wad in the can before saying with resignation, *Hell fire, son, what'd yore mama and daddy do? Cast ye outta steel? Sire theyselves a wolf pup? I've lived a right long time. I might as well die now as later. Yes, sir, I'll help ye. I can at least help keep ye alive until the law catches those bastards. Maybe we'll even get one or two of 'em our own selves, if'n Yellow Boy helps us.*

"I looked over at Yellow Boy who was watching Rufus wiggle around in his seat. I said, Will you help me, Muchacho Amarillo?

"His thin mouth cracked a smile and he said, *I no let gato catch little mouse. Si! I help. Yo su amigo, I your friend. We will take life for life many time.*

"Can we go after them tomorrow? I said, tingling with excitement. I'm sure I'll feel better then. Can we?

"Rufus roared with a laugh and choked on his fresh chew of tobacco. *Haw! Hi yee! And whoopy do! Listen to this little chicken hawk, would ye, Yellow Boy?* Yellow Boy's faint trace of a smile broadened to a big grin as I looked from him to Rufus and back again. I didn't see what was so funny. Now I had me some real fighters who could help me get even for Daddy. Yes, sir! I...uh...we were going to make Stone and Tally and Oliver Lee pay for Daddy's murder.

"When he finally stopped laughing and choking, Rufus looked at me with kind eyes and said, *Now, Henry, ye gotta start thinkin' like a smart scout. Ya gotta be cool and cakylatin'. Ye're a little boy, a mighty fine one, but still not close to growed yet. To go after these here killers, ye gotta get big and strong. Ye gotta be a expert with a weapon. I watched ye with yore Daddy's rifle and ye was good fer a little feller even if it was too heavy fer ye – but ye ain't nearly good enough to hunt men.* He nodded to the rifle hanging over the door. *I'll teach ye how to be a expert with that there buffalo rifle. Ye can shoot at those bastards from half a mile away and kill ever one of 'em with it if'n ye want to. Ye gotta be able to survive in this here desert to do it. Ye was lucky onct. Not likely to be again. I know a few tricks fer makin' do in the desert, but ole Yellow Boy there he growed up in it. He'll teach you to live in it and to make it support ye as if it were yore friend. He'll teach ye a lot of other Apache tricks too, of that I'm shore. When the time comes we'll saddle up and go get those bastards. But it shore as hell is gonna take a while fer ye to heal and grow and git smart and good with that there gun. It's a gonna be a powerful lot of work. Ya ready to work, and wait and learn?*

"I bowed my head and looked at the rough shack floor, realizing how big my talk had sounded without any idea of what it meant. It was embarrassing. Yes, sir, I said, I'll work real hard and I'll learn everything you can teach me. I promise. Just so's those murderers don't get away, I can wait.

"Rufus nodded and leaned over to give me a gentle pat on the leg. *Don't worry 'bout that. They's justice a coming. They ain't gittin' away. We're a gonna get 'em.*

"The need for more sleep suddenly rushed over me and I yawned and said, Rufus, I'm very sleepy now. He nodded, straightened the bed roll I was using for a pillow, helped me lie back, and then fixed my arm so it lay comfortably on my chest. I don't remember much after that except that he and Yellow Boy seemed to be talking far away as I drifted off. I woke up in the middle of the night with a thirst like I was wandering in the desert and needing to pee in the worst way. Rufus helped me up so I could water a creosote bush at the edge of the porch and then to get some water from the bucket on the table. It was cold on the porch, but the wind had died to a light breeze and the stars were twinkling in a smooth black sky. Yellow Boy was gone."

# 9

# THE GOING HOME TALK

**E**ven the gasoline stations along Route 70 were closed as the Plymouth passed through Tularosa. A few bare bulbs were lighted on walls near business entrances, casting shadows on squat doorways framed in adobe walls. A few blocks off Route 70, near most of the mercantile stores, a greater concentration of streetlights gave the appearance of more activity but not a soul could be seen anywhere. The Plymouth, appearing to float like a cruising shark from pool to pool of light cast by the streetlights, passed slowly down the wide road at the posted 25 mph speed limit.

Roberta ignored Tularosa as she stared at Henry in disbelief. He stared straight down the road. He was reluctant to look at her, sensing her confusion and incredulity, uncertain of the source of her furrowed brow and the fury lighting her eyes. He had told her the truth. Why shouldn't she believe him? She sighed and slowly rubbed her temples with the hand that supported her head as she forced her mind to grapple with the fact that Henry apparently refused to go back to his family. Finally, she said, "Why did he do it?"

"What do you mean, *Why did he do it*?" He volleyed back, stealing a quick glance at her while trying to avoid the angry fire in her eyes. Participation in many romantic liaisons had taught him that when women were angry, the best defense was to get out of their sight for a while. Trapped under the Plymouth's steering wheel, there was no place for him to hide. This time he had to sit and face the music.

"Rufus never took you back home, did he? He just kidnapped you and kept you, didn't he? Why didn't he just take you back home to your mother?" He slumped further under the wheel as the hurricane gathered force. "I can remember my father saying he never saw your mother in anything but black for years after you disappeared! How could Rufus...how could he, how could you, make her suffer like that? Why on earth didn't he take you back home? Why didn't you just go home on your own?" She emphasized her point by pounding her fist against the top of the seat where her arm rested. "Don't you understand? Rufus sounds as bad to me as Oliver Lee! Maybe he was even worse. He literally kidnapped you from your family!"

Henry grimaced as he shrugged his shoulders and wiggled more upright on the seat. That made Roberta even more angry and mystified by his seeming so-what attitude. They glided through the last street light in Tularosa and sped into the darkness on the final leg of their trip to Mescalero.

"Okay, okay, I understand now," he sighed. "On the face of what you know so far, you're exactly right. Rufus, in effect, did kidnap me. He, Yellow Boy, and I had a long talk about my going back home, oh...let's see...yeah,...about three years after Yellow Boy found me under that mesquite bush. Rufus wanted to take me home, but Yellow Boy talked him out of it. Besides, I didn't want to go and flat-out wouldn't go. In fact it was about ten or eleven years before I saw my mother again after Daddy was killed."

"You mean you actually saw your mother again?" Roberta shouted.

He nodded slowly, "Yeeeahhhh," he said, drawing out the word as though she wouldn't understand it otherwise. "I actually did. How do you think I got in medical school? My mother gave me the idea to be a doctor and pulled the strings to get me in Stanford. Maybe you'll be a little more sympathetic towards Rufus and Yellow Boy after I tell you about my early life with them and the talk with Rufus and Yellow Boy about my going home.

"When I awoke the morning after the Dripping Springs men had stopped by, an old coal oil lantern with a soot-blackened chimney was the only light in the shack. The most delicious smell of frying bacon, biscuits, and coffee I can remember filled the shack. The biscuits were cooking in the crusty old black Dutch oven I remembered from the day before. Beside it on the stove was an old beat-up coffeepot used over lots of trail fires, steaming away, making fresh-perked coffee smell the way I still hunger for to this day.

"I didn't see Yellow Boy anywhere. I panicked. We hadn't brought the killers to justice yet! I pushed myself up with my good arm and said to Rufus, Where's Yellow Boy? He promised to help us. Has he decided he won't?

"Rufus was frying bacon in a big old cast-iron skillet. He looked over his shoulder and grinned before spitting with unerring aim into his old spittoon can. *Naw, Henry! He's a gonna help us. He's just slipped back to the reservation fer a while a visitin' with his family. Oughter be back in a few weeks – maybe by the time ye're healed up.*

"My lower lip trembled when I whined, But he just got back from Mexico! His wife's down there. Who's he visiting on the reservation? He's not gonna help us is he?

"Rufus' grin spread another inch under his whiskers. He spat again and said, *Now don't git yore drawers in no wad Henry. Why shore he's a gonna help us. He's just a visitin' his wife. You remember? His number-one wife? He told you about her yestidy. See, son, some Apache men, dependin' on how well off they is, have more than one wife. Yellow Boy has two and they're sisters. One already lives on the reservation, but the other one won't come. She's too afraid of the soldiers. Old Yellow Boy could beat the one down in Mexico and make her come to the reservation, but he's smart enough to know that she'd wind up a hatin' him if'n he did, so he's jest kinda floatin' back and forth between his two wives until the one in Mexico changes her mind. 'Sides, he likes all the roamin' 'round he's a doin'. How'd ye sleep, little man?*

"His reassuring words had a soothing effect on my fears of being left alone to fight the killers. I said, yawning, "Pretty good I think. I don't remember any bad dreams. My arm doesn't throb anymore either, but my face hurts.

*Well, git on up then, if'n yore strong enough. They's some hot water and a towel over on that little table next to the door. Warsh the sleep outta yore eyes and see if'n ye can warsh off that there poultice on yore face too. It's a needin' changin'. I'll dress it with a new poultice. Then we'll eat and I'll show ye around the place.*

"He fixed us a breakfast of biscuits, bacon, and refried beans. I was starving and kept packing my jaws with victuals like a squirrel. I didn't want to stop eating. Rufus just spread some honey on a biscuit and dawdled with his eating pan while I stuffed my face. He kept saying, *Don't make yoreself sick eatin' too much now. They's lots to see. I want ye to see it all. Hope ye're a gonna like it here.*

"When we finished, he collected the plates and put the rest of the beans and the last bits of burned bacon in our leftovers. He put all the pans and plates out on the porch for Cody to lick clean."

Roberta made a face. "That was a little unsanitary, wasn't it?"

Henry smiled. "Well, a little maybe, but Cody was healthy and we rinsed the plates and pots off in water before we used them again." Roberta slowly shook her head in disgust. Men! They were all cut from the same mold – even doctors.

"After breakfast, Rufus helped me get up and dressed. My coat was ripped to shreds from crawling under the mesquite, so he threw a blanket over my shoulders to break the morning chill as we stepped out on the front porch. It was surprisingly warm outside, much warmer than it had been down in the basin when Daddy was murdered.

"Rufus's place was in an Organ Mountain canyon just south and east of Las Cruces. You know how the land rises up to meet the mountains. By the time you ride up to the mouth of his canyon and Rufus's shack, which sat a few yards from the entrance to the canyon, you've already climbed high above the Mesilla Valley. I'd guess his place must be about a thousand feet above the Rio Grande. The view from his porch was spectacular. Sitting there you could look around the western edge of the tall canyon cliffs and see the Florida Mountains about sixty miles away to the west, and it was easy to see the top of Tortugas Mountain, you know, the one the university kids call A Mountain, just outside of Las Cruces. You could also see a few out-buildings around Las Cruces, but most anything you might have seen in Las Cruces was hidden by that bald little wart of a mountain and the valley. At night, looking down the side of the Organs toward the south, we could see a weak sky glow over El Paso.

"The trail up to Rufus's shack from the desert floor was a straight two-rut sandy road that cut up from a slightly wider dusty road that ran alongside the Organs. That road passed Dripping Springs Ranch five or six miles away, crossed a trail over the Organs by Baylor Pass, and crossed the road that went over San Augustin Pass in a mile or two after that. The mesquites and creosote bushes along the road up to Rufus's place were just barely separated enough for a wagon to get through. You couldn't turn around on that road until you got up to Rufus's place. After you turned around and started back down the trail, you couldn't be seen from the shack after you'd traveled a hundred yards and your foot had to ride the brakes all the way down – it was that steep.

"Rufus had painted the shack a light turquoise-green color that matched the salt and loco weeds and a few old cactus that grew scattered around the front of his place. Its original color had faded from years of hard sunlight, but it still blended in well with the plants. The canyon walls rising like guardians on either side of the shack were rusty red with an occasional black streak down their faces. Those walls must have started out at least two or three hundred feet high and they got higher as you went toward the back. They shaded the canyon most of the time, except near mid-day and late in the afternoon, when the sun, setting behind the Floridas, caught the front edge of the shack.

"There was about a hundred yards between the south canyon wall to the side of the shack. The canyon wall on the north side was about thirty yards from the shack. On the north wall about thirty feet off the canyon floor and just about even with the shack was a wide ledge covered with piñon bushes. There were a couple more ledges like it further up the wall. Rufus had made a place to hide on that first ledge and had even chipped some hand and toeholds in the canyon wall so he could get up to it fast if he had to. He kept jars of water and some beans and salt pork stashed away up there in case he had to stay there a while to hide from Indians or bandidos. By the time I was ten, it was one of my favorite hideouts when I played 'Kill Stone and Tally'.

"Rufus used a small shed for a barn. It was about thirty yards southeast behind the shack. It sat by a corral and the privy was close by on the shack side of the corral fence. He'd stretched barbed wire from the corral all the way across the canyon to keep his cattle and his mules from wandering off. A little spring-fed stream wandered down a wide, shallow gully close by the south wall. He had damned it up into a nice little reservoir. Using planks he nailed and tarred together, he channeled the water from the reservoir to watering troughs and a holding tank he used for the shack. The barbed wire fence had a big pole gate at the corral that blocked a path disappearing back deep into the canyon. I could hear cattle occasionally bawling somewhere from deep within the walls of the canyon.

"When we walked over to his shed, I noticed a pile of rocks. It was about ten feet in diameter and three or four feet high at the center sitting between the house and corral. As I looked around I noticed other, smaller piles scattered back down the canyon. I couldn't contain my curiosity and asked Rufus what the piles of rocks were for?

"He stuck out his chest and says, *Well, boy, I intend to make me a first class place here one of these days. I'm a gonna use rocks like old Frenchy Rochas did over to Dog Canyon a few years ago. He even made his fences outta rock. So I's been gittin' my buildin' stones together 'fore I start.*

"Can I help you get your rocks together? Since you're helping me I want to help you all I can.

"*Shore, boy. That there'd be a mighty big help.* He chewed on the wad of tobacco in his cheek a couple of times and rolled a thought over in his mind before he spat again. He said, *Ye know, carryin' rocks to them there piles might be good fer ye. It'd help make ye stronger than a body might think ye was fer yore years.*

"Oh boy! Can I start this afternoon? I pleaded.

"Rufus laughed. *Naw, son! Ye gotta heal up first. They's plenty of time to work carrin' rocks to them there piles. 'Sides, they's some things ye gotta know 'fore ye start a pickin' up rocks in this here canyon.*

"I was puzzled and a little frustrated that I couldn't start getting big and strong right away. I sniffed, Rufus, what do you have to know to pick up and carry a rock? Don't you just pick it up and start walking? That doesn't take training, does it?

"Rufus's brow wrinkled and his eyes narrowed in disgust. *Naw, ye don't jest pick it up and start a walkin'! And don't go a gettin' smart-mouthed on me now, boy! Lots times they's bad critters under them rocks. Ye know, like rattlesnakes, or scorpions, or black wider spiders, or hundert leg centipedes. Those thangs'll bite ye. Aye God, ye know ye been bit when they do too! Why I see'd men lose a fanger after a centi-pede got 'em. Ye gotta be careful when ye pick up a rock around here son – they's things undert 'em that can kill ye.*

"I never smart-mouthed Rufus again. I made sure I gave him the same respect I'd always given Daddy. I understood then I had a lot to learn and a short time to learn it and that old tobacco-chewing man was all that stood between me and death before I was ten years old. He knew what he was talking about. I nodded and hung my head. Yes, sir, I said. I didn't mean to smart-mouth you. I won't do it any more.

"Rufus nodded and grinned. *Ye're a quick study, Henry. Ye'll do fine.* He was quick to try to make up, asking, *How's yore arm a feelin' in that there sling I made ye? Are ye warm enough with that blanket over yore shoulders? Ye wanta rest fer a while before we take us a walk up the canyon?*

"No, sir, I'm ready to go now. My arm's not throbbing and the blanket feels good.

"*All right then*, he nodded, *say ye feel like walkin' up the canyon? They's some places I want ye to see up there too.*

"Yes, sir! I want to see it all.

"We walked back past the shed where he kept his tools, harness and some grain for his mules. He pulled a couple of poles down to make getting through the fence easy. When we were on the other side he put them back in place and led off down the path through piñon bushes that disappeared around a curve in the canyon walls. He called back over his shoulder, *Be kerful and don't a go steppin' in no cow pies. It don't make the shack smell too good if 'n ye git that dirt on yore boots.* I saw the mischievous look on his face and laughed with him.

"We walked about a mile up the canyon. He had over a hundred head of cattle grazing on the best stand of gra'ma grass I'd ever seen. Stands of gra'ma that thick had been over-grazed and were for the most part long gone from around Las Cruces and the Tularosa Basin by then. As we neared the end of the path, the sheer face of the cliffs in which the canyon ended rose up before us, dark and overpowering in the shadows. Looking at their smooth walls for the first time, you'd swear they couldn't be climbed. But Rufus showed me a barely visible line of handholds that went right up the north wall and disappeared up over the top.

*I don't know who fixed them places. It's easy to climb up to the top of them there cliffs using 'em. Why I even done it myself onct. I 'spect it was Apaches made 'em. They's a fixing 'em a rabbit hole to 'scape down jest in case they got trapped in this here canyon. If'n ye foller them hand holds up over the cliff there ye'll find a trail that takes ye quick across the Organs and down the other side 'bout where Aguirre Springs is. Now don't ye go gittin' no ideas 'bout goin' up them thangs. One slip up high and ye'd be a goner fer shore.*

"I nodded. I could barely stand on my toes and reach the first hand-hold. It was way too hard for me to pull myself up to the first one, much less maintain my balance all the way up so I didn't fall back-wards. But you know Bertie, by the time I was twelve, I had gone up that cliff using those handholds and over to Aguirre Springs on the other side four or five times.

"Rufus pointed toward a small crack in the south wall that was maybe twenty feet wide and ran for several hundred yards perpendicu-lar to the main canyon before becoming impassable. To me it looked like a great place to play hideout. I noticed that there were mounds of dirt all the way down the length of the crevice, every fifty or so yards, and it looked like bits of glass were scattered on the tops of them.

*See that there crack in the world? What'd ye think I use it fer?*

"I could only shake my head at the mystery.

*See those mounds of dirt? I put 'em in there myself. They hold up my targets, usually bottles I git from the saloons. Them mounds is 'bout fifty yards apart and they's ten of them. That there is five hundert yards. It's where I practice with that there Sharps a hangin' over the door. Soon as yore arm's well, I'm a gonna teach ye how to be a deadly shot with that there old rifle. Think ye'd wanna learn that kinda shootin', do ye, son?*

"I was so excited at the prospect of getting to shoot that big old rifle hanging over the door posts I could only smile and nod. Rufus spat a long brown stream, smiled through yellow teeth and tousled my hair.

*Well, soon as yore arm's mended, we'll start a shootin'. I can see ye're gittin' tired so we'll git on back to the house. Oh! Almost fergot the main reason I brought ye up here today.* In the east cliff wall he pointed out the source of the spring that fed the little stream that watered the canyon. *That there spring, boy, is the reason this place survived the big drought. That there water is our lifeblood. Defend it with yore life if ye have to.*

"I will, I promise.

*I know ye will, boy. I know ye will,* he whispered as he headed off down the path. About halfway back down the path, he stopped and pointed my attention toward the canyon's north wall. *Notice anything peculiar 'bout them bushes over there?*

"I looked closely and couldn't see anything peculiar about the bushes he pointed toward. I stared at it for a few more moments before I realized there was a faint outline of some kind of depression about the size of a big door on the canyon wall behind the bushes. You wouldn't notice it unless you stopped and stared at it for a while. I pointed toward it, All I see is something that looks like a little depression in the cliff. It kind of reminds me of the door to a cave I used to hear Daddy reading to my brothers about in Aladdin's adventures. Is it a door? Will it open if I say Open Sesame?

"His grin covered both sides of his face and nearly jumped out of his beard. *I'll be a hornswoggled! Damn if ye ain't got sharp eyes 'n a good memory. Ain't nobody else seed that door 'till I point it out fer 'em. Yes, sir. It shore is a door. Made it and fixed it up to look like part of the mountain I did. It's to cover up the entrance to a little mine I started. It ain't very deep, but it's dry so I keep my extry supplies there. Wanna see inside?*

"Walking off the trail toward the door, it was easier to recognize it as a door as we got up close to it. Rufus had made it out of wood then covered it with a thin cloth sack that was filled with a layer of rock and dirt the same color as the canyon wall. Then he'd used plaster mixed with dirt to hide the doorframe that held it in place.

"He fished around near the bottom of the door to find the latch that held it tight and closed. A blast of stale, cool air came floating out as he swung it back. He lighted a coal oil lantern hanging on the back of the door and held it up so I could see inside. To me, the inside looked better than the US Treasury. It was filled with barrels of stuff, animal hides, an old saddle or two, harness, tools, some old apple crates filled with potatoes, and a stack of neatly folded canvas tarps. Toward the back, I could see the dim outline of a half a side of beef hanging from a small scaffold.

*Now, I'm showing this here hole to ye so ye know where it is, what's in it, and how to get in it if ye need to get supplies or tools fer us or to hide yoreself. Only thing ye gotta remember is snakes like this place too. They think it's a dad burn hotel. They'll generally mind their own business if'n ye don't bother 'em none. If they's one here, just take that stick there and toss him outside. Ain't no need to kill 'im, lessin ye have to. He'll keep the rats and other vermin gone. Do ye foller me, son?*

"I nodded, but in the back of my mind, I was certain I didn't want to fool with any rattlesnake, especially with just a stick. If I found one, he was a goner.

"Rufus closed the door and latched it again. He stepped back to admire it for a few seconds before he said, *Now don't fergit to latch it after ye're in there or they'll be more snakes than that there stick'll take care of.* I nodded I understood as he led me back down the path toward the house.

"When we got back to the house I was worn out. Rufus helped me lie down on the cot for a siesta, and said he was going to sit outside and whittle awhile and enjoy the sun until it was time to cook our supper. That old cot sure felt good. It wasn't more than two or three big yawns before I drifted off to sleep.

"Rufus took me for walks up and down the canyon nearly every day after that. He taught me about all the vagaries of the place like where to find plants that were useful for teas and medicines. I got stronger each time we went out. As the winter chill began to give way to the spring winds, I watched and learned how he did his chores – feeding the cattle, branding and castrating a few calves, and doing general handiwork around the place. I remember he taught me how to do my first operation – castrating a calf. It made me kinda nauseous the first time, but I got used to doing that surgery pretty quick. Sitting on his porch, we watched several big dust storms come rolling in out of the west and hide Las Cruces for two or three days at a time, but we got relatively little of the dust and wind. One day a big blow came up out of Mexico, a solid wall of brown dirt against an ugly gray sky. That time the dust practically hid the mountains. We couldn't see more than about a hundred feet outside, so we stayed inside the shack the whole time except to go to the privy. It was miserable. Dust finer than women's body powder was all over everything. It took a week or two to get it wiped off and shaken out of places in the shack.

"One day in late winter we were sitting on the porch step watching one of those brilliant sunsets over the Floridas. Rufus said, *Henry, what was the last thing ye read before ye left school to go to Lincoln with yore Daddy?*

"I thought for a minute, Well...Daddy taught Mama to read and write so he started us out early. We were reading before we went to school and he made us read out loud from his newspaper every night by the time we were in the first grade. That's how I learned about a lot things he did. I was given a copy of *Huckleberry Finn* for Christmas and I had read about half of it when we left for Lincoln. I took it with me to Lincoln, but lost it on that wagon ride when I was trying to get away.

*Well, sir, I don't think ye should be ignorant just 'cause ye a livin' here with me. Go inside there and find* The Iliad *in the stack of books over in the corner. That's a good 'un to start with. I want ye to start readin' some ever day. Can't have ye ill'itrate when ye git back home.*

"So I got up and went back inside to find *The Iliad*. The fire was low so I had to get the old coal oil lantern and fire it up to get enough light to read the titles. His two stacks of books over in the corner were nearly as tall as I. He read often himself so there wasn't much dust on them. I found *The Iliad* and *The Odyssey* in one volume about halfway down a stack. I had to unload the stack on top of it just to pull it out. It had been a beautiful book at one time, bound in green leather with gold letters for the title. Rufus had practically worn the gold letters off holding it and the leather had a smooth patina of wear. I stacked the books I had pulled off the top back on and wandered back outside with the book and lantern. I sat back down by Rufus and opened the book to the first page. He spat a long stream against the green creosote bush by the porch and said, *Read some to me, boy. I ain't heard that tale in a while.*

"It was one of the hardest books I ever had to read. I didn't know what many of the words or phrases Homer used meant. We'd usually sit on the porch or at the table with that old lantern casting its soft yellow glow, Rufus chewing and spitting, leaning back in his chair with his arms crossed and his eyes closed, listening while I tried to sound out the words. Whenever I asked him, he always knew the correct way to say the word and what it meant. I worked hard to learn fast and not forget what he told me. Rufus and I usually talked over dinner about what I'd read the evening before and what it meant.

"I'd say something like, That was a great trick the Greeks played with the Trojan horse. They didn't give up after ten years of war! I think it's funny they finally were able to beat the Trojans with a trick. Rufus would reply, *Yes, sir, that was purty clever. But it don't make no never mind that it took the Greeks ten years to beat the Trojans. What mattered was that the Greeks wouldn't quit no matter what, and neither should ye – ever. Ole Ulysses didn't quit a goin' home neither. When he got home he set things right even though he looked like a beggar an' they's men trying to take his wife and property. Shot 'em ever one with his bow 'n arrer 'n made thing right, aye, God! That's what ye need to do, Hombrecito! Ye gotta set things right fer yore family and fer yore daddy.*

"Of course, Rufus was just reinforcing what I had already promised myself and him. He was teaching me I wasn't the only one who had to struggle to find justice. I wasn't about to quit, no ma'am! No matter how hard it was to bring my daddy's murderers to justice, I was going to do it, and I was going to get back home and see my mama too!

"I read most of Shakespeare's plays and learned a lot about the doings of men and women, kings and queens, and human nature in general. I read *The Three Musketeers* and *Treasure Island* and learned the true value of friends like Rufus and Yellow Boy. I guess, by the time I was eleven or so, I was the best educated and the best shot, for a kid, in this part of the country. Rufus taught me to think logically with arithmetic and geometry too. He said a fellow couldn't make it across the country or the sea if he didn't understand Euclid."

Roberta squinted at him as the Plymouth steadily climbed toward Mescalero. "But you were just a little kid. I know how hard those books, especially ones like *The Iliad* and Shakespeare's plays, are to read and understand. Most kids couldn't have done what you did when you were ten or eleven. You must have been a genius to have read all that stuff."

"I don't think so. I just had a burning desire to know everything as fast as I could and to make my mama proud of me when she found me. Rufus, despite his rough edges, had read them all several times and had a sharp mind. He was a good teacher."

"The weeks sped by, the spring winds blew themselves out, and it began getting hot down in the valley. Yellow Boy had not reappeared. I was convinced he wasn't coming back. One day Rufus, as he usually did, examined my arm splints closely. After he felt my broken arm all over, he asked me, *Does it hurt anywheres, son?* When I told him it didn't, he pulled his long knife out of his belt, said he'd used it to take scalps back in his scouting days, and said *All right, looks like it's about time fer that thang to come off'n yore arm. Ye ready?*

"I said, Rufus, I've been ready for a long time! Yes, sir, cut it off and let me see how it feels being free of that thing.

"His scalping knife sliced up through the splint ties in one smooth motion without stopping for a double slice on a tie anywhere. The splint sticks fell away and there was my arm, although thin and wasted-looking, it felt good as new. It was filthy dirty because I had a hard time washing with a splint and bandages covering it.

130

*Does it hurt to move it around?* asked Rufus, a twinkle in his rheumy blue eyes.

"I swung it back and forth a couple of times and wrapped it around my body. It was a little sore, but nothing I'd complain about. I said, No, sir. A little sore maybe. But other than that, it's great. Thank you, Rufus. I'm going to need this arm when I get Stone, Tally, and Lee.

*Ye're welcome, Henry.* Rufus said with a nod and a grin. *Now, son, we can start a gittin' ye strong. We're a gonna start working on the rock pile tomorry, and we're a gonna start yore lessons with that there gun too.*

"The next morning we had breakfast while it was still dark and we were out the door just as dawn was bringing enough light to see by. Rufus rummaged around in his shed until he found a crow bar and an old pair of miners gloves he handed to me. He took a steel pry bar about his height and a pair of gloves for himself. He called Cody, who yawned and woofed as he watched us from the porch. We walked down to the stock gate and off down the path toward the back of the canyon.

"When we got to a rock pile, he said, *Now look at them there rocks. They's about the size of yore head. That there is the size ye wanta git. They's rocks scattered all over the canyon floor, but ye're most likely to find the right size uns up along the canyon walls. When ye find one jes pick 'er up an' haul 'er over to this here pile. Old Cody is gonna let us know if'n they's any snakes around. It's cool in the mornin' so them varmits can't move too fast and they's usually found a place to rest fer the day by the time the sun's up.*

"He started walking through the bushes toward the canyon wall and said over his shoulder, *Come on. I'll show ye how to get one without gettin' bit by snakes or them other critters I warned ye 'bout.* He walked about thirty yards before he stopped in front of five or six rocks scattered about that were just about the right size. He motioned me over to nearest one and said, *Now, first jes look all around to be shore they's no snakes around the rocks or the bushes. Usually, Cody will let ye know if they is, but sometimes the old fart fergits to do his job, so ain't no harm in bein' real kerful. If they ain't no snakes nearby, then all ye gotta do is roll the rock over with yore pry bar there so ye can see if'n they's any bitin' or stingin' varmits under it. If they is, crunch 'em with yore bar, then carry the rock over to the pile. Jes stick the bar in the ground where the rock was so's ye can find where ye found yore rock. Go head an' try it.*

"Eagerly, I walked over to the first rock, slid the crow bar under it and flipped it over with a little strain. I saw nothing on it or in the dirt where it had rested. I started to stick my pry bar in the ground to mark the spot, when the end of Rufus's pry bar landed with a thump in the center of the place where the rock had been. It surprised me and I jumped back. I looked at Rufus and cried, What're you trying to do, scare me? He grinned, took a chew, spat, and, nodding toward the place where the rock had been, said, *Naw, son. Take a look at the end of my bar there.* I looked. A small rattlesnake was twisting in its death throes. It was almost the same color as the sand under the rock and maybe five or six inches long. Rufus had squashed it in the middle with the end of his bar.

"Rufus spat again. *Ye gotta look close, boy. He ain't big, but a bite from that little bugger can make ye real sick or even kill ye. Now see if'n ye can carry that there rock over to the pile.*

"Humbled that he had saved me again, I bent over to pick up the rock, but before I could lift it off the ground Rufus said, *Not that a way, Henry. Bend at yore knees and use yore legs to lift it, not yore back. Usin' yore back to lift heavy thangs can ruin a feller.*

"I did as he told me. It was easy enough to lift the rock that way, but the reality was that it was a lot heavier than I thought. My arm, just out of splints, was sore and weak. I strained a little to hold it. It didn't look too far to the pile as I started walking. It was only about twenty yards. By the time I got half way I was struggling to keep hold on it. It got heavier and heavier, but I grit my teeth and strained to hold on until I finally made it to the pile and let it fall.

"Rufus watched me the whole time, his brow furrowed with concern. He said as I walked back to him, *Too heavy fer ye Henry?* I shook my head, although both arms felt like they wanted to float off my body now that the weight was gone. *I know that was a strain fer ye. But, ye held her. That's real good. Git the rest of them rocks there and call it a day. We'll do a little more ever day while ye git stronger. In a month or two ye'll be strong enough to work three or four hours like I do. Careful now an' don't drop one on yore foot!*

"I got the other four rocks. No more snakes, but I did uncover a couple of scorpions I promptly dispatched with my pry bar. Each new rock, although about the same size as the first one, was heavier than the last and the distance to the rock pile got longer and longer. The last one I carried, I dropped twice on the way to the pile. I was worn out after an hour of that heavy labor. When I got the last rock to the pile, Rufus, who had been carrying two or three rocks to the pile for my one, said, *Go on to the shack and git me some water will ye? Then ye rest some. I'll be along in a while.*

"I carried Rufus half a bucket of water that he nearly emptied. He wiped his face with an old red and white bandana dangling from his back pocket, then sent me back to rest on the porch. *Go on an' rest now. Ye'll be puttin' in long hours a totin' rocks here 'fore long.*

"Rufus was right. Within a month I was spending three or four hours a day carrying those rocks. Every step I took with one, I put it down to what I owed Stone, Tally and Oliver Lee. Someday...someday, I kept thinking over and over as I carried those rocks, Someday you're going pay and I'm going to collect for what you did to me and Daddy. Someday I'm gonna kill you. I promise you, someday I will.

"I was so tired after the days we carried rocks I slept soundly. I never had the bad dreams I had when Rufus first took me in. However, on Saturdays and Sundays, we rested, and for a couple of years thereafter, on Saturday and Sunday nights, I nearly always had a nightmare. I was chased by shadowy men who wanted to kill me. Stone's cold wolf eyes kept on sizing me up for a kill. Tally was jerking me up by my collar to go sit in the wagon while he watched Daddy die. Big bloody streams pumping out of Daddy's chest made rivers that drowned him in his own blood and swept me away. I can still remember details of those dreams to this day.

"My first rock-carrying day, Rufus finally came to the porch in mid-morning and had a cup of coffee off the stove. He sat on the porch and rested with his back to the wall, mopping his sweat-covered face with his old red bandana. After he sat there for about an hour, he pushed himself up, and, with poor circulation in his legs, staggered inside. I heard him rummaging around and a box of some kind sliding on the floor. Soon the door to the shack opened and out he stepped, a box of cartridges in one hand and the buffalo gun that hung over the doorpost in the other. He grinned at me. *Ready to start yore shootin' lessons with this here thunderstick?*

"I jumped up, my heart pounding, Yes, sir! He nodded and said, *Well, run in the shack and grab several of them there old empty whiskey bottles in the box close to the stove and we'll walk down to my shootin' range.*

"Grabbing some of the smelly whiskey bottles, I walked with him down the now familiar path to end of the canyon. When we got to his shootin' range, he said, *Put them bottles on top of that first pile of dirt where I told ye I practiced my shootin'.*

"I ran to the dirt pile and placed the bottles on top, side-by-side, and about six inches apart. When I turned around, Rufus was no where to be seen. I almost panicked until I saw him a few yards back from where

I'd left him, up close to the north face of the cliffs neatly camouflaged by the bushes and shadows. He was sitting in the shade of a big pinon bush about fifty yards away from the dirt mound. He motioned me to come sit next to his left side as I ran back.

"When I was seated, he said, *This here rifle is an 1874 Sharps. It has a barrel that's thirty-two inches long and it shoots a .45-70 caliber cartridge that has 'bout a ounce of lead in the bullet. It'll shoot all the way through a buffalo at a thousand yards. Ye know how far that is, Henry?*

"I slowly shook my head, my heart pounding harder with the thought that I might get to fire the cannon Rufus lovingly held in his hands. *Well, sir,* he said, *it's a little less than two-thirds of the length of the path back to the fence.* My jaw dropped in wonder. I was amazed at the idea that a gun, any gun, could actually shoot that much lead or anything, for that matter, that far. He reached in his pocket and pulled out a huge cartridge, its brass shining golden in the sun, its lead short, silvery, and flat-nosed protruding from the brass casing. Nearly two and half inches long, it was a giant compared to the regular .45 caliber shells I was used to seeing in Daddy's rifle.

"Rufus grinned at my awe. *Now pay attention, son. This here is how ye load her up. First ye pull the hammer here to half-cock. Half-cock is a safety feature. The rifle won't fire with the hammer there.* He thumbed the side-mounted hammer back until it clicked. Lowering the end of the barrel until it pointed toward the piles of dirt, he said, *Then ye drop the breech block.* He pulled on the wide, heavy trigger guard until it came forward and the heavy breech block dropped down from the stock end of the barrel. *Now ye're ready to slide yore cartridge in. Sight down the barrel to be shore its clear the first time ye shoot her. Be shore the cartridge is all the way in so's the breech block'll slide past 'er when ye pull the lever back.* He slid the cartridge into the breech end of the barrel, then pulled the lever forming the trigger guard back up so the breech closed with a reassuring snap. *Did ye git all that, Henry?* He asked with a smile. I nodded.

"He reached in his shirt pockets and pulled out a couple of lumps of bee's wax. He handed one to me and said, *Here. Pinch a couple of pieces off an' roll 'em up so's they'll fit in yore ears like this.* He rolled up two pieces of his wax and stuffed one each into his ears, and, grinning motioned me to do the same. *Ye need to do that when ye shoot this here rifle a lot of times at one sittin'. Ye can't hear a thang fer hours afterwards if 'n ye don't.* I nodded I understood. Later, I was surprised I could still hear as well as I did even with the wax blocking my ear holes.

"*Now watch, Henry. This here is how ye cock and fire.* He pulled the side hammer back until it clicked once more. Then he pointed at the triggers. I had always wondered about the triggers. The rifle had only one barrel, but two triggers and it didn't load two bullets. Rufus pointed to the back trigger. *This here trigger is the set trigger. Pull that trigger back 'fore ye fire and it'll set the front trigger so it's real easy to pull. See that there little screw between the triggers. Well, ye just back that there screw out until the first trigger has just the pull pressure ye want to use. Some folks want a hair trigger some don't. I like an easy pull, but not a hair trigger myself. Onct ye pull back on that set trigger, the pull pressure ye set will make 'er shoot. Ye ready to fire?* I nodded with excitement, trembling and unable to speak.

"Sitting in the dirt Rufus rested his elbows on his knees and sighted the rifle on a bottle. He squinted down the sights for an instant, then his trigger finger pulled back the set trigger. The front trigger made a little click forward. In a smooth motion his trigger finger found the front trigger and paused for half a heart beat before the rifle roared and the end of the barrel bucked up about six inches. Echoes filled the canyon and some cattle that had been watching us headed for the front fence. I was expecting the noise but I still jumped, amazed at the booming thunder from the report and obvious power in the weapon. It wasn't at all like Daddy's Winchester, which seemed a toy by comparison.

"Rufus grinned at me and nodded down range through the gray haze of smoke lying in the still air. One of the bottles had completely disappeared. *See if ye can do what I jes showed ye.* He handed the rifle over to me. I took it and almost dropped it, it was so heavy. *Be careful where ye point the barrel and always assume it's loaded. Here, sit cross-legged and rest it across your knees while a pointin' toward them bottles. Good. Now pull the hammer to half-cock and push the trigger lever down and it'll throw out the empty shell.* I had to strain and use my whole hand to pull the hammer back to half cock. The spring on the lever was stiff and I had to strain a little with both hands to get it to drop the breach, but the spring soon released and the shell came sailing out of the breech right into Rufus's waiting palm. *Save yore brass. It's costly and I reload 'em just the way I want 'em as often as I can.*

"He reached in his pocket again, brought out another cartridge, and handed it to me to load. I first squinted down the empty barrel like he had said do. It was still shiny and there was a little smoke curling out the end. The cartridge slid smoothly into the breech. I had to strain again to pull the lever up to close the breech, but it snapped into place when I was able to apply enough pressure. *Now see if ye're strong enough to hold it up with yore knees like I did.* I got the barrel pointed in the general direction but it waved all over the place. Rufus took it out of my hands grinning. *Still got a few more beans to eat ain't ye son. Here stretch out on the ground here at about this angle on yore belly and rest 'er on that there piñon stump.* Rufus positioned me at about a forty-five degree angle to the line of site, raised me up on my elbows, and fit the barrel of the rifle on the stump with the forestock in my left hand and the stock snug against my shoulder. It was a lot more comfortable and steadier that way but still a little heavy. *Can ye see the bottle through the sights?* I nodded. *All right, line up on a bottle. Aim about a third of a bottle low cause the rifle is sighted for a lot longer range. Got it?* I nodded. *Now pull the set trigger back until ye hear it click.* I pulled and it finally clicked. *Good. Now get your line of sight and put yore finger on the front trigger. Don't pull at all yet! Take a deep breath.* I did. *Now let about half of it out, and sighting where ye want, start squeezing the trigger.* I nodded. It was the same procedure Daddy taught me with his Winchester. I had just started to squeeze the trigger when the rifle roared, slammed up against my cheek, and kicked hard backwards. I felt like I'd been punched in the shoulder by my big brother Jack or kicked by a mule. I lay unmoving for a few seconds, stunned by the still unexpected roar from the Sharps and recoil punch. Slowly the smoke drifted away. A second bottle had disappeared.

"There was a big smile showing though Rufus's whiskers. *Henry!* he yelled. *Henry, damn if ye ain't gonna be a first-class marksman! One shot, one target, by damn!*

"I don't think I stopped grinning for the next two days. Rufus watched and coached me that afternoon as I shot about ten rounds before my shoulder got too sore to shoot anymore. Then he practiced some. He promised we'd practice nearly every day until I was consistently hitting targets at the end of the little canyon, about 500 yards away.

"Over time, as I got comfortable with that old gun, Rufus kept making me shoot at longer and longer ranges and at moving targets he set swinging off bushes near the whiskey bottles. I must have shot every cartridge he had in the first month of practice. Those cartridges were and still are expensive, so I had to learn to be very careful with every shot I took, and save the brass for reloads. Eventually, though, he started running out of cartridge supplies. Finally, Rufus told me we were down to his last box of cartridges for the old rifle and he had to save those in case he needed to defend his place against bandits or his stock from cats and bears. A week or two after Rufus stopped my target practice, Yellow Boy appeared with a pack mule carrying two cases of a thousand rounds each of .45-70 caliber ammunition. I think he stole it from government troops in Mexico. So I had lots of ammunition for practice and I was becoming an expert shot with what Yellow Boy called Shoots Today Kills Tomorrow. By the time I was twelve, I could hit a whisky bottle at 600 yards, five shots out of six. Yellow Boy, who was the best shot I ever saw, never missed at that range with his Henry and he was standing up without a rest for the rifle. Yellow Boy and Rufus taught me that accurate shooting is mostly mental. They made me learn to focus all my attention to the target and block out everything else that might affect my aim.

"The first day after shooting, when we got back to the shack, we had our afternoon siesta, then Rufus got up and made us some supper. As twilight came, Rufus and I sat out on the shack porch while I read *The Iliad* to him. As I was reading I noticed Cody's ears perk up. I looked up and jumped in surprise. There was Yellow Boy! He was always doing that, just appearing out of nowhere and making me jump.

"Rufus grinned. *Howdy Yellow Boy! Headin' to Mexico again?*

"Yellow Boy nodded. *Si. Mi mujer, my woman, she waits. The hombrecito, he is better, si?*

"Nodding, Rufus said, *Yes, sir, thanks to ye a savin' his hide, he's done healed up, I reckin. How long ye with us this time, amigo?*

"*One sun. I am back in a moon. Soon teach Hombrecito Apache ways. Make ready for war on men who kill padre.*

"Rufus nodded. *I reckin we got a lot of teachin' to do and him a lot of learnin'. They's frijoles and tortillas on the stove that's still hot. Go help yoreself. We'll talk while ye eat.*

"Yellow Boy grunted and disappeared into the shack. Soon he was gobbling down the remains of Rufus's cooking while they spoke of the latest news on the search for Daddy and me.

"That's the way it went for about three years. Carry rocks for three or four hours early in the day, shoot for an hour or two around mid-day, have an afternoon siesta, then supper, and finish the day looking out over the valley and reading to Rufus. The more rocks I carried, the stronger I got. In a couple of years the Sharps didn't feel so heavy and I could shoot without the stump for support if I had to. Yellow Boy appeared every month or two and stayed a little longer each time as he trained me to live and survive in the desert.

"We had the going-home talk in late spring on a Saturday afternoon after Rufus returned from one of his weekly visits to Albert Ellis's Barber Shop. He went down there nearly every Saturday to sit around and listen to the local gossip, read the paper, and, occasionally, get a trim. A lot of information flowed through Ellis's place. Truth be known, old Ellis kept his ear to the ground for Albert Fall and the Democrats. He'd pass along the latest gossip the townies, ranchers, and cowboys swapped. Rufus used those visits as a way to sniff the wind and find out what was happening with the investigation of Daddy's murder and where the men were I wanted to hunt.

"That day Yellow Boy had been showing me how to throw a knife so it always struck point first and it went where you threw it. Rufus came riding up the trail a little faster than usual on old Sally. He waved at us as he rode by the porch. He didn't say anything as he headed for the corral. After he took care of Sally, he lugged his burlap sack of supplies to the cabin with a grim look on his face and he says, *Come on in and eat, boys. We need to talk.* I looked at Yellow Boy, and he looked at me. Neither of us had any idea what was going on. So we just shrugged our shoulders and went inside. Rufus had his usual pot hung over the fire and served us up a supper of beans, chilies, steak, and tortillas. He didn't have much to say and we ate in silence waiting for the big news.

"It was strange for Rufus not to say anything. He was usually bubbling over with news from town, but during this meal he just stared, not saying a word, at the open door behind Yellow Boy. His mind was ten thousand miles way.

"Yellow Boy, as always, finished eating first, belched his appreciation of the dinner, and scratching around in his possibles bag found a Mexican cigar. He lighted it and squinting through the smoke said, *You talk now Rufus?*

"I said, Yeah, tell us what you found out today, Rufus!

"Rufus wiggled his nose, trying to nudge his wire-framed glasses up higher on his nose the way he did when he was thinking things out. He dropped his fork on his plate and said, *Well fellers, here it is. I's been a worryin' and a scratchin' my head about this ever since ye came here, boy. I ain't slept good fer a lot of nights a worryin' about what I oughter do. I's tried out all kinds of schemes in my head to make it happen, but I always find they ain't a gonna work after I thought out all the angles.*

"Yellow Boy took a deep draw on the cigar making the ash glow brightly in the gathering twilight gloom of the shack. He rolled the cigar between his fingers and said, *Speak straight Rufus. No comprendo when usted say not sleep good. Usted make big noise when sleep. Usted sound like usted sleep plenty damn good.* He grinned and winked at me.

"Rufus, however, didn't smile and remained grim. He pushed his half-eaten supper out of the way, reached in his vest pocket, pulled out a twist of tobacco and cut himself a chew with a short deliberate knife stroke. He chewed on it in silence for a while, resting his head on a hand with his elbow parked on the table. After a couple of direct hits in the spittoon and several nose wiggles, he sighed and said, *Boys, the problem here is, I's a kidnapper.* Looking sadly at me, he shook his head and moaned, *Henry, I shoulda carried ye back to yore mama a long time ago. But, I ain't. Maybe it's long overdue that I do. They was a talkin' today in the barber shop about how yore mama still wears black all the time and nobody ever sees her smile. Fact is, some folks in Cruces think she just went plain crazy with grief.*

"I wanted to cry. I remembered how sad she looked when Daddy and I left for Lincoln a lifetime ago. I knew it was me not wanting to go back, until I got even with Daddy's killers, who was keeping her in dark places. I could see her sitting by herself in that dark house going through hell.

"Rufus pounded his fist on his chest and spoke so loud he was shouting. *Damn it to hell! I'm the one who's made her crazy cause I didn't carry her son back to her.* His rheumy blue eyes behind those round wire-frame glasses were starting to collect water.

"Yellow Boy took a long draw on the cigar and stared at him, waiting. I was almost in tears.

"Rufus, you said if you took me back to Mama they'd kill us. You said I had to hide for a right long while and you'd take me back when it was safe. Every week you go down to old Ellis's Barber Shop and listen to the gossip, trying to find out what Jack Stone and Red Tally are up to so you'll know when it's safe to take me back home. You said if you took me back it'd be all over town in less than a day and Stone and Tally would know the next. You said my mama and sisters couldn't help spreading the good news I was alive, or one of the house help would tell, or a neighbor would see me. It wouldn't be long before the news was all over town and the newspapers would be telling it. The sheriff would have to pump me for what I knew. Stone and Tally wouldn't waste any time getting somebody to finish me off and kill whoever was with me. You and Yellow Boy promised you'd teach me how to be a warrior so I – we – can make war on those...those...bastards! That's what you said, ain't it? Ain't that what you said?

"Roberta that was the first time I ever used that word to describe anybody. Rufus flinched like I'd just hit him in the face because he knew where I'd learned that word and why I was using it. I kept after him, full of myself, now that I was using his very words.

"You didn't make my mama crazy, Stone and Tally did! I was shouting then. Rufus? Has any of what you told me changed? Are Stone and Tally still around? Is it safe to go home? Tell me if it is, cause then I want to go home just as soon as I can.

"Rufus sat rubbing his neck, slowly chewing, and staring out the open door, watching the last sunlight fill the doorway as he listened to his mouse roar. He shook his head and looked at me through those dusty wire-framed lenses illuminated with the dying sunlight.

"*Naw, Henry.* He sighed slowly as if the weight of the world was on his shoulders. *Naw, ain't nothin's changed, son. Not a damn thang's changed. They were laughing today in the barber shop about how fast Stone's herd's a growin' and Charlie Bentene ain't doing so bad nei- ther cept he's a gone off to fight Spaniards in Cuba. Red Tally, he headed up north to Wyoming to clean out some more farmers, but he's supposed to be back this fall to winter with Stone. Pat Garrett's been raising hell all over the desert looking fer Oliver Lee and his friends Gililland and McNew, cause he's convinced they did it. He found 'em too. They's a big shoot-out over to Wildy Well and they got away. But ole Lee's smart and after a while they turned theyselves in. Said they's innocent and knowed they'd git sonerated. Now they's about to go to trial fer yore Daddy's murder up to Hillsboro. Ye said they warn't there when the shooting took place. Lee musta had some hand in it. Ye said Tally went riding over to see him after he shot yore daddy.*

*Naw, Henry, the danger ain't less, but maybe the risk is. If ye went back now, those...bastards...would be watched like a hawk a wanting supper and sighted in on a rat. They'd have to be real fast, and it'd be real dangerous and incriminatin' to try and git ye. Still, I get a bad feeling ever time I think about a takin' ye home, cause they've got to get ye or they's dead. I don't believe ye'll ever be safe 'til they's wiped out or ye get so big, even yore own mama won't recognize ye.* He spat again, rattled the spittoon, and looked at me and Yellow Boy with one eye squinted and said, *Aye, God, ye're still gonna hold me to my prom- ise to help ye make war on those bastards and bring 'em to justice, ain't cha?*

"I looked him straight in the eye and said, Yes! I could hear Yellow Boy grunt, *Ummmph,* beside me.

"Yellow Boy had become adept at white ways. He could comforta- bly sit in a chair and eat with a spoon rather than his fingers or his knife. He sat in his chair, chewed on the cigar out the left side of his jaw, crossed his arms, and leaned back as he stared at Rufus. Rufus stared back slowly scratching the weekly stubble on his cheeks and chin with his stubby old fingers.

"Yellow Boy said, *What this word* kidnap *mean, Rufus?*

"The spittoon rattled again. *Well, I reckin it means grabbin' a body and a holdin' him fer money or as a slave. Hell, yore people used to raid down to Mexico, and up here too, fer women and young'ns fer slaves or wives or sons. Sometimes ye even sold 'em back again fer money or maybe guns.*

"I must have looked like I was watching a tennis match, swinging my head from one to the other as they volleyed back and forth.

*Rufus! Usted steal muchacho?*

*Naw! But, I shore as hell kept him.*

*Muchacho slave? Muchacho works mucho aqui. Usted make'm sweat mucho carrying rocks por casa nuevo. Muchacho use Shoots To-day Kills Tomorrow bueno. He shoot many time. Muchacho prisoner? Muchacho go in desert alone and come back. Ride Sally far, ride Sally close by. Mucho times ride alone. Ride con su. Muchacho free? Muchacho slave? Quien es, Rufus?*

"Rufus just shook his head. *Ye're right. He ain't no slave or prisoner. He earns his keep, but that ain't a making him a slave. No, sir, it shore ain't. He's a been making hisself strong a carrying those rocks. I've been a teachin' him to shoot over long ranges with the Sharps. Maybe he'll use that long gun to wipe out those bastards one of these days. I shore hope so. I'll give it to him if'n he does. He can come and go when he wants outta this here shack. Reckon, kidnap ain't the right word. Still I ain't took him home yet and it's a hurt his mama mighty bad to think her little boy's lying dead somewhere out in that there desert. Somehow it just ain't right.*

*Rufus! Muchacho es bueno dead or live?*

*Why hell! Live. Ain't no doubt of that there!*

"Yellow Boy set the chair back on all its feet. He leaned forward with his elbows on the table, his arms still crossed, and the cigar still stuck in his jaw. It was getting deep twilight outside and the colors in that sky still fill my mind as much as what he told Rufus. Yellow Boy stared straight into Rufus's eyes, the red glow from his cigar casting shadows on his high cheek bones as he said, pointing back at his chest, *Yo pull muchacho from mesquite bush. Bring su casa.* He slapped the table and almost whispered, *Yo take mouse from gato. Boy hurt muy mal. Almost die. You fix. You fix bueno. Arm strong. Face bueno. Good scar. Warrior scar. No muchacho. Poco hombre, Hombrecito, little man con heart grande. Hombrecito grande! Little Big Man! He lives now. No Yellow Boy, no Hombrecito Grande. No Rufus, no Hombrecito Grande. Usted y mi, we teach Hombrecito mucho. Hombrecito strong. Hombrecito sabe mucho. El sabe mucho mas before he make war on his padre's killers. Many seasons still before Hombrecito avenge padre. Hombrecito must learn. No learn from mamacita. Hombrecito hide aqui from enemies, learn good. No hide with mamacita. Hombrecito with mamacita die. Maybe mamacita die tambien. No bueno por mamacita if Hombrecito die.*

"Rufus stopped chewing and stared at Yellow Boy, then at me as the shack faded into darkness. The only light was from the glow of Yellow Boy's cigar and the coals glowing in the open door of the old iron cooking stove. Rufus didn't make any move to get up and light a lantern. Roberta, I tell you it seemed like time just stopped. Stopped like the pendulum in a clock paused at the top of its swing, it just stopped. He finally stirred and walked out the door. He stood leaning against a porch post, staring toward the brilliant orange glow outlining the Floridas at the far edge of the world and the purple and orange streaks filling the sky across the Mesilla Valley. The view from that little cranny stuck there in the Organs is one I've never found better anywhere when the sun goes down. I'll probably remember it on my deathbed.

"Rufus leaned on that post for a long time, staring at the sunset, before finally sending a stream of brown juice toward the base of the big creosote bush by the porch. It was greener than all the others in the yard because he watered it when he avoided going all the way to the privy in the middle of the night. He eased himself down and sat on the porch step. He stared off into the cool gathering darkness with his hands folded in a prayerful attitude and his elbows resting on his knees. Yellow Boy and I got up and wandered out of the dark shack on to the porch too. I sat down by Rufus. Yellow Boy squatted off to one side absorbed with the deepening twilight and making the ash on his cigar glow brightly as he puffed contentedly. Cody, got up from his corner of the porch, stretched, yawned, and padded over to flop down beside me. The only noise was the spring crickets and his tail flopping on the porch floor while I scratched his ears. Yellow Boy finished his cigar. He stubbed it on the porch, and tossed it in a bucket by the door as he got up and ambled over to the corral to rub the nose of his horse and whisper sweet nothings in its ear.

"Rufus still sat staring at the fading glow of the western sky. He smelled of sweat and tobacco with just a faint scent of lilac toilet water he had slapped on his face in the barber shop. He finally spat his chew out, wiped a brown tobacco dribble off the bottom of his chin and said, *Aw hell, boy! I tried maginin' ever way I can to get ye back to your mama. I ain't thought of one that won't get one of us killed pretty quick and most likely your mama or some member of yore family.*

*I thought about just riding up to yore family with ye and saying, Look a here who I found, but ye can't tell anybody he's here. They probably wouldn't tell, but a servant, a neighbor, or even a passerby might see ye or tell somebody else and the news would be all over town in a instant.*

"*I thought about sending yore mama a note. I'd say I had ye and she can come see ye any time she wants. Then yore brothers Albert and Jack would be up here a filling me full of holes fer kidnapping and Pat Garrett would be right behind 'em. I don't trust that son-of-a-bitch. He's a turned into more a politician than the hard lawman that killed Billy the Kid. Why there's even word a rattlin' 'round the barbershop that he'll probably try to get the customs inspector's appointment in El Paso when he's finished a sheriffing.*

*I thought about writing a note and telling yore mama to get on a train east and I'd meet it somewhere 'tween here and Dallas with ye and that she couldn't tell a soul. She'd do that, but all it'd take is fer someone on that train to know who she was and the news'd spread like wild fire.*

*Ye wanta settle accounts with the bastards that made ye half a orphan. Don't blame ye. So do I. That ain't a gonna happen if ye're a livin' in yore mama's house. She ain't about to lose ye again. Jack and Albert will go after 'em theyselves, half-cocked an' angry. Them bastards will murder 'em too and claim self defense. Yellow Boy and me's a pushing ye to get strong and to get good with weapons. We 'bout worked yore tail off, ain't we, boy? Look at ye though. Ye could pass fer an Indian young'un right now; ye're skinny but ye're all muscle and sinew. Few more years and we'll be ready to send those murderers straight to hell and Oliver Lee ain't gonna be far behind 'em if they ain't put him in jail or hung him already.*

"I said, I thought you said he was about to go on trial in Hillsboro. Why are we going to have to wipe him out?

*Cause they's saying down to the barber shop that the murder case is all circumstantial and that Fall will get him off. If 'n he does...well, we'll just have to hop that cactus when we're at it.*

*Point is, I'm in mortal fear fer yore life and I want ye to get some justice fer yore Daddy. He was a fine man. Maybe I've just got crazy with fear in my old age a fearing fer yore life. I don't know what to do no more. What ye want to do, Henry?*

143

"I could hear Cody's tail thumping on the porch, the crickets making music, and the occasional snort of Sally playing with Yellow Boy and his pony at the corral fence. The orange over the Floridas was nearly gone and the dark surrounded us like a cool blanket. I loved that old man. I knew he was struggling to do what was right.

"Inside I trembled. I trembled that he spoke to me man to man and was letting me decide what to do as a man. I said, I just can't leave now. I know Mama's still grieving, I know she is. I've got to do what's best for my family. I've got to make things right for my daddy. He always figured if something happened to him, Jack or Albert would make it right. They don't know who did it. They can't. One of these days I can make things right, and I will if you and Yellow Boy help me.

"Rufus turned his head to me and nodded. *Why shore we will son. Ye know we will. But it's a gonna take a few more years. We got to be patient. We got to be the hunters here. Ye understand?*

"Yes, sir, I do, I said. A few more years seemed like an eternity to me then, but I thought I understood what he was talking about for the first time. It was going to take a long time to get ready.

"Rufus stuck out his hand to seal the deal and I grabbed it. I jumped about a foot off the porch step when I realized Yellow Boy was standing right there in front of us.

"*So Rufus usted keep Hombrecito? We make a warrior? We settle blood for blood? No go mamacita?*

"Rufus nodded. *Yep. Ye got it about right, partner. We're a gonna do just that.*

"Yellow Boy smiled and said, *Muy bien! This night a warrior is born. Give hand Hombrecito.* I reached to shake with him. He took my wrist in a strong gentle grip. His big knife with the razor edge appeared in his other hand like magic. He said, *We are same blood, Hombrecito.* I felt the blade slice smoothly, but not too deep, across my palm, and the warm blood flowed freely. It didn't hurt at all then, but it did the next morning. My hand was sore for a couple of weeks. He put a slice in his own hand and held my cut against his. He said again, *We are same blood.* It was Rufus's turn to say, *Hmmmph.* Cody just kept beating his tail on the porch and the paint pony snorted as Sally maneuvered him away from the corral fence."

Roberta's brow was pinched in a frown. "So you and Yellow Boy became blood brothers?"

Henry shook his head. "No, I don't think Yellow Boy thought of us as blood brothers. It was more like uncle and nephew. He never really said, except that I understood then we were somehow family. Sometimes he calls me *Son*, sometimes *Brother*. It's been like that since I've known him. I guess he's much more a father to me than an uncle. I never mixed blood with Rufus, but I thought of him as an uncle too. I couldn't have survived without either one of them."

Roberta said, "So Rufus wanted to take you back to your mother, but Yellow Boy and you talked him out of it, and this was three years after Yellow Boy had found you?"

"Yes'm, that's right."

"Well, I still think it's shameful that happened but I guess I can understand why. How on earth was Rufus able to feed and clothe you?"

"Well, Rufus didn't by himself. The clothes I was wearing when Daddy was killed were coming to pieces after a couple of months living with Rufus. Yellow Boy started bringing me clothes Apache young'uns wore to replace the ones I had. I'm half Mexican anyway, and in the clothes Yellow Boy brought me I easily passed for a half-breed Apache child after my hair grew uncut for several months. All I needed was a breech cloth, boot moccasins, and a cotton shirt. The only reason I didn't look full Apache was because my hair had a little curl to it. As for food, Rufus had lived by himself most of his life and he wasn't a bad cook at all. In fact, I'd say he was a master at cooking with his old Dutch oven.

"Besides carrying those rocks, I helped Rufus with other chores around his place. I wanted to earn my keep. You know, feeding and watering the stock and chickens, carrying water and wood to the shack. When Yellow Boy came visiting, after the chores were done and it got cool, we'd sometimes walk or ride Sally back into the Organ canyons or down to the desert behind Tortugas Mountain. That's when he and Rufus started my desert training. You know – what plants could be eaten, how to find water in cactus or how to find springs and rain tanks, how to catch and cook rattlesnakes and other critters, and, most importantly, how to hide anywhere any time."

"Okay, so Rufus taught you the classics, a little mathematics, and to be a marksman, and Yellow Boy just taught you how to survive in the desert and knife throwing?"

Henry smiled. "Well, mostly he was my physical trainer. He taught me how to fight and to be pragmatic about life. For physical training, he started me out running. He made me run everywhere. When you're the age I was, nine or ten, running is natural. Kids run all the time. They have unlimited energy. They just run from place to place as they play. Apache kids are taught from an early age to run long distances and to run them as hard as they can. That's what Yellow Boy started teaching me. He started me out running up and down the length of Rufus's canyon. A round trip was about two miles, and he ran with me to see how fast I was running.

"It was real hard at first. I had pains in my side and usually had to stop and vomit before I completed the circuit. After two or three days of that, he said, *Usted, Hombrecito, no run so fast. You run, you finish, even if slow. Usted muy bien, you better, by and by.* I slowed down a lot after those first times and slowly built up speed. I learned to enjoy the early morning when the canyon bushes were filled with birds. The creosote bushes and the piñons have this smell about them early in the morning, especially if it rains in the night, that just makes you want to fly. I enjoyed the running more and more as I became better conditioned. The first few weeks I just ran the path back to the shooting spot once a day. Then, when I stopped breathing hard after I got back, he'd make me run it again. On the days when he was gone he had me run it early in the morning and again late in the evening. Then I had to run the canyon in the heat of the day. That was hard. The first time my lungs felt on fire and I was vomiting again. I slowed down again and built into it. Each time I ran, Yellow Boy said, *Su cabeza no es rojo, your head is not red. Andale! Get stronger. Go faster, Hombrecito!* After a while I had enough strength to run the distance flat out as fast I could. After those miles got comfortable, he said, *Now usted run in desert. Be fast as lion. Be steady as mule. Usted make mucho agua on skin. Make body strong! Go fast soon.* He had me run down the trail toward Las Cruces. He kept extending the distance: two miles, then three, four, and finally all the way to Tortugas Mountain, which must have been close to ten miles round-trip. He often ran with me over to Tortugas Mountain and coached me as we ran. After a couple of years of running I was taller and had a barrel chest. I could keep up with Yellow Boy in a steady lope for an hour or two in the middle of the day."

Roberta narrowed her eyes in disbelief. "Weren't you worried that somebody would see you running out in the desert like that – maybe even shoot at you if they thought you were an Indian?"

"That was part of the training. Yellow Boy said, *Hombrecito, you must be from the land of the grandfathers when you run.* It took me awhile to figure out that he wanted me to be ghost-like – you know – transparent to anyone that might see me. He taught me to be a desert ghost. He started out with a few simple tricks. Move when the light is bad – early morning, twilight, or even at night. Never wear anything that can reflect light. Never silhouette yourself against the horizon, stay down below the edge of ridges and hills. Move so you don't disturb bushes. Know where you are all the time and be prepared to hide at the first sign of detection. You'd be amazed at how effective the simple stuff is. Yellow Boy came and went off the reservation and crossed the Tularosa Basin as often as he pleased using those techniques and he never got caught. Of course, he had a lot of other tricks that weren't so simple he taught me later.

"When I finally ran to Tortugas Mountain and back, Yellow Boy showed me a trial that's used on Apache boys. He gave me a canteen one morning before I started and said, *Take water in mouth. Hold when run. Spit all out when come back. Now go! Be fast!* Then he climbed up on this big rock so he could watch me as I ran. The first time I tried it, I had it all swallowed or lost by the time I got to Tortugas Mountain. When I got back there wasn't a drop to spit out and I wanted water from the canteen. He climbed down off the rock. I've never seen him more disappointed. Looking at me he said, *No Apache aqui. Usted heart no strong. Usted weak man! Usted be strong in heart or usted die. Usted Apache boy; I beat! Usted must learn strength in heart! Now! Usted no muchacho! Usted Hombrecito. I go a Mexico por diez suns. I come back, usted do this, si?* I was shaken that he was so disappointed. I bit my lip to keep from crying.

"Rufus walked out of the shack and started arguing with him. He said, *He ain't old enough fer those kinds of tests yet, and ye know it.* Yellow Boy just laughed. *Any Mescalero muchacho that tall can run two times distance and no lose any agua. He no live all life like Mescalero boy, so he slow. He better soon. I know this is true. He Hombrecito.* Since I wasn't an Apache he didn't expect me to do as well! That made me mad and want to work harder to show him I was as good as or better than any Apache my age. Rufus just shook his head, but didn't say anything else. This was Yellow Boy's training and he wasn't butting in. The next day, Yellow Boy was gone. I tried again. I made it back with a little of the water that time. I kept trying and after about the fifth or sixth time I made the whole route without losing very much. When Rufus saw I had done it, he said, *Good work, Henry! That there'll show old Yellow Boy yore heart is the heart of an Apache.*"

Roberta nodded and sighed. "So Rufus thought Yellow Boy was being too hard in training you and Yellow Boy didn't think he was hard enough? How long did this training go on anyway? Until you were ready for your war?"

Henry smiled, "Well, it gets a little complicated."

# 10

# MESCALERO

The Plymouth passed the dirt road turn-off to Blazer's mill, and soon a light from the tribal center appeared – a big bright star against the coal-black horizon of the mountains. Henry slowed and turned up a dirt road torn by gullies washed out by the last rain. They bounced along, churning up the gravel until they reached a long concrete-block building with a single bare light bulb hanging over the front door. Built during the Depression, the building sat with it's long side pointed toward Father Braun's Apache Christ Church, a magnificent old world style cathedral rising inexplicably out of the dark shadows.

Henry glanced at Roberta. She sat biting her lip and smoothing the strands of hair that had managed to escape from her tightly pulled bun. With a worried smile, she said, "At last!" He parked next to the front door of the tribal center. Pushing open the heavy car door he slowly and stiffly eased himself out of the driver's seat as the cold night air slapped him awake and quickened his blood. He walked briskly up to the door, and, cupping his hands to the sides of his face to block out glare, put his nose to the glass and looked around inside. Lights were on up and down the center hallway, but he saw no signs of life, and trying the door found it locked. He stepped back and glanced around the building, trying to decide if he should just go on up to Yellow Boy's house or wait to meet John Burning Tree. His gaze fell on the bulletin board next to the door. Seeing a page of ruled notebook paper containing a hand-written note thumb-tacked over several government notices, he tried to read it from where he stood but couldn't. His hands were getting cold; He slid them into his pants pockets and made three three sliding steps over to read the note. It said:

148

*Dear Doctor Grace,*
*Sorry I had to leave. My husband is just home on leave from the*
*Army. John Burning Tree is with Yellow Boy. I'll be here tomorrow if*
*I'm needed.*
*Maria*

Henry tore the note off the bulletin board so Maria would know he had the message and got back in the car. Roberta raised her brow in a silent "Well?" Wordlessly, he handed the note to her. Cranking the engine, he turned around in the parking lot, his spinning tires throwing gravel against the building in his hurry to get back to Route 70. Henry drove too fast, literally bouncing from rut to rut down the tribal center road. Roberta held on to the dashboard and door pull with a strength only genuine fear can produce. After a last mighty bounce over the remaining gullies, the Plymouth leaped on to the paved road and raced forward. Driving up Route 70 past Father Braun's cathedral, Henry sped along in the inky darkness before turning east up another dirt road. It wound through tall pines and then up a canyon until it stopped in a yard fronting a small frame house. Henry grinned every time he saw it. He felt as if he had come home. Roberta sighed her relief they were finally there and silently prayed they weren't too late.

Yellow Boy built the place years ago. He had stubbornly refused to build a wooden house at the urging of the hated agent Stottler who tried to force the men into cutting their hair and wearing white man's clothes. However, a few years after Stottler left, Henry and Father Braun helped Yellow Boy build his house. For a long time it was the best house on the reservation. It was something of a copy of Rufus's shack, although it was better built and over three times as large – Yellow Boy had two wives, two sons, and a daughter with whom to share it. It was sturdier than Rufus' shack – the winters up in the mountains were harder and the wind blew colder than in the little canyon in the Organs. It also had five rooms while the place in the Organs had only one. The same style chimney as Rufus's shack was in the back toward the middle of the house, a stoop-covered porch ran the width of the house, and there were four long windows in front rather than the one in Rufus's shack. White paint was peeling off the wide sheeting planks that covered the outside. A corral sat toward the back and to the left. Three horses stood with their heads over the fence, watching the approaching headlights with their ears up. The corral was connected to a small barn sitting under three large pines. To the right sat a large pile of logs cut for firewood, ready for splitting. A big two-foot tall section of a tree three feet in diameter was used for a chopping block. The hickory handle of the single-bit axe buried deep in the chopping block cast a long narrow shadow in the Plymouth's headlights. A few yards beyond the woodpile sat a two-hole privy, terminating a well-worn path leading from the house. On the north side of the canyon, a small spring-fed stream bubbled out of a shelf of bare rock. It flowed into a reservoir made by a small dam. There were two streams from the dam's overflow. One stream supplied water to a series of wooden troughs that ran to the house and then down to the second reservoir. The women had only to step out on the back porch and hold a bucket under the flow falling about three feet to get a quick bucket full. Then, a second set of troughs carried the water back to join with the second stream. Near the barn the second stream had been dammed up and provided a pool of water for the stock. Henry had helped Yellow Boy and his sons lay it out so the work of managing water for family and livestock without access to mechanical pumps was minimized.

Soft yellow light filled the window curtains. As they pulled into the yard, the house door flew open, silhouetting a short, powerfully built man. He headed for the Plymouth, his breath making little clouds that surrounded his head before quickly vanishing in the cold night air. His hand was on Roberta's door almost before the car came to a stop. He pulled it open for her and looked in at them with relief in sad dark eyes as Henry was opening his door.

"Thank God you're here, Dr. Grace and Nurse Gonzales!" he said breathlessly. "I'm afraid Yellow Boy's time is near. The medicines you left for him last time don't seem to be doing any good. I've sent Redondo to find Father Braun and Sara is here now." John Burning Tree, always the dutiful son, was doing everything he could to make his father's last hours comfortable. His face sagged with fatigue and worry.

As she swung her knees out of the car, Roberta, almost in tears, said "I'm so sorry we weren't here sooner. It's all my fault."

Henry, out the car door as soon as he turned off the engine, began rummaging in the back seat for his coat and doctor's bag. He wished Roberta wouldn't dwell on her oversight and said firmly, "No matter. We're here now and we'll do everything we can for him. It's good to see you old friend. How're Ninyeta and the children?"

"Oh they are very good, Dr. Grace." John managed a weak smile. "Ninyeta, she asks after you often. Tina just finished cutting her last tooth. We're glad of that. She's kept us up for many nights. Her sore gums made her whine and complain a lot. The boys they are becoming good outdoorsmen and in school, they do okay, I guess." Like most reservation children, they hated the white school system. John had attended only under a threat of being beaten daily. Yellow Boy told him and his brother, Redondo, many times that they must learn to read and to write and be smart like Henry if their sons were to survive. John repeated that story often to his sons, but rarely beat them. If Yellow Boy died, he alone must insist his sons educate themselves and he knew it would not be easy.

John was obviously very glad to see Henry and Roberta. He felt helpless to do anything. If only this sickness was a man or an animal, he knew he could fight it and save his father's life. Fighting this sickness, this unknown spirit demon, it was like trying to grab the wind. Only a man who knew how to fight things unknown and unseen, like Henry, had the power to save his father now. In silent prayer, he asked the Apache Christ that Yellow Boy's salvation be near at hand.

They covered the ten yards to the house in long, fast steps. John reached the door first and opened it to let them in. Yellow Boy was on a thick pallet in front of the fireplace. Thin pieces of orange and brown-streaked stone formed the fireplace. It held a crackling fire that provided most of the light in the room and its smoke filled the air with the intoxicating incense of burning juniper. An iron crane over the fire held a couple of fire-blackened pots, one of which bubbled and boiled with some kind of meat stew. Above the mantle hung the Henry rifle that had made Yellow Boy famous as the best shot in the Tularosa Basin. Its brass receiver, Yellow Boy's namesake, glowed like gold in the flickering light. A circular rough-cut plank table, its top smooth, shiny, nearly gleaming from years of use, sat in the room's front corner ringed by straight-backed cane-bottomed chairs. A shiny, zinc-coated, five-gallon bucket with a dipper on the side sat on a curtained cabinet next to an old unlit iron cooking stove in the opposite corner. Rough wooden shelves above the cabinet held a few pots, pans, and some tableware. Large, beautifully made, tightly woven baskets hung on the walls. Coats, shirts, and an ancient battered cavalry hat hung from pegs by the door. On a peg next to the fireplace hung a two-inch-wide belt holding a nickel-plated, long-barreled revolver in a two-loop Mexican-style leather holster and a large bone-handled hunting knife in a beaded sheath.

Sara, Yellow Boy's daughter, kneeled beside him, sitting on her ankles. She cupped a glass of brown liquid in both hands as though holding a libation for some ancient god. A cup and coffee pot sat on the floor beside her. Her loose hair, black like a crow's wing, but accented with a few traces of gray, reached almost to the floor. She wore a heavy red-and-black-checked wool shirt over her blouse, with the shirt's sleeves rolled half way up her arms. She used the shirt each time she visited Yellow Boy to ward off the chill in the back corners of the house. The shirt almost swallowed her, making her appear surrounded by a little tent with her head poking out the top. She slowly turned her dark brown face toward them. Unlike her brother's moon-round face, her face was sharp and finely cut like her mother's. Her sad eyes confirmed what Henry already knew from the labored breathing he heard standing in the doorway.

Henry took two long strides to reach the pallet. He was opening his bag and already reaching for his stethoscope as he kneeled beside her. "I'm sorry I'm late, Sara. Roberta and I got here as soon as we could. Did you give him a little whiskey from that glass there?"

She looked at the glass and slowly nodded. "Yes, John said you told him it would be all right if we gave him tea and whiskey if he asked for it. He wanted a swallow, but took only a little before he drifted off to sleep. He has the sweats often, but, once in a while, when the fever breaks, he is clear in his head and speaks sense. The whiskey, it seemed to perk him up. He laughed and said, *Be careful, daughter, or you'll have an old drunk Indian on your hands. Perhaps it is a good way for an old man to die – in a bed and drunk.* Then he drifted back to sleep after tossing around in a heavy sweat and speaking to the grandfathers."

Henry pulled back the light blanket covering Yellow Boy and opened the first three buttons on his denim laborer's shirt. He put the stethoscope in his ears and warmed its big shiny button with his breath before holding it to the old man's smooth mahogany chest. His heart sounded regular and reasonably strong, but it was clear from the wheezes he heard that the infection has spread to both lungs. Unless the penicillin he brought acted quickly, his old friend and protector would soon be joining the grandfathers.

Roberta pulled off her coat. Fatigue was settling like a warm fog on her brain. She focused to help Henry and to comfort John and Sara. She and John knelt on the other side of the pallet. Her trained ears listening to Yellow Boy struggle for air told her they had to do something quickly if they were to have any chance to save the old man. She reached over and felt his forehead. It was warm and moist. She looked at Henry and said, "He has a light fever."

Henry nodded, and, looking up, croaked, "He has double pneumonia. We have to get some pure oxygen in his lungs. There's a surplus high-altitude airman's oxygen unit in the trunk of my car. I bought it just the other day to try out for emergencies like this. You and John get it and see if you can make it work. Be careful, the tank is heavy and the regulator delicate. Let John lift it out of the trunk for you. I'm going to give our friend here a shot of the most potent penicillin I have. If it's too strong he may die, but we've got to risk it, or he'll die anyway."

Roberta and John pulled themselves up from the floor and began their work. They found the oxygen bottle and mask in the Plymouth's trunk and brought them inside. Roberta carefully unpacked the mask from a box that was still sealed. Good, she thought, never used. It took her a few moments to figure out how the mask was supposed to fit and how to strap it to the user's head. She did a practice fit against John's face and fiddled with the regulator values. She worked until she made the gas flow correctly with the mask's check valve and John could breathe easily. She checked to be sure the sides sealed correctly against his face. She took the mask off John and cleaned it with alcohol for Yellow Boy's use. John moved the heavy bottle of oxygen over to the head of the pallet so the supply hose easily reached from the tank to Yellow Boy. The close proximity provided enough slack from the hose to the mask to keep it from becoming disconnected or breaking the regulator if he stirred too much from the hallucinations that came with the sweats.

Henry loaded a syringe with penicillin and gave Yellow Boy an injection. He helped Sara pull Yellow Boy out of his clothes. She rested her father's head on her knees while Roberta and Henry gave him an alcohol sponge bath to lower his body temperature. John watched and waited for instructions from Henry and Roberta. Henry had seen the old man naked, except for a breach cloth, many times in his younger days. The others had not seen him without his shirt before and marveled at the trophy case of warrior's scars Yellow Boy's body carried. There were several old bullet wounds, two or three ugly knife welts, and ancient burn scars on his chest and belly.

They dried him carefully and turned the pallet so his feet pointed toward the fire. They covered him with a wool Pendleton blanket covered with geometric designs in black and red. Yellow Boy wasn't conscious while they worked. Listening to him struggle for breath with the deep wheezing in his lungs and the occasional racking cough made them all flinch as a black cloud of gloom spread through the room.

Roberta showed Henry the oxygen mask set-up she and John had rigged and he nodded approvingly. The regulator was adjusted, and the hose to the mask uncoiled to be certain the oxygen flow was about right. They fitted the oxygen mask over Yellow Boy's face, fixing the straps behind his head so it sealed correctly. Henry set the flow rate from the bottle and watched the rise and collapse of the sides of the mask reservoir to be certain it was working. When they were satisfied Yellow Boy was no longer struggling to pull air into his infected lungs, they relaxed a little.

Sara said, "Henry, I know you and Roberta must be starving. John told me you were driving straight here from Las Cruces. Let me get you some stew and tortillas. The meat is from an elk my husband shot yesterday. It's good."

Henry nodded and said, "I could sure eat. How 'bout you, Bertie?"

Roberta was ready to collapse. "That would be wonderful. I'm about out of gas. Let me wash my face and visit outside first, then I'll be ready."

Henry said, "Yeah, me too. Give us a few minutes and we'll break bread with you folks."

Soon they were dipping big stainless steal spoons into tin plates of stew, tearing off pieces of tortilla to sop up the gravy, and drinking hot coffee. Roberta thought she had never eaten anything so good and asked for a second helping. Not much was said. Henry only ate one plateful. He wasn't hungry. Pushing the empty plate aside, he lighted his pipe, sat back in his chair holding his coffee, and stared at the fire, lost in memories covering over half a century. John got up from the table and sat down cross-legged by the old man, listening to Yellow Boy's every breath as he drank his second cup of coffee.

Roberta and Sara washed the dinner dishes and caught up on the latest news about family and friends in whispered volleys of gossip. It had been four hours since Roberta and Henry had sped out of Las Cruces. It seemed a lifetime.

An hour passed. Henry occasionally timed the rate the oxygen mask's reservoir bag expanded and collapsed. Yellow Boy's breathing appeared to grow more regular and stronger. Henry felt drowsy and stepped outside to let the cold air bathe and refresh him. He squinted at the hands of his watch in the light from the window and saw it was nearly eleven. Alert once more, he stepped back inside and said, "It's going to be a long night, folks. It may be a day or two before we know if the infection is under control and he starts coming back. We need to pace ourselves. I'll take the first watch. You all find a place to rest and I'll call John when it's time to start rotating. How does that sound?"

John and Sara nodded and found blankets in which to roll up on the rough frame beds in two of the adjoining bedrooms. Roberta was tired but not sleepy. Too many thoughts were bouncing around in her head and caffeine had locked her eyes open. She found a blanket, walked over to the table, took a chair, and then sat it by Henry who watched her quietly out of the corner of his eye. She threw the blanket over the back of the chair to keep her backside warm, and, sitting down, wrapped it about her shoulders and legs. She looked over at Henry and smiled, saying, "I'm worn out, but have too much on my mind to sleep. Can you use some company for a while?"

"Sure." Speaking through teeth clamped on his pipe bit, Henry put his arm across the back of her chair, making her feel welcome and her company desired. "It's always a pleasure to have your company. I was just remembering old times with Yellow Boy."

Folding her hands in her lap, she nodded toward the old man who was breathing easier in the military surplus oxygen mask. "Is he going to make it, Dr. Grace?"

Henry sighed as he blew a stream of smoke toward the fireplace. "I don't know. He's close to ninety. He's a tough old bird and has a powerful will to live, but you never know about these things. We'll just have to wait and see. I pray to God he makes it. I owe him a lot, as you've probably guessed by now."

Now it was Roberta's turn to look at him out of the corner of her eye. "I suspected as much after you left me hanging in mid-conversation when we got to the Tribal Center. Tell me the rest of it," she said in a throaty whisper, trying not to disturb John and Sara.

Henry knocked his pipe ashes into his palm and tossed them in the fire. He nodded, but first got up and made an outside visit to Yellow Boy's primitive facilities and gathered more wood for the fire on his return. He placed the rough logs carefully on the stack in the fireplace so they wouldn't shift as they burned, then slipped back to his chair. He sat down heavily, crossed his arms, and tilted back staring at the fire. She waited, watching Yellow Boy fight for his life, and prayed he be spared once more.

Henry took a deep breath, filled his cheeks and made a soft whistling sound as he blew through pursed lips. "Yeah, I guess I did leave you hanging."

"Yes, you did." Henry heard the impatience in her voice.

"Well, I think you understand that Rufus and Yellow Boy were training me to war against Stone, Tally, and the others we believed had murdered my father, and, no doubt, had planned to kill me too. Rufus figured, given my age, they'd have to wait at least eight or nine years before I was ready to even plan how to go after them. Over on the west side of the Organs, I was living well-hidden at Rufus's place. Yellow

Boy visited us often, but he had problems of his own. The BIA was a disaster at managing the reservation. There were quick turnovers of agents. Each one came in convinced that he, by God, knew what was best for the Indians." Roberta saw Henry's face turning red with anger as he thought about it.

"Those idiots tried to make the Mescaleros wear white man's clothes and cut their hair short. They starved them by saying they ought to work for their food but found them no jobs. They stole their children and sent them to special schools for their so-called education, where they tried to make them forget their language and their culture. There was an Indian School during that time in Albuquerque you know. They tried to make them take individual ownership of the reservation land, which the Indians thought was immoral. Teddy Roosevelt gave away part of their land to a national forest governed by the Secretary of Agriculture. Taft gave it back to them. Washington politicians just didn't have the sense or desire to understand these people. Things have been a mess and in turmoil here for a long time." He sighed again, weary with what his memory brought back.

"Yellow Boy refused to tolerate the bureaucrats. He came and went as he pleased. He stayed on the reservation just long enough to assure the agents that they couldn't make him leave. He kept his families free and lived the old ways in the Sierra Madre until he moved his second wife back to Mescalero. I came back from medical school and convinced him that I would do everything in my power to make sure the agents and the government left him alone. That's when he finally built this place. He's made enough from the cattle herd and horses to live comfortably. Compared to his neighbors he's done very well."

Roberta smiled and nodded. "I thought you might have a finger in that. But what happened to the plan to train you for war against the men who murdered your father?"

Henry grimaced, baring his teeth against the stem of his pipe as he thought about those years. "Some eggs get laid, but don't hatch. Some get dropped and break. A few produce roosters. Our nest had a few eggs that didn't hatch, some got broke, and, luckily, some produced roosters."

Roberta looked at him, the firelight twinkling in her eyes. "Don't spare the details!"

# LONG RUN HOME

**"I** must have been close to fourteen. I had spent about six years helping Rufus carry twenty-pound rocks to the piles we made for his new shack and fences. I was very strong for my size, my muscles as hard as those rocks I'd carried. I must have weighed about one-twenty and I could lift my body weight over my head. Rufus trained me to be a sharpshooter with the Sharps. Even though it weighed close to ten pounds and kicked like a mule, I hit bottles or cans ten times in ten shots at four hundred yards from a prone position or with crossed sticks for resting the forestock. Most folks don't realize how great a distance 400 yards is for iron sights. Whiskey bottles are so small that about all you see is an occasional glint. When I was a young man in my twenties I could consistently hit something the size of a bucket at a thousand yards. I read *The Iliad* and *The Odyssey* twice for Rufus, the Bible, and some of Shakespeare's plays. I understood what I read and that was even more important than just the reading. I was probably more literate at fourteen than ninety-five percent of the grown men in southern New Mexico.

"Yellow Boy taught me to live alone in the desert and survive, to run miles in that searing heat without water, and to be dependent only on myself. His lessons were in natural history and in the physical and mental discipline that had made my mind tough and my body capable of extraordinary endurance. Rarely was an Anglo or Mexican, rancher or townie, able to endure the desert as I was taught to do, or even as much as Apache children. I knew I was tougher than most white men who worked the ranches and cattle, and, at fourteen, my hormones were raging for a challenge to prove I was a man.

"Early one morning I had already started down the trail on a run to Tortugas Mountain and back when I caught sight of a cowboy riding up the trail toward Rufus's shack. He was just jingling along with his head tilted back and his eyes closed, letting the rising sun warm his face. I swung off the trail and hid, perfectly still and close to the ground, just the way Yellow Boy taught me. It wasn't long before the cowboy came riding by, never dreaming I was hiding within ten feet of him. As he rode by, his horse flicked his ears like he heard or saw something. I heard the man say, *Damn horse! If we was still fightin' Apaches I'd have my hands filled with cocked guns the way yore a flickin' yore ears around. What're you seein'? A snake?* Lucky for me, he never guessed why the horse was curious; he just kept riding.

"There was just enough light to recognize him. It was Buck Greer. His old gray hair poked out from the edges of his hat like straw, and his big bushy eyebrows lay under a forehead covered with wrinkles that looked like the network of dry washes up by Hot Springs. I remembered when he rode by Rufus's place right after Yellow Boy had found me. I saw his face through a crack in the door as they talked. He rode with two men from the Dripping Springs Ranch to search for Daddy and me, and they had stopped by to ask Rufus if he wanted to come along. He came back about three weeks later and told Rufus the story of their fruitless search all over the Tularosa Basin and up into the Sacramento Mountains. He said he believed Oliver Lee was behind us being wiped out. I sat behind the shack's door and listened to his story, nursing my broken arm and trying to keep from crying. I was grateful that they had worked so hard to find us, but I was afraid he would find me and carry me back to Mama before I settled my business with Stone, Tally, and Lee.

"Following Buck back to the shack without getting caught was a game for me. I did it too. I got within ten feet of the shack porch where he and Rufus were talking without either of them knowing I was there. I heard Buck say, *Yep! Cap'n Van Patten's a using three or four of his hands to drive wagons back and forth from Cruces carrying eastern dudes up to that hotel he's a building.*

"Buck chewed about as much tobacco as Rufus and sent a long brown stream towards Rufus's creosote bush growing next to the shack porch. He was sitting on the porch steps leaning back on his elbow next to Rufus, his hat pushed back, watching the morning shadows of the mountains creep toward them as the sun floated higher.

*Pretty mornin', ain't it, Rufus?*

"Rufus took his turn to spit, and said, *Shore is, Buck. What brought ye over this a way? Not that I ain't damn glad to see yore old ornery hide onct 'n a while.* They chewed in silence as they stared out toward the Floridas lit with early morning gold.

"I saw Rufus frown just a little when I crept into my hiding place behind some creosote bushes. I knew he thought I was probably there even if he couldn't see me. Cody caught my scent, lifted his head, and cocked his ears. Looking straight at the bushes where I was, he gave a little *woof!* Buck looked at Cody and said, *What's the matter with yore hound?*

"Rufus rolled his jaw a couple of couple of times before he spat and said, *Aw, they's a wild bitch in heat he's been after for the last three or four days. She's out there in bushes a wanting him to come out and play. I think she's done wore the old fart out and he don't wanta get up this early to fool with her.*

*Hot damn, Rufus!* Buck laughed. *Yore ole hound's a doing better'n both of us put together. Best I'n do is 'bout a once a month visit at Carmela's down to Juarez. I ain't seen you down there in a long time. How's you and the widow lady in Lincoln a doin'? Not much, I bet. She's too proper for old geezers like us. There's yore old hound and the ladies is a coming to him. Damn, if that don't beat all.* Rufus, who had started whittling while they spoke, grinned big, nodded and put another brown stream on the creosote bush as he grimaced on the side of his face Buck couldn't see.

"Buck laughed again, then got down to business, *Naw, reason I come by was old Cox, Jack Stone, and Oliver Lee is puttin' a herd together to sell to the Army. They plan to drive it down to Ft. Bliss next week. Cap'n Van Patten is gonna sell a few head to 'em. We're a little short on the number of cattle he promised to sell to 'em and thought maybe you'd want to sell a few yore self. We could round 'em up for you and drive 'em over to San Augustin Ranch with our herd if you want. Course you understand you'd have to wait until we was paid before you got yore money. I believe Stone plans to pay us off when we deliver our stock on Saturday over to Cox's corral so I could bring yore money over on say Monday or Tuesday, if that'd be all right.*

"Jack Stone! The name hit me like a slap in the face. I grew nauseous and hot in the face every time I thought of him. Here Buck was wanting to sell some of Rufus's herd to the man who murdered Daddy! Well, I thought, it'd be a cold day in hell before that happens. Nevertheless, Rufus grinned and said, *Why shore. That's mighty neighborly of Van Patten and yerself. If yore boys will take about twenty or thirty head, I'd be grateful. That money'll keep me in beans fer another year or two.*

"I was madder than a stepped-on rattlesnake. Why was Rufus helping that low-life murdering skunk? I couldn't understand it. I wanted to shoot him and here these two old geezers were selling him their stock!

"Rufus and Buck chewed and spit while they talked cattle and politics for nearly an hour. The sun was a quarter of its way to its zenith and I felt the sweat rolling down my face when Buck finally got up and stepped off the porch. He tightened his cinch, climbed in the saddle, and leaning over his saddle horn said to Rufus, *I'll send some boys over to get yore stock in two or three days. You just show 'em which ones and we'll take care of gettin' 'em over to Cox's place.* Rufus nodded with a grin and saluted, touching the edge of his raggedy old hat with his left hand, he said, *That's mighty neighborly of ye. 'Preciate it! I'll be lookin' fer yore crew in two or three days. Ride kerful now. Adios.*

*Adios.* Buck turned and rode off down the trail. He hadn't gone ten yards, when, laughing, he called over his shoulder, *Get that old hound to teach you a trick or two, Rufus! Then I'm shore Carmela'll be glad to see you and yore money! Haw!*

"Rufus laughed and yelled back, *Hell, he's taught me too many tricks already.* He sat on the porch step and watched Buck disappear down the trail. In a few minutes he said, *Ye gonna stay hid out there all day, boy? You'n come on out now.*

"I appeared from behind the creosote bushes and flopped down by Rufus on the porch step. Cody came over and stretched out beside me, yawned, rolling his long red tongue, and waited for me to scratch him behind the ears. A flock of quail, three adults and eight or nine chicks ran out of cover across the trail and disappeared under some mesquite. It was quiet and getting hot quick. Rufus could tell I was mad. He wasn't any too happy either. He said, *Ye're lucky, son! Ye hid well. But damn it, don't ever try to hide when they's a dog close by. They'll give you away ever time. That's why the Apaches always tried to kill the dogs around a house before they snook up to git the rancher living there. You's this close*, he made a narrow gap between his thumb and forefinger, *to old Buck catching yore tail. Then, aye God, I'd a had some fancy explaining to do about why some Indian kid was a hiding on my place. It's a good thing I'm a damn good liar!*

"Humbled by his review of my bush craft, I wasn't too mad anymore about Rufus selling Buck those cows, but said anyway, Rufus why are you selling stock to Jack Stone? You're helping the man make money who helped kill my Daddy! It's not right.

"Rufus spat on the green bush and wiggled his nose to edge his glasses up. He said in a soft voice I had to lean into to hear, *I know how you feel, son. I need the money and it's time to sell. Buck's offer couldn't a come at a better time. It don't make no never mind if I sell them cows to Stone or Mary the Virgin. They's gonna be et all the same. Jes get down off yore high horse now and get to runnin'. We got a lot to do to get ready fer them riders from over to Dripping Springs.*

"In my heart I knew Rufus was right, but it still stirred anger and hate down in my guts. As I was runnin' up the trail back to the shack that morning I kept saying over and over to myself, Someday I'm gonna kill you, Jack Stone. Someday I'm gonna kill you, Jack Stone. You know, running really gets the adrenaline flowing. A running man is just about as dangerous and irrational as they come. I was nearly finished with my run when I thought I had just about the best idea ever. I couldn't believe how clever it was. Rufus always got up early on Saturday to go down to Ellis's Barber Shop, listen to the latest gossip, and pick up supplies at Lohman's in Las Cruces. As soon as he left I'd take the Sharps and, following the shortcuts over the Organs at the back of the canyon Rufus showed me, I could run over to San Augustin Ranch in two or three hours. Or, I could even sneak around through Baylor Pass and still get there in four or five hours. Once I was at the Cox place, I'd pick me out a good spot where I'd hide and watch where the cattle were penned up. If I was lucky I'd get a good sight picture on Jack Stone and put a .45-70 slug right through his head. If I was real lucky, I might even drop Oliver Lee.

"I told myself I had been waiting six years for this opportunity and I was ready. I had carried tons of twenty-pound rocks, shot hundreds of shells through the Sharps, and run hundreds – no thousands – of miles all over the Organs and Mesilla Valley getting strong and smart. Wasn't I a crack shot? Didn't I know how to hide and survive in the mountains and desert? Why, I'd be back before dark and Rufus wouldn't even know I'd been gone. I sat down on the porch to catch my wind as my idea grew into a full-fledged plan. It occurred to me that what I'd read in the Bible about God delivering David's enemies into his hands was the same situation I had. David was just a little boy and he killed a giant. That was me. I was going to kill a giant, maybe two or three of them. God was about to deliver my enemies into my hands and I meant to kill them just like David, who, when he was about my age, had hit the giant right between the eyes with a rock. I was gonna put a bullet right between Stone's eyes.

"Yes'm, I was having myself a real epiphany sitting there on Rufus' porch. He was sitting there whittling before we went out to tote rocks. He sniffed and spat before asking, *What ye thinkin' so hard about, Henry?* It was the first and only time I ever lied to him when I said, Oh nothing except how hot it's getting. Makes it hard to run. He nodded, *Yeah, but doin' hard stuff 'll make a man of ye.* I just smiled and felt the lowest of the low for lying to him and for what I was planning, but I believed it was my destiny. I was going to do it regardless of what I'd promised Rufus and Yellow Boy when I was just a little kid."

Roberta shook her head and marveled that Henry had survived and had survived to become a healer of men, not a destroyer. She lit a cigarette and slowly exhaled, letting the smoke calm her anguish and sooth her curiosity over how much Henry had suffered as a child. She waited patiently while he stuffed his pipe. She had worked for and had been friends with Henry for over twenty years. Her curiosity about him now was like a fever on her brain. Once they were only friends. Now, besides friendship, she felt a strong physical attraction toward him. It was unlike any she had ever known for any man.

Before lighting his pipe Henry kneeled by Yellow Boy and listened to his chest with the stethoscope. There appeared to be no change, but at least he wasn't getting worse. With the oxygen, the old man appeared to be resting easy and he was cool - no fever. A sudden racking cough filled the oxygen mask. Roberta stuffed her cigarette and sprang to help Henry. They tore the mask off Yellow Boy and held him up so the fluids he was trying to get out of his lungs could be expectorated. He coughed and wheezed in to a clean towel for a couple of minutes, his eyes squeezed tightly shut in pain. The coughing stopped. Yellow Boy opened his eyes and smiled weakly when he saw Henry.

"Henry! Hombre! I must still be in the land of the living unless you have died too." He saw Roberta's face filled with concern, peering at him from his other side. He nodded at her. "Perhaps we are in the land of the grandfathers ..." He choked, gagging and wheezing, then coughed again for another minute. Managing to clear his airways, he wheezed, "I see an angel is with us."

Henry nodded. "Si, un angel es aqui, but we are still in the land of the living. We're trying to keep you out of the land of the grandfathers. It's hard. You must help us, even as weak as you are. Can you help us?"

Yellow Boy wheezed and coughed again before finally clearing the sputum from his throat. He said, "Si. I will try."

Grasping the oxygen mask in his right hand, Henry held it so Yellow Boy could see it. "This carries special air so it's easier for you to breathe. You must wear it. It has power over the demon in your body. Can you do this, mi hermano?"

He rolled his eyes toward the mask and frowned questioningly when he saw it, saying through a wheeze, "Whatever you ask, I will try."

"Bueno! Roberta and I will put it on you. Don't worry. I've given you stronger medicine. This and the special air will make you better.

Try to rest. We're sitting next to you. We're here." Henry motioned toward their chairs. Yellow Boy nodded he understood even as his chest heaved with short barking coughs.

Roberta and Henry fixed the mask back on him, twisted it a little to make sure it sealed well on his face, and laid him back down on the pallet. Henry checked the regulated flow and Roberta straightened the blanket and fluffed the old man's pillow. She squeezed his shoulder reassuringly and felt the thin tight muscles ripple under his shirt. It amazed her that a man his age still had muscle tone as good as most of Henry's thirty-year-old patients. The oxygen reservoir rose and fell at a regular pace.

Henry checked the towel Yellow Boy had coughed into and saw traces of pink in the sputum, but no red blood. It was a good sign. He put the towel in a bucket on the back porch and hurried inside to wash his hands and take his seat by Roberta. She had just lit a fresh cigarette. Leaning back in his chair he lit his pipe, took a deep draw making the coal glow, and then tossed the match into the fire that was rapidly being reduced to deep red coals.

Roberta pulled the blanket up around her shoulders. She nervously ran her hand over the tendrils of hair that steadfastly refused to stay in the bun. She said in an anxious, throaty voice "So did you make it to Cox's ranch?"

Henry nodded. Crossing his legs and stretching out in the chair he put his hands behind his head. Holding the pipe clamped in his teeth and speaking in a soft voice said, "Yeah, I made it.

"Rufus was usually up by four-thirty every day. He'd scratch around putting wood on the fire and making something for our breakfast – usually beans and tortillas. On Saturday mornings he'd saddle up Sally, stoke up the fire, put some coffee on and eat a little something with me. He'd tell me with a grin, *Now, Henry, don't go a gittin' in to any mean-ness, or if'n ye do, don't git caught.* Then he'd stomp out into the cold early morning air, climb up on Sally, and disappear in the coming dawn down the trail toward Las Cruces. That particular morning when he told me not to get into meanness, he gave me an evil-eye squint that said not to do what I had in mind. At least that's how I read that look. I knew Rufus couldn't read my mind but it sure seemed like it.

"As soon as Rufus left, I climbed up on a chair and took down the Sharps. I kept it well oiled and cleaned, making it gleam in the lantern light. I ran my hands over it, feeling the smooth octagonal barrel and easy-to-grip stock, fantasizing how it was going to be my sword of jus-tice. Touching it made me believe anything was possible.

"Scratching around the cabin, I put ten cartridges, the old brass naval telescope he'd found in a wagon train massacre years ago, and some jerky and roasted corn in the possibles bag he had given me. I filled a canteen half full of water – I wanted to keep the weight down so I wouldn't wear out with all the running I had to do. I tied my hair back and stripped down to just my breach cloth and soft boots for a long hard run.

"I decided I'd take the long way around, over Baylor Pass. I didn't want to risk dropping the rifle trying to hump it up the little trail of toe holds over the cliff at the end of Rufus's canyon. When I started running the cold air and darkness painted with black shadows made me feel as though I was in the nether regions of some womb, surrounded and safe. The trail along the western side the Organs toward Baylor Pass passed tall cliffs, making it hard to see for a while, but I had run it so often I could do it with my eyes closed. My feet knew every stone and pebble along the way. The Sharps' weight was a bigger burden than I thought it would be and I was glad I hadn't tried to climb the cliffs with it. I was ready to rest when I topped Baylor Pass on a thin little path through the piñon and yuccas that ran within several yards of the old trail the cowboys used. The sun had been up a couple of hours, but, high as I was, the air was still very cool and comfortable. I drank from the canteen and ate a little corn. Sitting concealed on a boulder back in the bushes, I used the telescope to find Cox's cattle pens before I eased on down the trail toward the ranch.

"A while before mid-day I found an ideal spot where I was able to watch the cattle pens and set up to shoot. It was a large reddish brown boulder sticking up out of the ground at about a thirty-degree angle in the middle of a good stand of grass and a few small mesquites. When I crawled up on that boulder and looked over the top, I was just below the top of the grass. Perfect! I studied the area for a rabbit hole in case I had to hide or get out of there quick. There was a large dark-green thicket of piñon bushes back toward the pass. I decided it gave me the best opportunity to hide or escape if I had to run. I lay down across the top of the boulder and balanced the Sharps in a prone position to feel how steady the sight picture was. Stone was a dead man! I picked out a corral fence post close to six hundred yards away and held on it steady as the rock. I was sure I'd hit a target at six hundred yards or more. My spot was about four hundred yards from the cattle pen fence. If Stone showed up, I knew, even with pounding heart and sweaty hands, I had a real opportunity to kill him.

"I pulled the old brass telescope out, put a little dust on it so glints wouldn't give me away and surveyed the cattle pens. The Dripping

Springs herd had arrived early that morning. There must have been a couple of hundred head squeezed inside the pen fence. There were five or six cowboys lounging around like they were waiting on somebody. I took that to mean Stone and his partners probably hadn't come yet to look over the final herd. This was finally going to be my lucky day! I crabbed back down the boulder backwards and sat with my back to it, ate some parched corn and jerky, and drank from the canteen, while I figured out what I'd do to get away after I killed Jack Stone. I thought, God, for sure, has delivered my daddy's murderer into my hands. There's gonna be justice this day!

"As I looked back toward the way I had come, I decided that I'd use my *rabbit-hole* piñon thicket for escape after I shot Stone. I knew there was a good chance of being caught if I tried going back along the Baylor Pass route without hiding in the piñon. It was way too dangerous to try to go straight up the spires and over to the handholds in the canyon cliffs at Rufus's ranch. From the piñon thicket I'd make my way back up to the same trail I had come down to get back to Rufus's place. I hoped – no, I was sure I was strong enough to outrun anyone that came after me, but I didn't know exactly where I was.

"It was getting hot and I was restless just sitting and waiting. I decided to ease back up the boulder. That rock was hot out there in the sun. I gritted my teeth against its red skillet heat when I put my belly to it as I stretched out to survey the cattle pens. I used the telescope again and studied all the cowboys at the pens. Buck Greer and a couple of the hands from the Dripping Springs Ranch were familiar, but none of the others. Swinging it towards Cox's ranch house, there were several horses tied to the hitching post in a shady spot. A couple of Mexican women were working in the plants around the front patio, but still no one that grabbed my attention. I waited.

"The sun was just past mid-day and turning my brown skin to burnt black when four or five men walked out of the ranch house. They were rubbing full bellies, engaged in jovial conversation, and smoking cigars. One of them stood out in a brilliant white shirt, a vest and a string tie. Rufus told me one time about how peculiar W.W. Cox was about wearing clean clothes and a string tie. These had to be the men putting together the herd. I studied them through the old brass telescope. My whole body twitched; a wave of fright and hate rolled through me, making my heart pound and sweat roll off my forehead in rivulets. The telescope showed me Jack Stone as he unwrapped the reins from the hitching post at the patio and swung into his saddle. Laughing and joking with the others he didn't have a care or any sense of how close to death he was. There was no sign of Red Tally.

"Hearing the rapid thump, thump, thump of my heart beating a tattoo in my ears, I eased the rifle forward to a shooting position. Pulling the hammer to half cock, I dropped the breech block, slid a shell slowly in, closed the block, and laid out three more shells within easy reach in case I had the opportunity to use them. I was determined to have a shot at Stone. If I had to, I'd try to shoot him at Cox's front door. I guessed it was nearly 600 yards from where I lay. The chances of me hitting him at that range weren't nearly as good as they were if he came in closer to the cattle pens. Cox and the others climbed on their horses too, and they all rode toward the cattle pens together. They wanted one more look over the stock before they started the drive toward Fort Bliss in El Paso.

"I tried to steady my nerves by breathing in long steady breaths, and by focusing on the spot by the pens that would give me the best shot to kill Stone. I guessed that he and the others would ride over to the ranch house side of the pens and sit in their saddles while they did a final look-see and head count. That's just what they did too. I picked a spot about the middle of the fence line and at about the height Stone should be on his horse. At that range it was an easy shot. Trying to focus and calm myself, I waited. I knew I had him. At least Daddy was going to get a partial payback that day. All those days of practice staring through the sights on the long Sharps barrel and feeling the now familiar punch in my shoulder from the recoil, all those days of carrying rock, all those days of running, all those days were finally going to bear fruit.

"The cowboys gathered around their bosses as they rode over to the pens. Stone was the middle rider in the group of five. They all rode up to the spot I had picked. I took a deep breath and felt as steady as the big rock under me. I sighted down the long octagonal barrel and thought, God is with me this day. Vengeance is mine! This is for you Daddy. Stone, you sorry bastard! Today you're gonna pay for your evil!

"Cox climbed off his horse and started to climb up to the top rail of the cattle-pen fence. The man riding next to him started swinging off his horse too. Stone paused. I remember his image as if it was frozen in a photograph. He turned to say something to one of his men. God is with me this day. I pulled the hammer back to full cock. The smell of gun oil was strong and intoxicating in the hot bright light. I sat the Sharp's double trigger, took a deep breath and aimed for Stone's head. It was just like shooting bottles back in Rufus's canyon. Oh joyful God! This day is mine. Die, you son-of-a-bitch! I let half my breath out and carefully laid my finger on the hair trigger. Stone moved, starting to dismount. I tried to relax my finger. Too late! The trigger setting was too sensitive and the Sharps roared my rage. Stone's hat went flying, but his head stayed on. The bullet thunked into a big fence post on the far end of the pens and sent big splinters flying just as the men heard the whistle of the bullet burning through the air past them. Thunder from the shot snapped across Cox's cattle pens, making men and animals show the whites of their eyes, big and round in fear. Stone continued his dismount as a flying belly flop on the ground in front of him.

"The cowboys around the pens hit the ground, their revolvers instantly out, cocked, and pointing in every direction as they jerked about under whatever cover was available, desperately trying to find their attacker and defend themselves. They frantically turned their heads in every direction. The roll of thunder from my rifle echoed off the mountains, confusing them about my location. Cox had jumped off the fence into the cattle pens, finding protection behind its rails. Horses bucked and jumped around until they jerked free of their bridle ties then ran off down the wide trail to the ranch house.

"I was frozen in disbelief, suspended in time as my brain tried to digest the situation. I missed. It was an easy shot and I missed! Wasn't God supposed to help me? A murderer is supposed to get justice! I had failed Daddy! Again!

"The sound of men yelling started to penetrate my daze. Cox's arm was through the fence, pointing to my left. A little cloud of smoke from the Sharps drifted on a whisper of breeze about ten yards from where I lay. Some of the men began firing toward the cloud, but it was much too far for a revolver. The shots fell way short, kicking up dust and sand far in front of me. One cowboy with hair so gray it was nearly white rose up on one knee and held his revolver in both hands. He fired a long arching shot that struck a boulder about five feet below my spot and ricocheted away with a sound like a broken guitar string.

"That shot jolted me into action. The old cowboy was on his feet, bent over and running side-to-side. He was headed in my direction. I scooped up my extra cartridges, scrambled back down the boulder, collapsed the telescope, threw it in the possibles bag, and, grabbing the canteen, ran in a crouch below the top of the grass toward the piñon thicket two hundred yards away. I stepped on as many exposed rocks as I could. Yellow Boy's lessons taught me to leave no trail wherever I went, and there was very little sign around the boulder that I had been there. Reaching the thicket I was sucking wind and the disappointment I was feeling made my legs feel as if they were wooden posts with no bounce at all. I passed the first of the bushes, and, stopping, crawled up under one to scan my shooting place. I was shaking with rage and fear as I levered the empty shell out of the Sharps and put a new cartridge in the chamber. In a couple of minutes, I saw several hats floating above the grass near the boulder as they looked for signs that could point them toward the shooter.

"I pulled out the telescope and watched them stomping around in the grass, looking in every direction. The gray-haired cowboy found my boulder and climbed up on it. He lay down on top of it like I had and yelled something at the others. He turned around and squatting on his heels, looked back toward the mountains, and slowly, deliberately surveyed the near rocks and bushes where I might be. He stared toward the pinon thicket where I was hiding for a good while before turning his attention to other spots.

"Stone and the other ranchers rode up to the boulder, their men right with them and everyone with a rifle set on full cock. There was a nice round ventilation hole on both sides of Stone's big flat-brimmed Stetson, just above the top of his scalp line. His face, even under the shadow of his hat, was pale, grimacing, and filled with rage. His partners and the men continued to swing their heads, scanning the mountains in front of them for some sign of the shooter

"From where I sat, I heard him screaming, *Find him! Find that son-of-a-bitch! A hundred dollars to anybody that finds him! Just don't kill him. I got to talk to him before he's hung!* He pointed his rifle toward Baylor Pass, *Damn it! You're letting him get away! Come on, boys! If we ride hard, we can catch him before he gets to Cruces.* They thundered off in a cloud of dust. Cox rode up to the boulder and said something to the old-timer who shook his head and stayed where he was before pointing toward my stand of piñon. Cox nodded then rode off to join the posse heading toward Baylor Pass.

"I knew I was in trouble. The old-timer was coming my way and he knew what he was doing. I had to find a place to hide and fast. He'd come slow, looking for signs. That was to be my only advantage. I could try and out-run him or I could hide and get behind him and take my time to get home. Either way, I wasn't about to shoot him. He just happened to be at the wrong place at the wrong time.

"I decided to put some distance between us, then hide, and let him get past me. I grabbed the rifle, canteen, and possibles bag, and took off, trying to keep the stand of juniper between the us. After about half a mile, I stopped. Looking back, I saw him studying the ground around the piñon thicket with his revolver drawn. I ran on.

"The weight of the rifle was tiring me out faster than I had expected. I was a mile or so from Baylor Pass and breathing hard when I found a good place to hide under a shelf of rock fronted by some piñon bushes growing a few feet below it. Wiggling up under the shelf so I could watch back down the trail, I had just managed to get organized and laid out straight and comfortable when I saw the old-timer slowly riding up the trail, a bloodhound hot on the scent.

"I eased the Sharps up alongside me until it was in front of me and I could reach the trigger if I had to. In the gloom of the dim light under the shelf, I glanced back in the direction of the old-timer trying to find my trail. There lay the biggest rattlesnake I had ever seen. I'd missed seeing him in my scramble to get under the shelf. He was a foot or two longer than I was tall and he must been four or five inches in diameter. There was a big lump in his middle section. I guessed he had made a kill earlier in the day and had expected to lie there in peace for a few days while his dinner digested. It stared at me, but didn't rattle. I stayed perfectly still while it raised its head a few inches and flicked its tongue at me trying to figure out what I was. I didn't move. I tried not to even breathe.

"The old-timer stopped on the trail just in front of my hiding place. He stared at the bushes in front of the shelf crevice for a long time. Finally, he threw one leg over the saddle and slid off. He drew his revolver. I heard its hammer click back, cocked and ready to fire. My mouth was dry, but my heart had stopped pounding and my nerves were steady. He started moving toward the shelf. The snake turned its attention from me to the new creature advancing on its sanctuary. In the dim shadowy light in the crevice, I could see its forked tongue flicking faster than when there was just me as it sampled the confusing air we created. It was cool there under the shelf, but I could feel the sweat running off the end of my nose. I was trapped in a hole with a snake on one side and a smart old-timer with a cocked revolver on the other. The snake still refused to give itself away with a warning rattle.

"Watching where he put every foot, the old-timer moved closer. It was obvious he wanted to look exactly where I was hiding. When the old timer wasn't more than fifteen feet from the piñon in front of the shelf, I picked up a hand full of dirt and gently threw it at the snake, hitting it about where its lunch was digesting. It didn't do anything except continue to flick its tongue toward the old-timer, who stopped and cocked his head, listening. It was quiet as a tomb. He swept the revolver back and forth toward the shelf, trying to see through the bushes and the dark shadowy underbelly of the crevice. It was either a mad rattlesnake or the old-timer with the revolver. I grabbed another small handful of dirt and threw it again. This time bits of gravel hit the snake on his head. That made him angry. He raised his head almost to the top of the crevice, rapidly flicking his tongue toward the man outside, furiously shaking his rattle.

"The old-timer's eyes got wide. He kept his revolver pointed at the crevice but slowly backed toward his horse. I heard him mutter, *No thanks, brother. Don't think I want to poke my nose in yore house today.* The horse was nervous and ready to run, but the old-timer grabbed the reins, holstered his revolver, and swung into the saddle in one smooth motion. He trotted away from the crevice smartly, following the trail up through Baylor Pass where Stone's posse had ridden not more than a couple of hours before.

"After the old-timer rode on, the snake finally stopped rattling and laid there watching me with unblinking eyes. After waiting a bit, I wiggled back out from under the shelf, took a long swallow from the canteen, and started running up the little path that paralleled the Baylor Pass trail. I wanted to catch up with the old-timer and keep him in sight so he wouldn't wind up behind me. I still hadn't found him when I topped Baylor Pass, but I found fresh horse apples that told me he was no more than a few minutes ahead. I found a place to stay out of sight of the trail and sat down to rest. I'd been running with that heavy rifle and possibles bag up the steep path to the Pass for nearly two hours. Despite my conditioning, I was leg-weary and needed a rest. I drank the canteen almost dry, ate the rest of the corn and jerky, and lay back against a boulder for a few minutes watching the western sun casting long shadows on the Mesilla Valley. It was late mid-afternoon when I forced myself to start moving again. I had four or five more miles to go before I was back home.

"I stayed high up on the Organ ridges and followed the path that cut past the southern wall of Baylor Canyon, expecting the old-timer to keep on into Las Cruces with the rest of Stone's posse. I followed the path all the way around to the western side of the Organs, found the dry wash the drovers used to push the herd over to Cox's ranch, and followed it all the way down to the road that ran in front of Dripping Springs Ranch. I followed that trail back toward Dripping Springs until I found a spot where I could get back on the trail I had run along going to Cox's ranch. I ran easily, thinking that I might even beat Rufus back home.

"Stopping to rest, I was about to start on when I heard a horse snort on the trail below and behind me. Looking for the horse, I blinked in surprise when I saw the old-timer standing off the south side of the trail with his back to me, relieving himself on some bushes. Easing down behind a thicket of cactus and creosotes, I waited for him to get in front of me again so I could keep an eye on him. For some reason he had decided to turn down the road that ran past Dripping Springs rather than head toward Las Cruces. I realized then how lucky I was he hadn't caught me. He was trail-smart and relentless.

"The old-timer got back on his horse and rode on. He rode slowly, studying the ground in front of him for signs, often stopping to look back over his shoulder like he thought someone was following or watching him. I ground my teeth that I couldn't go any faster, get around him, and get home before he caught me. I realized, that to throw him off the scent, I needed to go a mile or so past Rufus's place and cross the trail again to make him think I was headed for El Paso. I saw him turn from the southern trail that ran parallel to the Organs and follow the one toward the Van Patten place. That was my chance to get around him, so I ran past Van Patten's on my path then moved down the slopes and crossed the trail toward Rufus's place, making sure I left little hard-to-see signs to show that I was still on the trail south. Then I got back on the path above the main trail and followed it past Rufus's place for another mile, crossed it again and back-tracked back toward Rufus's. I found a place to rest and drank the last drops of water in the canteen. I was worn out. The sun was nearly down and the breezes off the Organs were cool and sweet after that long run across the mountains.

"It was a good two hours after the sun dropped behind the Floridas when I finally got back to Rufus's place. Coming up the trail I saw Sally watching me from the corral. My heart sank. I knew that if I hadn't beaten Rufus back from town, he'd know I'd done something stupid and be mad, and he had every right to be. I had taken his rifle and tried to shoot Jack Stone, despite my promise that I'd wait until we were ready. I didn't have any idea what he'd do. He was sitting on the porch step, watching me come up the trail. He was resting his elbows on his knees, his hands clasped together between them, and he had a big wad of tobacco in his cheek. Cody stretched out on the far end of the porch, woofed at me and beat a thump-thump hello with his tail.

"Rufus nodded at me, *Howdy, Henry! Glad yore back. I'm a just sittin' here thankful I ain't gonna have to saddle up Sally and go over to Cox's place to get yore body in the mornin'. Are ye hurt?*

"Wha...Why would you think that, Rufus? I stammered, not having a clue how he had known I had been at Cox's place.

"He spat toward the big green creosote bush and squinted at me through his dusty round lenses. *Aw, old Pete Catron was by here 'bout sundown. I rode with Pete years ago when we wuz a tryin' to catch Victorio. Told me about how somebody had nearly put a bullet through Jack Stone's head. Said he thought he might be on the assassin's trail, but that whoever he was trailin' was mighty crafty. He thought maybe whoever he wuz might be an Indian or an Indian fighter. He just wasn't shore he had come this direction, although he saw signs that maybe he had. He was just following a hunch. I give him some beans and tortillas, we chewed the fat about old times fer awhile, then he went on his way.*

"I was as weary as I've ever been. I just nodded to Rufus, went inside, and drank several dippers full of water. I unloaded the Sharps and dragged the stool over to the doorway so I could reach the pegs to hang the Sharps up until I could clean it. I filled a tin plate with beans out of the pot hanging over the fire, took a couple of tortillas, and walked outside to sit down beside Rufus.

"Those beans and tortillas tasted like a gourmet meal after covering nearly fifteen miles of mountain trails and eating nothing but parched corn and jerky. Rufus didn't say a word or look at me. He just chewed and spat, watching the stars fill a cloudless night. I finished shoveling down the beans and tried to apologize for my fool trick. *Rufus, I'm sorry. I understand now what a fool trick it was, and –*

"Rufus spat and looked at me a moment, his jaw slowly turning the wad of tobacco in his cheek into more brown juice. He shook his head and said, *Don't never back up, boy. Say what ye mean to say and do it. Yore mighty young and inexperienced to do what ye did. But, aye God!* He reached over and grabbed my shoulder with a big grin on his face. *Ye nearly pulled it off! Just the luck of the draw you missed. It's even luckier ye weren't caught. Tell me what happened!*

"So I did. I told him everything. From how I had decided to do it because David had been able to kill the giant with God helping him. I figured God wanted to punish Jack Stone, so He'd help me too, but He didn't. I didn't understand why. Rufus just sat and nodded as he listened. I told him what an easy shot it had been and how I couldn't understand how I'd missed. I told him about my get away and how Pete Catron had nearly caught me and a rattlesnake under that shelf. Rufus laughed out loud at that one. I had to laugh too when I thought about it. I told him how I'd back-tracked from further down the trail trying to throw off old Pete Catron. When I finished Rufus was quiet for a long time, just sitting there in the dark, chewing and spitting as he whittled a stick down to a toothpick.

"The moon began to fill the canyon with its soft yellow light and stark black shadows. A warm breeze rolled up from the valley floor. Rufus spat and sighed, *Henry, ye did all right! Ye just made one or two big mistakes and several small ones, but, for a child yore age, ye did mighty fine. Yore blood uncle, or whoever he thinks he is, Yellow Boy, will be real proud of ye too.*

"My weary body, once near collapse, wanted to stand up and dance in the light of that praise from a man with years of fighting experience. All I could say was, I did well? I thought you would want to beat me for taking the Sharps without your knowing it or being with me to guide me along. What were the mistakes I made?

"Rufus leaned back on his elbows and looked at me. Even in the dark I felt his eyes fully on my face. *Yore biggest mistake was ye didn't go fer a body shot. It's mighty hard to hit a man in the head at a long range, son. A feller's head moves a lot. If ye'd gone fer a body shot ye'd probably have hit him in the heart or lungs and he'd been dead one way or the other fore ye topped Baylor Pass. The other big mistake was ye should have shot through a hole in some bush so the smoke from the shot broke up and be a lot harder to see. But ye was smart hangin' back and followin' the people tryin' to catch ye. That there's an old Apache trick. Did Yellow Boy teach that to ye?* I shook my head. *Well, son, yore a natural then. Only difference 'tween yore trick and theirs is the Apaches would have attacked again from the rear and wiped out the ones chasing 'em. Ye oughter've thought about how to hide out until everyone was a chasing some phantom up the trail and not got in front of Pete. If he'd just realized ye was a little fart he'd probably caught ye right there in that shelf. Might even have shot ye trying to shoot the snake through those bushes. He just didn't want to waste cartridges. Ye understand what I'm a tryin' to tell ye?*

"I nodded, Yes, sir. I know you're right, Rufus, except ...
*Except what, son?*
"Why do you suppose God didn't help me today like he did David?
"Rufus was quiet as he tilted his face up to look at the stars and scratched at the stubble on his face. He said, *What makes ye think He didn't help ye today? Physically yore just a boy. Ye covered about fifteen-mile worth of mountain trails today, packing a ten-pound weapon and another five pounds of food and water. Ye came within a couple of inches of puttin' lead between the eyes of the man who had yore Daddy killed. Henry, ye survived when by rights ye oughter be dead! Don't tell me God didn't help ye. Why, it's a damn miracle yore alive!*

"I nodded I understood. Rufus was right. It wasn't luck that got me through. It was providence. Maybe next time the giant would fall. I said, Rufus, can we name the Sharps?

*What do ye mean, son?*

"Well, I want to name the Sharps Little David. You know, like David and Goliath? Because today I almost brought down the Giant in front of everybody and it was like using little David's slingshot.

"Rufus grinned. *Well, that old rifle ain't had no name before 'cept when ole Yellow Boy calls her Shoots Today Kills Tomorry. I reckon Lil David is a good name, especially if ye use it to wipe out those men who killed yore daddy. Ye just be shore you clean Lil David first thing in the morning. We a goin' to need him.*

"Why are you saying that?

*Well, I spec we oughter to see Jack Stone and his boys by here in two or three days. He's a goin' to be madder than hell 'cause somebody took a shot at him. He ain't got no idea why exactly, but I bet it could be fer all kinds of reasons. Old Pete will think he might have trailed the shooter past my shack. He told me he believes it was a Sharps that was used to shoot at Stone and he knows I got a Sharps too, and that I ain't got no reason to be shootin' at Stone with it. We got to find ye a good hidin' place and figure out how to handle Stone when he comes. It ain't goin' to be pretty. I jest hope Yellow Boy gets back here soon to help us.*

"I nodded and yawned. I was ready for sleep. Tomorrow's problems would be there tomorrow."

# 12

# JACK STONE COMES CALLING

Yellow Boy was resting comfortably. The oxygen mask reservoir bag rose and fell regularly. His breathing was still filled with loud wheezing, but the blood-spotted sputum no longer came when he coughed. Henry had placed his stethoscope to Yellow Boy's chest twice since he had begun the story of his first attempt on the life of Jack Stone. Each time he listened, he nodded approval at the old man's improvement.

He made a fresh pot of coffee while Roberta made a dash down the path for the little wooden house in the cold night air. When she returned her teeth were chattering. She wondered how pioneer women had ever hardened themselves to using those kinds of sanitation facilities. Sitting down next to the fire Henry had just built up, she rubbed her hands, calling circulation back to ice-cold fingers. Without the extra effort, her fingers were always cold and stayed that way in the drafty old house. She accepted the speckled enamel cup of black coffee Henry offered her and took a sip of the scalding black brew. It burnt the roof of her mouth, but she didn't care. It had a pleasing bitterness that brought back childhood memories of her father's coffee.

"What time is it?"

She slipped off her coat, stretched her left arm out of her sleeve to see her military nurse's watch in the flickering firelight, and said, "Nearly two."

They could hear John and Sara softly snoring through the doors to the bedrooms. "I think Yellow Boy is going to make it. Go wake John and get some sleep yourself. I'm too wound up about the old days to sleep. Maybe I'll nap some tomorrow when we're sure he's not going to the grandfathers."

They sat side-by-side, soaking up the warm glow of the fire. She hesitated, then impulsively reached over and laid her hand on his forearm. She said in a low whisper, "Please don't send me away to bed. I can't sleep either. Maybe I can sleep in a little while. I just can't get my mind around what you've told me. It's not that I don't believe you. It's just so hard to accept that your perception of people you think you've known most of your adult life can be changed by their past so fast. They become completely different persons than you imagined them to be. It's very unreliable to try and guess the future or assume the true past, isn't it?"

She gave his arm a little squeeze and looked into his weary eyes, pleading for more time with him. As he looked in her eyes, Henry realized he felt something more than the affection and friendship for her he had known over the years. His smooth hand caressed her cheek. He smiled as he whispered, "Your loyalty to this old man knows no bounds, does it? Most people would have laughed me right out of this old house if they had heard a tale like I just told you. If we stay up, we'll be exhausted tomorrow. But, John and Sara ought to be able to take care of him. He'll be safe if we're sleeping nearby. Stay up with me if you like, but I'll continue only under one condition."

Her eyes never left his face as she arched her brows in the obvious question. "When we're alone, don't call me Dr. Grace. For you, I'll always be Henry. Calling me Fountain or Grace doesn't make any difference for us now. It pleases me for you to just call me Henry."

She swallowed against the little tickle in her throat as she nodded and felt her heart open like a budding flower that had waited years to bloom. Henry, like a teenager on a first date at the movies, hesitantly placed his arm across the back of her chair and around her shoulders. She trembled as she thought, Oh God, can this night be real?

"Are you cold? I can put more wood on the fire."

"No...Henry. I'm not cold at all. Your arm is all the warmth I need." They sat content in the yellow glow of the fire, surrounded by the big room's dark corners and the sleeping sounds of Yellow Boy, Sara, and John. Roberta said, "So was Rufus right? Did Stone show up?"

"Yes, he did. He and four other riders showed up at Rufus's shack about suppertime a couple of days later. Rufus was just serving up our plates when he looked out through the window and saw the first rider top the trail to the house. He rode into the yard, followed by the other four, like he owned it. I was at the spring getting a bucket of water. Rufus came out of the shack, careful to close the door behind him. He hoped I had heard the men come up and was hiding. I was about half-way back to the house when I heard Cody barking, and then strange voices. I hid the bucket behind a bush and tried to find a place where I could hide and see and hear what was going on.

"When I finally maneuvered within sight of the yard, there sat Jack Stone, Charlie Bentene, and three cowboys I'd never seen before. Those three stayed back on the edge of the yard. Stone and Bentene had ridden up close to Rufus. Stone was resting his forearm on his saddle horn and leaning forward. Bentene, with his big hooked nose, sat straight in the saddle with his hand on his revolver watching every move Rufus made. As soon as he came out the door, Rufus had tied Cody to a porch post. Cody stood with his teeth bared, a low growl in his throat, and, his usually happy tail, was still.

"I heard Stone say, *Sorry to intrude on you like this, Mr. Pike, but some son-of-a-bitch put a big hole through my hat a few days ago. We've been looking for him ever since. Pete Catron thinks the rifle used to do it was a Sharps and that the shooter came this way. Told me he thought you had a Sharps. That true, Mr. Pike?* He bared his teeth in a menacing grin.

"Rufus spat a stream at the green creosote bush and stared back at Stone unblinking. *Yep, I own a Sharps. So do about a hundert other folks on this here side of the mountains.*

"Continuing to show his teeth, Stone said, *Yes sir, you're right about that. But you're the only one that does on this trail, and Catron thinks the shooter rode by here or to here or near here. You got anybody living with you inside that shack, Mr. Pike?*

"Rufus stared straight at Stone and said, *Nope.*

"*Well, do you mind if my partner Mr. Bentene here takes a look?*

"Rufus spat another stream in the dirt where Bentene would have to step and said, *Hell, yes, I mind. I'm a telling ye now to git offa my place. Ye ain't got no business in here.*

"Stone drew his Colt. He pointed it directly at Rufus. Slowly cocking it as his finger curled around the trigger, he said with malevolent sarcasm, *Oh, we got business here, and you don't care if we look...do you? Step inside and look around, Charlie.*

"My heart was pounding. I was crazy with anger and scared to death they were going to do something to Rufus. If Bentene looked inside, he'd know that there were two of us. I was going to get caught, and I still owed those two for my daddy. I tried to think what Rufus would tell them, but he said nothing as Bentene swung down off his horse, pulled his revolver and cocked it as he walked around Cody, who was making a deep-throated growl. Pushing the door open, he stepped inside.

"In a couple of minutes Bentene came out grinning like a coyote that's caught a quail. He had the Sharps and said, *He was getting sup-*

per ready for two people, Jack, and there's a bedroll on the floor next to the fire. Here's the Sharps. Looks like it's been shot often, but it's clean. There ain't no telescope for it that I saw.

"Stone said with a coyote grin and a barely concealed snarl, *Two people? Why, Mr. Pike, you said nobody else was living here. Two people, eh? Charlie, see if you can't persuade Mr. Pike to tell us who the other fella or lady is.*

"Bentene nodded. In one smooth motion he viscously swung his revolver into Rufus's face, making his head jerk to one side and his glasses go flying. The blow bloodied the left side of his head and knocked him backwards, but he caught himself on a porch post before he fell. Cody was going wild, barking, straining with all his might on the rope to go for Bentene's throat. I was sick about what they did to Rufus. It was all my fault. I wanted to kill 'em and I would have too if I'd had the Sharps. I did the only thing I thought I could do. I appeared from behind the bush and walked over to the house ready to die, ready to confess that I had shot at Stone.

"I wanted to vomit and my knees had turned to water. I had failed Daddy. I'd never see Mama again. Now Rufus would probably get shot or beat up or worse. It was all my fault. I gritted my teeth and forced my feet to move forward. The riders stared at me like I was a ghost. Stone's ugly grin turned to a snarl as he squinted at me with his wolf's eyes. A shadow of uncertainty fell over his face. He hadn't expected a kid to come walking out the bushes. I saw him frown, obviously trying to remember where he had seen me.

"I started to speak, but Rufus spoke up and said, *The kid's just helping me fer a few weeks with chores. He ain't nothing or nobody ye're a wanting. His Daddy lives over to the reservation. He ain't hurting nobody. He don't even speak good English. You afraid this kid's gonna shoot you, Stone? Leave him alone!*

"Stone looked from me to Rufus and said so low I could barely hear him, *Calm down that goddamn dog or I'll kill him. Give me that rifle and get on your horse Charlie.* Bentene holstered his gun. He stepped off the porch, tossed Little David up to Stone, and swung up on his horse. The coyote grin never left his face. Rufus stumbled inside, dragging Cody. I could hear him speaking soothingly as he tied Cody to a bedpost. Stone and Bentene sat on their horses, waiting for Rufus to come back outside. Cody still barked but he wasn't going crazy any more. Rufus had blood running down the side of his face. A big ugly bruise was forming around the gash on his face. He wobbled back outside, squinting hard to get a little focus as he looked around the porch until he found his glasses in the dirt at the bottom of the step. The left lens was cracked and the frames were twisted. He put them back on just as they were. He spat toward the creosote bush and stared up at Stone unafraid, waiting for his next move.

"Stone wasn't laughing. His frown and piercing wolf eyes were deadly serious as he searched my face for some landmark of recognition. *You look like some kid I've seen before. You remember me?* I just looked at him, pretending I hadn't understood a word.

"*I told you! He don't speak or understand English too good. Now, damn it, leave him alone!* Rufus stood there like nothing had happened, his hands in fists, blood running down his face. He was in charge, ready to attack. They'd have to kill him. He wasn't being bullied.

"*Shut up! Shut up, before I bend this rifle barrel over your head, and we have to dig a grave up here for you, you old bastard,* Stone said, gritting his teeth and waving the heavy weapon a few inches above Rufus's head.

"Stone continued to stare at me over Rufus's shoulder. He leaned toward me and shouted *Como se llama?* as though I was deaf. I just stared at him and didn't say anything. He looked at Rufus and said, *What is he? A deaf half-breed? He's too light to be full Apache. Must have a Mex mama. All right, Pike, so you got a kid working here. Chores for beans, huh? Mighty charitable of you. I bet you're working his tail off for them beans too, ain't you?*

"Stone let the hammer down slowly, holstered his Colt, and scratched his stubble-covered neck as he looked around. He turned back to Rufus. *I know this kid from somewhere. Funny I should remember a kid, I usually don't pay much attention to 'em. Maybe I've just seen him around.* He laughed. *I guess it don't make no difference, does it? He ain't gonna be shooting no rifle this heavy, especially at me seven or eight miles from here. Pike, I'm thinking all the shooter signs point to this here shack. Even so, it just don't make no sense for you to go to all the trouble to be tryin' to bushwhack me at my friend's ranch, 'specially if you got this kid helping you with the work.*

"He tossed the rifle over to Bentene and said to Rufus, *Old Charlie's gonna keep that good-for-nothing old thunder gun of yours, just in case you were involved in my hat trick. You lost a rifle and got tapped a little on the side of the head. That's nothing. Mister you got off lucky. Hear me now. If there's ever another shot from somebody ain't facing me and the trail signs even point to the west side of the Organs...I'm gonna come back here and burn this place to the ground with you and anybody else that's here in it. Don't ever cross me, Pike. I'll blow a hole in you big enough for that damn dog to run through if you do. Adios, kid. I'll remember where I've seen you one of these days. Let's go, boys.*

"Stone jerked his horse around and trotted off. His men pulled back, waiting for him to take the lead back down the trail. Rufus stood there watching them go. Blood was running down his face, covering the front of his dirty long johns. He stood there unflinching, his lips silently swearing vengeance, waiting for them to disappear. I ran up to him in tears. I was so sorry I'd caused his misery. I wished I'd waited for a better time to take a shot at Stone. But I'll tell you, I wasn't a bit sorry I had nearly killed him.

"When Stone and his men were out of sight, Rufus swayed, staggered backwards a couple of steps, and sat down hard on the porch step. He laughed and slapped his knee. *That there is one scared son-of-a-bitch, Henry. Ye flat put the fear of God in him, ye did!* He rubbed his aching head and said quietly, *Let Cody outta the house, boy, 'fore he gets loose and eats our grub. Then bring me a bucket of water and a rag to wash this blood off, will ye?*

"I let Cody out of the shack and ran to get the bucket of water I left behind the bushes. When I got back to the porch, Rufus said, *See if ye can find a clean rag over by the wash bucket to clean me up. This 'un I got here in my pocket is dirty. I been wiping dirt and sweat and 'baccer juice off my face with it.*

"I found a clean rag, wet it, and began to dab at the blood on his face. The bruise continued to get uglier. His eye was swollen shut and the broken skin across his cheek bone must have been two or three inches long. I knew he must be hurting bad, but he sat there stoically on the porch step with his hands on his knees while I fumbled around trying to doctor him. When I finished washing him he said, *Now, fetch me a mirror and that half bottle of whiskey under my bed. Here, give me that rag and I'll do a little extry washing while ye look fer 'em.*

"The whiskey bottle was right where he said it was, and half of it was gone too. I gave him the whiskey and ran over to the corral where he kept a wash basin. He had a broken piece of mirror there he occasionally used when he shaved. He looked at his reflection with his one good eye and grunted. He winced a few times when he probed around the cut area with his gnarled forefinger. I stood there watching Rufus doctoring himself and marveling at how much damage the barrel of a gun could do to a man's face. He took a long pull from the bottle, smacked his, lips and said, *Reckin I'm lucky. Don't think my cheekbone's broke. Does look like we'll have to do a little sewing though. Go get my possibles bag, will ye, Henry?*

"I found the bag next to his bed. It was a soft buckskin pouch with fine beadwork on the flap. When I brought him the pouch, he rummaged around in it until he brought out a small piece of folded leather. He carefully unfolded it and took out a curved needle about two inches long and several pieces of sinew. He popped the sinew in his mouth to soften it, and struck a big sulfur match to sanitize the needle. *Remember how I taught ye to sew up yore breech cloth when ye tore it a slidin' across them rocks?*

"I just nodded. I didn't want to hear what I knew he was going to say next. *Well, now we're gonna see what kinda doctor or tailor ye'd make. Ye're a gonna hafta sew up this here cut fer me just like ye was sewing up that there breech cloth. I ain't got no depth perception with just one eye or I'd a do it myself. I know ye ain't never done nothing like what I'm asking ye to do, but I'll shore as hell make a mess of things if ye don't sew it up for me. It'll almost be like sewing on yore breech cloth, 'cept ye make one loop at a time and tie it off, then do another. My old hide ain't too tough to sew. Ye don't have to dig way down in my cheek meat to sew this one together either, cause the cut ain't that deep. I figure maybe seven or eight stitches ought to do it, and them right across the top of the cut. Ye'n do it. Help an old man out here now. A couple more swallows of this here firewater 'n I'll be ready. Grab that little three-legged stool in there by the fire and sit down here beside me so ye're comfortable while ye work.*

"He reached in his mouth and pulled out the sinews he'd been softening. *This here is yore thread. It's deer sinew. When I'm healed up you'll be able to cut the stitches offa my face easy. They's some little sewing scissors in that there sewing kit. Ye'll need 'em to cut the sinew after ye make a loop and tie it off. I ain't gonna feel much so don't worry about hurtin' me. Now git to it.*

"That was the first time I ever put a stitch in anybody. I was scared and a little shaky at first, but I knew I had to do it for my friend. I threaded up the needle with a long piece of sinew. I stared at the cut for a while and kind of eyeballed about where I thought the stitches should go while Rufus swilled down some more of his whiskey. It was easier sewing than I imagined. I pulled the two sides of the cut together with my thumb and forefinger with my left hand. I didn't have to push hard with my right hand to make that sharp needle pass right through the skin on both sides of the cut. I tied the first stitch in the middle of the cut. Then put three on either side of the first one, halving the distance each time. Rufus never flinched or showed the first sign of pain. When I was finished I poured a little whiskey over the cut like Rufus told me. That made him groan and grit his teeth some.

"I handed the piece of mirror to Rufus so he could see what kind of job I'd done. I was proud of the work. It felt good to help Rufus after he had done so much for me. He looked at each stitch carefully. *Damn, Henry! You'd make a right fine doctor. That there is a first-class sewing job!* I reveled in the glow of his praise, and I guess that's where the idea for me to go to medical school was first planted.

"*Now go get ye something to eat. I ain't hungry. I'm just gonna sit out here and watch the sun go down while I finish the rest of this here bottle.* I got a plate, sat out on the porch step with him, and ate my supper while he got drunk. I hung my head in bitter disappointment. Little David was gone. I'd probably never have another chance at Stone. I'd never be able to set things right for Daddy, and I had endangered the life of one of my best friends. It was the worst day I could remember since Daddy died.

"For the next four or five days we went about our business like nothing had happened. I ran twice everyday and carried rocks while Rufus started stacking some of them to make the new house over by the barn. I could tell Rufus's face hurt, though, and that he was giving something a lot of thought. Saturday morning came. He saddled up Sally, as he always did, to ride into town for supplies and a visit to Albert Ellis's Barber Shop. Just before he left he said, *Now don't get in no more trouble. Stay hid if anybody else comes. I'll be back 'fore sundown.* I slowly nodded. He grinned and winked as he rode off.

"The sun was beginning to send streaks of gold and purple across the sky when Sally and Rufus topped the trail into the yard. I ran to meet them. Rufus had new glasses. They had silver wire frames and were a little smaller in diameter than his old broken pair. He had bought an old 1873 Winchester. It lay across the saddle along side a burlap bag of groceries and a few other supplies. As he handed me the rifle and climbed down from Sally I said, How were things in town? Do you like your new glasses? Where'd you get this rifle? What's –

"He laughed. *Slow down there, Henry. Jest one question at a time, if ye please. I got my glasses at Lohman's. He just got in a new shipment from back east. I had to get two pair, one pair fer reading and one pair fer long distance. Reckon my old lamps are a goin' out. Ain't they fine ones, though. I saw a feller selling this here rifle to Lohman fer some groceries. I knew how much old Lohman paid him fer it, so I offered Lohman a dollar more and he give it to me. So now we got us some long-range artillery as well as that damned old pistol of my mine.*

*Everbody wanted to know how I got beat up so bad. Told 'em Sally run me into a post when I wasn't lookin'. They all laughed in Ellis's cause the talk was several people over on this side of the Organs had run into posts this week too. They's all speculating about who took a shot at Stone. Ellis laughed and looked at me when he said he thought there might be several to shoot at him now. Stone and Bentene are supposed to be up in the Sacramentos lookin' over abandoned homesteads to get some more land and water to support their herds. Soon as Yellow Boy comes in from Mexico, we're gonna go get Little David back, and I'm gonna settle me some business with Mr. Bentene. Now let's eat. Ye go set out the meal and I'll feed and water Sally.*

"It was monsoon season, raining three or four times a week. Rufus and I loved to sit on his porch watching the lightning shows start far down south or to the west, then roll east toward Las Cruces and El Paso. The night sky lighted up with streaks of lightning for hours. We could feel the cool breeze and smell the rain as the columns of water rushing out of the heavy black clouds marched toward us on giant stubby legs with thunder beating their march. Those storms are fearful to watch from down in the valley. When you see them from half-way up the Organs, they're flashing wars, clouds striking each other with fiery crooked strokes that hang in your eyes long after the dark returns. Yes, ma'am! They'll make you fearful watching 'em from the valley. Up higher, where Rufus had his shack, they make heathens into God-fearers.

"After supper that evening, Rufus and I sat out on the porch watching clouds gather over the Floridas. The big blue bruise on his face was starting to heal and turn yellow. The swelling had gone down enough that he could see out of his left eye. In another week I knew he'd want the stitches cut off of what was going to be an ugly scar. He sat on the porch step, his elbows resting on his knees and his hands clasped together. He had a big chew in his jaw and was using the green creosote for a regular target as the lightning began. We already felt the whisper of a cool breeze and there was the faintest smell of rain. We could tell that the storm wouldn't waste any time coming this way and back up on the west side of the Organs. We'd probably get enough water to fill to overflowing all the natural and other water tanks we had. No doubt this rain would fill the trail to the shack with washouts.

"Rufus what are we gonna do?

"Rufus spat and said, *You mean about those bastards that stole Lil David?*

"Yes, sir, that's what I mean. Them that stole it, they're the ones who killed Daddy. I felt tears of frustration rising to my eyes, ready to embarrass me in front of my mentor. They're getting away with anything they want to do. It's not just or fair or any of that stuff! I can't stop them, it's my fault we lost any advantage of surprise. We both know it's only gonna be a little while before Stone figures out who I am, and then he'll be back to finish business. I'm the one who's got you into all this trouble. Maybe I ought leave. Just go back to Mama and hope for the best. At least then, maybe, they'd leave you alone.

"Rufus chewed and stared at me for a moment, snorted and shook his head. *Whatever give ye the idee that life's fair? Let me tell ye, it ain't. Men have justice in their lives by puttin' honor first even if it means loosin' their own lives. That's what we're gonna do. We're gonna git us some justice even if it means our lives. As fer ye leavin' in the hope the bastards will leave me be, well, it just don't make no never mind, Henry. They know ye're staying here with me and it's likely ye told me what ye knew about 'em. They's a gonna have to wipe me out too when they come after ye. So don't go down yonder to yore mama and put her in danger fer me, 'cause they's gonna come after me anyway. Ye didn't get me into this mess 'ceptin I wanted to be in it with ye. It was gonna happen sooner or later. It's just happened sooner is all. The ace we got in this here war is Yellow Boy. They don't know about Yellow Boy and that he's yore uncle or whatever that bloody hand ritual meant. They don't know he's vowed revenge for ye. And, let me tell ye, I nearly laughed out loud when Stone said ye was too little to put that hole in his hat, then outfox Catron to get back here. But, ye did it, didn't ye? Ye was able to do that 'cause Yellow Boy taught ye how to think and we helped ye get strong in yore body and yore mind.*

"He shifted his wad to the other jaw and turned his head to spit at his creosote bush. As he turned back to look at me his jaw dropped and his eyes got wide. *I'll be damned! Buenos noches, Señor Yellow Boy! We been hopin' ye'd show up.* I jumped and looked over my shoulder where Rufus was staring. There sat Yellow Boy, leaning against the porch corner post. One foot was on the porch, one on the ground, his rifle was between his legs, the barrel resting on his chest.

"I shouted, Yellow Boy! I jumped up, and in three steps was kneeling by him. Up close he looked tired and worn out. I hadn't a clue when he had joined us on the porch.

"He held up a slow hand to greet us, *Hola, Rufus! Hola, Hombrecito! I ride hard por tres sols y tres noches. No eat, only rest horse. Esta carné in su pot Rufus? Esta agua aqui Hombrecito?*

"Rufus had a smile on his face and his eyes sparkled with new fire. He was chewing twice as fast as his normal I'll-get-to-it-mañana rate. *Three days and three nights? Damn! They shore as hell is some grub in the pot, hombre. Be right back with a plateful,* he said as he stepped inside. I ran inside too, and grabbed the water bucket and dipper. I handed Yellow Boy a dipperful that was gone in three long swallows. He sipped the next dipperful.

"I studied his face as he drank. He looked weary beyond anything I had ever seen. I could tell he hadn't slept in days. He was covered with dust and the sweat falling out of his hatband made rivulets in the dust down the sides of his cheeks. Normally he stayed very clean, but this night he had the sharp pungent smell of old sweat, his and his horse's, and miles of desert trail dust. I didn't care. I was so relieved to see him I felt as if I'd just been saved from drowning. Maybe our trouble with Stone was going to be set right after all!

"Where's your pony? I'll feed and water him.

*This I do already, Hombrecito. He eats and drinks con Sally.*

"I looked around the side of the shack. Sure enough there was the paint pony next to Sally, with their rumps pointed out of the shed, its covered sides shielding them from the gusting wind and coming storm. Rufus came out of the shack with a tin plate piled over with what we had left in the cooking pot.

"Yellow Boy took it and ate like a starving man. He filled both cheeks as he chewed while the gravy ran down his chin. He wiped it off with his free hand and licked it, not wasting a drop. Rufus, his smile made crooked by his swollen face, leaned against a porch post watching him eat. I was grinning myself as we waited for him to finish.

"He wiped the plate clean with the last tortilla, emptied another dipper of water, belched loudly, sighed with relief, and leaned back against his post, closing his eyes for a moment. When he opened them, he looked at me, then Rufus, and nodded. *You are safe, mi compañeros! Bueno! Vamos! Pronto!*

"Rufus and I looked at each other with frowns of surprise. We had a lot to tell him. What did Yellow Boy know that we didn't? His voice was earnest as he said, *Sally run you into a tree, Rufus? Why are your anteojos nuevo...why are your glasses new? Que is Shoots Today Kills Tomorrow?* He stared first at Rufus's face then mine and saw only confused stares back. Sighing, he said, *I dream. I come quick. Darsé prisa! Vamos! Hurry! We go!*

"Rufus's jaw dropped and his brow shot up. *We have to go? Now? Ye had a dream? Ye rode nearly three hundert miles in three days and nights because of a dream? What kind a dream made ye do that?*

*I dream in sweat lodge while my woman has child. Shoots Today Kills Tomorrow finds Hombrecito's enemy. Enemy does not die. Enemy medicine is strong. He has many riders. He searches far for Shoots To-day Kills Tomorrow. He finds. He takes. He goes. He knows Hombrecito. He returns. I know I must ride plenty quick, or Hombrecito dies. The enemy he comes pronto! We go quick! Vamos pronto!'*

"I stared at him with my mouth open and felt myself trembling down in my gut. Rufus's eyes narrowed and his jaw moved slowly on his tobacco. It took a moment for the fog to clear. Then he spoke with urgency, *Good Gawd! Henry, run get Sally and the paint. Take 'em up the canyon. Hobble 'em. Rope off a little corral around that old log back in the corner of the canyon. You know, where we usually try our longest shots. This here storm's a comin' and it'll likely scare hell out of 'em. They'll try to wander back here if they ain't fenced in back there. If you hear shootin', you hide up in the juniper behind where we put targets. Be kerful and don't get on no glass. Don't come back here till I call ye, if they's shootin'. If it's quiet, ye come back on the side trail to that overhang I fixed fer us to hide on. Ye understand me boy?'*

"Yes, sir, I do.

"I was off the porch and down to the corral faster than a quail crossing the road. There was already a strong breeze filling the air with the coppery smell of rain and faint thunder off to the west. The storm would be over us in less than an hour. The paint stood with his head down, little strength left except to eat. He was easy to halter. Sally was skittish with the coming storm, but I knew her tricks and got the halter rope around her neck before she ducked out into the corral.

"I led them up the canyon to the log Rufus mentioned. It was actually just an old juniper tree that had fallen over. I rested Little David many times on it shooting the bottles Rufus used for targets. The paint and Sally were easy to hide and protect from the storm there. The wind was swirling up and down the canyon when I finished a little rope corral and their hobbles.

"I strained to listen for the sound of gunfire against the increasing moan of the wind high above the canyon walls. There was none. I ran along the path on the north canyon wall about ten feet above the path we usually took to shoot. I had to run in stops and starts, waiting for the lightning to show me the way. I knew I needed to get to the overhang before the rain came because the path would become slick and dangerous when it started raining. There was a pause in the wind and a bright flash and crack of thunder just as I got to where I had to climb up to the overhang.

"Rufus and Yellow Boy were stretched out on their bellies, staring out into the darkness through the juniper bushes fronting the ledge. I could hear the low mumble of their voices as I came down the path. I had nearly climbed up to the ledge when I heard Rufus say, *Come on up here beside us, Henry.*

"I stretched out by Yellow Boy. The old rifle resting in his hands was on half-cock, a cartridge in the chamber ready to fire. Rufus was loading the rifle he had just bought. Three boxes of cartridges lay between them. Cody was tied in the shed, chewing on a piece of meat left to keep him quiet. It was darker than a tomb up there behind those bushes except when lightning flashes spread a quick search light over everything. The wind began to pick up and blow dust up the canyon, swirling little dust devils up and down it's sides. There were droplets of rain mixed with it. In the lightning flashes we saw a big cloud with a column of rain over on the western edge of the valley and knew it wouldn't be long before the storm was on top of us.

"Are we going to shoot them if they come? I whispered as the wind moaned and the dust picked up. *Now,* I thought, *now we'll see if you're such a big dog, Stone! Yellow Boy's gonna cut your nuts off.*

"I'm sorry to be so crude, Bertie, but that's just what I thought. I can remember every detail of that night." Roberta covered her mouth and smiled. She nodded her head that she understood and wasn't offended.

"Yellow Boy shook his head. *No, Hombrecito. Es mal...It is bad...place por un ambush. Es no way out. Aqui no extra bullets, no frijoles, no agua if el gato stays aqui and shoots back. If gato leave they get away too easy. They warn others. Then we no avenge su padre. We wait. We find bueno place to spill blood. No es aqui. We trapped here. If they find us, we must kill them all. Everyone. Comprendé Rufus?* Rufus spat and nodded once that he understood perfectly. *Shore, Yellow Boy. What yore sayin', that there's a fact.*

"There was only the moan of the wind through the canyon. We lay there without moving, feeling the wind rise and fall, the smell of water on creosotes from down in the valley getting stronger. I opened my mouth to tell Yellow Boy about my adventure when he reached over and grabbed Rufus's forearm. He nodded toward the trail and cocked his head to listen. The wind was getting stronger and dust was pelting our hiding place. I was gritting my teeth. You know how blowing dust makes your skin feel like fire ants are biting it. The wind was blowing so hard I couldn't hear or see anything. It was darker than Stone's soul. I barely saw Yellow Boy's head and he was right next to me. There was a sudden short pause in the wind. I heard a stone rattle down the trail.

My heart was thumping so hard it was about to jump out of my chest. I'd have sold my soul for a swallow of water to wash away the dry cotton in my mouth.

"There was a tremendous flash of light. A wicked bolt from the cloud over Las Cruces split and thumped three different spots with a roar of white blinding energy and thunder that ricocheted off the mountains. I sucked in air through my teeth, surprised. The flash revealed four riders reined up in the middle of the yard, their rifles across their saddles. The man closest to us had a red beard. Red Tally! One of the other riders had been with Stone and Bentene when they pistol-whipped Rufus. I didn't recognize the other two. They all wore long black dusters with collars turned up to fend off the wind, and their horses were black. They'd be hard to see anytime. I clinched my teeth, and heard my heart pounding in my ears. I wished to God I had Little David. I'd settle accounts right then! I didn't care if I died on the spot. At least I'd have gotten the man that shot Daddy.

"Red Tally bent his head and cupped his hands as he lit a cigarette. His collar was turned up on one side of his face to provide a windbreak. He cocked his rifle. The others cocked theirs too, then pointed them at the shack door. Tally nodded toward one of the other riders, who then tried to yell above the roar of the wind swirling in the canyon, *Come on out, Pike! Bring the kid with you! Come out now or we'll burn you out!* Kerosene lanterns hung off the saddles of a couple of the riders.

"Flashes of lightning were becoming brighter and more frequent as the storm began skirting the Organs and moving off toward El Paso. Tally looked at the rider next to him and motioned him forward with a wave of his rifle. The rider climbed down and stepped on to the porch, his rifle ready. He walked up to the shack door. He kicked it open, jumped inside, firing several times as he went. Rufus sighted on the doorway and brought the hammer back on his Winchester. Yellow Boy grabbed him by the arm and shook his head. Rufus spat a heavy brown stream in disgust and put his rifle back on half-cock. The man in the shack came out and yelled into the wind's fury, *Ain't nobody here. They was though. Fireplace is still hot. You wanna burn 'em out?*

"Tally looked around, and, apparently not liking the odds, especially if they went further up the canyon, shook his head. Up the canyon, the advantage fell to us; they might even be boxed in. Raindrops the size of marbles began to pelt us.

"He pulled his horse around and yelled, *No! Leave it. Wouldn't burn now anyway and I ain't riding up that canyon in this rain and dark. I'll finish the job in a day or two. That kid ain't gonna get away from me a third time. Come on, let's get down that trail before it's too slick and washed out to ride on.* They started back down the trail as the clouds eagerly dumped their water on us.

"I raised up on my knees, ready to run back up the canyon and get the paint and Sally. Yellow Boy grabbed me by the shoulder and held me with a powerful grip. He nodded toward the yard. In a moment, a weak flash showed a rider sitting motionless, waiting at the edge of the yard, rifle drawn, and collar pulled up to his hat. We waited, feeling the cold rain washing us clean and new.

"The rain passed. As the lighting flashes became further and further apart, and the thunder rolled away toward the south, the lone rider turned and slowly headed back toward the Dripping Springs road, letting his horse pick his way through the myriad of little streams racing down the trail. Yellow Boy turned to me, *Vamos! Bring horse and Sally to shed, Hombrecito.*

"I made my way back up the canyon. It was tricky business. There were gushing rivulets everywhere, pouring toward the big wash that ran on the south side of the canyon. The paint and Sally were soaked but no worse off than I. We returned to the shed without drowning in the roaring run-off or falling on slippery rocks. I gave them an extra ration of oats; they needed it. Rufus had the fire going and most of the water that had blown through the open door swept out by the time I got back. He fumbled around with the fixings and finally got a pot of coffee started on the fire.

"Yellow Boy sat on the edge of the porch calmly smoking one of his Mexican cigars. I walked over and sat down next to him. He clasped my shoulder and gave it a little shake, *So, Hombrecito, Rufus say you open un grande box of trouble, si? Es bueno. You have a brave heart. Bueno! You do a powerful thing against this man Stone. I am proud. You have warrior's heart, pero usted no sabé mucho. We take our enemies' lives por su padre. This we must do pronto or die by the hand of this man who comes like the hunting lion. When Rufus ready, we talk.*

"I nodded at his words and sighed. How was it, I wondered, that the strongest purposes of our hearts often had the weakest outcomes in action, while the weakest had the most profound effects on our lives? It was my first lesson in being careful for what you asked, because you just might get it.

"Soon Rufus brought the coffeepot and three enamel cups out to the porch and poured us each a cup. The stars came out and fog rose from the ground, swirling about our feet like smoke from a dying fire. Crick-

189

ets began their orchestra. It was late and very peaceful. The danger had blown through, the strong wind filled with uncertainty gone up the canyon until the next storm.

"I had to blow the steam off my cup and slurp loudly to make the hot liquid cool enough to drink. Rufus and Yellow Boy just smacked their lips and drank it scalding hot. They never taught me how they did that.

"Rufus drank about half his cup and said, *Well, boys, what're we a gonna do. The fat's in the fire now ain't it? I say we ambush 'em on the road somewhere, just the way they did Henry and his daddy. That there'd be poetic justice.*

"Yellow Boy looked puzzled. *Que es poetek justez Rufus?*

"Rufus grinned over the steaming cup and shook his head. *No never mind. It'd take the rest of the night fer me to explain it to ye.*

"Yellow Boy's tactical mind sought the most effective way to assure we got results with minimum danger. *How many must we fight, Rufus?*

"Rufus thought for a minute and said, *Well, they's the two big ones, Stone and Tally. Tally is the one with the red beard on his face. They's Bentene – I want the pleasure of guttin' that son-of-a-bitch fer a pistol-whippin' me. They's three that always rides with Tally, and they was three with Stone and Bentene the other night. I reckon they's maybe nine we might haffta to take care of. Henry did you know any of the other riders besides Tally tonight?*

"I shook my head.

"Yellow Boy blew a puff of smoke that hung in the cool night air like a small cloud that stayed behind from the storm. *Dondé esta ranchos de Stone y Tally y Bentene? Sabé, Rufus?*

*Shore I know. Stone's place is down towards the malpais and up against the San Andres. Bentene's place is next to Stone's. I hear Tally stays the winters with Stone, then rides the train with his crew up to Wyoming country to murder homesteaders. I's surprised to see him here tonight. Stone musta sent fer him all the way up to Wyoming. Bentene ain't got much of a place. He's mostly Stone's partner. Stone ain't been doing too good lately with his stock though. They say Lee's been a tryin' to buy him out, but that there is another story. Henry thinks Lee was in on shootin' his Daddy – just warn't there is all. Why do ye wanna know?*

"Yellow Boy's eyes narrowed to match the coyote grin on his face. *Hmmmph, usted know Rufus. Mountains good place for ambush like wolf hunting deer. Rancho casa es good place por ambush when enemy sleep there. If we were sleeping, when Barba Rosa come, he kill us, si? Meat for the wolf es meat for the lion, si? What works for Barba Rosa es bueno por us tambien. Stone y Bentene in mountains, now, pero come back to rancho casa. First we find Shoots Today Kills Tomorrow. Maybe find at Bentene rancho. Take back por usted y Hombrecito while Stone y Bentene en mountains. Then Rufus, Hombrecito, y Muchacho Amarillo hide on Sierra Blanca en mi land. Maybe we find Stone and Bentene while we hide. Maybe kill, si? We go once more a Stone y Bentene ranchos. Maybe burn. Maybe kill, si? Maybe we am-bush 'em on road. Maybe kill, si? What usted think, Rufus?*

"Rufus spat on the green creosote bush as he thought about Yellow Boy's proposal. *Aye God, Yellow Boy, I wouldn't want ye fer an enemy. We'll rest ye and the paint up tonight and most of tomorry. Then we'll take the path Henry used and go on over Baylor Pass late tomorry. We'n lay low in the Jarillas day after tomorry, then hit Stone's and Bentene's places fer Lil David that night. I got all the supplies we need. We need to git outta here purty quick though. The Tally bunch'll probably burn the place tomorry night. Henry and me's gonna build us a rock house anyways. If'n we get those bastards, Henry can go back to his mama. If we don't, he ain't gonna be goin' nowheres and neither is we. Ain't that right, Henry?*

"I nodded. I had to clinch my teeth to hold my cup steady I was so excited.

"Rufus and Yellow Boy laughed. They understood what I was feeling. Things were happening much faster than any of us had imagined. They couldn't happen fast enough for me. I didn't care if I was fourteen years old. I wanted blood. I wanted it right then. I wanted to see my father's enemies choking on their own blood like he did. Most of all, I wanted to see my mother and tell her I had settled accounts for Daddy and her dead son had come back to her still living."

# 13

# HIDING ON SIERRA BLANCA

R oberta was floating on the surface of a dream, tethered to reality through her fingers resting lightly on Henry's warm hand. The flickering fire stirred golden light into the late night darkness, creating a screen on the walls where her mind projected images from Henry's story.

"Henry, are you telling me that Yellow Boy rode three hundred miles in three days without rest because he dreamed you had tried to kill Stone and that Stone was coming back to Rufus's ranch to kill you? How can that be? You're a physician, a man of science. Do you really believe that he dreamed all that?"

Henry listened with his head bowed, and then gave her hand a little squeeze. "Yellow Boy told me he did. He's never lied to me. I have no reason to believe that he ever would. I know Rufus never doubted him. We acted as soon as he told us about his dream. I don't know how our subconscious works or what its sensitivity is to events far removed from our physical location, or even in the future. I do know there are many stories told in the Indian nations about the foretelling of events that most people wouldn't or couldn't believe."

Henry held up his thumb first, then his index finger, and finally his middle finger as he counted. "For example, I know Geronimo had a vision that he would never be killed by a bullet, and he died in his sleep. Crazy Horse dreamed he'd be killed as a result of the foolishness of his own people, and he was betrayed. Sitting Bull dreamed Custer would be wiped out, and you know what happened there. The list goes on and on. I've even had one or two dreams that came true, and I bet you have too. I know, I know. There are a lot of liars about such things. But since you ask, yes, I really believe Yellow Boy's dream saved Rufus and me. Come on, haven't you ever had a dream or a vision come true?"

"Well, no...yes...well...maybe." She frowned and pursed her lips as she remembered a time, several years past, when she turned down a

192

marriage proposal from a man she liked very much. She rejected him because of a dream she had of her man robbing a bank and disappearing into the desert. She shrugged off any idea that the dream had anything to do with reality, and told herself she just wasn't ready for marriage. A week later her former boyfriend was killed trying to rob a bank in El Paso. She remembered the dream when the sheriff told her what happened. She marveled at how good her instincts were and how lucky she was.

Henry looked at her for more information, but she shook her head and was silent. She had decided to put all this confusion about dreams on a shelf and wait for more information.

Yellow Boy had not coughed in over an hour. The wheeze from his chest was less noticeable. The oxygen reservoir bag rose and fell in a steady rhythm. He was cool to the touch – no fever. Henry knew his old friend was further away from the land of the grandfathers than he had been in days, but he might still hear its call. Perhaps, in another day or so, he'd be safe.

As Henry told Roberta more of his story, he felt a sense of exhilaration, freed at last from a self-imposed exile, freed to begin a new life. The realization of his true feelings for her was even more liberating. Loving a woman who loved you was fulfillment. Loving a woman who was also your best friend was the completion of your true self. He had waited over forty years to find her. He smiled – she was worth the wait.

He put another log on the fire, poking the coals until the flames grew high again. Pointing to the old enameled coffee pot he raised his brows. She shook her head and patted his chair for him to come back to her. He sat down with a sigh and stretched out as her arm lay across his shoulders. They were both tired, their eyes red with fatigue, but sleep was still far away.

They were quiet for a while, enjoying the solitude, the warm crackle and glow of the fire, and their friend's slow return to the land of the living.

"So – the next day the three of you just got on your horses and rode off toward Stone's ranch?"

Henry smiled at the memory. "Well...it wasn't quite that simple. Yellow Boy disappeared down the trail toward the back of the canyon. He found a place to sleep the rest of the night and most of the next day in a juniper thicket close by the back cliffs.

"The next day Rufus got me up at daylight. We worked our tails off right up until the time we left, late in the afternoon. Most of my work was at his mine, you know the place I told you about where he stored his valuables, about half way up the path to the back of the canyon. I had been in it only once or twice since he had first showed it to me, and had ignored it so much I'd nearly forgotten it was there. I must have walked past it a thousand times going to practice with Little David and not paid it any attention.

"It was dry inside despite the hard rain we had the night before. After he opened the door he took a stick and beat around to be sure there weren't any snakes staking a claim to his territory. He found one and tossed it, twisting and rattling, outside, just like he'd taught me to do. He put me to lugging stuff in the shed and shack, mostly books, tools, and pots and pans, up to the mine while he rode over to Van Patten's place to buy a pack mule and a horse. He asked Buck to keep Cody and to watch over on the place while he was gone. Buck was right fond of Cody after Rufus told him that tall tale about wild bitches coming to court him.

"When Rufus returned, he gave me the horse he'd bought from Buck. He said Buck called her Midnight, and she was the first horse I'd ever owned. She was small, black, and shiny as tar with a white blaze on her face and three white stockings. I watered her and curried the dust off her while we got acquainted. She was a friendly little horse and got along well with Sally. I liked her as soon as I saw her. Rufus said, *Buck says she'll never win any flat land races, but a man could ride her right over the Rabbit Ears and she'd never miss a step. He wanted to know why I wanted a horse when I had Sally. Told him I was gonna do some cattle drovin' and prospectin' down to Mexico and Sally was just getting too durn slow – which ain't true, but it was a good enough reason fer Buck. That there mule answers to Elmer. Buck swears by him too. Says he even lets some of the fancy-pants tourists that come over to the Drippin' Springs Reezort take him fer a ride cause he's so reliable and gentle.*

"We led Midnight and Elmer up to the storage mine. Rufus dug around inside for a while before he came out with an old dust-covered McClellan saddle, a rough saddle blanket, and an Army bridle. He wiggled his nose and said, *I ain't used this rig since I done a little scoutin' fer the Army back to '68. Reckon it'll be easier sittin' than bareback, but not much.*

"I was thrilled. I was going to be riding across the desert, just like a trooper back when Daddy led men against the Apaches and bandits. Rufus went back in the mine again, rummaged around some more, and came out with a pack frame for the mule. He sent me to fill a small keg with water. After some shifting around of barrels and sacks, he found a case of .45-70 caliber ammunition for Little David, and a case of .45 caliber cartridges for his and Yellow Boy's rifles. He threw the coffee pot, a skillet, his Dutch oven, some eating pans, spoons for eating and cooking, beans and cured meat, coffee, flour, and grain for the horses and mules into some old worn-out panier sacks that went on the pack frame. He rummaged around in the shack and found his medical kit, odds and ends to use around a camp, and herbs he used for everything from snake bite to constipation. They all worked too, although to this day, I still don't know what half of them were. Yellow Boy does.

"Yellow Boy appeared at the shack in mid-afternoon. He yawned and stretched as Rufus gave him the last of the breakfast beans from the pot left hanging over the fire. When he finished eating he went down to the shed and sat in the watering pool for a little while and bathed. Clean and refreshed, he helped us load up the mule and saddle the horses as the sun began falling behind the Floridas.

"Before we mounted, Rufus showed Yellow Boy the cases of cartridges and told him to help himself when he needed ammunition. Yellow Boy nodded his head and looked at Rufus solemnly. *Es war Rufus!*

*Ye're a damned right it's war! We're gonna kill those bastards or I ain't comin' back here alive. I done kept this boy from his mama too long and put up with those bastards a whuppin' my head fer too long. Now they's gonna come back here and burn us out! Hell, yes they's gonna be a war and they ain't a gonna see it comin' till they's a big hole right 'tween their eyes.* He said it with such anger and vehemence, that I was a little taken back.

"Yellow Boy stared at his eyes for a few seconds. *Bueno, Rufus! Es war! Hombrecito will become a great warrior. There will be much blood por revenge y Alberto Fountan will rest en paz con the grandfathers. Vamos, amigos!* We made some final adjustments to the pack on Elmer and the saddle gear, took a last look around, and mounted up.

"The shadows were long in the desert, the canyon slowly drifting into soothing dark and chirping crickets, as Yellow Boy led us down the trail that ran from the shack around the back side of Van Patten's ranch and up over Baylor Pass. Buck was right. Midnight was easy to ride and sure footed as we cantered down the trail. Her steady gait made me less fearful I'd embarrass myself riding her in front of Rufus and Yellow Boy. I didn't ride often, and when I did, it was just a slow walk on Sally. I just followed the run, run, run, run-all-the-time schedule Yellow Boy demanded of me. Now traveling was easy, the McClellan saddle was like a rocking chair compared to pounding the ground with my feet. We stopped a couple of times in the early going for Rufus to rearrange the gear on Elmer so it couldn't be heard rattling around or bumping together as he trotted along. We hurried because we wanted to be well beyond Van Patten's ranch before Tally and his men came back. We were strung out over about two hundred yards with Yellow Boy in the lead, me in the middle and Rufus in the back leading Elmer. It was a dark night, nothing but deep black shadows and bright stars overhead. But, Yellow Boy rode down the trail as though it was full daylight and we made good time. As we neared the top of Baylor Pass, he turned and galloped back down the trail past me, stopped to speak with Rufus for a moment, then continued on to disappear in the blink of an eye into the inky black shadows of the Organs.

"Midnight had her ears up in curiosity, watching Yellow Boy ride back down the trail while we waited for Rufus to ride up. He nodded back down the trail and said, *Ole Yellow Boy's a gonna ride back to the shack and keep watch down the trail fer Stone. We're a gonna wait fer him at Aguirre Springs on the other side of this here pass and give these animals a breather. They ain't use to runnin' up and down these here mountains like you did.* Even in the dark, I could see his yellow teeth shining in a big grin as he gave me a wink and a nod. I suspect he could see my teeth too because his little backhanded complement made a big smile appear on my face there in the chilly night air.

"We followed the trail over Baylor Pass, carefully picking our way until a big yellow moon finally popped up over the Sacramentos and made the trail easy to see on the way down to the springs. It was so bright we stayed in the shadows from bushes on the up side of the trail. No one could see us in those shadows even if they were coming toward us on the trail.

"As we approached Aguirre Springs, I saw Rufus stop, pull his Winchester out of its scabbard and lever a round into the chamber while he waited for me to come up.

"What's the matter? I whispered.

*They's big cats in these here mountains and they might wanna use that spring to get a little water and maybe get a little dinner from some idjits dumb enough to be stumblin' around in the dark. They's also the chance there might be some fellers a camped in there. Here, ye take the reins fer Sally and Elmer. I'll walk in. Ye ride in behind me. If any of the animals start acting up, it's likely they's probably smelling a cat or a camp's horses and mules. Ye whistle in yore hands like a dove if that happens and ride back up the trail a ways until I come get cha.*

"I nodded. I was scared. A mountain cat was big enough to carry me off or easily kill the horses and mules. I didn't have a weapon except for the throwing knife Yellow Boy taught me to use. Right then a knife didn't seem like much of a defense against a big cat.

"Rufus disappeared down the path into the springs and I slowly followed, my fast breathing leaving a little cloud of vapor behind us. Midnight, Sally, and Elmer moved along with no signs of fear or that they smelled other stock. We found water from the springs running down the mountain in a little stream, but no mountain cat or campers. Rufus put his rifle on safety, spit a stream of brown juice between his boots, and said through the little cloud his breath formed, *I spec Yellow Boy will be another two or three hours. Let's loosen the cinches on Sally and yore horse, take the load off Elmer, and get us some rest. Yellow Boy's a gonna want to move soon's he gets here. We need to be in the Jarillas before dawn or likely as not ranch hands will spot us.*

"We loosened cinches, unpacked Elmer, and hobbled the stock so they could graze on the bushes and grass around the little stream. We found us a big smooth boulder to rest against and watch back up the trail for Yellow Boy. It was chilly that time of night, but the water rippling over the rocks and the moon glowing over the Sacramentos made the evening mighty pretty and peaceful.

"We sat in silence for a while, watching the moon sail across the night sky toward the western horizon, lengthening the stark black shadows cast by the bushes, but bending them away from us. Rufus cut a fresh chew, and stuffed it in his cheek. He crunched down and sucked in some wind to get the juices flowing as he nodded toward me and said, *Are ye fearful, Henry?*

"I never really thought about being afraid, I said. I was half trembling from the cold air and half from the trip's excitement. I'd had plenty of nightmares about Tally and Stone hunting me down and killing me. I had those dreams nearly every night for about a couple of years after Daddy was killed, but I hadn't had a nightmare after that for two or three years, maybe more. Now my friends and I were finally going after the murderers. We were in the right. Stone and Tally deserved killing and we were going to make things right. Why should I be fearful?

"What do you mean? I asked Rufus.

"He spat and said, *Well, sir, ye've been a hiding fer about six years. Here ye are, maybe fourteen year old, a running around in the desert with an old fart and an Apache who won't stay on the reservation. They's hard men who want ye dead and they almost killed ye too. Ole Red Tally, he'd just as soon cut yore throat as look at ye, and ye can bet he'll do it if he has even a little bitty chance. Stone, he's got to have ye dead. If ye ever talked to the law, Garrett would come get him and he'd be swingin' from a gallows shore as hell. That jackass Bentene, he just does what Stone tells him, so he'll want to kill ye too. They probably got fifteen or twenty trusted cowboys that'd ride through hell with 'em, and they's no doubt they'd not hesitate to try to run ye right into the ground if they's the chance. Those men know ye're alive now. They's comin' after ye, and here ye are, by God, a goin' after them. That there is yore best defense. Ye think ye're just a gonna ride up behind some bush and shoot 'em all at a distance like ye tried to do with Stone? They ain't gonna let that happen. Wished I could say it'll be that easy, son, but these here hombres are gonna be hard snakes to kill. Git my drift now?*

"Yes sir, I said, I guess I do. What you're sayin' now is enough to make me right fearful. I just know it's something I've got to do. If they kill me, then at least I can rest easy knowin' I did the best I could to make things right for Daddy. Ain't nobody gonna care if I kill or am killed except you or Yellow Boy 'cause everybody else thinks I'm dead anyway. I'd have had a better chance of livin', I know, if this thing we're doing now had started when I was older. But I just couldn't let a chance at killin' Stone slip by. I almost had him too. Somehow, someway, I'm gonna get Little David back. I'm gonna try again and again, until Stone's lying on the ground with a bullet hole through his heart. Then it's gonna be Tally's turn, 'cept I'm gonna stake him out over a slow fire and boil his guts in his own juices like Yellow Boy says the Apaches did to the enemies they hated most. I'm gonna settle my score with Bentene too, and I'm gonna finish with Oliver Lee. He's gonna suffer for what he paid those killers to do!

"The more I talked, the angrier I got. We'd never really talked before about what it was we were going to do. It slowly seeped into my head that we were aiming to kill, at least, three or four men. All of them had nerves of steel. They were used to facing death and were not afraid of being killed. They were hard men. They wouldn't hesitate to kill any of us in an instant. I didn't care. I wanted payback.

"I whispered, I hate 'em. I want to tear their hearts out while they're still livin' and dance on their graves.

"Rufus sat there for a while not saying anything, just looking at me in the soft glow of the moonlight. A little stream of tobacco juice trickled out of the wad in his cheek. After cogitating for a while, he spat a mighty brown stream then said, *Gawd amighty, Henry! I didn't know ye'd gotten so blood-thirsty. When did that happen?*

"I wiped my runny nose and sniffed. Aw, I don't know. Every time I ran in the desert, every time I picked up a rock for your house, every time I hid when you had company, I thought about it. I thought about how I was lucky to be alive and having you and Yellow Boy teachin' me how to survive. I'd think the reason I was with you was 'cause those killers almost put me in the ground when they murdered my daddy in cold blood. I thought, every time, as I was working or training, those men are gonna pay. They're gonna pay every last pound and pennyweight that's owed justice, or I'm a gonna die tryin'!

"Rufus spat a stream of brown juice on a big beetle that had started across a rock next to him. *That there is a mistake, a big mistake.*

"What are you talkin' about? Those murderers got it comin' and I'm the one who's owed to givin' 'em a start toward the arms of hell.

"Rufus shook his head and stared off across the basin aglow in the moonlight. *Ye got to be cold and cakilatin'. If ye want to survive bringin' justice to those men, ye gotta be thinkin' all the time. Yore daddy's killin' and them chasing ye is the best of reasons to go after 'em fer shore. But ye can't let yore feelings about 'em tell ye what to do. Jest like ye a goin' after Stone with Lil David. Yore feelings on that one left ye high and dry when the nut cuttin' time come. Ye're lucky boy, damn lucky, to be alive.*

"Well I almost killed him, didn't I?

"Rufus spat again, then looked at me with a squint of cold rationality. *Almost don't cut it. Ain't no reward in that. Almost ain't never killed nobody. Almost ain't brought nobody to justice. Ever time ye try to kill a man, be damn shore ye do it. Ye ain't likely to get another chance 'fore he kills ye, and he's in the right to do it too. Now I ain't sayin' ye ain't brave and showed lots of courage and shootin' skill tryin' to kill Stone, but this here range is covered with graves of brave men with a lot of skill who didn't cakilate what they was a doin' 'fore they made a challenge. Ye got to be smart when nut-cuttin' time comes. Ye got to be real smart.*

"I knew Rufus was right – almost didn't cut it. All I could say was, Yes, sir. I know you're right. Well...what're we gonna do now?

"He was still for a while, his jaw working hard to mash down the chew he had just started. After three more splats on the beetle he had hit earlier he said, *Well, we need to swap idees with Yellow Boy, but I'm a thinkin' we oughta go after Bentene first and get Lil David back. He's the weakest of the three and oughta be the easiest to git. Then we need to try to pick off Stone and Tally separately if we can, even if it means ridin' up into Colorado or Wyoming. Shoot 'em from a mile away if we need to. Hell, I don't care. I ain't proud, as long as we get the bastards. Oliver Lee? He's different. People round here, they's loyal as dogs to him. He's a good man to have on yore side in any fight. He lives by a strict code. I ain't so shore he was responsible fer getting Stone and Tally to murder yore daddy. That there is something ye gotta decide for yore self. Just be shore yore right about him bein' guilty. If we kill him, this here whole countryside is gonna come after our tails.*

"I nodded I understood, but deep in my heart I knew I was gonna kill Oliver Lee. I was sure he had it coming. There was no doubt in my mind that he needed killing.

"Rufus reached over and grabbed my forearm and gave it a little squeeze for me to be quiet. We cocked our heads to one side, listening. Rufus cupped his left ear with his hand to hear better and pulled the hammer back to full-cock on his rifle with the other. I could feel my heart pounding and my breath coming in short quick puffs. Out in the cold moonlit darkness, a rock bounced down the trail, making an irregular clicking sound as it rolled from one stone to the next. We rose up in a squat and stretched our necks trying to see over the bushes and into the shadows. We waited, straining to hear the next sign, or to see the first motion of what was out there in the cold gloom of the moonlight.

*Que pasa?*

"Rufus and I jumped like we'd been jabbed with cactus thorns. There was Yellow Boy, squatting behind us like he'd been there all night. I laughed aloud and sagged back down in relief. Rufus was gagging and wheezing. He'd nearly swallowed the big wad of tobacco in his cheek.

"He managed to sputter as Yellow Boy squatted there, grinning at us, *Damn ye, Indian! Ye scared me clean into tomorry. How'd ye do that?*

"Yellow Boy swung his arm back toward Baylor Pass. *Many big rocks to springs. Easy walk. No sound. Make caballo walk down trail. Usted turn ojos to him. Bueno trick, huh? Plenty easy find you. Su hablar mucho. I hear. I come.*

"Rufus raised his brow wordlessly asking the dreaded question. Yellow Boy didn't need to hear him speak. *No fire on su casa. Water still good. Cattle still graze. Stone y Tally they come. No Bentene. Stone calls for you. Shoots many time en su casa. Glass in windows gone. Roof leak more now when rain comes. Tally laughs. Say Stone fool. Stone say he think usted y Hombrecito vamos a Mexico. He wait. He say usted come back. He kill you next time.*

*Well, boys, I reckon we got off lucky.* Rufus stood and spat all the way across the little stream of water. *Now all we gotta do is find 'em fore they find us. Let's git outta here and on down to the Jarillas 'fore the world wakes up.*

"Yellow Boy disappeared, but soon came back with his pony. Meanwhile Rufus and I loaded up Elmer and tightened saddle cinches on Sally and Midnight. Yellow Boy led the way, staying in the same formation we used riding up Baylor Pass. We traveled slow and quiet through the creosotes and mesquites, bypassing little groups of grazing cattle owned by the Cox ranch. The curious cattle watched us with their ears up listening. They seemed to wonder why these odd-looking cowhands were out in the desert on the far side of midnight. Once in a while, we saw the low red glow of a banked fire from ranch hands staying out to keep an eye on the stock. We got past the Cox ranch and breathed a sigh of relief, for it was unlikely we'd see any more cowhand camps or run into any other night riders. Finally Yellow Boy set his horse to a good canter and pointed straight for the middle of the Jarillas painted in stark shadows from the setting moon.

"We reached a little canyon in the Jarillas just before dawn. Yellow Boy often used it to rest and take cover on his travels back and forth from the reservation to the Sierra Madre, and we planned to hide and rest there for the day. Its entrance was hidden by mesquite and tall ocotillo with long cable like stems that sunk sharp thorns into you for every wrong move you made passing it. There was a thin trail only Yellow Boy's sharp eyes could pick out in the early morning gloom that wound through the thicket and into the canyon's entrance. Once through the mesquite and ocotillo, it was easy going for several hundred yards on a little winding trail down the center of the canyon. Near the end of the canyon, Yellow Boy showed us a large rock shelf that we could crawl under to get shelter from the mid-day sun.

"*Rufus y Hombrecito, usted rest aqui 'til el sol es aqui.* Yellow Boy pointed straight overhead. *Yo cuidado. I watch por riders from lookout. You watch until sol es no mas. I sleep, si?*

"Rufus spat and gave his head a quick nod of approval. Yellow Boy climbed up the canyon wall on a series of foot and handholds, leading back toward the mouth of the canyon. Rufus and I unloaded the stock, tied them where there would be shade, rubbed them down, and fed and watered them. We ate a little of the cold beans and meat Rufus brought from his last cook pot back at the shack.

"We had come a long way. I was sleepy and so sore in my crotch I could barely walk. It was just beginning to sink into my young brain what hard work this war for justice was going to be.

"As the sky in the east started to brighten and long shadows from the mountains began to form, Rufus found an old ocotillo stalk and swept under the ledge for snakes. Finding none, we spread a blanket, crawled up under it, and stretched out for some sleep. Rufus was snoring in minutes, but the night's excitement and the coming light kept me awake until I finally pulled a bandana over my eyes and passed out from exhaustion.

"Mid-morning sunlight was creeping down the canyon walls, driving the dark cool shadows away from where we rested, when I snapped awake, startled by the sound of distant bawling cattle and human voices. I raised up on an elbow and started to get up, but Rufus grabbed me by the arm and shook his head and said in a coarse whisper, *They's just some stock being driven by here; probably just headed fer the stockyards in Alamogordo. Nothin' to worry about. Go on back to sleep. We're fine until Yellow Boy tells us otherwise.*

"Rufus was snoring again in less than five minutes, but I had a hard time getting back to sleep. It was hot, and since it was the monsoon season, the humidity was high. Some insect kept biting me, raising little bloody whelps on my arms.

"I was slowly drifting back to sleep when I felt Yellow Boy gently tapping my foot with the barrel of his rifle. Rufus was already up and pulling on a canteen in long slow swallows that made his Adam's apple bob up and down like a fishing line float. I crawled out from under the ledge and had a long drink too. Yellow Boy put his finger to his lips to indicate we should be quiet. He showed us by pointing and using hand signs the handholds and foot notches up the side of the rust colored canyon wall and where to sit while on watch. Then he sat down, lay back, and instantly fell asleep. Rufus climbed up the handholds to the lookout where a mesquite bush had somehow precariously grown on a wide ledge and provided a little shade and perfect cover against being spotted by someone on the desert floor spread out below us. I scrambled up behind him to take my turn watching so he could nap if he wanted.

"The lookout spot was on a ledge about fifty feet up from the canyon floor; it gave good protected lines of sight everywhere on the west side of the Jarillas. The monsoon rains had changed the range from dull summer browns to a mottled patchwork of dark cedar green creosote bushes and delicate light green mesquite thickets on a carpet of turquoise-colored succulent grasses and weeds. Delicate little flowers in blues and purples, red poppies, and large white and yellow gourd flowers were blooming everywhere. I could see little wisps of smoke from some activity far away at the Cox ranch, its buildings against the Organs lost in the hazy distance. There were small groups of cattle scattered everywhere, filling their bellies with the new green grass. I could see the occasional cowboy far in the distance, trotting his horse down the cattle trails through the creosotes and mesquites. Sometimes only a hat or a horse's head were the only things visible until they broke into a small opening that provided a quick glimpse of the full man and his mount.

Rufus and I surveyed the countryside for a while, then, handing me his rifle, and pointing toward the middle of the sun's arch on its downside, Rufus said *Here Henry, ye watch till the sun is right there, then I'll relieve ya.* As I took the rifle, he pulled his beat-up old hat over his eyes and lay back in the shade. He was asleep again in short order. I wondered how he and Yellow Boy managed to sleep so soundly so fast in the heat and with the worry of discovery hanging over them. I wasn't a bit sleepy and my heart was pounding as I watched the range and tried to be careful not to miss anyone who might ride toward us. The rock where we sat had been absorbing sunlight all day and was hot to the touch. Although I was dressed like an Apache boy with high moccassins, a breech cloth, thin cotton shirt, and a head scarf to keep the sweat out of my eyes, sweat poured off me. I drank the canteen nearly dry. The discipline and self-control of Yellow Boy's training helped me endure the tedium and discomfort of being a lookout. Even so, I needed all my will power to keep from dozing off. Being a lookout was not a full-time job I thought I'd enjoy or want again. But, I realized it was all part of our need to not be detected, and it ensured we didn't have to endure someone questioning us with guns to our heads.

"I shook Rufus awake in the mid-afternoon. His eyes blinked open instantly, immediately alert. When I shook my head to his inquisitive look, he took the rifle, scratched his scraggly beard and yawned like a big tomcat just getting up from a nap. He motioned me back into the shade then crept up to the place just behind the bush where I'd sat and began surveying the scene. I laid back and swatted at insects trying to get to the sweat that bathed my face. I yawned once or twice in the soggy hot air then fell asleep. Rufus woke me up gently shaking my foot. The sun was nearly gone. A cool breeze floated down the canyon giving the evening a pleasant, easy feel.

"Getting down from the lookout was harder than getting up. Some of the foot and handholds were hard to find in the dark shadows filling the canyon. Yellow Boy had made a fire in a shallow pit while it was still light. He let the wood burn down to hot coals so its glow couldn't be seen after dark. He cooked us some fry bread and beans. All that remained of the fire when Rufus and I came in were a few hot coals, but they were enough to make coffee and keep the food hot. After being up on that lookout through the hot part of the day, I thought that meal had to be about the best I ever ate.

"Yellow Boy sat with us with his rifle between his legs while we ate. He said nothing as the sun slowly faded behind the San Andres and long shadows crept silently down the canyon walls. After Rufus and I gobbled down the beans and bread, we gave the tin plates a sand wash and began loading the gear on Elmer and saddling the horses and Sally. When we were ready to travel Rufus cut himself a chew and sat back to wait for full dark. Yellow Boy rolled himself a cigarette and lighted it in his cupped hands. The cool air made the heat from lingering fire coals feel good. We could hear doves calling as they settled in for the night. I lay back, resting my head on my hand, watching down the canyon.

"Yellow Boy said, *Esta mucho hombres between here and sharp mountains today, Rufus?*

Rufus nodded. *Yes, sir, seems like a right many more than I thought they'd be. They's more stock than I thought they'd be too. It looks like the range is really bein' pushed too far and too hard to support 'em fer long.*

*Ummph,* Yellow Boy grunted. *These little mountains aqui closer to Tally and Stone than place near Mescalero, pero place en Mescalero more better and safe than here. You think this is true, Rufus?*

"Rufus spat into the fire's coals, causing a little puff of steam to rise. *Yes, sir. I reckon that's about right. Do ye know a place we can hide and scout round from Mescalero, Señor Yellow Boy?* I was listening to them carefully and cupped an ear with my free hand to be sure I didn't miss any of their conversation.

*Si, know place. Good agua. Plenty wood. Soldier no find. No long time ride to Lincoln. Close to my woman. I sleep warm in the night. Good place, Rufus. Good place even if winter come and we still there.*

"Rufus spat on the glowing coals again and grinned. *Close to Lincoln, eh?*

"Yellow Boy grinned and nodded. I didn't understand the joke between them about Lincoln, but I grinned too. They just looked at me and laughed, sharing pleasure in the ignorance of my youth.

"*Well, can ye get us there tonight so we can burry in and get us some rest? Then tomorry night I'll take a little ride into Lincoln and see what I can find out from Mrs. Darcy. She oughter know the whereabouts of them fellers we're a lookin' fer.*

"*Si, vamos tonight. Be there by sol, if no rain.*

"I spoke up and said, Rufus, won't somebody see you in Lincoln and let Stone or Tally know where you are? For all we know they might even be there now. I thought we wanted to stay outta sight till we found 'em. I was sure what Rufus was planning would get us caught. I was beginning to worry that maybe he was getting too old to think straight and was going to get us all in trouble.

*Naw! I ain't gonna be seen crawling through Mrs. Darcy's bedroom winder in the middle of the night 'cept by Mrs. Darcy herself. Git my drift, son?*

"I nodded. Yes, sir, I think I do. Mrs. Darcy knows about everything that goes on in that town. She'll tell you what's goin' on for certain. That's good. Can I come with you?

"Rufus and Yellow Boy laughed again. *Naw, Henry. We need ye to stay and guard the camp. Yellow Boy's gonna spend time with his wife while I'm in Lincoln and I wouldn't want Mrs. Darcy blabbing it about that you're a still livin' if she recognized ye. Can ye guard the camp while we're out, uh, scoutin' around?* They both laughed again.

"I grinned and nodded. Sure I can. Just find out where those killers are and let's get 'em.

"Rufus spat in the dying coals again, got up and started kicking sand over the ashes. *Well, come on then. Let's haul ourselves on over to Mescalero so's I can rest up fer my ride to Lincoln tomorry night.*

It was full dark when we rode out of the canyon and across the northern end of the Jarillas by Monte Carlo Gap in the same formation we'd used the night before. Yellow Boy led us toward the edge of White Sands, but stayed back in the shadows of the bushes away from the Sands gleaming in the moonlight as the moon came up big and bright over the Sacramentos.

"We passed to the west of Alamogordo, tracking along the edge of White Sands. Yellow Boy turned northeast after we passed to the west of Tularosa. We rode along at a pretty steady pace, but stopped several times to rest the animals in the dark shadow side of big creosote bushes.

"Once past Tularosa, Yellow Boy rode up the right branch of Temporal Creek and into Dry Canyon. It was dark and scary down deep in that canyon with the moon casting tricky shadows as it sailed across the night sky. I felt safe enough knowing Rufus was behind me and Yellow Boy was in front. We followed along a thin little trail that climbed up out of Dry Canyon. The moon began to set and it was down-right scary looking off the trail back down into the dark pit from where we were climbing. When we topped Dry Canyon we rode across a gentle slope that paralleled Pete Gaines Canyon and was covered by a stand of juniper bushes among long fuzzy shadows of tall scattered pines.

"When Yellow Boy finally stopped I could see the first faint glow of dawn. We were above and within a mile of Jose Second Canyon. It was pitch black under those trees. Every clearing was filled with juniper bushes and covered with short, deep green grass that cattlemen often killed for. It was hard for me to imagine how anyone could find us, much less how we would find our way back out. Yellow Boy apparently knew the area well and easily led us to a thicket of large junipers in front of a small spring. A clear half-circle-shaped area lay in front of the spring, which dribbled out of a shelf of rocks and collected in a little pool before rolling down into Pete Gaines Canyon. Yellow Boy slid off his paint and motioned us to dismount. He led the paint over and let it drink long soothing draughts from the pool. Rufus came up with the other animals and we gave them all a good long drink. We had stopped three times to rest and water the stock, but, even so, we made good time and easily beat the sun's rise.

"In the receding gloom Yellow Boy swung his arm around the site and said, *Agua bueno, wood bueno, ground soft, plenty grass for horses and mules. Hard to find. Not far to woman, less than half day to Lincoln. Good place, Rufus?*

*Yore eye fer hideouts is as good as it is with that there rifle Yellow Boy. Good? Hell, it's perfect! Suit you, Henry?*

"I was cold and tired and the insides of my thighs were on fire. I doubted if I'd ever walk again. If my protectors thought it was good, it was fine with me. Yes, sir! I like it fine.

*Good! Boys, let's get the stock taken care of, make us a camp, cook a little breakfast, and get some rest. Don't reckon it's necessary fer lookouts in here, is they, Yellow Boy?*

*No lookouts por hombres. Horse and mule say when bear or cat come. Little fire keep away. Estamos muy bien.*

"Bear or cats! Fighting or running off one of those things was not my idea of a good time. But I wasn't about to say I was fearful to Rufus or to Yellow Boy. After all I'd been through at the hands of men, a bear or a cat was the least of my worries. We unloaded the stock, fed them some grain, and put hobbles on them. Rufus set up a little fireplace under a big pine tree a few yards from the spring so the smoke diffused before it could be seen. He made a little lean-to with a piece of tarp next to it so that we could cook and sleep when it rained and keep our gear dry and a fire going. Yellow Boy and I gathered in a pile of wood, careful not to leave any signs for wandering eyes.

"Sunlight was finding its way through the juniper and lighting up the morning mists floating through the tall pines when Rufus poured us each a cup of black coffee and we sat back to eat the last of his beans and tortillas. The air was cool, almost cold, and filled with the smell of pines. It was paradise, and, although I was having trouble keeping my eyes open, I wanted to dance a jig to celebrate our safe journey and for getting closer to the lair of the men we were after. Rufus and I washed up the pots and pans. Yellow Boy checked his weapons and sat and smoked. I don't think I ever saw him do any camp maintenance while we were there. It was just not proper for a warrior to do camp work.

"We all stretched out on our blankets to rest. I fell into the deepest sleep I can remember. Rufus woke me as the sun was starting to slide behind the mountains, casting long shadows from the peaks and hills. Yellow Boy was gone and Sally was saddled. After I came back from relieving myself, he handed me a cup of coffee and a hot plate of beans.

*Here ye go. Careful now, it's hot! I'm a gonna light out fer Lincoln now and visit Mrs. Darcy. Yellow Boy has gone down to visit his wife. Said he 'spects to be back sometime tonight. I got to take the rifle. The only thing ye gotta worry about til Yellow Boy gets back is cats and bears. I scouted around fer an hour and ain't seen no sign, so ye should be fine. If'n one shows up, remember they's afraid of fire, or ye can climb that tree where we got the supplies hung. Ye'll be all right, won't ye Henry?*

"He spoke with such concern, but with such obvious longing to be gone, I had to laugh. Sure, Rufus, I'll be fine. Yellow Boy will be back soon enough. I ain't afraid. You go on and see Mrs. Darcy. Find out what you can. How soon you reckon you'll be back?

"Rufus nodded, still a little concerned about me, but anxious to get down the trail to Lincoln. *Aw, I'd guess in a couple or three days. I'll put a bee in her bonnet about what we need to know and then wait a day or two while she sniffs around. Don't worry. I'll stay hid.* With that he swung up on Sally. I handed him the rifle and he was off through the juniper bushes and trees down into Pete Gaines Canyon to find the trail to Lincoln.

"I spent the rest of the daylight hours scouting around the area where we'd camped. I learned where hiding spots were, paths through the bushes that led into camp, and potential getaways down into the canyons or across the ridge back toward Tularosa. I felt free and easy, somehow released from a burden I'd felt for a long time. At last, we were going after Daddy's killers.

"The sun dropped behind Sierra Blanca and it was soon full dark. I stayed close to the fire, my only concern was that a bear or cat might attack me. In my wandering about the camp area, I found a nice straight aspen sapling near a tree that had been struck by lightning. The sapling was cooked from flames of the struck tree, and it was hard and smooth under the bark that fell off in my hands. It was about an inch and a half in diameter and nearly ten feet tall. I cut it, trimmed the blackened branches and twigs and carried it back to camp to make myself a spear.

"I had some supper and spent most of the evening smoothing and straightening my spear shaft, although it really didn't need much. I was hardening the point in the fire when Yellow Boy appeared in the fire's circle of light. I jumped up in surprise and relief. I never knew he was there until I looked up and saw him against the darkness of the piñons. You know, I've been around that old man for nearly sixty years and I have yet to figure out how he was so quiet when he moved.

"He grinned and motioned me down with his hand. *Rufus travels to Lincoln, si? Que es, Hombrecito? Make big spear with fire point?*

"I nodded feeling a little foolish. I knew I wasn't much of a weapons maker and I hadn't trimmed the length so it was still nearly ten feet long. I said, Yes, sir. Rufus is gone to Lincoln. He left with the sun. I'm trying to make a spear, but I don't think it'll be much of a weapon. I haven't trimmed the length yet and the center is soft. How long do you think I should cut it? What else do you think it needs?

"Yellow Boy looked it over carefully running his hands up and down the smooth wood. *Wood es muy bien, Hombrecito. Too long for you. Need point of iron to make hunting spear. Aqui, you stand straight.* I stood up. He held the shaft against my back and stretched to make a notch in it about two feet above my head. He handed it back to me and said, *Cut at notch. Smooth fired end. Length is right for you. I bring iron point and leather to bind in place mañana. You cut. I come back.* With that he disappeared in the darkness. I thought he had gone for the night, but he soon reappeared holding a short bow and a quiver full of arrows.

*You learn bow while Rufus gone. My people use the bow since before the grandfathers. It is good weapon. I make this one for you. Give sooner, but Rufus teach you Shoot Today Kill Tomorrow. I wait. Even Apache muchachos no use bow now. All want rifle. Army say no. They still no use bow. Now Shoot Today Kill Tomorrow taken by Bentene. We find. Take back. You use then. You learn bow now. I teach. You will be strong warrior, Hombrecito. Rufus and Yellow Boy will search for Shoot Today Kill Tomorrow. Kill Bentene. Take back. Take blood por Alberto Fountan su padre.*

"I nodded in gratitude without saying a word as he put the bow and quiver of arrows in my hands. It was a short recurved bow, no more than about four feet long, the kind used by horsemen. It was made of dark mesquite wood carved and scrapped smooth with the heartwood on the inside. It had been reinforced on the back with sinew. The handle was wrapped by a continuous cord of leather that gave it a steady grip even in a sweaty hand. I could pull it back to full draw and hold it for a few seconds before my arms started to fail me. It was a work of art and I wanted it as soon as I saw it. I still have it at home. I'll show it to you sometime.

"The arrows, made of cedar, were tipped with sharp iron points and fletched with wild turkey feathers. They were a little longer than my arm and when Yellow Boy showed me the balance point on one, all the other arrows balanced in almost exactly the same place on the shaft. The quiver was made of coyote hide because, as Yellow Boy said, *Coyote trickster. He quiet in hunt. He always finds game.*

"I was so thrilled I could only mumble as he lay these fine gifts in my hands. Muchas gracias, Señor Yellow Boy. Es muy bueno. I will make you proud. I will shoot a strong bow.

*Ummph, Hombrecito. It is not the bow that is your strength. It is the arrow. Find a good arrow. Shoot straight with any bow. You kill. These arrows good. I make. Mañana you begin.*

"Bueno. I will work hard to learn this new weapon. I put the bow and quiver of arrows by my blanket. Yellow Boy pulled a cigar from inside his cavalry jacket and lighted it with a twig. He lay back with his hands behind his head and stared up at the night sky, puffing contentedly. I came back to the fire and carefully cut the spear off where he had notched it. He showed me how to cut a long thin notch in the hardened end to hold the knife blade he would bring me for it. After a couple of hours of steady work and little wood chips and shaving scattered all over where I sat, I had finished the notch for the knife blade. Cobwebs started filling my brain. I put the spear shaft aside, told him good night, crawled under my blanket, and drifted off into a dreamless sleep.

"Early next morning, when the sun had just floated over the mountain tops and the shadows from the ridges had pulled away from our spot, the bow-shooting lessons began. At fifty yards, Yellow Boy could easily put all twenty of my arrows in a tree a foot in diameter. I was lucky to hit the forest, but he was patient and taught me how to balance the arrow, aim, and follow through. I soon learned accurate shooting was having the concentration to keep your eye on the target and to concentrate on form and follow through. We quit after a couple of hours. I was getting tight and tired in my back muscles and the tips of my draw fingers were nearly bloody from the horsehair string. As I got sore, my accuracy became worse.

"We sat by the fire for a while and had some coffee and bacon. The air was cool and birds sang in every bush and tree. Yellow Boy finished his coffee, handed me his cup, and went for his pony. He brushed him down while I cleaned up the frying pan and got a bucket of water from the spring.

"When I returned from the spring, he handed me a piece of buckskin that had an odd design laid out on it and said, *Cut leather. Follow line. Usted make shield for bow fingers. Fingers not understand string, must grow hard. You learn while fingers get hard. You shoot many times today. Get better. I go now. Quando sol es no mas, I return. Adios.*

"I saluted him as he disappeared through the junipers and down the little trail. I worked on the bow shooting nearly all day. My target was a big piece of elk hide strung between a couple of saplings. As I learned to focus on the elk hide, shutting out every distraction, the arrows clustered closer and closer to its center. When the light began to fade, I was shooting twenty arrows out of twenty into the elk hide at a range of fifty yards. My shoulders and arms ached, but the leather shooting patch I'd cut from the buckskin, using Yellow Boy's pattern for my fingers, saved the day.

"That evening, true to his word, Yellow Boy walked out of the darkness just as the moon began to rise. He had a rusty old butcher knife stuck in his gun belt. It was dagger-shaped and perfect for a spear point. It had a handle made of wood wrapped by a long buckskin cord. He handed it to me.

*Make sharp, polish blade smooth. Then we tie in notch you make.*
"Gracias, senor. I will. Esta bien en su casa?
"Yellow Boy grinned and nodded. *Muy bien. Juanita es mujer buena.*

"I spent over an hour sharpening and polishing the blade on a piece of stone until it looked practically new while Yellow Boy sat and smoked by the fire. When I finally showed it to him, he inspected it carefully. Taking his knife, he cut the buckskin cord around the handle and unwrapped it letting the wood handles on each side fall off. He motioned me to bring him the spear shaft. He fit the blade into the notch I'd cut. The notch was about an inch shorter than the handle, but it seemed to me there was plenty left with which to tie it and still have a first-class spear.

*Cut notch long as knife handle. Then we mount, Hombrecito.*

"I raised my eyebrows in question. He understood immediately. *Blade and shaft must be as one. You make weak weapon, you die. Build strong. Build right. Live long. Comprendé?* He shook his fist to show strength. I nodded and worked for a while to get the notch the right length. After I lengthened the notch, and he was satisfied the knife fit in the notch correctly, he dug a small bag of powder out of his saddle bag and mixed some with boiling coffee in a rock depression. He stirred it constantly. The mixture soon turned thick and gooey. He spread it on the wood in the shaft slot, then spread some on the bare knife handle, and slid the pieces together. He wrapped a thin piece of buckskin around the shaft slot, and holding the knife blade in place, used the cord off the handle and more of the goo to wrap the cord tightly around the buckskin then tied it off.

"Yellow Boy found the balance point in our spear and decided it was too far forward for good throwing. He cut a small marker notch where he thought the balance point should be and handed the spear back to me. *Cut grande blood drain lines on four sides. Cut each same. Fly straighter when you throw.*

"I cut some zigzagged lines along the shaft from the point so blood would flow more easily out of a wound. I handed it back to him. He determined the balance point and said, *Cut a little deeper.* We repeated this process several times. Each time I handed it back to him, the balance point moved closer to his mark. Finally, he hefted it, found the balance point and said, *Bueno. Mañana you learn spear.*

"For the next three days, I was instructed by a master in the use of primitive weapons. Yellow Boy was patient. He knew many tricks in the use of the bow and spear. As I learned to thrust, parry, and throw the spear, and as the circle of my arrows grew smaller, I began to feel more confident I could survive anywhere.

"Yellow Boy started me running again. At midday, every day, I ran up a path through the tall trees toward the peak of the mighty mountain, Sierra Blanca, and back down again. We were above five thousand feet and the air was thin. It was harder to breathe than when running behind Tortugas Mountain, but the air was cool and fresh. The running was exhilarating. Yellow Boy cautioned me to run quietly and be aware of my surroundings. Bears were there and men might be nearby.

"Five days passed then six. Rufus had not returned. I was worried and so was Yellow Boy."

$14$

# FINDING LITTLE DAVID

As the night drifted toward morning light Henry and Roberta moved from sitting on the straight-backed chairs to a spot on the floor near the fire. She put pillows behind their backs and they leaned against the wall. Henry stretched his legs out in front of him and held Roberta's strong, comforting hand as he continued his story. Gray light began to fill the windows as the dark dawn began to give way to sunlight slowly burning over the Sacramentos. The old man still rested easy, but Henry, feeling the pinch of old age in his nether regions, excused himself and stepped outside. Wisps of fog, like pools of water, collected in the low places up and down the canyon. The gray morning air, thick and still as he stepped briskly down the path to the little outhouse, made his bones creak and his muscles tighten. The cold air awoke his body and made his mind whir with memories long forgotten, memories that he needed, now, for Roberta.

A fresh pot of coffee was percolating over the fire when he returned. Roberta sat in their spot with her legs crossed, the hem of her nurse's uniform pulled modestly below her knees. Having pulled the pins from her hair, she was running a comb down the long black tresses, making them radiant in the firelight. Kneeling next to his old friend, Henry listened to Yellow Boy's chest again and was satisfied. The oxygen mask was helping him breathe and the penicillin finally appeared to be winning against the infection. Henry wasn't sure how long he ought to keep the oxygen mask on him, or even if it worked as well as other respirators he had seen and used in the hospital in El Paso. He left it in place since it seemed to do no harm. Checking Yellow Boy's pulse, Henry found it strong and regular, another encouraging sign.

Roberta rubbed some Jergen's lotion on her hands and face, finishing her toilette. "Henry, can I get you some fresh coffee? I'm having a cup."

212

Putting his stethoscope back in his black bag, he scratched at the stubble on his face, and looked at his watch. It was nearly five. He probably should get John and Sara up in another hour, and then he and Roberta might catch five or six hours of sleep to be ready for any afternoon emergencies. He nodded. "Sure. We'll get John and Sara up in an hour or so, then we can get some rest."

She rinsed out the cups they had used earlier in the evening and filled them. The old blue-and-white speckled pot was so hot she had to hold its handle with a dish towel. She handed Henry a cup, holding the rim with her fingers so he could take it by the handle. "Please excuse my delicate manners señor, but it's too hot to hold anywhere else except the handle. Why don't you put a blanket on the floor and lie down? You can put your head on my lap while you tell me the rest of your story."

The dry wash of wrinkles around Henry's eyes crinkled as he looked at her over the rim of his cup and took a sip. He smacked his lips and gave a little sigh. "If it were just us two here I wouldn't hesitate to do just that. But Sara is the biggest gossip on the reservation. If she got up and saw us cuddled up with my head on your lap, by the time we got back to Las Cruces, the story would be all over the reservation that we had been fornicating next to my dying friend's bed. Will you give me a rain check until we have some time alone?"

Roberta smiled. "Of course. I know you're right about Sara. Just promise you won't change your mind after we leave. There is a real yearning in my heart to be close to you, Henry Grace."

Henry nodded as he stepped toward his space on the floor beside her. "That's a bona fide, señorita. My heart desires to be with you more than I've wanted to be with any woman in a long, long time." He slid down beside her. "How could we have passed through twenty years together and not become more than good friends? The mysteries of the human heart will never be understood, will they?"

She took a sip, careful not to burn her lips, then sat the cup aside to cool as she straightened the pillow against his back. Smiling, she said close to his ear, "We've been more than friends for a long time. You just weren't conscious of it. So tell me, did Rufus make it back to camp? Was he just slow getting back because Mrs. Darcy's bed was warm and she was giving him some much needed comfort?"

Henry looked at Roberta and smiled his possum-eating-yellow-jackets grin. "Well, now that you mention it, I learned a few years later that she gave him more comfort than he could just about stand. They were lovers, but very discrete. With her boarding house business, there couldn't be any hint that she and an old desert rat were more than just employer and employee. There would have been ladies of the evening wanting to set up business in her house and every old coot lined up outside her door thinking he could get in her...good graces if word had leaked out that Rufus was in her bed. And, no doubt, the Ladies' Auxillary of Lincoln would have made her an outcast. So Rufus, not wanting to be seen himself, was very conscious of the need not to be seen at her house unless he went in the front door like all her other guests.

"He was still gone after eight days, and it was hard to do anything except worry about him. I was sure something bad had happened to him. I thought maybe Stone or Tally had murdered him like they had Daddy. Maybe Sally had stumbled and thrown him or rolled over on him, breaking bones or killing him. Maybe he had been snake bit, or a cat or a bear had killed and dragged him off. When I broached these ideas to Yellow Boy, he just shook his head and said, *No! Rufus es bueno. He comes back soon, Hombrecito.* But I could tell he was trying to decide what to do about finding him.

"On the night of the eighth day, I lay down to sleep in a black despair. I was certain Stone or Tally had killed Rufus, while they were trying to find me. Rufus, like my daddy, must have disappeared into some canyon crevice or be under some cairn we'd never find. Now I had two murders to avenge, and I had no idea how to go about it. I twisted around in my blanket trying to figure out what to do next. The coals from the fire and a nearly gone quarter moon were the only light. It was darker than my worst nightmares.

"I felt Yellow Boy squeeze my arm, his face close to mine. He put fingers to his lips for me to be quiet, and sat up on his blanket. He cupped a hand to his ear. I strained to hear anything for a couple of minutes, then I heard the steady breathing and push of bushes as some animal moved toward us. My heart was pounding. There must be a bear coming for us. I slowly picked up my spear and held it tight with both hands, pointing it toward the faint sounds as they got louder and moved toward us. I heard Yellow Boy cock the Henry and saw him looking in the same direction. I moved up on my knees and waited. Yellow Boy was on one knee, in a crouch, with his rifle sighted toward the marauder. The sounds drew closer and stopped. My heart pounded harder. Whatever it was, it was sizing us up. Yellow Boy had taught me how to use that spear and I was ready! He was the best shot in the country. Let it come. Then we heard, *Now where in the hell did I leave that boy?*

"Rufus! I don't have to tell you how overjoyed and relieved I was.

"Yellow Boy said, *Aqui Rufus!*

"I put the spear down and started to put wood on the fire, but Yellow Boy grabbed me by the shirt tail and shook his head. We didn't know if Rufus was alone. We waited.

*Don't kill me, boys, I'm a comin' in.* Yellow Boy nodded at me and I started adding wood to the coals. In the time it took for a nice flame to grow, Sally's long mule face moved into the light and there sat Rufus, big as you please, with his rifle across the pommel of his saddle.

"*Howdy, ladies! Did ya miss me?* He tossed me the rifle and swung down from Sally. I saw Yellow Boy give a quick nod and move toward the fire. I yelled, Rufus! You're all right! I thought you must be killed. I ran up to him to hug him, but he stuck out his old gnarled hand, so we just shook hands like grown men. He wasn't about to let me act like a little boy anymore.

"Where were you? I shouted. We were…I was scared Stone or Tally and their crowd had caught you and made you disappear like Daddy!

"Rufus casually waved his hand down toward the ground. *Just relax, Henry, everthang's fine. Fact is, it couldn't be better. Unsaddle Sally and brush her down fer a tired old man, will ye? I'll have a little coffee, then tell y'all about my little trip. We's gonna have to move fast to take ker of business.*

"He glanced down at my sleeping blankets and saw the spear. *Great day in the morning, Henry! Where'd you get that sticker? That there would make any Apache or Commanche proud! You know how to use it?* He looked over at Yellow Boy and winked. Yellow Boy nodded and grunted.

"I led Sally up to the spring pool for a drink before I pulled the saddle and began rubbing her down. I called back over my shoulder, *I found the shaft and straightened it up like you showed me. Yellow Boy found me the point, it's from an old butcher knife he had and he showed me how to attach it. He's been teaching me how to use it too.* Rufus nodded, clasp forearms with Yellow Boy and wearily sat down by the fire.

"It wasn't long before we were all sitting around the fire having coffee. Rufus had pulled off his old miner's boots and was wiggling his toes next to the flames to get the blood circulating. He pulled out a briar pipe and a tobacco pouch I hadn't seen before and made himself a smoke while Yellow Boy and I leaned forward, waiting to hear his story.

*This here pipe and tobac is a present from Mrs. Darcy. Seems some drummer left 'em at her place when he was passing through. She didn't have any idee where to send 'em so she just give 'em to me. Said she'd rather kiss me if I smoked than if I chewed. Still got my chewing tobac fer working though. Guess chewin's jest too nasty fer her.* I thought, Why would he kiss Mrs. Darcy? Only married people do that?

*Well, boys, I got to Mrs. Darcy's 'bout midnight the day I left. It's dark down in those canyons and slow goin', let me tell ye. But I got there without a gittin' killed. Old Sally must have eyes like a cat. I woke up Mrs. Darcy by a scratching on her winder screen. Guess I's lucky she didn't plug me when she stuck her dead husband's big dragoon pistol under my nose and nearly dropped it when she saw who I was. Well, sir, she let me crawl in and visit with her. We musta spent several hours a...talkin'. Told her I needed to know the whereabouts of Bentene, Stone, and Tally, and that I didn't want 'em to know I was a lookin' fer 'em. She told me the last she'd heard, Tally was a whorin' and raisin' hell in El Paso. She'd overheard some of Stone's cowboys talkin' about how Tally planned to winter and hunt with Stone. Stone's expectin' him to keep an eye out fer cattle thieves next month or two as they pull another herd together fer the Army. She was shore somebody had mentioned just last week that they thought Stone was down to Ft. Bliss with Cox trying to haggle a new beef contract with the Army fer Bliss and Selden. He's supposed to catch the train up from El Paso to Alamogordo and meet the ranchers he's a representin' fer the contract four days from now. She understands he'll tell 'em the terms of the contract with the Army and git 'em started a gatherin' the herd. I tell you boys, that woman is one pure fountain of knowledge.*

*I asked her about Bentene and she just laughed. Said two days 'fore I showed up ol' Bentene come into town with some of his hands to get supplies and hang around 'til Stone come back to Alamogordo. He had a bottle or two while they's a killin' time there in Lincoln. Damned if the night 'fore I scratched on her screen, Bentene didn't git juiced up and take a little target practice on the post office sign and the winders of a saloon. The deputy threw him in jail and kept him all night and most of the next day. He finally let ol' Bentene out and told him he'd better not catch him in Lincoln when the sun was down or he'd put him in irons, trot him down to Las Cruces, and let him deal with the sheriff down there. Ole Bentene said he was right sorry fer shootin' up the place and he'd just camp outside of town with his men and come in sober durin' the daylight until he was ready to ride down to Alamogordo. Deputy said that was fine. So ol' Bentene, rather than sleeping in a nice comfortable house like Mrs. Darcy's, is a sleeping on the ground and steering clear of that deputy. Guess where ole Bentene's a sleepin', right now, this minute?*

"I didn't have any idea and just shook my head.

*Remember that there little canyon two or three mile out from this side of Lincoln where ye, yore Daddy, and me went a target shootin' one Sunday? You remember the Bonito River run through it. Well, he's a right there! Big as you please. He stays about half drunk most of the time. His boys, they's in Lincoln right now blowin' their pay on whiskey, cards, and whores and jest havin' a good time! But ol' Bentene - he'll git outta his blankets when the sun comes up in the mornin', go to Lincoln to eat, maybe visit a whore, or play cards mosta the day, then buy another bottle and ride back to camp with his cowhands that's too broke to sleep with a whore. He always comes back to his camp 'fore dark, studies some kind of map while he drinks a while, then passes out. His men gits up way fore he does and rides into town to eat and swap lies in the saloon. He's just like a watch. I know 'cause I've been a watchin' him fer the last three days. He's supposed to leave fer Alamogordo tomorry, and meet up with Stone and Cox in a couple or three days.*

*You know what else? He's got Lil David in his camp gear! Yes, sir! He shore does! I seen it!* Rufus was practically shouting with excitement when he told us this last piece of news.

*I think we oughta go over there tonight, git my rifle back, and settle accounts fer yore Daddy. That's what I think. Ain't gonna be no better time. What'd you fellers –* Yellow Boy, his mouth set in a straight line and eyes narrowed to fine slits was up and moving toward the stock. *Where you goin' Yellow Boy?*

*Get pony. Ride. Vamos now, es still dark when we find Bentene!*

*Well, what'd you think, Henry?* I just nodded and shook my spear; my grip was so tight I was grinding wood grain into my hand. *Reckon that answers that question. Let's go then.*

"I saddled Midnight for myself and Elmer for Rufus. He thought he needed a fresh mount if we were to get to Bentene before sunrise. We moved out through the juniper and down the trail into Pete Gaines Canyon a quarter of an hour later. Yellow Boy led the way. He knew a faster, but rougher trail than the one Rufus had taken to Lincoln. We stayed close together and rode as fast as we dared along the dark trails. I was glad I was on Midnight. She was surefooted and seemed to anticipate every move Yellow Boy's pony made as we crossed running creeks that were usually dry and moved over rocky ridges and up and down steep passes into and out of canyons.

"I wasn't good enough yet to use the bow as a weapon so I took the spear. As we rode, I began thinking about what we'd do when we found

Bentene. I wanted to kill him. He was part of the group that murdered Daddy. Yet, it just somehow didn't seem right to kill him in his sleep. Maybe Rufus should put a gun under Bentene's nose and swear at him for keeping Lil David and beating him with his pistol? Didn't we want to give him a chance to defend himself before we killed him? Didn't he need to know why I was gonna run my spear through him? Was it justice if we just rode up and killed him? Wouldn't we be as bad as him if we did? Shouldn't we turn him over to the sheriff or some other law officer?

"I imagined running up to him when we got there. Rufus and Yellow Boy would be hiding in the brush, covering me. Bentene would have this surprised snarl on his lips and freeze in disbelief as I told him who I was. He'd reach for his revolver and I'd stick him in the guts with my spear then Rufus and Yellow Boy would shoot him before he could get his gun out of his holster. I'd make a speech to him about how justice always gets you. Then he'd die there with my spear in his guts and blood running out of his bullet wounds. After that we'd ride off to get Stone and Tally. I even made up a speech or two in my head that I'd give to Bentene as he was dying, about how he was paying the price for killing Daddy and how we were going to get Stone and Tally too.

"The stars were disappearing and it was the deep black just before dawn when Yellow Boy dismounted and motioned for us to do the same on a high ridge next to a spring trickling out of a little collecting pool. He signed for us to be quiet. We fed and watered the horses and Elmer, tied them for a quick getaway, then carefully worked our way down toward the bottom of the valley below us. When we got to the bottom, Yellow Boy stopped, kneeled by some juniper bushes, and pointed toward a dark mass of trees to our right. I heard Rufus say under his breath, *I'll be damned.* There was a rutted road not fifty feet in front of us and the mass of trees were not more than two hundred yards beyond and below it. As we squatted there, it began to dawn on me that we were directly across from the little canyon where Rufus, Daddy and I had been shooting on that Sunday so long ago.

"I heard some faint noises down in the trees. It sounded like horses or cattle moving around. Then the faint tinkle of steel cinch rings knocking together and leather being slapped. The low red glow from a small fire began to grow down in the trees and I heard occasional grunts and curses as Bentene's camp began to stir. I heard the distinctive clicks as Yellow Boy and Rufus half-cocked their rifles to safety. The grip on my spear tightened and my heart began to pound. The sky was just getting gray when a cowboy rode up out of the trees and on to the road, his horse kicking up little puffs of dust as he cantered toward Lincoln. Two others soon caught up with him. We waited another half hour as the day became steadily brighter, but there were no more sounds from across the road.

"Yellow Boy rose in a half-crouch and motioned for Rufus and me to follow. He was hard to see in the dark as he moved from juniper to juniper, then across the road. Birds began to call from the bushes as it got lighter. When we were across the road and well into the trees, it was easy to see a bright flickering glow from the fire, but we heard nothing. We crept closer, a hundred yards, seventy-five, fifty. Yellow Boy stopped, kneeled on one knee in a clump of grass, and motioned us to stop. Rufus was about five yards to his left and I was just to the left of Rufus. A nice fire was burning under a big cottonwood tree. We could see empty bedrolls laid out around the fire and a black coffee pot sitting on a flat rock next to it. There was one horse tied to a picket rope. I saw the blanket from one of the bedrolls fly up and a dark figure stagger upright. He stretched, yawning, and scratched himself in the firelight. Bentene!

"I felt my heart thumping in my chest and my grip on the spear got tighter. It was hard to get my breath. Then I remembered what Rufus had told me about being cold and calculating and tried to force myself to be that way. I wondered how Yellow Boy and Rufus were going to get the drop on him so I could give him my best speech about Daddy before we killed him.

"Bentene reached down for his hat, turned away from the fire, and staggered a couple of steps before he hiked a leg and let a tremendous fart, followed by a drowsy giggle. He wandered into the dark shadows cast by the rapidly increasing light, and, in a couple of minutes, we heard water splashing. I heard Yellow Boy bring the Henry to full cock, but in that gray light I never saw him move, or even his chest rise and fall. He stared toward Bentene like some hunting wolf waiting to pounce on a rabbit. Rufus was a statue too. When I heard Bentene peeing I felt a tremendous need to do the same myself, but gritted my teeth and waited.

"Soon Bentene reappeared back in the firelight. He picked up his blanket and threw it over his shoulders. He yawned mightily, stretched again, and moved up against the big cottonwood. Easing himself down against it and stretching his legs out, he yawned again. He pulled the blanket over his shoulders, then his hat over his eyes so the edge of the hatband lay just over the bridge of his big hook nose and would block any light after the sun was up. He didn't move for a couple of minutes. Then I heard a little snore.

"I was ready to move closer and looked toward Yellow Boy for some sign to creep forward. He didn't move. He continued to stare at Bentene in the flickering yellow and red light of the fire and the receding gloom from the steadily brightening dawn. The Henry came up to Yellow Boy's shoulder in one smooth motion. I could see the reflection of the fire in the brass receiver. He sighted down the barrel for an instant before pulling the trigger. The bright flash from the end of the barrel momentarily blinded me and its thunder echoed up and down the little canyon, making my ears ring. Yellow Boy was up and running toward the fire through the smoke of his shot, levering a new round into the chamber, keeping the stock against his shoulder, sweeping the area around the fire for anyone we had missed as he ran.

"Rufus paused for half a heartbeat staring toward the camp for any movement. Then, he too was running toward the fire, crouched over his rifle, ready to shoot if anything moved. I was frozen in place. I just couldn't move. It was like a dream. I could see every move they made. It was like everything they did had been slowed down. The ringing in my ears disappeared and my eyes gradually adapted back to the gray dawn light. I realized I was being left behind as Yellow Boy and Rufus ran toward the fire. I started running too, crouched over my spear like Rufus was over his rifle. Yellow Boy jumped the fire and stood waiting with his rifle still shouldered as he stared at Bentene not six feet from him. In a few moments the Henry came off his shoulder and his knife flashed in his hand.

"Rufus said in a hot whisper, *No! If you cut him, they'll think it was an Indian that done it and there'll be trouble at Mescalero. Let him be. That there was too good a shot fer 'em to believe an Indian did it anyhow. They'll never guess an Apache done it. Help me find Lil David, then let's git 'fore anybody else shows.*

"Yellow Boy nodded and slid the knife back in its sheath. He started poking around the bedrolls with the barrel of the Henry. I ran up breathing hard and stopped to stare at Bentene. He looked as though he was still sleeping except there was a greasy looking, perfectly round hole in the hat's headband where it crossed the bridge of his nose. I could see the firelight reflecting off dark liquid running down the bark of the tree and there was a strong smell of fresh feces. I suddenly felt sick and wanted to vomit. This wasn't at all the way I'd imagined it would be. Yellow Boy murdered Bentene just like Tally had killed Daddy.

"Rufus walked up beside me and put his hand on my shoulder. *That there is justice. Take a good look at it. Just the way it oughta be, swift and clean. No jawin' about nothin'. You ride with somebody that does a killin' you're just as guilty. You're gonna die fer murder too. Only thing wrong with this way is that the son-of-a-bitch never felt a damn thing. He just ain't livin' no more. The bastard didn't suffer like yore daddy.* Rufus turned and spit in the fire. *The damned son-of-a-bitch. I hope he's a burnin' in hell right now.*

"I nodded I understood while I swallowed several times to keep from vomiting. Rufus, what's that smell?

*Nothin' unusual son. That there is the smell of death. Man dies like that, his bowels usually turn loose, and they's blood and brains blowed against the bark on that cottonwood. Come on now. Let's find Lil David and git fore some early riser comes down the road.*

"Just as we turned to look for Little David, Yellow Boy said, *Here! Here is Shoot Today Kill Tomorrow!* He held up a beautifully finished saddle scabbard with the Sharps pulled halfway out of it and handed it to Rufus.

"Rufus grinned with delight. *Got him! I shore am glad to have ye back, Lil David!* He pulled the rifle out of the scabbard and admired it like some men admire a beautiful woman. He wasted no time shoving the Sharps back deep into the scabbard. *Yes sir, welcome back. Now let's git.*

"Yellow Boy motioned us back up the ridge. *Usted y Hombrecito vamos. I wipe tracks. We ride muy pronto.*

"Rufus and I ran crouched over so we'd be harder to see in the fast coming morning light. Yellow Boy took some twigs from the firewood and lightly brushed away any tracks as he backed up, moving toward the road. Rufus and I tried to step on big rocks as we moved up the ridge toward the trees where we'd tied the horses and Elmer. Yellow Boy took his time and did a thorough job on our tracks. No tracker would be aware we were there unless they found where we had tied our animals, and that wasn't likely. We were saddled and heading down the backside of the ridge as the sun rose over the mountains, and the shadows began falling away from the canyons.

"We spread out like we usually did when we traveled and stayed down in the canyons, using the wet-season streams in the rocky creek beds to hide our tracks. Yellow Boy moved much slower than he had during the night, stopping often to listen for other riders, but we heard and saw no one.

"We were back in our camp on the ridges of the Sierra Blanca by mid-afternoon. I was so tired and emotionally drained I was ready to fall off Midnight. Yellow Boy and Rufus didn't move too fast either.

We took care of the stock and ate. Yellow Boy and Rufus had a smoke, but I laid down and fell into a deep sleep. I dreamed about Daddy being murdered again and seeing Bentene just sitting on his horse, watching him die. In my dream I was standing in front of Bentene on a big stage in front of hundreds of people. His hands were tied and they all knew he had been sentenced to die. I gave him one of the speeches I'd made up when we rode over to Lincoln to kill him, then a deputy handed me my spear and I jabbed him with it, right in the throat. His blood flew everywhere, especially all over me. I wanted to yell obscenities at him but his blood got in my mouth and started choking me. I kept trying to yell but couldn't. Bentene's blood kept pumping out of his jugular drowning me.

"Rufus shook me a wake. *Henry! Henry! Wakeup son! Ye're just having a bad dream!* I left my nightmare startled and thirsty. It was dark and the stars were out. Rufus was chewing and Yellow Boy still smoking, as they sat by the fire talking about how to get to Stone and Tally. I went to the latrine bush and relieved myself, got a drink from the spring, and walked back to the fire. The cool night air jolted me out of my sleepy fog. When I sat down, Yellow Boy smoked and Rufus chewed and spat in silence. They were apparently finished with their plan.

"Yawning a couple of times, I poured some coffee and sat down between Yellow Boy and Rufus.

*You having a bad dream, Henry?*

"I felt empty and hollow inside. I didn't feel like I thought I would after catching one of Daddy's killers. Yes, sir, I said. I guess I was. I told them about my dream.

"Rufus nodded, wiggling his nose to pull his glasses up closer to his eyes. *Well, you ain't got to worry about Bentene no more. We took care of that son-of-a bitch this mornin'. We got Lil David back too. Even have a day to renew acquaintances with him 'fore we head down to Alamogordo to take care of Stone and Tally.* He spat a long brown stream into the fire, sending sparks up into the trees as he winked at me.

"I nodded and grinned. I enjoyed shooting that old Sharps even if it was hard to hold steady and had a good kick. I turned to Yellow Boy. Can I ask you question?

"He was stretched out, looking up through the edge of the tree at the stars and contentedly puffing a cigar. *Hmmmm. Que es, Hombre-cito. I will answer.*

"I'm glad Bentene is dead. He deserved to die. But, why did you just shoot him between the eyes? He never knew what hit him or why he was dying. He didn't have time to think about what he'd done. He never knew who killed him. Shouldn't we have told him? Maybe even turned him into the law? I mean, we killed him like they killed Daddy, except his dying was a lot faster than Daddy's. He didn't even suffer. Shouldn't he have suffered? Was there any honor in killing him that way?

"Yellow Boy said nothing for a while. He just puffed on that cigar and watched the stars. Finally he said, *You ask many questions, Hombrecito. Pero, yo hablo usted answers.*

*Si, Bentene die quick. Not know who kill or why. Die easy. Bentene was weak man. He cannot die like a warrior. I no honor him so he no suffer. You are my blood. You think this?* He held up his palm and showed the scar left by the knife when I became his blood. I held up my hand to show my scar and nodded. *Yes, sir, I am your blood.*

"*Usted son hombre in heart, usted warrior in heart, pero usted have mucho to learn before killing men who murder su padre. I take your part, I kill. I help you kill. This I must do. It is the way of my people. Man must die who takes life from my family. This I do as your blood. Comprendé?*

"I nodded. I'd never thought of dying slow as an honor. If it was, then Bentene died as he should have, alive one second, dead the next.

*Palaver con hombre before he die gives nada. Bentene is gone. Bother you no mas. Kill men in desert, no mas. Lay with woman, no mas. Drink burning water, no mas. See sol nuevo, no mas. It is enough por Bentene. It is what he deserved. It is justice. I speak no more of this dead man. Comprendé?*

"Rufus sat and nodded at what Yellow Boy was saying. He put two fingers to his lips and moved them away in a wave as he said, *Yellow Boy speaks well, speaks true.*

"I nodded. *Si, comprendo. Muchas gracias por mi protection ye su counsel. What will we do about Stone and Tally?*

"Before Yellow Boy could answer, Rufus spoke up. *Here's the plan. We'll sleep tonight and spend first thing tomorry gittin' ready. Then we'll ride across the reservation using a trail 'round by Cloud-croft and over to the Eyebrow Trail that leads down into Dog Canyon. Dog Canyon's where ol' Frenchy Rochas used to live 'til he was murdered back in the winter of '95. Ain't nobody much been back in there since. Yellow Boy and his people know it well. They used to sucker their enemies into chasing 'em up the Eyebrow, then roll rocks down on 'em to knock 'em off the trail and hear 'em yelling all the way down. Must be a two-thousand-foot drop. I reckin that there trail climbs up nearly three or four thousand foot. They's real good water there in the canyon and plenty of places to set us up a ambush with good close lines of fire.*

*I figure Stone knows Bentene's been shot by now and is startin' to sweat a little, what with the long-range bullet ye put through his hat and all. It coulda been anybody killed Bentene. Stone probably thinks we lit out fer Mexico cause we was gone when he come to git us, so it ain't us he's a got to be worried about. He may come down to Alamogordo a day earlier than he's supposed to 'cause he wants to sniff around and try findin' out who mighta killed Bentene. Or maybe he'll think he ain't got a prayer a findin' out who did it, or maybe he jest don't give a damn and come the next day when he planned.*

*In any case, when he steps off that train in Alamogordo, we're a gonna make sure he sees us. We'll just ride along the road outta town like we didn't have a care in the world. He'll send somebody to follow us and find out where our camp is 'til he and Tally can come after us. We'll ride back to Dog Canyon, which ain't but maybe a hour or two's ride from Alamogordo, and set us a little surprise party fer 'em. If we can't kill 'em and help comes then we'll ride up the Eyebrow and hope they follow. If they do we'll take care of 'em just like the Mescaleros used to wipe out the cavalry that chased 'em. If they don't follow us, then we'll just have to wait to catch 'em again. It might be a long wait too, Henry. I spect we'll have to hide out with Yellow Boy's people down to Mexico fer awhile. Now, ol' Yellow Boy's gonna cover us from off the road when we ride back to Dog Canyon from Alamogordo, just to be shore those murderin' bastards don't try to kill us fore we can set up our trap. Course if they make it to Frenchy's shack when we bushwhack 'em, it could be a long standoff, but I think it's a risk worth takin'. What'd ye think, Henry?*

"Rufus, you mean I'm gonna get another chance to drop Stone and Tally with Little David?

*Yes, sir, that's just what I'm a tellin' ya. We need yore fire power with that big gun. You just might drop Stone the second time around. I'm also tellin' ya, they's no shore thing when it comes to killin'. We might be the ones gits kilt.*

"My eyes got a little watery. I don't care. Just so I get another chance at Stone and Tally.

"Rufus looked over at Yellow Boy who just nodded and puffed his cigar.

*Good. Looks like yore 'bout three or four days from havin' some long-delayed justice fer yore daddy.*

"I'm counting on it.

"Rufus served up some chilies, beans, and tortillas for supper. I ate and listened while he and Yellow Boy discussed what to do if we had to high-tail it out of Dog Canyon and head for Mexico. When I was full, I lay back down and instantly went to sleep again while they were still talking.

"Next morning, after eating and cleanup chores, Rufus tossed me the scabbard with Lil David. *How 'bout checkin' him out and cleaning him up, Henry?*

"I was thrilled to hold the weapon again. It was like finding a long-lost treasure, which I guess it was. I checked it over. It was in good shape. I don't think Stone or Bentene had even fired it. The saddle scabbard Bentene had it in was like something professional big-game hunters might use, even today. Oversized, bigger and longer than the gun, it was a light mahogany color and had pockets on the side for cartridges and cleaning gear. I sighted down the barrel and dry fired it a couple of times, dropping the breech each time. I decided they hadn't moved the set trigger screw either; the hammer fell with just the right amount of pull on the trigger.

"Giving it back to Rufus, I said, I don't think they ever fired it. It's clean and the trigger pull is still the same.

*Hmmph.* He grunted. *Well, Henry, this here '73 Winchester works just fine fer me. Why don't ye take Lil David and use it on this here hunt, unless I need to swap with ye?*

"Rufus laughed at the expression on my face. It was one of surprise and pure joy. Yes, sir! I said with a big smile, every tooth showing. I put it with the things Rufus wanted me to carry on Midnight.

"Where's Yellow Boy? I asked. He was nowhere to be seen.

"*Aw, he rode down to Mescalero to visit his wife fer a while. He'll be back later today 'fore we're ready to go. Here, come help me slice up this haunch of venison and get these here supplies ready to go.*

"We worked through the morning. Everything was set to travel by mid-afternoon.

"When Rufus gave me two hundred rounds to carry for Lil David I said, Two hundred rounds! Rufus looks like we're goin' to war!

"He looked back at me with just a crack of a smile and said, *Yes sir, we are! Here, maybe ye'd better take another hundred rounds now that I think about it.* I took the extra cartridges, never believing we'd use anywhere near that many.

"Yellow Boy appeared just as we finished eating an early supper. Rufus offered him some meat and beans, but he said, *No, gracias, Rufus. Mi mujer, she feed her hombre. We travel now?*

"Rufus nodded. *Just as soon as we get this here pot warshed and the animals saddled and loaded.*

"Yellow Boy shrugged his shoulders. *Hmmph. I smoke by fire. I wait.*

"Rufus just said, *Bueno,* and we set to work. In half an hour we were moving down the trail. We had about three hours of daylight left and Yellow Boy set us a good pace over the ridges and canyons around to the little village of Cloudcroft. He swung around it and followed a thin little trail through the tall pines along the western edge of the Sacramentos. It was easy riding and we made good time. He stopped where the trail appeared to drop off into a steep dark hole in the steadily falling night around us.

"He spoke softly to Rufus and me. *Aqui es trail down into Canyon of the Dog. Rest horses and mules now. Rest till light is good. Then go.* Pulling his pony off the trail a few yards and tying its reins to a bush, he sat down with his back against a tree. Rufus and I unloaded the horses and mules and made ourselves comfortable near Yellow Boy. I was too excited to sleep and took the first watch. When I shook Rufus awake I was ready for some sleep.

"I woke up to the singing of thousands of birds down in the canyon and sunlight casting misty beams through the shadows of the trees. Rufus and Yellow Boy were already up saddling the animals and putting the supplies on Elmer's rig. Throwing off my blanket, I walked over to the opening in the trees a few yards away. The opening was at a cliff's edge that just seemed to roll off into space and the view of the other side, the basin flats, the far Organs, and White Sands took my breath. The Organs must have been thirty or forty miles away. They were clear as a close-up photograph. The view across to the south-side cliffs made my heart stop. They were gnarly, nearly vertical, walls that would give a mountain goat nightmares much less hold a path of any kind for man or beast. The treetops far down at the bottom of the canyon looked the size of pinheads. The exposed stone cliffs on the south side had rust reds, soft pinks, an occasional dark green splotch from some bush that managed a toehold in the smooth stone faces, and there were soft brown beiges and dark, almost purple colors in some places. They were spectacularly beautiful. With their sheer height and vertical reachs, I just couldn't believe there was any kind of passable trail down those walls. I turned back ready to vomit, the sound of my heart pounding in my ears. I wasn't afraid of heights, but the trail down and around those walls just had to be too dangerous. What was Yellow Boy expecting us to do? Go down those walls on a rope?

"Rufus laughed when he saw me. *Henry, did you see a ghost? Yore's pale as milk. What's the matter?*

"I swallowed to keep the contents of my stomach down, and said, Rufus have you been down the Eyebrow before? I don't see how we can ride or even climb down those walls yonder.

"Rufus nodded toward them. *Kinda scary, ain't they? Yes, sir, I been down and up 'em a time or two. Couple times when we was chasing Apaches and praying they warn't a waiting to pitch a rock in my pocket and send me and my horse to the grandfathers via quick trip to the bottom. Reckon I was just lucky those times.*

*Ain't no need to be fearsome, Henry.* He spat a brown stream toward the edge and nodded. *Yellow Boy's rode up and down the trail many a time. It's not a bad trail except in the part that's called the Eyebrow. The trick is when we start down the trail, just sit back, relax, and let yore pony find her way. She's shore-footed. Ye'll be fine. Don't know nothin' about how Elmer'll do on a narrow windin' trail, but I think he's got the right temperament fer it and he'll follow Sally near anywhere. I'll be fine too. You ride down 'tween Yellow Boy and me jest, as usual.*

"All I could do was nod and swallow the bile filling the back of my throat. Yellow Boy and Rufus checked the cinches on the horses, Sally, and the pack rig on Elmer twice. Then we mounted and followed Yellow Boy down and around the winding steep curves off the top ridge.

"The trail we followed off the top started in the north corner of the canyon and tracked down the eastern back wall. It wasn't as bad as I thought it would be, until we got about down on the eastern wall and hit a steep part that was a narrow squeeze between the cliff and a two thousand foot drop straight down. This was the part called the Eyebrow. It hung on that vertical cliff like an eyebrow on a giant. There the Apaches used to push boulders and throw big stones down on their pursuers. I still remember feeling the cool morning air floating up around me from below, the calls of thousands of birds in the lush trees down in the bottom, and above us nothing but a great empty hole with blue sky. I thanked God we didn't have to worry about Apaches trying to force us off the edge.

"I did what Rufus told me and let Midnight pick her way along as she chose and we just eased past that scary narrow stretch. Elmer jogged along like he had lived on that trail all his life, and, for all we knew, he might very well have been up and down the Eyebrow a few times in an earlier life. Past the Eyebrow, the trail widened out and the descent, while steep, was much easier.

"It took us most of the early morning to work our way down the five or six miles of trail. As the trail incline became less and the trail widened, we crossed several small streams. Down near the bottom of the canyon, I saw the remains of a rock wall someone had put a lot of labor into building. I looked back at Rufus and pointed my thumb toward them.

*Frenchy Rochas built those 'bout twenty year ago,* he called back to me.

"As we neared the mouth, but still well into the canyon, a small stone house stood lonely watch. Rufus pointed toward it, and, in an admiring voice, said, *Old Frenchy built that too. It's only got one or two rooms, but it's built like a fort. It's the reason I decided I'd build us one too. Spect it'll last a while, that one will.*

"Yellow Boy stopped and surveyed the scene, looking toward one particular spot, then another, as if weighing the value of each. In a few minutes he turned back up the trail and led us unerringly to a small spring hidden by a thicket of bushes next to the northern wall. It was within a quarter mile of Frenchy's cabin. The canyon here was passable on a mount for no more than two or three hundred yards before a rider had to get off and walk. A good stream of cool water ran right down the middle.

"Turning to Rufus and me Yellow Boy said, *Safe here. Agua es bueno. See all range toward south. See riders when they come. Rest animals now. Then ride to Alamogordo.*

"Rufus and I unloaded, fed, watered, and rubbed down the animals. Then we all lay back and rested. I stared up at the cliffs back up the canyon and found it hard to believe I had ridden down them. Looking south, we were still high enough to have good view back toward the Organs and White Sands, and could see little black groups of cattle scattered here and there over the range.

"Looking out on the range Rufus pointed toward some buildings at least three or four miles away. *Know what those buildin's are Henry?*

"They were obviously part of a ranch, but whose ranch I had no idea, so I just shrugged my shoulders.

*Well, sir, that there ranch is owned by Oliver Lee.*

"He had my attention then and I studied Lee's ranch house and out buildings closely. How ironic that we were planning to kill, within sight of his own ranch house, the very men he paid to murder my father. I hoped when he heard what we'd done, he'd know I was coming for him.

"As we rested, Rufus and Yellow Boy looked over the canyon and picked out some spots from which to form a crossfire in the canyon.

The locations of the shooting spots formed a triangle. There were two places on either side of the canyon and a point further up the canyon well-protected by brush and boulders. The strategy was to get Stone, Tally and their riders to ride up the canyon past Frenchy's house. As soon as they were well past it, the shooters on either side could lay into them. The shooter on the up-canyon point would keep them from escaping that way. The major weakness with this plan, it seemed to me, was that if they were able to retreat and reach Frenchy's house, it would be mighty hard to get 'em out. We debated about whether one of us should get in the house, but decided that if any escaped they would ride past it to try and get away. If the house wasn't occupied, at least they'd run for cover there and we'd have them. We chewed on that for a while and decided it was worth the risk to leave Frenchy's place open. Yellow Boy took the up-canyon point. Rufus and I took side positions.

"After a couple hours of dozing, we saddled the horses and Sally and rode out of the canyon and across the hot flats toward Alamogordo. After we found the dusty road running to Alamogordo from San Augustin Pass we made good time. Yellow Boy hung off several hundred yards to one side of us and just out of sight, in case we needed him. Within a half mile of Alamogordo he pointed toward a thicket of mesquite where he'd wait to escort us back to Dog Canyon.

"Rufus and I planned to ride into Alamogordo, visit some stores and get a few supplies, ride up and down the streets and generally make sure anyone from Stone's outfit knew we were there. If we were lucky we would be followed back to Dog Canyon. Then all we had to do was wait for Stone and Tally to arrive expecting to get rid of the niggling details that could get them hung – namely Rufus and me.

"Alamogordo was a railroad town built in 1898. Not having seen it up close before, or, for that matter, not even having been in a town for over six years, it seemed very busy and filled with people. There were businessmen providing ranchers and miners supplies, and ranchers and cowboys in town for a little entertainment or to buy, sell, or ship cattle and horses. Mexicans and a few Chinese laborers working for merchants hurried up and down the streets or sweated in hard labor around the rail station. There were hundreds of horses, tied to anything that wouldn't move or in corrals. Fancy women walked up and down the street under colorful parasols. There were saloons and whorehouses over in what was called Block 50, but nowhere else. There were cottonwood saplings planted everywhere. I'd never seen so many small trees in one spot before. A train filled with passengers and cattle was just starting to roll toward El Paso and gave a long farewell whistle as it chugged passed us. I realize now that I must have looked like an ignorant Indian kid staring at everything like I was seeing a town for the first time. Rufus laughed in good humor, as he watched me take it all in.

"We rode up and down several streets in Block 50, but saw no one we recognized. Rufus said, *Henry, what's say we tie up to that store over there and get me some chewin' tobac? We'll find you a cold sarsaparilla and then sit in the chairs there in the front of the store fer a while to see who we can see?* I nodded, still speechless at all I was seeing.

"We rode to the store, dismounted, and tied Sally and Midnight up to the hitching rail. Rufus motioned me to sit in a chair while he went inside. I could hear him talking and laughing with the man at the counter like he had known him for a long time. I looked down the street from where we had just come and noticed a cowboy leaning against a post under a big red sign for a gun and ranch supply store. He was staring hard at our side of the street. I had the uneasy feeling I recognized him, but had no idea where I had seen him before. I watched riders and buggies moving up and down the street. Each time I took my eyes off one and looked back, the cowboy was still staring.

"Rufus came out and handed me a cool bottle of sarsaparilla. Before I took a swallow, I said, That cowboy, the one leaning against the post under the big red sign down the street, has been staring over here ever since you went inside.

"Rufus nodded. *Yeah, kinda thought he would be. I noticed him when we rode by and he pulled his hat down over his eyes and kept on watching us. I'm purty shore that there is one of the fellers with Stone the first night he come up to the shack and stole Lil David. Finish that sarsaparilla, son, and then we'll mount up and see if we got us a fish a trailin' our bait.*

"The sarsaparilla was a real treat. I hadn't had anything cool and sweet like that since Mama had made lemonade at home. It was so good. I swilled it down in about four swallows and then we mounted up. The cowboy under the red sign hadn't moved. Rufus swung down the street toward him and I followed. We just ambled along down the middle of the street looking in storefront windows. When we reached the cowboy Rufus paused and strained to look at the guns on display in the window behind him. He looked down and stared for a few seconds at the cowboy watching us. The cowboy stared back. Rufus's eyes got large, his jaw dropped, and he quickly turned his head and set Sally at a trot down the street. I had to kick Midnight to keep up with him. It was the finest acting job I've ever seen, including anything by John Wayne or those other Hollywood actors in the movies. I shot a quick look back and saw the cowboy climbing into the saddle on a dun-colored mustang.

"I caught up with Rufus well outside of town. The cowboy followed at a distance, trying to stay inconspicuous. Rufus looked over his shoulder at me, grinned, and said in a voice filled with mischief, *Howdy, Henry. Glad you showed up today. Looks like we found us a fish. Yes, sir, a fishing here in the desert is fun, ain't it?*"

# 15

# THE AMBUSH

**T**he morning came running through the mists and shadows of the night. Henry gave Roberta's hand a little squeeze. He yawned and stretched forward, touching the tips of his socks. Roberta steadied herself with one hand on his shoulder, wobbling from side to side as she stood up, her joints creaking as they pulled against gravity. The gray light of dawn was giving away to brilliant golden sunbeams piercing the dark tree tops and pools of cold misty air down the canyon. Rather than standing, taking three steps, then kneeling again, Henry rolled to all fours and crawled around the end of the fireside pallet to check on Yellow Boy. Roberta threw a blanket over her shoulders and stepped outside.

Yellow Boy was awake, his eyes staring at the ceiling rafters, his mind focused on events lost far away in time. Gently removing the oxygen mask, Henry reached and twirled off the oxygen tank valve. The old man's ancient dark eyes turned slowly toward him and he smiled. He spoke in a low rasping whisper that Henry had to lean forward to hear.

"At last you are telling someone else the truth of your life, little brother. I remember those days well. It was not so long ago, was it? It is a good thing for you to speak of those days to your friend. She is a good woman, strong and she speaks true ..." The dark eyes twinkled with a question, the answer already known. "I saw you take her hand. Your eyes looked like those of a young man wishing for a maiden. Is she more than a friend?"

Yellow Boy's I-know-a-secret smile turned to a frown as his lungs ran out of wind and forced a deep, phlegm-filled cough. When his breath returned he said, "Soon I will go to the grandfathers. Then, only you will know the truth of your life unless you pass it to your friend. It is good to do this thing. I have not spoken of our time together to anyone, not even to John, Redondo, or Sara. Perhaps you will tell them too sometime?"

Henry smiled and nodded. "Yes, uncle, I am telling our story to my friend. Soon I will tell your sons and daughter too if you wish. But it is better for you to speak of your life and what is in your heart, rather than for me to speak for you. Only you can truly speak of these things. And, yes, I have been blind; Roberta is much more than a friend. I have not yet spoken with her as a man speaks of his heart with a woman. Soon I will. But enough of me. How is your strength this sunrise? Are you stronger than yesterday?"

"Si. I am stronger, but still weak. My water sack is very full," he said with a groan. "And I have hunger. Perhaps Sara will make us enchiladas? Then I can rest more and get stronger. Can you stay awhile?"

"Yes, we will stay today and tonight. If you grow stronger today, then we will leave tomorrow or the next day. Here put your arm over my shoulder and I will help you down the path."

Henry slid his arm under the old man's back and helped him stand. Yellow Boy lay his bony arm over Henry's shoulders as he came to his feet. Henry hated to have him waste his energy on an outside toilet break rather than use a bedpan, but he knew the old man would let himself die if he thought he couldn't perform his normal personal needs. The deep phlegm-filled cough returned as they stood up. Henry paused to let him cough and catch his breath then started moving toward the door. Before they made two small steps, the door swung open letting in a swirl of cold air. Roberta walked in, vigorously rubbing her arms trying to get warm.

"Ah! You are up, señor! Bueno!" she exclaimed. "I've cleared the path and warmed the seat for you already!" She pulled the blanket off her shoulders. "Here, let me put this blanket over your shoulders. There is no wind, but the air is still and cold!" She covered him and Henry so the morning air wouldn't have too much bite. She looked at Henry as if to ask, *Do you need some help?* Shaking his head, Henry eased Yellow Boy out the door and down the path.

Roberta stoked the fire's coals and added the last chunks of wood in the firebox. She heard a bedroom door creak open. Sara stepped out of her room, plaiting her long black hair into a single long braid. She looked toward the empty pallet by the fire and frowned. "Is Father all right, Roberta?" She asked through a little barking yawn.

"Yes, I think he is some better. Dr. Grace is helping him down the path. Did you get any rest last night?"

Sara nodded, her face a little red with embarrassment. "I was very tired and so relieved when you came, I don't think I moved after I went to bed. You were supposed to call us hours ago! Aren't you about to drop?"

Roberta stood warming herself with her back to the blazing fire. "I'm tired, but, you know, doctors and nurses sometimes have to stay up long hours with their patients. Hen...uh... Dr. Grace was telling me about the old days with your father and the time just galloped by. We thought it would be better to let you rest all night, then we could rest all day and not get worn down in case we had to be up later."

Sara nodded, and, without another word rolled up her sleeves and stepped out into the icy air on the back porch to wash up. When she returned her teeth were chattering, and her face and hands were bright red from a vigorous scrub.

Roberta was making up the pallet next to the fire when John opened the other bedroom door, eyes squinting mole-like at the bright beams of light beginning to stream through the window. He flopped down in the nearest chair as he shook his head to clear the cobwebs from his brain. Rubbing his eyes, he yawned and said, "Roberta, you were supposed to get us up hours ago. Where're Yellow Boy and Henry? Is he any better?"

She greeted John with a cheery "Good morning! They've taken a little walk down the path. He seems better this morning."

Sara said, "Go wash up, John. I'll start a fire in the stove and make some enchiladas for the morning meal, then Roberta and Henry can get some rest."

He stood, shaking and stretching himself out of his sleepy lethargy, and said with a grin, "Best idea I've had all day. I'll get wood for the stove and the fire before I wash. Is there anything I can get for you, Roberta?"

She spoke over her shoulder as she went out the back porch door for her wash water, "Nothing but a good bed after breakfast. That'll be wonderful. My eyes feel like they have half of White Sands in them, and just the thought of Sara's enchiladas makes me hungry."

John smiled and nodded as he went out the door toward the woodpile. Henry soon appeared, helping Yellow Boy totter slowly along. Little clouds from their breath surrounded their heads. Yellow Boy continued to fight a wheezing gurgle deep in his chest that John heard from the woodpile. Sara and Henry eased Yellow Boy down on the pallet. Roberta, just in from her wash in the freezing cold water, rushed to put a fluffed pillow under his head, then she took his pulse and temperature. His pulse was strong, but he still had a low-grade fever.

Henry considered keeping the oxygen mask on the old man but decided to try his recovery without it. He'd become stronger faster if his lungs had to work to get the air he needed.

John put a day's wood supply by the fire and in the stove's wood box while Henry washed up. Sara worked fast to prepare her enchiladas. When they were ready, she helped Yellow Boy eat while Roberta set the table and served the plates. The old man ate a plateful, belched loudly, and lay back content. Sara joined the others as they greedily finished off big stacks of tortillas covered with her fiery green chile enchilada sauce.

After breakfast, John and Sara shooed off Henry and Roberta when they offered to help with the morning chores. Before going to bed, Henry left John with instructions to get him up so he could turn on and adjust the oxygen mask if Yellow Boy's breathing faltered. Retiring to John's disheveled bed, Henry mummified himself in a red and black Pendleton wool blanket with geometric designs, and lay down in a fetal position. He fell into a deep, dreamless sleep.

Roberta, sitting on Sara's made-up bed, pulled off her white nurse's shoes, swung her legs up on the bed, and pulled a heavy comforter up to her chin. Exhausted, she lay back and closed her eyes as she waited for sleep to relax and fill her. It held back from coming for a while as her mind raced with images of the story Henry told her. Her eyes fluttered shut, her brain drifting into unconsciousness as she thought, *less than twenty-four hours since the woman from the tribal center called. It seems a lifetime ...*

She awoke with a start. It was nearly dark. She sat up, looking around in confusion, trying to remember where she was. Looking at the luminous hands on her watch, she saw it was a little after five o'clock. Her mental fog began to lift and she realized she had been sleeping in a bedroom at Yellow Boy's house. She swung her legs off the bed, found her shoes, and wiggled her feet into them. She stood and straightened her dress and underclothes, then sat back down again on the bed and tied her shoes. Rummaging through her purse, she found her comb and pulled the knots out of her long hair, then twisted it into a bun on the back of her head. Recalling yesterday's unexpected turn of events, she yawned, stretched, and made the bed before opening her door into the main room.

Light was fading quickly from the windows. A large pot of green chile stew bubbled like volcanic magma on the old iron stove. A warm delicious smell of freshly made fry-bread filled the room. Henry sat cross-legged on the floor next to Yellow Boy, leaning forward and cupping his ear to hear the old man speak. John, his head cocked to one side, listened too as he leaned forward with his elbows resting on his knees while sitting in a chair next to Henry. Sara sat in a rocker at the head of Yellow Boy's pallet. She was listening too as she rocked and sewed a button on a shirt.

After being under the warm comforter for so long, the air in the room at first felt cold. Roberta rubbed her arms to get her circulation started. Henry looked over his shoulder when he heard her door creak open and smiled with delight when he saw her wobble into the room, covering another big yawn with her hand. "Glad you could drop in today, Nurse Roberta!" Henry teased. "Did you sleep well?"

She yawned again and nodded. "I was a little slow finding dreamland, but once I did, I don't think I moved the rest of the day. I was tired. How long have you been up?"

"Oh, about an hour, I guess, but I slept like I was on the wrong side of the dirt."

Sara smiled a pleasant good evening and said, "As soon as you've visited outside and washed up, I'll put supper on the table. I hope you're hungry."

"Yes, I am! I'll be ready in ten minutes."

"Bueno! I'll set the table."

Yellow Boy lifted a hand to her and waved, smiling. She waved back and asked, "How's our patient?"

Henry nodded for emphasis and said, "He's getting stronger. He should be up and moving around by tomorrow."

Roberta grinned at the good news as she threw her coat over her shoulders for her trip outside. By the time she returned, shivering and washed up, Sara had set the table and filled big thick-walled bowls with her stew. Sara again helped her father eat as the others began.

Yellow Boy had been awake most of the day, telling John and Sara about old times and swapping stories with Henry after he awoke. As the light faded, and with supper past, he drifted off to sleep. He had made it all day without the oxygen mask and his strength was returning at a remarkable rate. The wheeze in his chest was still noticeable, but wasn't as nearly as bad as before.

As the four of them sat back from the table, full and content with the fiery stew in their bellies, they swapped news about the reservation and what was happening at White Sands. During a lull in the conversation, Henry said, "John, why don't you and Sara go on home to your families tonight? I think he's through the worst of it. Roberta and I will keep an eye on him. If he continues to improve, we'll leave sometime tomorrow, or, if need be, we'll certainly stay longer. I know your families need attention. Go on and go, we'll be fine."

John and Sara looked at each other and nodded. John said, "Are you sure, Henry? Our families know where we are and that father is very sick, it's okay if we stay here."

"I know, but everything's fine now my friend. Go on home."

Sara said, "We'll be back before first light. I am a little worried about my youngest daughter getting the attention she needs from her sister and brothers. My husband has been on a hunt over on the other side of Ruidoso. I don't know if he's back yet."

"That's fine, Sara. Go. You're needed at home. You too, John. I know you need to be home."

"Thank you, my friend. Before we leave, we'll get the evening chores done."

There was a flurry of activity as John and Henry brought in wood, and went to the barn to water and feed the animals. Sara and Roberta washed the dishes, cleaned up the cooking area, and put fresh sheets on the beds. In less than an hour, Sara and John were in John's old pickup truck heading out of the canyon.

Despite the constant movement by others in the big room, Yellow Boy slept peacefully. Henry checked his pulse and temperature. The fever was nearly gone. The stethoscope indicated the infection in his lungs was fading. More penicillin would do the trick. He should be able to do without the oxygen mask for the rest of the night.

Roberta pulled a slat chair up next to the cozy fire, sat down, slid off her shoes, and wiggled her stocking-covered toes in its heat. Henry pulled up a chair beside her, slid his boots off and did the same. She felt perfectly at ease and relaxed, wishing the feeling could last a life-time. She lighted a cigarette, blew the smoke toward the chimney, and, taking Henry by the hand said, "So how do you feel now, Dr. Grace?"

He gave her hand an intimate little squeeze and smiling said, "A lot better than twenty-four hours ago, Nurse Gonzalez. I've unburdened my soul after nearly fifty years. My old friend isn't dead and is getting better. I think I've discovered a treasure I was too blind to see for many years. It's been a very important time for me. And you?"

"I'm much better than twenty-four hours ago. I've not let your friend die without hearing us say good-by. I'm one of probably three people now living who knows that Henry Fountain survived. My heart is filled with a man I've known and admired for many years, but didn't dare hope he might truly care for me in more than just a professional way." She let out a low whispered whistle. "I've never known such a twenty-four hours."

He smiled and nodded as he reached in his pockets for his pipe and tobacco. Stuffing the old briar bowl with the long thin strands of Flying

Dutchman, he leaned over, pulled a flaming splinter off a log in the fire, and lighted it. Pulling hard, he formed a bright red coal in the tobacco. He crossed his arms and leaned back in his chair, blowing smoke toward the ceiling.

Roberta took another draw on her cigarette and said, "You really are a mean man, Henry Grace!"

"What! Me? Why?"

"Yes you! I've had to wait all day to hear what happened in Dog Canyon. I want to know right now!"

"Oh, okay. I didn't know if you were still interested in a story over fifty years old."

She punched him on the shoulder, laughing. "You know very well I am! Now get on with it!"

"Well ..." He let the pipe dangle momentarily at the end of his thoughts as he collected his memories, then began as if he had never stopped the story. "Yellow Boy confirmed that the cowboy who followed us out of Alamogordo came all the way to the mouth of Dog Canyon, then turned back toward Alamogordo, riding at a pretty good gallop. We figured Stone's cowboys might be back that night. Didn't happen. But we were ready and kept a good lookout, watching in shifts, all night under a bright moon that would let us see them coming from a couple of miles away.

"When dawn came, Rufus cooked us some trail biscuits in that Dutch oven of his, then he and Yellow Boy jawed for a while. They decided Stone must still be coming in on the ten o'clock train from El Paso that day or the next. Rufus wanted to be sure Stone and Tally came after us while we had the advantage in Dog Canyon. So we saddled up again and trotted off toward Alamogordo. We left Yellow Boy at the same big mesquite thicket outside of town as the day before. It was close to train time when we got there and a small group of ranchers were waiting on the passenger platform when we rode by. Rufus had tied Little David in the expensive saddle scabbard so it was easy to see on his saddle from Sally's right side.

"We rode a couple of blocks up the street past the train station. We stopped and dismounted, leading Sally and Midnight into an alley to wait for the train's arrival. Rufus said, *Now, when that train comes, we're a gonna ride back down the street slow and easy, like we're a ridin' to church. I'm gonna be on the side closest to the tracks. When he comes in, I want Stone to see us. I want him to see Lil David tied to my saddle. He's gonna believe right off I's the one put a hole through Bentene and he's gonna know I ain't hidin' out in Mexico a peeing-in-*

*my-pants 'fraid of him either. I'm hopin' that when he sees me and you ridin' down the street big as you please, he's gonna git mad as a cornered rattler and not waste any time 'fore comin' after us. He ain't gonna be cool and cakilatin' – just mad. If'n that happens, we got him.* Rufus clinched his fist and shook it as if he had Stone by the collar. *You understand, boy?*

"Yes, sir, I sure do. I just hope he takes the bait. It's time for Daddy to get some justice.

*It is boy. Yes, sir, it is. I'm a bettin' it's gonna happen today too!*

"We waited about half an hour before we heard the train's whistle moaning on the tracks back toward El Paso. We mounted and eased part way out of the alley so we could look down the street toward the train station. Several people were coming out of the train station with bags and looking down the tracks toward a distant low-lying black cloud where the tracks lay hidden in the creosotes and mesquite bushes. Soon the engine with a couple of passenger and several freight cars rumbled into the station and stopped with the passenger cars even with the platform. Rufus and I slowly rode out of the alley and down the street toward the station.

"We saw several women and children followed by Stone, Red Tally, and a couple of well-dressed men in derby hats stepping down from the train just as we started moseying along. The small group of ranchers and cowboys waiting on the platform walked over and surrounded Stone and Tally. They were shaking hands, slapping backs, and laughing at jokes when we rode by. I saw Tally's eyes catch sight of Rufus and me and begin tracking us like some radar-controlled gun. Rufus stared right back at him. Tally gently put his hand on Stone's shoulder and wrinkled his brow toward the street to turn his attention toward us. Stone paused in the middle of a big belly laugh, his eyes narrowing to slits when he saw Rufus and me sauntering down the street. Rufus looked toward him, nodded with a grin, and spat a tobacco-juice challenge toward the train as we continued leisurely out of town. The last time I saw Stone and Tally in Alamogordo, they were still in the middle of the ranchers and cowboys surrounding them, and staring after us like hunting hawks after a rabbit.

"When we were out of sight, Rufus said, *Won't be long now, boy, let's git.* We rode at a fast canter back to Dog Canyon. We occasionally looked back over our shoulders but saw no one following us. We unsaddled Sally and Midnight at our little camp behind the thicket, then tied them to bushes next to water and grass about three hundred yards up the canyon from Frenchy's cabin. We took care to be sure they were hard to see but still visible if a person looked hard enough. Further up the canyon Rufus built a small fire that put out just enough smoke to smell and for someone to see if they were riding up the canyon looking for camp signs. Rufus figured Stone and Tally would believe he was too smart to stay in something as obvious as the cabin and that we probably hid out and camped further up the canyon.

"From the canyon entrance Yellow Boy kept watch for riders while Rufus and I set our trap. It was well into mid-afternoon when he rode up and said, *Cinco hombres, they come. They are here when the shadows reach that tree.* He pointed toward a scraggly apple tree Frenchy had planted years before. It still had one or two branches producing leaves, but mostly it looked dead and mournful.

"Rufus nodded, *Good. We got 'bout an hour. Henry, you take the spot we picked on the south side. The cover's good there. Keep the barrel of Lil David back in the leaves so some eagle-eye in the bunch don't spot it. You'll be in position for good shots there, and some protection if'n they have a chance to shoot back. I'll take the north wall. Yellow Boy, you go up the canyon. With me and Henry lightin' their fire from behind, you oughta be able to pick 'em right off if'n they ride forward.*

"*I figure they'll stay in a group like they did when they come to my place. Henry, you been wantin' a second chance at Stone. You take the first shot. I'll try to get Tally. Yellow Boy you drop the others then shoot fer Tally too. He's the most dangerous of the bunch an' he'll be hard to kill. We gotta get him fer shore. If'n they turn back and run, shoot the horses. That'll make 'em run for Frenchy's cabin. They ain't gonna git outta here alive without no horse. I know ye ain't reluctant to shoot Stone. Can ye shoot horses too, Henry?*

"My heart was pounding and my mouth felt dry when I said, Yes, sir, I can.

"Rufus squeezed my shoulder and smiled. *Good! I know you can. This here is judgement day, boys! Henry, be shore an' set yoreself out plenty of cartridges. Likely to need all of 'em. Take yore time pickin' yore targit, but kill him when ye shoot. These here skunks ain't gonna go easy. Git on up there now and git sighted in and ready. Good luck, fellers.*

"Yellow Boy nodded, and, without a word, started his pony up the canyon. Rufus and I ran back to the thicket. I pulled Lil David out of the fancy saddle scabbard and picked up the saddlebags with cartridges. Rufus loaded his Winchester and put an extra box of cartridges in his grimy old vest pocket. Handing me a canteen, looking me square in the eye and squeezing my shoulder again with his gnarly old hand covered with liver spots, he said, *Today's payback Henry. Don't be shy 'bout shootin' the sons-of-bitches. They earned ever' round we can put in 'em. Don't be foolish and aim for Stone's head. Put one in his lungs or heart and it'll all be over fer him. Now git up there and drop Stone like I taught ya.* I nodded without a word and took off for my perch.

"My spot on the south side of the canyon was about ten feet above and a hundred yards from where we hoped to catch Stone and Tally in a cross-fire. Some piñon bushes stood right in front of two big rocks that lay side by side forming a nice notch in which to steady the rifle while sitting down behind them. I opened a box of cartridges. I was so nervous I wanted to vomit but the velvet smoothness of the stock, the smell of gun oil, and the feel of that first .45-70 brass cartridge in my hands made me steady up.

"I dropped the block on the Sharps and slid a cartridge into the breach calmly and deliberately. I tried, as Rufus taught me, to be cool and cakilatin' as I pulled the Sharp's breach closed. The words Judgement Day ran through my mind over and over. I rested the barrel forestock in the rock notch and looked along the sights, trying to imagine the sight picture where Stone would be. Sighting on the notch of a nearby tree limb, I found I could hold the rifle steady on a sharp point. It was a good day for vengeance, and if we weren't successful, well, it was a good day to die. I pulled ten more cartridges from the box and laid them side-by-side on a little shelf protruding from the right hand rock forming the notch. I dropped the breech, reloaded, and sighted several times for practice. Then eased the rifle out of the notch, and sat back to wait.

"The water running down the middle of the canyon helped make the air much cooler than out on the desert, but the air was still hot enough to bake bread. As I sat back against the canyon wall and waited, I could feel the sweat running out of my hair and down the back of my neck and face in cooling little rivulets. I closed my eyes and remembered the last time I had seen Daddy. He was lying on the ground, wheezing and gasping for his last breath of air; his chest held two dark bloody holes. Stone and Tally sat watching him die, glad to be rid of him, and patting themselves on the back for the superb job they'd done in killing him. I remembered sitting in the wagon frozen in shock, not believing or fully understanding what had happened. I remembered the confusion I felt when Daddy didn't get up and use his Schofield to run them off and get us on home to Mama. I thought about hiding under the tumbleweeds caught in the big mesquite bush and the big tumbleweed I was under flying up in the dark when Yellow Boy found me. I was so cold! I've never been that cold again in the fifty-five years since. I remembered all the years I'd worked with that Sharps, all the rocks I'd carried for Rufus to get strong, all the miles I'd run in the desert, and all I'd learned in order to survive and be as tough and hard as any Apache. I thought of my mother and how I'd waited all these years to see her. I hoped that I'd be a living son to her again soon. Perhaps I'd get my life back again if I tore it away the from the men who murdered my Daddy and stole my childhood.

"Birds were everywhere. Large flocks of canyon wrens covered the bushes chirping. I could see hummingbirds as they sped from flower to flower feeding on sweet nectar. An hour passed, shadows were touching the scraggly apple tree and there was still no sign of the riders Yellow Boy said were coming. I wiped the sweat off my face with my sleeve and looked out through the notch hoping for some sign of the men we meant to kill. A covey of Gambel's quail, three adults and a string of six or seven chicks, ran out from under some bushes a few yards below me and headed up the canyon. On the northern wall close by Rufus's spot, a coyote loped down a path through the bushes. His tongue was hanging out and he stopped at the water to lap up a drink, roll in the stream, shake dry, and then lope on down the path on the other side. I sat back and had a pull from the canteen. The shadows were becoming longer and starting to fill the canyon. I wondered if Yellow Boy had misinterpreted the direction of the riders he had seen and that perhaps they were not Stone and Tally at all. Maybe they were just some of Oliver Lee's cowboys coming in from work.

"It got quiet in the canyon. Even the breeze was still. The wrens stopped chirping, then, as if on command, they flew up the canyon in several clouds that grew in number as they disappeared toward the east wall we had come down the day before.

"I heard two rocks grind together and a splash or two in the little stream that shouldn't have been there. My chest tightened as I plugged the canteen and sat it down carefully before creeping up to look through the notch.

"Five riders were spread out across the center of the canyon, about five yards apart. They were moving slowly, looking quickly from side to side with rifles drawn, pointed up, and cocked, ready to fire. The riders on the wings held back about ten yards from the point man, who was splashing in and out of the winding little stream. Stone was on the south side between the point man and the flanker, Tally on the north side between the point man and his flanker. Their arrangement couldn't have been better if we had designed it. They passed Frenchy's house; a rider stopping momentarily to look in through a window, I assume to verify we weren't hiding there, and then continued up the canyon.

"My heart was pounding and my breath was coming in long puffs like I was running. I felt the quiet stillness around me as I picked up the rifle and felt a serene calm as I pulled the hammer to full-cock. Stone couldn't have been more than fifty yards away. It was a shot I could make with my eyes closed and had trained to make perfectly for years. The riders had stopped and were standing in their stirrups straining forward to look up the canyon. The lead was pointing with his rifle toward some bushes further up the canyon. Sally was sticking her head right out where they could see her and pricking up her ears in curiosity. Putting the sight picture in the middle of Stone's back, I pulled and felt the reassuring light click of the set trigger. Stone nodded toward Tally who started to dismount. It seemed there was no resistance at all when the firing trigger came back.

"A roll of thunder, the voice of judgment, echoed up and down the canyon as the Sharps thumped against my shoulder like a hard punch thrown with a fist, the long barrel kicking up three or four inches. I threw the breech down; the ejector sent the big shell case flying. I focused on being steady as my fingers slid a new cartridge in the breech and flipped the block closed. I heard Rufus's Winchester roar three times, its echos in time with mine as they bounced up and down the canyon. Yellow Boy's Henry, adding to the raging cacophony, roared out two evenly spaced shots, held two counts then fired again. I looked through the notch to find a new target.

"Chaos whirled below me. Stone lay on his back staring at the sky, a bright red stain on the front of his shirt just below and to the left of his heart. The two outriders were down, and, like Stone, unmoving. A bright red stain spread on the head of the man who had ridden next to Stone up the canyon. A horse kicking in its death throes pinned the leg of the rider closest to Rufus. His pistol was drawn and he was wildly firing in every direction, the bullets ricocheting off nearby boulders. I sighted on his head and cocked the Sharps. There was a loud report from up the canyon and his head jerked like he'd been hit with a club as he wilted before my eyes. The outrider closest to me was on the ground screaming in agony with his hands pressed over his belly. Tally had a crease of blood across his left cheek that was starting to color his beard a deeper red. His horse lay kicking in its final death twitches. Two horses bucked and kicked as they nervously danced around, screaming in fright, the whites of their eyes showing their terror. They tore off up the canyon as fast as they could run. Stone's horse also bolted up the canyon, straight toward Yellow Boy's position. One of the bucking horses gathered his wits and ran toward the mouth of the canyon, and then, inexplicably, stopped, not a hundred yards down the trail from Frenchy's cabin.

"Tally managed to reach the cover of a boulder and returned Rufus's fire. The bushes at his back blocked Yellow Boy's line of sight. The point man had escaped unscratched. He lay behind some boulders near the stream, levering fire toward Yellow Boy's position. He fired several rounds then stopped, waiting for the shooter above him to make a mistake and show himself. Stone lay on his back where he had fallen, unmoving, not making a sound, just staring at the sky with open eyes. The bloodstain was spreading across the entire front of his shirt. The stain was too low for him to have been hit in the heart and killed instantly, as I wanted. He was still alive, but he wasn't going anywhere.

"Yellow Boy dropped four or five rounds close by the bush that screened Tally, then stopped. He wouldn't shoot at a target he couldn't see. I figured he must be coming back down the canyon to get a better shot. If that were so, then he was in immediate danger as soon as the point rider saw him. I saw brief snatches of Tally's shoulders behind the rock he used to screen himself as he raised up to squeeze off a shot at Rufus. Although it wasn't a long shot for the Sharps, his motion and small exposure made it a hard one. I tried anyway and missed. The thunder of the Sharps mixed with his return fire and Rufus's shots, filling the canyon with an apocalyptic roar. He snapped off a shot in my direction, the bullet ricocheting off the canyon wall a couple of yards to my left. As soon as he fired toward me, Rufus covered the rock he was hiding behind with five or six quick shots then stopped.

"I dropped the breech and reloaded again. Rufus couldn't see the point man on the ground. I had to kill him or see Yellow Boy put at high risk. I couldn't stand that thought. Less than sixty yards and a still target, it was an easy shot, even though I could only see the point rider's legs sticking out behind the boulder where he waited. I pulled the hammer back and held a cartridge between my fingers for a fast re-load. I knew as soon as I shattered the rider's leg his reflex to the brutal pain would make him jerk and show himself. I aimed for his knee. The Sharps roared and there was a scream of pain as the rider jerked forward and momentarily exposed his upper body. I was reloaded and aimed before he sat fully upright. There wasn't any sound of pain with the second shot. He flopped backwards and was still. I could only think, Ride with murderers, die with murderers.

"The echoes from the shots faded away and it was quiet except for the pitiful moans and pleading for water from the gut-shot rider on my side of the canyon. Soon I heard a long sigh and his moaning stopped. There was no sound anywhere. It was still as death. I heard my heart pounding in my ears it was so still. The shadows grew longer. No birds, no breeze, there was nothing to rattle the bushes as the shadows got longer. Then the steady clop of horse hooves filled the stillness.

"I saw Yellow Boy's pony moving down the stream. There was no sign of Yellow Boy anywhere. I knew he wanted to get Tally alive if he could. He wanted to show me how Apaches made their enemies pay blood for blood. I saw the barrel of Tally's Winchester roll up and over from the direction it had been pointing toward Rufus. It pointed back toward Yellow Boy's paint. Tally fired and a bright red stripe appeared on the pony's rump as the bullet bounced whining off the walls up the canyon. The horse screamed and kicked, then disappeared running back up the canyon. There was kicking and bucking from Sally, Elmer, and Midnight as they jerked free behind their bushes and followed him. I shot at Tally's rifle barrel, the only thing I could see close to him, and I missed. He must have seen the smoke from my shot because he returned fire and splattered lead on the boulder not a foot from my notch. Rufus covered his hiding place again with a quick succession of rounds, stopped, and waited, hoping Tally would make a mistake and show himself.

"Suddenly Tally was up and running, weaving and bobbing, toward the protection of Frenchy's cabin. Yellow Boy's rifle poured round after round after him. Some ricocheted off the boulders and stones around him. I saw two rounds pass through his shirt, and the heel of a boot went flying. I took a shot with the Sharps and saw his hat go sailing off and an ear disappear. Another round from Yellow Boy knocked Tally's revolver holster right off its belt, but he got to the cabin and disappeared inside. Not only was he the most murderous man I've ever known, he was the luckiest.

"I swept the cabin, looking down the barrel of the Sharps, but saw no sign of him. Rufus was crouched over and running down the canyon from boulder to boulder toward the house. Yellow Boy soon joined him. Rufus waved, motioning me to stay where I was and cover them. I waved back I understood. I watched them study the cabin for a couple of minutes. Before they made a move, Tally dived out a window on the far side of the cabin, rolled to his feet, and bobed and weaved from one boulder to the next, a crazy heel-and-toe gait to compensate for the missing boot heel. He was headed for the outrider horse that had stopped below the cabin. Like a fool I didn't shoot the horse, but tried to hit Tally again and missed. I yelled at Rufus and Yellow Boy, Shoot! Shoot! He's running for the horse! They ran toward the cabin. By the time they got there, Tally was already mounted and headed down the trail. I cursed with skill far beyond my years. Would I ever learn? Just like Stone, I had missed him, and, because of my bad judgment, he was getting away.

"I looked up from the Sharps' sights and through the small cloud of gunsmoke surrounding me. Yellow Boy was in a rush to undress down to his breechcloth, long knife, and his moccasin boots as he talked to Rufus. I grabbed the Sharps, cartridges, and canteen and ran down to them.

"As I ran up, Yellow Boy kneeled by the stream and drank deeply. What are we going to do? I asked, overflowing with guilt at not shooting the horse. I let Tally get away and knew we were in big trouble.

"Rufus rolled a quid he had been chewing to the other cheek and spat. *It's liable to take an hour or more to run down them animals. By then Tally'll be long gone or have found help to come back and git us. Damn it! I knowed we shoulda shot the horses right off! Hell, Yellow Boy said we oughta, but I wanted to save 'em and wouldn't listen.* He put his hand on my shoulder and gave it a reassuring squeeze. *It'll be all right, Henry. Yellow Boy's a gonna run him down.*

"Yellow Boy dunked his head in the cold stream, then pulled it out to swing it back and forth, flinging silvery threads of water from his hair everywhere. How's he gonna do that, Rufus? You just said it could take an hour to round up the stock? Tally'll be long gone by then.

"Yellow Boy stood up. He took me firmly by the shoulders and looked squarely into my eyes. *I run. I catch. I kill.* He drew a quick finger across his throat.

"But, but...you can't catch a man riding a horse when you're on foot. I sputtered.

"He smiled patiently. *Si, I catch Tally, Hombrecito.* He held up two fingers. *In two days at the canyon in the Jarillas, I come. Adios.*

"He set off down the canyon in a long easy stride carrying his rifle in both hands and his cartridge belt strapped across his chest. I stood speechless staring after him. As he disappeared in the late afternoon light, Rufus spat again. Wiping his mouth with the back of his hand, he said, *A strong man with good wind has more endurance than a horse. They's plenty of tales floatin' around 'bout how Apaches a foot have caught horses by runnin' 'em down. I was almost kilt by an Apache a foot-chasin' me and me on my horse back in my scoutin' days. You push a horse hard, you might get sixty or seventy miles in a day out of him, if he's in good, real good, shape. I've seen Apaches run a hundert miles in a day across a hot desert that'd kill a horse. Hell, they's tales in the cavalry 'bout an ole Indian in Californy that run nearly a hundert mile across the desert to a fort. He took a little rest when he got there and then run back making the entire trip in less time than it takes fer the sun to rise, go down, and come back up again. That there was a two-hundert mile run in a day and a night Henry! My money says Red Tally is a gonna be in hell come first light tomorry.*

"I shook my head, finding what Rufus told me hard to believe, but I didn't dispute him. He said, *Come on, let's round up the stock and git over to the Jarillas 'fore first light. Somebody at Lee's place might a heard the shootin', get a little curious, and come a lookin' tomorry mornin'.*

"We started walking up the canyon. What're we gonna do with the bodies, Rufus?

"Rufus spat a stream of brown juice on a lizard scurrying across a boulder and said out the side of his jaw, *Soon as we get the animals, we'll load 'em up on Sally an' Elmer, haul 'em up the Eyebrow and toss 'em over. Toss 'em off that there bluff and they'll fall two thousand feet an' hit where it's real hard to git to. Thought we'd never git to those cavalry boys that the Apaches sent over the edge back in eighty-two. We'll have to ride the trail in the dark, but they's near a full moon tonight and we ain't goin' over the Eyebrow proper so we oughta be all right. Suit you?*

"I nodded. I knew it would be hard, nasty work but it needed doing if we weren't going to bury the bodies. We were lucky. We found all the animals grazing together after walking about fifteen minutes up the canyon. The hide on Yellow Boy's pony had an ugly cut from Tally's bullet grazing him, but it wasn't life-threatening and Rufus said he could doctor it right up. We led them back to our supplies, and after Rufus put a poltice on Yellow Boy's paint, we harnessed the others up. We decided we'd ride the horses and carry the bodies on the mules until we got to the steepest part of the trail, then lead the mules on foot to the spot on the Eyebrow where we wanted to toss the bodies over. The animals were skittish and hard to handle. The smell of death, drying blood, and feces was everywhere.

"*That smell's gonna draw varmints fast Henry. Best have us a gun ready in case a cat or a bear sniffs us out. Bring Lil David and some cartridges with you, will ya?* He said over his shoulder as he walked away leading Elmer. I grabbed Little David and caught up with him.

"We picked up the north side outrider and threw him over Elmer's back and tied him in place. Then we got the point rider. I led Elmer over to the equipment and tied him off until we could load up the other two. Rufus walked over to Stone and spat a brown stream of tobacco juice on Stone's shirt. *That there is what I think of yore sorry tail, Mr. Stone.*

"I was leading Sally over to help pick him up when I heard Stone wheeze in an agonized whispered groan, *Why'd you back-shoot me, you old bastard?*

"Rufus grinned from ear-to-ear, showing his old yellow teeth through his scraggly beard. He leaned forward, resting his elbows on his knees as he brought his face up close so he could look in Stone's eyes that were slits locked shut with pain. With a snort of defiance and victory he said, *I'll be damned if ye ain't still alive! I's delighted to tell ye, we a gonna give ye a free ride offa the Eyebrow. If'n ye can keep on breathin' till then, why ye'll have 'bout four or five seconds to yell fore ye hit the rocks. Hell's fire Stone. I didn't shoot ye. Henry Fountain did. Just like I taught him. Reckin' this here's payday jes like it was fer yore pard Bentene.*

"As I walked up Stone coughed and groaned again, *God! This hurts...I knew that sorry little pup would get me someday if I didn't find him first.* He coughed again and said through clinched teeth, *Guess this just ain't my lucky day. It ain't yours either, you old bastard!* With his last bit of strength he threw his revolver up and fired. The bullet caught Rufus in the side and spun him around. His teeth clinched in pain, and, holding his hand over the wound, he began to sit down slowly.

"With the thunder from the Colt echoing up and down the canyon, I screamed in a sick rage, No! No! I dropped Sally's reins and grabbed the Sharps by its barrel with both hands. I ran up to Stone and swung it as hard as I could into his face. Blood flew everywhere, all over Stone, on to Rufus's back and neck, and on the front of my shirt. Half of Stone's face disappeared into the back of his skull. He didn't move or make another sound.

"I ran to see how badly Rufus was hit. He sat there his face twisted in pain, laboring in long slow pulls to breathe. *A dead man shot me, Henry, and damn if it don't hurt. Never thought no dead man would shoot me, but he did. I ain't dead yet though. Don't look so scart. Here, help me over to the supplies and find my doctorin' bag.*

"I sat him down and began rummaging for his medicine kit. It didn't take long to find it and give it to him. He pulled out some dried moss and a roll of bandaging. *Look at my back, Henry. Did the bullet pass through?* I looked, lifting his bloody shirt. The exit wound was there, a big black hole oozing blood. I wanted to vomit, but I knew I had to stay calm and strong. It was our only chance.

"It definitely went through, Rufus.

*"That's good, that's good.* He groaned as sweat ran down his face in little rivulets. *I might make it yet.* He coughed a little blood, spit, and then tore off two wads of moss. He dug around in his kit, found a sack of evil-smelling powder and dusted the moss with it. Handing a piece of moss to me, he said, *Here, boy. Wet it a little, then put it over the hole in my back. Start wrappin' this bandage around me whilst I hold some over the front.* When we finished, he sat back against a rock. *Don't reckin I'll bleed to death now, thanks to you. I shore don't feel like packin' any bodies up the trail. Can you do it by yore self while I rest?*

"Yes sir, I can do that. You just rest here. I'll be back in a while. He coughed and nodded as he held his hand against the bandage as he took a long swallow from a canteen.

"I tied ropes around the feet of Stone and the outrider. I tied Sally up next to a dead apple tree. Using Midnight to pull the bodies up on her, I balanced them once they were across her back and tied them on. She pranced around a little, her eyes still wide with the smell of blood and all the shooting that had gone on. Stone's head was leaking blood and the stench from the gut-shot outrider was terrible. I made sure Rufus was comfortable before I led Sally and Elmer up the trail toward the Eyebrow.

"I was lucky the moon was full and was up early that night. There was plenty of light to see the trail. When we got to the narrow neck of the Eyebrow, I nearly slid off the edge myself getting the bodies off the mules. Stone was the last to go. Before I pushed him over, I took two cartridges from his gun belt, one to remember that day and one for the day he had Tally murder Daddy. I expected to put one of them in Oliver Lee. I sat Stone on the edge of the Eyebrow, his face and head smashed nearly beyond recognition in the soft yellow light. He appeared to have already fallen over the edge once.

"I looked at his corpse and murmured, *Nothin's ever gonna bring my Daddy back Stone, not even killin' you – twice with the same gun. I just hope Daddy, somewhere, somehow, is resting easier. You got your due this day. Good-by...I'm sure we'll meet in hell.* With that I heaved him off the side and listened as his body bounced down the bluff wall to crash into the trees and rocks at the bottom with a dull sound, like a boot dropping on a thick carpet.

"Mounting Midnight, I led the mules back down the trail and didn't waste any time getting back to Rufus. He was sitting against the same rock where I'd left him. He had his rifle across his knees and was smoking his pipe like nothing was wrong at all.

"That job's done! You any better? Why do you have your Winchester out and cocked?

"He nodded. *Good man. Those bastards oughta not be found for a right long time once the varmints get their fill. I'm a hurtin purty bad, but I can ride. Done had a coyote through here sniffing at the bloody spots. Warn't gonna take no chances that cuss was gonna come sniffin' after me.* He groaned as he shifted position. *Now, Henry, if you can load up Elmer and saddle Sally, we'll get on over to the Jarillas.*

"He sounded so sick and weak, I said, I can load the animals, but are you sure you can ride, Rufus?

"*Yeah...umph...I can ride. A 44-40 slug just ain't nuthin' I'd want regler fer breakfast. Know what I mean?*

"I managed a smile and nod as I began loading Elmer. *Yes sir, I do. I wouldn't want none either.*

"When we rode out of the mouth of Dog Canyon, the moon still hadn't reached midnight. Rufus rode bent over, holding onto his saddle horn with both hands. I led the way, taking paths that avoided the glow of campfires in the distance and making as straight a line as I could toward the Monte Carlo cut in the Jarillas. Thankfully, it was a fairly easy ride. We didn't stop to rest the whole way. Rufus wanted to get where we were going, change his bandage, and then rest.

"Crossing to the west side of the Jarillas, I found the ocotillo thicket in front of Yellow Boy's canyon and threaded our way through to the little stream toward the back. I helped Rufus off Sally, got him some water, laid out his bed, and unloaded our gear at the overhang next to the little wet-season stream of water. He lay back with a hard sigh and motioned me to rub down and feed the animals before I did anything for him. When I finished with the animals we changed his bandage. The bleeding had stopped. Rufus thought that a good sign. I unsheathed the Sharps, wiped the dried blood off the stock, loaded it, and lay down next to Rufus. I was exhausted. I was even more tired than the night after I had taken my first shot at Stone. Well, at least I hadn't missed today, and Stone lay somewhere at the bottom of a two-thousand-foot bluff with wolves and coyotes sniffing around for a piece of him. My father had a measure of justice. If Yellow Boy caught Tally, the debt would be paid in full except for settling with Oliver Lee. I was proud of the work we had done that day. I was in a dreamless sleep in three breaths.

"I awoke to hundreds of birds twittering in the bushes up and down the canyon. The sun was up and it was already starting to get hot. I looked over at Rufus. His eyes were squeezed shut and his teeth were ground together. His face was covered with sweat and his breathing was labored. I knew he must be in a lot of pain and felt helpless to do anything.

"Rufus! What can I get you? Do you need water? I was frantic to do something.

"*Ummm...ph.* He groaned. *A sip outta that canteen is gonna taste mighty good.*

"I got the canteen and helped him sit up to drink. After a couple of swallows he lay back and said, *Been needin' that fer a while. They's been a herd went by here 'bout first light. That oughta wipe out any tracks we made gettin' in here. You all right son?*

"Yes, sir, I'm fine. You look like you're hurtin' bad.

*Reckin' I ain't ready to swing no gal in a saloon jig.* He ground his teeth again as a new wave of pain swept over him. He panted a little then seemed to relax. *By damn! We got ole Stone, didn't we? He shore as hell ain't gonna pull any more sorry shootin's on this here range. Tally ain't gonna be a shooter anymore either. Ye'll see when Yellow Boy gets back. Ye'll see, ummmph, just wait.*

"He waited for the pain to pass. *Henry, I want ye to slide yore hand agin that hole in my back and show me the blood.* He looked at my face and managed a grin. *Remember, son, cold and cakilatin'. Go on now. Do it. It ain't a gonna hurt that much and I need to see. Gimme a stick to bite on 'fore ye start.*

"I cut a stick off a piece of mesquite and gave it to him. He clamped down on it and nodded. I slid my hand up under his back as carefully and easily as I could, but he groaned deep in his throat and his breath came in short desperate pants over the mesquite stick. I felt around on the wet spot under the bandage and pulled my hand back. It was smeared with dark blood, not the bright red kind I had seen when he was first wounded.

"Rufus squinted at my hand through his dust covered glasses as I held it up for him to see. He nodded and relaxed. I guessed that the dark blood was a sign the poultice we'd rigged up was doing some good. The bleeding didn't seem to be that bad, just a slow low-level ooze. The pain seemed to recede and I took the stick out of his mouth.

"He was quiet as I stepped over to the little stream and washed the blood off my hand. I came back and sat down cross-legged beside him. I felt the warm sun on my back. It was quiet and peaceful with only canyon wrens chirping in the bushes.

"He saw how serious my expression was and managed a smile. What does it mean? The blood was dark – almost black. Is your poultice workin'?

*"Naw. Ain't no poultice gonna fix me. Dark blood means I'm liver-shot. I ain't gonna make it more'n a day or two at best. I'm bleedin' inside.*

"You're not gonna die, Rufus! You can't die!

*"Yes, sir, I reckin' I am. They's nuthin' anybody can do about it. I'm done. We got to figure out the best thing fer ye to do next. Stone might a told somebody he was a goin' lookin' fer ole Rufus and his kid. If'n he don't come back, they's a gonna come lookin' fer us too. Ye oughta lay low fer a while fore ye go back to yore mama. Yellow Boy is still yore ace. Ain't nobody gonna guess ye're with him.*

"I felt sick, enraged, and alone. I was helpless to stop the death of my friend. He was going to die because he'd helped me. I wanted to cry in shame and frustration, but didn't dare do it in front of him. All I could do was sit, stare at him, and chew on my lip. This couldn't be happening to me again. Stone had murdered Daddy. Now he had killed the man who raised me like I was his own. It wasn't fair! I wished I could kill Stone again as the memory of smashing in his face filled my mind.

"Rufus squeezed his eyes shut again and clenched his teeth as another wave of pain rolled over him. When he began to relax he looked over at me. *They's nearly a full bottle of laudanum in my kit. It's the dark brown one with the red thread tied around it. Guess now is as good a time as any to use it. It'll make me easy in a little while. Get it fer me, will ye?'*

"I found the laudanum and gave him a good swallow. He took a big swig of water, then lay back in his pain. As the air got hotter and the sun rose higher, he began to relax and drift in and out of sleep.

"The animals were getting restless. They hadn't been fed or watered since we found our way into camp. I took care of them, straightened up the camp, and found some more cow chips and wood for the fire. The work dulled the ache I felt in my heart and gut knowing Rufus was about to die. It was like I was staggering around senseless in a nightmare.

"I sat by him through the rest of the day keeping the flies off the bloody bandage, and giving him water and laudanum again when he asked for it. He became peaceful and slept easily through the heat of the day. I was hungry as the sun was going down and shadows filled the canyon. I made some stew and ate. Rufus awoke and watched without speaking. When I asked if he wanted to eat he shook his head.

"Is the laudanum working?

"He nodded. *It's a doin' its job, son. I ain't a hurtin' much now. Just feel kinda dreamy. Havin' a hard time a thinkin' straight. See if'n ye can find a bottle of whiskey in the grub sack and give me a swaller or two, would ya?*

"I found the bottle and he took two or three long pulls. He smacked his lips and said, *That there stuff ain't gonna do my liver no good, but it shore warms a feller up on the inside. Sit down here next to me, Henry. I'll tell ya what I'm a thinkin if'n ye'll fire up my pipe fer me.*

"He corked the bottle and sat it beside him. I found the pipe in one vest pocket and tobacco in the other. I filled and lighted it like I'd seen him do many times. It took some coughing and wheezing on my part to get a good coal in it, and he grinned while he watched me struggle with it. I handed it to him and sat down cross-legged next to his chest so I could see his face. I stared at his rheumy blue eyes behind his dust-covered wire-framed spectacles, waiting for him to speak as he pulled long and slow on the pipe.

*Don't feel so bad about me dying, Henry. I done lived several year past seventy. Shoulda been dead a few times 'fore this. My string just run out is all. Bible says we're done after three score and ten and that there is seventy. Guess God gimme me a little extry time to take care of ye and help settle the score with Stone and Tally. It's time fer me to go an' I'm ready.*

"There were tears rollin' down my face. I don't want you to go, Rufus. I need you here. Please don't die.

"He patted my knee. *Yore a man now, son. I'm mighty proud of the way you handled yore self yestidy. Yellow Boy's gonna help you along till yore full growed. Ye gonna be fine, boy, just fine. Gimme another swaller of that whiskey, will ye?* I uncorked the bottle and he took a couple more long pulls before lying back with a sigh. He was quiet for a while as he pulled on his pipe and sent puffs of smoke floating up into the still cool air.

*I ain't got nobody else 'cept you, Henry. I want you to have all my stuff and the ranch. Git a piece of paper outta my medicine kit and write what I tell ya.*

"The only paper I could find was folded up in a flat leather pouch along with a lead pencil. On one side of the paper, creased and yellowed by the years, was a letter from Mrs. Darcy. I've looked at it so much I memorized it. It reads:

Dear Rufus,

Thank you for bringing my Charlie home to me after the Apaches shot him. He was a fine man and he liked riding with you. Now that he's gone, I'm selling our place and starting a boarding house in Lincoln to support myself. Our children are gone. All I have left that's of any value are good friends like you. Please come and expect to stay at my boarding house whenever you're over in this part of the country. I look forward to seeing you soon.

Your friend,
Sarah Darcy.

"I showed the letter to Rufus. He brightened at seeing it and said, *Sarah Darcy. Damn good woman fer any man. Go ahead and write on the back of it, Henry. She won't mind 't all. Now write what I tell ya:*

*Bein' clear headed and thinkin' straight, I, Rufus Pike, leave all my possessions includin' land, cattle, mule, dog, and guns to my friend Henry...Henry I don't think I oughta call you Henry Fountain, everbody thinks ye're dead and they might think I's crazy and you's a thief...What's a good name to call ye in this here will? Uhmmmm...I think ye's saved from Jack Stone by the grace of God...I'm a gonna call ye Grace, Henry Grace. Is that all right, Henry?* I nodded. Anything to make him easy.

*Henry Grace you are then. Where was I? Oh yeah, to my friend Henry Grace. Signed this date 1 September, 1902, Rufus Pike. I know it ain't the First, Henry, but I know it's September so the exact date don't make no never mind. Hand it over here and let me sign it.* I gave him the pencil and paper and held the skillet I had turned over to write on. He struggled to sit up straight, sweat pouring from his face. He signed it with strong strokes, and then lay back exhausted. I folded the letter back up and put the paper and pencil back in the leather pouch.

"He took another pull on the whiskey bottle and sighed. *It's a gettin' cold ain't it? Bring me another blanket, will ya?*

"It was dark, but the air was still warm in the canyon. I was sweating and he had a blanket wrapped around his legs. I couldn't understand why he thought he was cold, but I got him another blanket, anything to make him comfortable.

"After I spread the second blanket over him, he said, *When ye're ready to use the will, take it over to ol' George Adams in Las Cruces. He's a lawyer who helped me git the ranch recorded and rode with me in the old days. He'll know my signature and he'll make shore things is done right.*

"He coughed, spat some blood, and then took another pull on the whiskey bottle, but most of it dribbled down his chin. I reached to steady the bottle for him. He coughed and choked a little as the liquid fire flowed down his throat.

"Rufus was still for a while, then he turned and looked at me. *Henry, I just remembered, they's four sacks of gold coins under the porch post closest to the barn. I took 'em off a freight wagon Apaches wiped out years ago on the San Antonio road. I buried 'em fer when I needed the money, but never touched it. I spec they's about twenty thousand dollar there. Ye take it and get yore self a good education and a good start. Ye got the guts and brains to be anything ye wanta be. Never stop trying at anything ye wanna do and it'll happen. Understand me, son?*

"I nodded. I couldn't speak. I knew he was slipping away. The tears trickled down my cheeks, bathing my face in sorrow. I felt so helpless. There was nothing to be done to save him.

"He was quiet, breathing easy for a while with his eyes closed. I sat by him cross-legged, rocking back and forth, my hands clasped together in an attitude of prayer, hoping against hope that somehow he'd live. The moon swung up over the mountains and climbed high in the night sky against puffy, slowly drifting clouds. Stark shadows mixed with golden light filled the canyon. When the moon began it's downward arc, his eyes flickered open. He looked at me with a peaceful smile.

*Good-by, Henry. Live a long time and do good.* His spirit left with a deep sigh as he closed his eyes and was gone. I wasn't able to cry for my father when he was killed, but I cried for Rufus. I cried like a man cries, from deep in my gut feeling the springs at the bottom of my soul opening and flooding a great empty place left in my life.

# 16

# THE COST OF HONOR

Roberta felt tears running down her cheeks and reached for the handkerchief she kept folded in her uniform breast pocket. She bowed her head and looked sideways at Henry, afraid for him to see her feelings. His faced was filled with sad melancholy. She felt pulled into the deepest recesses of his heart. He had opened its door by telling her of some of the most intimate parts of his life; now, she felt part of it too. It was obvious to her that Rufus's death was the genesis of Henry's choice to be a physician. She dabbed away her tears, squeezed his hand, and gave him a little peck on the cheek.

He sighed and looked into her eyes. "I've lost lots of friends and patients in my time. I've never wept for them as I did for Rufus. I was too young to fully understand what happened to Daddy when Stone and Tally murdered him. I was virtually grown when Rufus died in that little canyon. Sitting there with Rufus's body, I wondered if my life had a chance ever to be right again. It was like...it was like I was the only person left in the world. I thought that maybe God had cursed me for some reason, and that my destiny was for those close to me to die before their time so I'd suffer. I thought about that for a long time. Then I remembered that Rufus often told me that we mustn't blame God for the bad things that happened to us. God wanted justice, and one way or the other, justice happened. Either we helped it along or we didn't, but it happened. *Henry,* he used to say, *it's all gonna come out even, regardless of what we do. The Book says cast yore bread on the water and it'll come back to ye a hundert times over. That there means ye do good, ye'll get more back than ye ever intended and maybe in ways ye never believed. If yore doin' a good thang for the right reasons, ye don't expect nothin' back anyways. If'n yore works is bad, the payback is a hundert times worse.* Church-going hasn't been on my life's page, but I read the Book like Rufus taught me, and I think, even to this day, he had it about right...You want some coffee?"

She nodded. He stood up to fill their cups while Roberta knelt and checked Yellow Boy's pulse and felt his brow for fever. He was cool to her touch. The old man was resting easy; most of the wheeze in his chest was gone.

They put the chairs back by the table, and then sat down against the wall once more. Henry filled his old briar pipe and lighted it with a splinter from the fire, and Roberta lighted a cigarette. They sat close, arm in arm, enjoying the mutual warmth of their bodies in the cool cabin air, and watched the smoke from their tobacco twist and curl in the flickering light.

Roberta nodded toward the old man peacefully sleeping in front of the fire. "Was he able to catch Red Tally?"

Henry's crooked little, are-you-kidding smile appeared. He nodded, "Yes, he did.

"The river of grief pouring out of my soul finally stopped. I felt drained and empty. I cried all I was going to cry. I sat beside Rufus's body the rest of the night. The times we'd spent together tumbled out of my memory fresh and clear. As I thought about it, I realized Rufus must have spent a fortune on cartridges teaching me to be a marksman with the Sharps. I'd bet I shot well over three thousand rounds at the targets he put in front of me. By the time I shot Jack Stone, I was about as good with Little David as I am now. We probably carried a hundred tons of rock, twenty or thirty pounds to each stone, to make me strong and to build the cabin and fences he wanted like Frenchy Rocha's. The hours we spent in the desert with Yellow Boy, and them teaching me how to live off the land were long and hard.

"He didn't have much of a repertoire when it came to cooking, but I was never hungry and he taught me to keep beans in the pot and coffee on the fire. I read every book he had stacked in that corner of his shack, and we spent many a long evening talking about the ideas and beliefs they held. He taught me all the mathematics I needed to know for surveying and for using the stars to navigate across the desert. That meant he had to teach me some trigonometry and algebra. He once told me how he'd come to learn all those things in the New Mexico wilderness, but that's another story, and it's a good one.

"The stars were beginning to fade when I realized I wasn't alone. I jumped in surprise and started to get up, but Yellow Boy, standing behind me, put a firm hand on my shoulder and nodded toward Rufus's body. *Que esta Hombrecito?*

"I had to bite my lip to keep from crying again. I mumbled and choked on my words as I told Yellow Boy the whole story.

"When I had finished, he flopped down beside me, exhausted. He sighed as he stared off into the dark shadows along the canyon walls as the sky got brighter. After a long while he said, *So, at last Rufus goes to the grandfathers. He goes with a strong arm and courage in his heart. He is welcome there. We lose friend and brother. There are no women to mourn for him here. We will smoke and fast to remember him when the sun comes. Tonight we go to his rancho. I know place there for his bones. Do not be sad for Rufus, little brother. Be sad for yourself. You are still in the land of the living. Rufus has trouble no more. Our friend has left us. You must be strong for yourself. Your friend wants you to be strong.*

"We sat together with Rufus's body and watched the morning light find the high puffy clouds and creep through the shadows in our canyon. Birds began singing in the mesquite and creosote bushes. I could hear the trickle of water in the little stream just below us and the mules and horses beginning to stamp around. I looked over at Yellow Boy. He was gaunt and dirty. Salt sparkled in the light where streams of sweat had run down his shoulders and belly. I looked up the canyon and saw the horse Tally had taken tied with our mules and horses.

"I stared at Yellow Boy's eyes, eyes white and clear like those of a big hunting cat. Did you get Tally?

"He nodded toward a greasy-looking sack sitting by the fire. *Look.*

"I threw a little extra wood on the fire. As it blazed up I saw the sack was a bloody pair of long-johns with the arms and legs tied in a knot. I kneeled down beside it, untied the knot, and pulled open the cloth.

"The bearded head of Red Tally stared back at me, a bullet hole through his good right eye. Yellow Boy had made sure Tally's head was blind if it made it to the land of spirits. I clinched my teeth to keep from gagging and stared at the head of the man who had brought me so much grief and nearly killed me. The patch over the left eye was gone, and the socket stared back at me never having known my image. The heavy red beard seemed to engulf the rest of the face in a ball of fur smeared with dark dried blood.

"The nausea passed. I felt grim satisfaction settle in my belly, a meal fully consumed, but leaving a bitter aftertaste. There was nothing but a great feeling of emptiness left in the middle of my chest. What Stone and Tally started so long ago was nearly finished. I still had the bullet I promised for Oliver Lee. Now I wondered if I would ever use it. My thoughts formed an image of a naked, headless corpse lying somewhere out in the desert for the coyotes and buzzards to pick over.

How ironic, I thought. The man who made my father disappear will also vanish without a trace, and here I stand holding the sack with his sorry rotting head. What was it Rufus had said? *Cast yore bread on the waters.* I retied the long-john sack and sat it where I knew it would stay in the shade. It was already starting to stink.

"Yellow Boy hadn't moved. I sat back down beside him and whispered, Tell me of this victory. I want to know all.

*First I will drink and wash. Find my cigarros, little brother. I will tell you while we watch the day.*

"He got up and drank deeply, then bathed in the little stream by the fire. I covered and wrapped Rufus's body in his ground canvas and blankets and pulled him up under the ledge where it was cooler. I rummaged through our gear until I found Yellow Boy's shirt and coat and handed them to him as he pulled the water from his hair, sliding it through his fingers. He tied off his hair with his big yellow bandana, pulled on the shirt, and slipped the army jacket over his shoulders. I looked over at his rifle leaning on Elmer's pack rack. One cartridge was missing from the tube magazine. He found his gun belt and checked the revolver's load before buckling it on. Stuffing some rags, a straight stick, a small bottle of coal oil, and a box of cartridges in an old flour sack, he picked up the Henry and nodded toward the Sharps. *Hombrecito, take Shoots Today Kills Tomorrow and a blanket. We climb up and watch the day, clean guns, smoke and speak of the end of Tally.*

"From up on the watch point we saw a beautiful, clear morning covering the valley. The air was cool. The sky colors over the Organs were delicate gauzy purples, reds, oranges, and a soul-lifting turquoise that glimmered for a while to the south before it faded into a brilliant morning blue. Small groups of cattle moved through the grass and mottled delicate light-green mesquite thickets and rugged pine-green creosote bushes spread below us. There were no riders anywhere in sight.

"We spread the blanket, sat down shoulder to shoulder with our backs to a boulder, and began cleaning our weapons. I had to work to get the stain left by Stone's blood off the Sharps stock. For all the abuse I'd given it killing Stone, the stock still showed no cracks and stains that couldn't be removed with coal oil and a little frantic rubbing. Yellow Boy's stick was just long enough to push a coal-oil-soaked patch down the long Sharps barrel. It took several cycles of soaked patches followed by a clean dry one pushed down the barrel to get the rifling to shine again in the morning light. Yellow Boy was smooth and efficient cleaning the Henry. Soon he raised the loading spring tab and twisted the loading gate at the end of the barrel. He carefully slid back down the barrel the cartridges he had levered out of it before cleaning. After the last of those was in place, he pulled one cartridge out of his gun belt and let it ease down the remaining three inches left in the magazine tube. The bullet made the magazine full again. He carefully closed the loading gate, gently eased the spring tab back down on the cartridges, laid the Henry across his knees, and watched with satisfaction as I finished the Sharps. After I cleaned and reassembled the breech gate, I slide a cartridge in, closed it, and let the hammer down. Done! He grunted approval. *Ummmph, Rufus taught you well.*

"He reached inside his coat and produced two cigars and a box of sulfur matches. He cut the ends to be lighted off, and then handed one to me. He bit off the mouth plug and spit it away. Copying him, I did the same. He stuck his cigar in his mouth and clamped down on it with his jaw teeth. I imitated him with mine. He lighted the end of each one while we pulled hard to get a good coal burning. I coughed and cleared my throat pulling in the smoke until I learned how to blow it back out without inhaling. We sat silently for a while in our little cloud of blue smoke as the morning began its race for midday. I trembled inside a little. I knew Yellow Boy smoking with me meant that I'd been accepted as a man. I was a boy no more.

*Now I speak of end of Tally?*

"Si, por favor! Tell me your story; I very much want to know what happened.

*When I run out of canyon, I see the dust from Tally horse in the distance. He rides toward El Paso y Rio Grande. Es perhaps tres o quatro long shots for Shoots Today Kills Tomorrow. He rides hard at first and the distance between us gets longer. Then he slows un poco and soon stops to look back. He stares a long time; it is not wise thing for a man riding away from death to do, pero he no see mi. I raise no dust and his eye cannot find me in the mesquite. He stops too long. I get a long shot closer. After long time, he turns and rides at easy trot straight for Mexico. I run easy. I run steady. The earth is warm, pero the air es frio. It is good to run. Tally knows he must not ride hard or his horse will not make the rio. I gain on him.*

"I envied him that run. Loping through the desert in the heat of the day takes a lot of strength and endurance. But if you have it, if you train for it as he did and had taught me to do, after a while, you get in a kind of a rhythm. You feel and hear the whoosh of your breath, the steady thump of your heart, and your feet rippling across the sand. Somehow it all gets synchronized. With every stride your body starts to feel like you're just floating along, like you're an animal running wild and free, like there isn't anything you can't do. You feel so good! It's a narcotic! I knew Yellow Boy probably was not even breathing hard as he gained ground on Tally's horse.

"Yellow Boy took a long drag on his cigar and slowly blew the blue-white smoke in a long stream into the morning air above his head. *I know he will stop and give horse water at Jacob's Tank. Perhaps, I think, if I am lucky, he is foolish enough to rest there. It took two steps of the sun,* which is about three hours, Bertie, *to reach Jacob's Tank. He rides, I run. Soon night comes. The moon climbs the mountains and watches the race. Tally stops at Jacob's Tank. I pass Jacob's Tank and find place to watch Tally and rest. Tally gives horse water, drinks, and washes in tank. He hobbles horse, eases saddle. He sits by tank. He rests as moon climbs high. I rest and watch for a while then run on toward river until moon is setting. I run far around Jacob's Tank. Tally knows not I was there. Tally rests, I run. I stop at place you call Boat Rock.*

"Not many people know about Boat Rock. It's way off the beaten path, a few miles this side of the Rio Grande. It looks like the upside down hull of a New England fishing boat and the keel sticks about ten feet up out of the sand.

"Yellow Boy took another long drag on his cigar, and stared over the valley. I waited for him to come back to me. *I stop. I climb up on rock and rest. I know I will face Tally at Boat Rock when birds sing and sun is behind me. He will know who takes his life. I wait.*

*Sun comes. Birds sing. Soon Tally comes. I stand on Boat Rock. Sun warms my back. Raise arms, hold Yellow Boy high to the grandfathers. I sing. I ask help from grandfathers to kill my enemy. Tally stop one long shot from Shoot Today Kill Tomorrow. Sit on horse. Watch. I see him but no move. I sing with my arms high toward the west. I hear him laugh. See red wool on face shine in the new sunlight. See black patch on eye.*

*He say, 'All right, you dumb red nigger, stand there and I'll kill your ass.' I no move. He aim rifle. Shoot once. Bullet hit far in front of Boat Rock. I no move. I sing. No sound comes from birds. They watch. I hold Yellow Boy high.*

*Tally ride forward, half long shot from Shoot Today Kill Tomorrow. Still on horse. Raise rifle sight. Shoot once. Bullet low again. Hit Boat Rock and sand. I no move. Hold Yellow Boy high. He say, 'Dumb red nigger, you do wanna die don't you? My pleasure to oblige you, señor. Mexicans will give me a little spending money for your scalp. You're just a little hard to see against that damn sun is all.*

*He walk horse toward Boat Rock slow. He careful. He watch and
wait for me to move. He ready to spring like lion on deer. He ride to me
until he sits a bow shot from rock. I see face, see eye, see beard. I no
move. Hold Yellow Boy high, sing to grandfathers. He stop. He lowers
rifle sight. He laugh mighty laugh. Raise rifle to aim. I drop to one
knee. I fire. Yellow Boy shoots straight. Bullet hits aim eye. He falls
backward from horse. I watch. He no move.*

"I had to laugh when he said, *Red nigger not dumb. Red nigger
lives. Tally dead. Tally dumb. Climb off rock and walk slow to Tally.
Want to take all scalp. Take hair and beard. Take his man parts, make
him eat.* He raised the index finger on his right hand as if he had an
idea. *No. Rufus speaks true about Bentene. Bentene and Tally same.
Others find body. No man parts, no scalp, they think Apache rob, kill,
use torture like old days. Mescaleros on reservation suffer. I think I
take head. Leave body. No clothes. No man can know him. He has no
head on other side. Head blind on other side. He is fool forever. Pull
body into mesquite. Take clothes. Take guns. Take head. Wrap head in
clothes Rufus call long-johns. Leave body there. Vultures and crows
come. Coyote come. Wolf come. Big cat come. Soon body of Tally gone.
When I leave, I take tracks away. Ride Tally horse to resting place in
mesquite until moon come. Moon come I ride to Jacob's Tank drink,
rest. After rest, I come here. Bring head of Tally, guns, saddle. My
story es no mas Hombrecito. Tally es no mas.*

"We sat and made smoke until the cigars were gone. *Rest now,
Hombrecito. I watch. You watch when sun is there.* He pointed toward
the mid afternoon sky. Suddenly, I was very weary. I stretched out on
the blanket and began to doze.

"It seemed only minutes before Yellow Boy shook me awake. He
shook his head when I asked if there had been any riders. The rest of
the day passed quickly and uneventfully as I sat and watched and
thought of Tally's final payoff.

"We climbed down as it got dark. I cooked us some hardtack and
beans over the little fire. After we ate, I took a shovel and walked to the
end of the canyon. I climbed up high on a sloping bank and buried Tally's
head so it wouldn't get washed away and perhaps found after a thunder-
storm. I shoveled the dirt in on top of it, packed it down and swept the area
so it looked unused. I stared at the spot for a while, prayed that the price
I'd paid for that head was worth it to Daddy, wherever he was, and I
thanked the grandfathers for my uncle, Yellow Boy.

"We loaded the gear on Elmer and Rufus's body wrapped in the
canvas groundcloth across Sally. She was skittish at first, rolling her

eyes and not wanting to carry the smelly canvas-wrapped body but, after Yellow Boy settled her down, she was steady the rest of the night. With the moon on the rise and rifles across our saddles, we trotted out of the canyon, and made a long flat arc south by southwest around Cox's ranch, up over Baylor Pass, and down the other side. We stopped to rest the animals a couple of times before we cleared the pass, and again near the backside of Van Patten's ranch. A good hour before dawn we rode up the trail to Rufus's shack. It had been a hard ride, and a hard return knowing only Rufus's body was there with us.

"We left Elmer and Sally loaded and the horses saddled while we watered and fed them at the corral. I didn't want Buck to look in on the place and find a couple of strangers there with Rufus's body. There was no telling what he might think or tell the sheriff. As the sun began to brighten the eastern sky, we led the animals up the trail toward the back of the canyon as the cattle stared at the familiar strangers riding among them.

"We off-loaded Elmer at the storage cave. I was wondering what Yellow Boy had in mind for Rufus's body when he led Sally further up the canyon. After about three hundred yards he stopped at a pile of rocks against the canyon wall and motioned for me to come help him as he picked up the stones, one by one, and put them to one side. Soon the rectangular mouth of a small cave appeared. It was about waist high and three or four feet wide.

"Yellow Boy nodded toward it. *One time Rufus dig new mine. Find no gold. Find no silver. Stop pretty quick. Work too hard for no money.* When we finished moving the stones I knelt down and looked inside. It wasn't more than ten or twelve feet deep. It was a perfect burial vault for our friend.

Gently we took his body off Sally. Yellow Boy passed me a canteen and I washed him as best I could, crossed his arms, and wiped the dust off his glasses. I backed into the shaft, pulling the body on the groundcloth all the way to the back. By the time I crawled out the sun was high, and it was getting warm.

"We rubbed the animals down and hobbled them so they could graze nearby while we washed, ate, and rested. We slept through the heat of the day in the shade of a big boulder on the south wall of the canyon. I was physically exhausted and emotionally drained. My sleep was deep and dreamless. When I awoke, Yellow Boy was up and had built a small fire near the mouth of the mine. He sat cross-legged near it, facing toward the sun in an attitude of meditation, his lips moving in a wordless chant.

"I washed the sleep from my face and walked about collecting a few wild flowers. I brought these back and left them floating in a bucket of water. I walked down to the shack. It was lonely, unkempt, deserted. I stepped on the porch, the boards making a mournful creak, and opened the door. Sunlight streamed through the broken window highlighting dust motes slowly drifting in the warm stifling air. A smell of old smoke, the residue of iron stove cooking over many years, seeped from the dry, cracking, wooden walls. A thin blanket of dust covered everything. Memories of happy times, struggles to learn, cleaning guns, stories of battles fought and won, treks made, and thoughts about what the writers stacked in the corner said flew at me from everywhere. I stepped to Rufus's old cot and his little bedside table. I found what I had come for: his Bible. I saw him read it often. He hadn't carried it with him on our trip. He thought it was hypocritical to have it in your pocket when you had decided you were going to kill someone, but it was all right to read it after you'd done your crime and made penance. I blew the dust off the old book, looked around the room once more, felt a shudder of grief, and then closed the door.

"As I walked back up the canyon, the sun was beginning to slide behind the Floridas turning the long streaking clouds a brilliant red and orange. Yellow Boy still sat in quiet contemplation, the little fire burning some kind of pungent smelling sage. The air was very still and the smoke rose in an arrow-straight plume slowly disappearing into the darkening sky. I carried the bucket of wild flowers into the mine, and laid them near the canvas that wrapped Rufus's body. I found his rifle with my gear and was carrying it to the mine to leave with the body when Yellow Boy raised his hand for me to stop.

"*Why you do this Hombrecito?* he asked, puzzled. *He will not use or want this weapon on the other side. He will want you to live a long time. It is of value that you keep it and preserve your life with it. Do not give it to a body that will soon be part of the earth.*

"I'd never been part of a funeral before. It seemed natural to leave a person's things with them when they died. But, what Yellow Boy said made sense, so I deferred to his judgement and kept the rifle.

"I asked him if it was appropriate to read some scripture over Rufus that he read often. Yellow Boy had been a scout for the Army in his younger days and understood what the white eye did with his dead.

*Yes, the book has words that are wise and it sings good songs. Read the words. Read while there is still enough light.*

"The dark shadows of the dying day steadily crept up the canyon. The perfume from the cactus flowers in the mine floated out to us. I stepped to the opening with the Bible, faced toward the setting sun, and turned to the third chapter of Ecclesiastes. Earlier in the day Yellow Boy had dusted off his Army jacket and rinsed the dirt and salt from his bandana. As I read, he came and stood beside me, tall and straight, with his rifle held in the crook of his arm.

> *For every thing its season, and for every activity under heaven its time:*
> *a time to be born and a time to die;*
> *a time to plant and a time to uproot;*
> *a time to kill and a time to heal;*
> *a time to break down and a time to build up;*
> *a time to weep and a time to laugh;*
> *a time for mourning and a time for dancing;*
> *a time to scatter stones and a time to gather them;*
> *a time to embrace and a time to abstain from embracing;*
> *a time to seek and a time to lose;*
> *a time to keep and a time to discard;*
> *a time to tear and a time to mend;*
> *a time for silence and a time for speech;*
> *a time of love and a time to hate;*
> *a time for war and a time for peace.*

Roberta watched Henry as he spoke. His eyes were closed and he spoke as if he were reading the words from a sheet of paper, never missing its cadence or stumbling over them.

Henry opened his eyes and saw her watching him. "How long have you had that memorized?"

"Since the day I read it over Rufus's body. I just never forgot it."

"Remarkable," she murmured. "Did Yellow Boy do anything special?"

"Yes, he did. He sprinkled some golden pollen on the canvas along with the flowers. Then he made a complete circle about the fire stopping to face each of the four directions and say something in Apache I didn't fully understand, but I heard words like *power* and *grandfathers*. I stood by, as respectful for what he did as he had done with me.

"When he finished, he said, *Now we close the door for this place that holds Rufus' bones, Hombrecito.* He picked up a stone and put it in the entranceway. I picked up one and placed it beside his. We worked into the night. The last stone was in place as the shadows from the moon came.

"When we finished, he took four stones, each the same size, and put them together in a square in front of the pile of stones covering the entrance. Each corner of the square pointed in a cardinal direction. Then he sprinkled golden pollen in their center. He stood up, facing the west. Putting his fist over his heart he said, Adios, *mi amigo bueno. Ride with the sun.*

"He turned to me. *It is for us to eat and smoke. I will sweep the tracks away from here. No one will know this is where Rufus Pike rests. Only me, only you. Go. Fix our food.*

"I dug a pit and built a small fire near the corral. I didn't want to go back in the shack again, at least not for a while. I cut venison steaks Yellow Boy had taken earlier in the day and put them on skewers to cook slowly over the fire, cut some potatoes and put them on to boil, and made a pot of coffee. My stomach felt bottomless and reminded me I hadn't eaten much of anything in three or four days. I was hungry.

"Yellow Boy soon came and sat by the fire. Neither of us spoke. Somehow it didn't seem appropriate to say anything. The smell of fat dripping in the fire and watching the steaks turn dark with flavor made us ravenous. We soon pulled the meat off the skewers, still hot and dripping, and wolfed the meat and potatoes down like starving men. When we finally sat back to blow cool and slurp the boiling coffee, Yellow Boy offered me a cigar. I shook my head. I remembered how raw my throat felt from the last one. He lit up and studied my face as I watched the fire.

*Will you find your mother now Hombrecito?*

"I don't think I can for a while yet. If those men we killed are found, riders will come looking for us, maybe even the sheriff. They'll figure out Rufus and I suckered them into Dog Canyon for an ambush. They'll be wanting payback regardless of why we did it. They won't care. Rufus told us Stone was liked and respected by most of the little ranchers. They won't stand for letting somebody get away that they think might have murdered him.

"I doubt anybody will ever find Red Tally. We'll saddle his horse and turn him loose down on the edge of the Van Patten ranch and scatter his clothes around down there. When the horse comes in without Tally, they'll think he was thrown or killed by somebody on this side of the Organs. I doubt there'll be much investigation of his disappearance because he comes and goes all the time anyway. Rufus said most folks were afraid of him. They'll be glad to see him gone.

"There's also a score I have to settle with Oliver Lee before I can go back and face my mother ...

"*You come to Mexico with me. Stay with my woman's people in Sierra Madre. No one knows they hide there or where. You safe. I teach you more. You learn to shoot with pistola. Maybe you find wife too. I know good woman for you.*

"I'll think on it. I know it is a good thing to do. But I'll have no wife for a long time. I have much to do yet. A woman will only slow me down or hold me back.

"Yellow Boy grinned. *You think muy bien, Hombrecito. You come with me. A woman is good for a man. Gives him children. Cooks. Builds wickiup. Keeps his bed warm in the cold winter. You are young. You will see. A man needs a fast horse, a straight-shooting rifle, and a good woman.*

"I don't know about the woman. I never had one. But, you're right about needing a fast horse and a straight-shooting rifle. I just haven't figured out yet what I'm going to do with my life.

"Yellow Boy's brow wrinkled, puzzled. *You live your life. Your padre plants you in your madre. Of this you no change. Pero, you make your honor, you make your body strong, you have courage, you fight, you live as a man, and you die as a man. What else is there you can do? When you know what you do with your life, tell me. Perhaps yo comprendo.*

"I try to make usted sabé now, uncle. He looked at me with his black-as-midnight eyes boring into mine and waited. It was hard to argue with him for he usually had a ready answer for everything. I said, Among the Apache, do not some men choose to be warriors? Do not some choose to be hunters or to make weapons? Do not some choose to work at the sawmill with Doc Blazer? They have chosen their work. In the white man's world there are many things a man can choose as his work. I must choose mine.

"He shook his head. *They no choose. Their power chooses them. My power told me to be a warrior. My power tells me to go where I want. My power tells me a bullet will not kill me. I know Tally cannot kill me with a bullet. My power told me this many seasons ago. My power says I must live free with my wife in the Sierra Madre far across the river and with her sister in Mescalero. My power chooses how I will live my life. My power helped me find you and make you a warrior too.*

"I do not know this power uncle. How will I find this power?
*Come with me to the Sierra Madre. Fast until it finds you. Pray on the mountains. Feel the cold wind, the rain, the snow, and the hot sun on your body. The power will find you. You will know.*

267

"I stared at his black eyes and the firelight etching the sharp outlines of shadows on his face. Either I had to go with him or go back to my mother. I couldn't face her yet and I didn't want to be hanged for killing Stone. If I hid for maybe as long as a year with Yellow Boy in the Sierra Madre, then things should be calm enough for me to come back to my family. There really wasn't much choosing to do.

"I go with Yellow Boy.

"He grinned and nodded. *Bueno! You will find your power in the Sierra Madre. We rest until the sun leaves mañana, then vamos.*

"I cleaned up our cooking site and covered over the fire pit. We left no sign of anyone being around the cabin and kept the animals out of sight up the canyon. We spread our blankets and took our weapons up on the ledge where we had watched over the shack for Stone to come back to kill Rufus and me. We laid back and watched bolts of lightning being pitched back and forth between clouds collecting over the Floridas and south toward Mexico.

"Resting there watching the distant sky flash against puffy black clouds and red mountains, doubts grew in my mind about the rightness of what we had done. Revenge left me a hollow vessel with no bottom. Revenge left one of the men dead who saved me as a little boy. Revenge was keeping me from my family and had placed a seed of desire in my soul to kill again.

"Uncle?

*Ummmph? Que es, Hombrecito?*

"We have killed those who murdered my father. You have cut off the head of Red Tally. I shot Jack Stone and smashed in his head. You shot Bentene in the head. The others with Stone, I think we also killed them in Dog Canyon. They are no more. The price has been high. Rufus is gone to the grandfathers. I would give them all back their lives if Rufus still lived. This thing we have done, was it a thing that must be done?

"He was quiet for a long time, not moving. I expected to hear him snoring at any moment, but after a while he raised up on one elbow and spoke to me looking straight into my eyes.

*What is worse than death, Hombrecito?*

"My mind was blank. I can think of nothing worse than death.

"*Ummmph. You are very young, but you have seen death many times. Still, you do not know? I tell you there are many things worse than death. To be separated from your power, that is worse than death. To live in fear, that is worse than death. To live without honor, that is worse than death. To have no courage, that is worse than death. To leave your family to the mercy of wolves, that is worse than death. Comprendé?*

"Si, comprendo. Perhaps what you speak is true. I do not know.

"He nodded. *Si, you have not lived enough to know this is true. It is true. Your power is your guide. It shows you light in your life. If you find your power, and are not true to the vision it gives you, the light is gone. You may live, but your life is dead. Fear comes and stays. Fear is a wolf. It always hunts you. It is always there in the dark waiting for you. If you run, it will come after you. It will not let you live as a man lives. It will run from the shadows and tear you to pieces. You will live as a coward, bent over with your burden. You cannot stand straight and face the sun. Your honor, Hombrecito, it is the will to keep the law you make for yourself, the law your father gives you, and his father before him, the law you choose. Honor keeps you a man. It says to the wolf you have no power over me. Without honor there is no light in your life. Without honor, there is no peace in your spirit. Walk a straight line, let no man push you from it. Always keep your honor.*

*Other men must know you have no fear. Other men must know you will not let them dishonor you. If they strike you or your family, you will strike them even if it means dying. There is no higher price. There is no greater value than your life lived with honor. Men speak of courage and admire it. What is courage? Courage is to know the wolf, but keep your honor even if it means you will lose your life. Su padre, he kept his honor. He kept his courage. He lost his life for his honor. He lived well. You are proud. This I know.*

*When Tally, Stone, and Bentene took his life, there was no turning from your honor. They had to die by your hand. That is justice. That is the law my father taught me, and his father before him. It is the law Rufus knew. It is the law even the white man believes, but chooses not to follow. The white man gives the burden of his honor to others to carry. You did not do that. Rufus did not do that. I did not do that. We paid the debt ourselves. It is finished. Rufus has gone to the grandfathers. There are many things worse. He had rather be with the grandfathers than for his friend to live without honor. That too is my belief. The debt has been paid, Hombrecito. Now sleep. We must travel far when we leave this place.*

"I knew what he told me was true. I wanted the burden of courage and of honor. I wanted to be a man, a man who was like Yellow Boy, a courageous and honorable man. I would never give that burden to someone else. I knew what I had to do when I came back from Mexico. There had to be a final accounting."

# 17

# YELLOW BOY GOES
# TO THE GRANDFATHERS

They sat silent, arm in arm, for a long time, listening to a gentle wind caress the big pines up and down the canyon. The fire was dying, it was time to bring in more wood, but Henry felt so warm and comfortable with Roberta he was reluctant to move. In the deep stillness, they heard an owl call, first in the distance, then again closer to the house.

Roberta felt Henry squeeze her hand, his whole body suddenly stiffening, as he muttered under his breath, "God!" He was looking directly at Yellow Boy, whose eyes had fluttered open. No longer asleep, he was staring at Henry, a slight smile across his lips.

"I heard the owl call my name, Hombrecito."

"I heard it too, uncle. What do you need me to do? Are you in pain?"

"No, my son, I feel no pain. I am ready. I have always been ready. Will John, Sara, and Redondo be here soon?"

"Not for a while. Redondo still searches for Father Braun. John and Sara sleep in their homes. The moon is not yet falling. Shall I get them for you?"

"It is a good thing, if you will. Before the sun is high tomorrow, I will sleep with the grandfathers. If Redondo is not here, it is as it should be. His ways do not follow the sun's rising and falling, the hours of the white man have no meaning for him."

"I will come soon with John and Sara. Roberta will stay here and help you if you have need."

The old man smiled. "It is a good thing to be in the eyes of a young woman who draws her beauty from Mexico."

Henry turned to look into the bewildered face of Roberta. Her hand held his shirtsleeve tightly as she looked in his eyes. "Henry? What in the world is going on?"

"Nearly all the old ones believe that when an owl calls at your window you will die soon. Yellow Boy heard the owl. He thinks the owl we heard called his name. He believes, no, he knows now he's about to die – probably within the next day. He says before noon. I wouldn't dare argue with him. I've seen this happen too many times to say he can't die just because he seems to be getting better. I'm going to get John and Sara. I know he wants to talk with them before he goes. There's no telling where Redondo is or if he's found Father Braun. I should be back in less than an hour. Just make him as comfortable as you can while I'm gone. Give him anything to drink or eat he asks for."

Roberta sat and stared at him for a few seconds without moving. Yellow Boy had been getting steadily better now he believed he was about to die because he heard an owl call and Henry believed it too? She shook her head. Henry knew what he was doing. "Okay, I can do all that. Any special instructions?"

"No, just hang in there. I'm in bad need of your help and support." He looked at her with sad, pleading eyes. He whispered as he squeezed her hand, "I'll be back as soon as I can."

She nodded. "Go ahead, I can manage until you get back. Whatever I can do I will, you have to know that. Please be careful on those dark roads."

Henry slipped on his heavy leather coat and the big brimmed Stetson. He waved at them before going out the door and roaring down the canyon road in the Plymouth.

Roberta sat with Yellow Boy in the soft silence of the flickering fire without speaking. She rubbed her brow as she tried to make her mind disengage from Henry's story and focus on Yellow Boy. In a while, he pushed himself to one elbow and said to her, "Nurse Gonzalez, can you spread a blanket there by the wall where you sit and help me to move there? I need to be sitting up when I speak with my children."

Roberta nodded. "Of course, señor. I'll get you one."

She found the nice red-and-black wool trader's blanket covered with geometric designs. Spreading it out and folding it so she could pull it up behind his back, she helped the old man stand and walk a couple of steps before sitting in Henry's place against the wall. He felt even more frail to her than when she had helped move him earlier. Breathing easily, he seemed content and relaxed sitting against the wall.

"Is this a good spot for you, señor? Would you rather lie down?"

"I am fine, Nurse Gonzalez." He spoke in a raspy whisper. "I ask only two more things of you: a dipper of water and my rifle. Can you bring me these things?"

"Of course, señor." She brought him a dipper gourd of water from the water bucket.

He drank long and greedily then wiped his lips with his shirt sleeve before saying, "El agua es muy frio y bueno, eh, señorita?"

She nodded and smiled. The water from that gourd dipper was cold and good. Stepping over his legs to the fireplace, she reached for the rifle with the brass receiver as she looked at him and raised her brows questioningly. He nodded yes and smiled. Surprised at how heavy it felt, she noticed the cartridge spring three quarters of the way up the magazine barrel. It was loaded. She guessed, from what Henry had told her about it, that there must be about eight cartridges in the magazine. The hammer was set in the safety position. The receiver blazed brightly enough to reflect a golden spot on the ceiling as she took it down from its support hooks.

Pointing it toward the ceiling, she let her hand glide over the smooth patina of the walnut stock. Yellow Boy watched her retrieve the old Henry without blinking. When she handed it to him, he gripped it as though shaking hands with an old friend, and he nodded to her gratefully.

"I would hold this weapon once more and gain strength from it before I leave. It has been my friend for a long time now, killing many enemies, and saving me from being wiped out when I was a much younger man." Holding it upright between his legs while resting the butt plate on the floor, he ran his right hand up and down the barrel and over the brass receiver and stock smoothly and tenderly, as if caressing a woman. He lifted it, his weakened shoulders straining against its weight, placed its butt plate on the floor next to his right hip, and held on to the barrel as though it were a staff.

Roberta couldn't help herself as she blurted out, "Be careful with your rifle, señor, it's loaded. I think there are at least eight cartridges in the magazine."

"Of course it is loaded. It has never been unloaded except when I cleaned it. What is the use of a gun unless it is loaded? No! Wait!" He said with a smile. "I have broken many heads swinging it as a club. It was easier to use with bullets."

"I am just concerned there might be an accident. I just don't want you to shoot someone you do not intend to harm, señor."

"My power has never let a bullet leave my rifle without my sending it. It will not now. We are safe."

"I know we are, señor."

"Now, may I once again ask two favors? Will you bring me my scout hat? And, will you speak to me and remember me by my name?

It is Muchacho Amarillo, Yellow Boy, Nurse Gonzalez, Yellow Boy son of Caballo Negro, Yellow Boy, Army Scout and tribal law officer." he said proudly.

Roberta smiled at him. "I will be honored to call you by your great name...Yellow Boy...if you will call me by my name. It is Roberta. Now let me get your hat."

He nodded and smiled as he waved his hand, palm parallel to the floor, in a sweep of acceptance. She stood, walked to the front door-jamb, and retrieved the battered old cavalry hat from a peg. Returning to his blanket, she kneeled beside him and placed the hat on his head as she had seen him wear it, with the front brim folded up. He reached up, and making a small adjustment said, "Bueno, Señorita Roberta, y muchas gracias."

She nodded. "De nada." Folding her feet under her, she sat down beside him, and, leaning forward on one arm, gazed past him, staring at the fire and pondering all the unbelievable things she had heard in the last two days.

He patted her hand, gently, a falling leaf in the wind, and smiled to reassure her. She looked so solemn and sad. "You look like a wise woman my child. What do you think of my brother Henry? He is a hombre bueno, si?"

Roberta smiled. "I believe he is a very good man. There is none better."

"You have spoken truly. I have seen you when you look at each other. Will he take you for a wife? He has never married or been close to a woman since the years in Mexico. Has he told you of the years in Mexico?"

She looked at the floor and shook her head. "I do not know if he wants me for a wife. He hasn't asked. If he does, I will proudly accept. He has told me many things on this trip, but he has not told me of the years in Mexico. Was there a woman for him there?"

"Si, there was a woman, a very fine one. He must tell you of those years himself. She is no more. All that is left of her is the turquoise eagle he carries with his clock. I have seen his eyes, he will ask you to come to his hacienda and be his woman."

"I do not know this, Yellow Boy. Your eyes are older and wiser than mine." Roberta felt her heart beat faster, but she shook her head. How did Yellow Boy know this? She knew in the deepest well of her heart that she loved Henry, and now knew she had loved him for a long time, but...to think he loved her that deeply too? Only Henry knew his true feelings. She might have to wait a while to see if Yellow Boy's prophesy came true. This was something only she, Henry, and time must workout. She changed the subject.

"How did you come to have your rifle?"

Yellow Boy smiled as the memories came fluttering back, a mixed flock of good times and bad roosted before his ancient eyes. "Mi padre esta Caballo Negro. Hombrecito has spoken of Rufus Pike?"

She smiled. "Yes, he has told me much of Rufus."

"Then you know mi padre was given the life of Rufus by his uncle, Fast Hand. It was a good thing Fast Hand y mi padre spared Rufus. Until he goes to the grandfathers, Rufus raised Henry like a son. Mi padre took this rifle from a wagon train we ambushed on my first raid. There were no survivors. Mi padre found it in a wagon and gave it to me. It was not as good as his, but was better than any of the others mi amigos had. I was a very bad shot. I shot over two boxes of cartridges we found at the wagon train at targets my father picked and hit nothing. Caballo Negro took me to the rancho of Rufus. He told Rufus he must teach me to shoot well or he would demand his life, the one he had spared so many years before. For many moons Rufus taught me to shoot just as he taught Hombrecito many years later. I became a better shot than Caballo Negro. From Rufus, I learned to point true. From my power, I learned to see the bullet on that point. The bullets from this rifle, they go where I see. My power now rests in this rifle. Comprendé an old man's words?"

"Comprendo señor, comprendo mucho." Now that Henry had opened his life to her, Roberta was brimming over with desire to know every detail of his survival and life after Albert was murdered. She couldn't resist asking, "How did you come to find Henry the day his father was killed?"

Yellow Boy's brows raised in surprise and question. "He has told you what happened? That I found him that day?"

"Si. He has told me all the story until Rufus went to the grandfathers and you took him to Mexico."

He smiled and nodded. "Ahhh, bueno. It has been a heavy burden for him to carry all these years. He must trust you without question. It is a hard story to keep buried here," he said motioning to his heart.

Roberta did not move as she listened to Yellow Boy tell his long hidden story. The room suddenly felt very cold and she shivered. Staring at the floor, she could only shake her head. She marveled at how such a well-loved doctor, who had saved and made better so many lives, had taken cold and calculated revenge on his father's killers. Looking up, she saw an old Apache man's face staring back at her from a porch window.

She caught her breath as she put her hand over her mouth in surprise that turned Yellow Boy's attention to the window, but he saw nothing. The door swung open, the wind blowing the fire and making shadows dance in a frenzy around the room and on the two men who stepped inside. The Apache, his hair very long and mostly gray, had a pockmarked face, a finely sculptured straight nose, slits for eyes and mouth, and, by Roberta's guess, must have been in his fifties. The Anglo man with him was older. He looked frail and used up far beyond his years.

The Apache stepped over to a smiling Yellow Boy and kneeled on one knee as he gently held the old man by his shoulders and looked in his eyes.

"I bring Father Braun, Yellow Boy. It has taken a long time to find him. He was high up on the side of Sierra Blanca with the Ortegas. Are you better?"

Yellow Boy nodded. "Si, Redondo, I am better. Tonight I heard the owl call my name. Tomorrow I go to the grandfathers before the sun is high. I am sorry Father Braun has traveled far only to see me go."

"Insignificant!" the priest cried. "It was a short road to see my friend of so many years. We will all be poorer without you, Yellow Boy. It warms my heart to see Nurse Gonzalez here with you. Is Henry nearby?"

Roberta held out her hand to Father Braun who took it firmly and hugged her. "Henry has gone to get John and Sara at their homes, Father," she said loudly enough for Redondo to hear.

Redondo nodded he understood, sat down at the feet of Yellow Boy, and crossed his legs. He stared at his father in sad contemplation and waited without speaking.

Father Braun knelt slowly on his arthritic knees next to Yellow Boy. "Old friend, did I hear you say the owl called your name?"

Yellow Boy nodded still clutching the Henry tightly for support. He looked relaxed and at peace as he stared into Father Braun's eyes. "It is so, my friend. Before the sun is high I will go."

"Then, after you speak with your children, may I perform for you the church's ceremony for those going to the grandfathers?"

"Si, mi amigo. Por favor, give me this ceremony. You are a good shaman. Our hearts understand the same medicine. I will need help on my path to the grandfathers. Muchas gracias."

"Then I will wait, my friend. I will wait at your table." Slowly Father Braun pushed off the floor, and, limping, sat down at the big round table in the room's far corner. He rummaged in the black bag he carried with him everywhere and found what he needed to prepare a last mass for his friend.

It was quiet in the room. Yellow Boy sat holding the rifle, staring off into space. Redondo hadn't moved since he sat down. Father Braun sat on a table chair leaning forward with his hands clasped between his knees and his head bowed in an attitude of prayer. Roberta stood awkwardly in the middle of the floor until she excused herself and stepped outside. She breathed deeply a few times in the cold air to steady her emotions, and gathered several sticks of firewood before returning to the door.

Father Braun looked up as she came in, and, seeing the wood, asked, "Can I help get some more wood Nurse Gonzalez?"

"No Father, I think this will be plenty for a while, pero, muchas gracias."

She knelt by Redondo and wordlessly tossed the wood on the fire one stick at a time. She washed her hands on the back porch, and then sat down in one of the old slat-backed chairs so she had easy access to Yellow Boy if he needed her. She glanced at her watch and decided Henry was likely to be back soon just as car lights lit the curtains over the windows. She smiled. She and Henry marched to the same beat.

Car doors were still slamming shut when Sara pulled open the door, her eyes red. "Father! Thank God you're still here. I'm so sorry I went home," she cried as she knelt beside him and put her hand to his ancient face.

Yellow Boy slowly shook his ancient head. "Do not weep, daughter. I am still here. You should have been in your own bed. I only call you so I can speak once more with my sons and daughter before I go to the grandfathers."

John stepped through the door followed by Henry who glanced at Roberta, a questioning look in his eyes. She nodded all was well. John knelt by Redondo, and, putting his hand on his brother's shoulder, gave it a comforting squeeze. He said, "We are all here now, Father. Give us your wisdom." He turned to look at Father Braun who was shaking hands with Henry. "Thank you, Father. It is a long way to travel in the middle of the night. It is a hard time for us all."

"The distance and the time of day are insignificant, John! I'm honored you have called me to my old friend's bedside in this time of tears and good-by." John nodded and sat down by Redondo.

Sara sat down where she had first knelt on the floor by her father. Roberta saw Father Braun speak softly near Henry's ear and saw Henry shake his head, then Henry moved over by Roberta and sat cross-legged on the floor, his hands folded in his lap. She started to get up and join Father Braun who stayed at the table back in the flickering shadows, wanting this to be a family matter in which he did not intrude unless asked. Henry nodded at her, motioning her to sit down beside him. The only sound in the room was the slow crackle of the fire and the occasional rustle of the wind through the pines.

Yellow Boy began with Sara, then studied the face of each one, even Roberta's and Father Braun's, slowly and carefully as he drew his memories of them from deep in his soul. At last, he said, "Por favor, Padre come join us." The priest moved from the table and slowly sat down in a chair next to Roberta, who held her hand up to steady him.

Yellow Boy began to speak as he leaned forward, supported by his rifle and carrying the weight of years on his sloping shoulders. His grip on the rifle's barrel made the blue veins on the back of his hands stand out as though framed by fine parchment paper. "My children, tonight I heard the owl call my name. Soon I will go to the grandfathers. Father Braun will give me his ceremony for going to the grandfathers before I go. I want you to hear my last words and to have my blessings. I have lived summers beyond counting. I had two wives who cared for me well, and gave me five healthy children. Two of those I lost to enemies in Mexico. I have adopted one son I call brother. I have paid all debts of honor. Now I sit in mi casa, a man of wealth for many summers. I have lived a good life.

"I have owned many horses. I have traveled many miles on this side of the great river and in Mexico. I have seen the sun rise and set in the Sierra Madre and on the bosom of Sierra Blanca. I have drunk from cold water in the high sierra and chewed cactus in the low desert. I have felt the cold breath of the high sierra and the fire of the desert. I have known many happy days and many hard moons with my brothers.

"I have killed many men. Some were white, some were Mexican, and some were my own people. I chased my own people for the Army. Some men I killed I did not know and they did not know me. They wanted my death because I am Apache. I did not die. They died. I killed them with my knife, my bow, my spear, or my rifle. I never took scalps; even when it was right, I never did this thing. I have never disgraced my name as a warrior. I have survived many battles. Scars from bullets, knives, arrows, and fire are on my back, chest, arms and legs to prove this. My power has lived with my Yellow Boy, my rifle. I have always followed my power. It has always spoken the truth, and now my power says I will soon go to the grandfathers." He paused for a moment and gathered his strength.

"Now I tell you this. Redondo is a wolf. He is the Apache like my uncles and father. He is the old Apache. Cunning and hard he desired war when there was no war. He was born too late for old Apaches. He has yielded to the reservation, but his heart does not live here. He has found no peace in mescal or whiskey. He seeks peace, but finds only the demons he cannot destroy. He has lived too long this way and must change." Redondo stared at his father and nodded.

"John is a horse, a wild horse tamed for reservation work. He is a horse to be ridden. He is a horse who works. He will help the Mescalero survive and prosper in the white world. He is no warrior, but he has courage to face the day and to live in it. He can read the signs of the white man and knows their meaning. It is good that he knows this. John is strong and wise in council. He thinks before he speaks. John is the future." John bowed his head and stared at the floor.

"Henry is an eagle. He has known the air of the highest sierra and the lowest desert. He has flown from the deepest pit of darkness to the highest mountain of light. He is my adopted son. I found him just before the grandfathers claimed him. I pulled him from the cold sand. There are few men like him. He is a warrior with wisdom. He is a man of many faces who has saved many lives. He has saved many more lives than he has taken. He is a true son of the Mescalero. When he became my son he was the weakest, now he is the strongest of my sons. He knew a woman in Mexico. She was taken from him. He found the demons in mescal, but he fought them. He was very strong. He is an Apache of my fathers. He avenged his woman. The men who took her life are no more. Henry has never taken another woman to wife. Now his heart is opened. He dreams of another. Soon he will have her. The last season of his life will be longer than mine and his heart will be full once more. He will continue to restore life to many." Roberta's eyes filled with tears and she covered her mouth with her hand. Henry glanced at her and gave his head the smallest of shakes as if to say, how did he know?

"Sara is the moon, a guiding light in a black night over many miles of travel. She covers her family with warm blankets in the night and gives them her strength. She arises before the dawn and makes the fire bright and the food hot. The sons and daughters she has given her husband are strong. They delight my eyes. Many Mescalero hear her voice and it is wise. Sara is a mother to her people. She will live many summers." Tears slowly rolled down Sara's cheeks.

"I go to the happy land of the grandfathers. Put me high on Sierra Blanca. Put me where my bones will see the forests of the Mescalero, the canyons of the Sacramentos, and the white sands resting against the mountains. Let my bones rest between my two wives. My sons know this place. When you are on the desert you will look toward Sierra Blanca, standing tall and tipped with white in the distance. You will know it is the bosom of my life and its stone marks the place of my bones. Now, Father Braun, brave friend of many summers, come forward and bless me with your ceremony. I am ready."

Father Braun stood in a groan of age, walked over to the table, gathered his tools of worship, and came back to creakily kneel by Yellow Boy. He brought his book, the sacraments, holy water, and oil. Yellow Boy removed his hat but continued to support himself with the rifle. Unlike he was taught, Father Braun gave Yellow Boy his last sacrament in English, translating the Latin liturgy as he read so they all understood. Henry, as a physician had seen this ritual many times. He understood the comfort it brought Catholic families and believers. John and Sara were members of Father Braun's flock. He and Redondo were not. Henry wasn't sure if his beliefs matched any formally recognized religion, only that he believed a just God ruled the affairs of men. Redondo didn't believe in the Apache Jesus. He believed only in the grandfathers, but he respected and admired Father Braun. Redondo and Henry were grateful for the blessing Father Braun was giving Yellow Boy. Roberta was Catholic. She understood perfectly every nuance in this, the last sacrament. That Father Braun was not binding himself, as tradition dictated, to speak the liturgy in Latin, deepened her appreciation of the faith she had since girlhood.

Father Braun ended the sacrament with, "... the Lord Jesus bless and keep you my son." He made the sign of the cross over Yellow Boy, arose, stepped back to the table, and sat down, fatigue showing in every line in his face.

Yellow Boy raised his head. He looked at each one and spoke clearly, a man at peace with himself. "Redondo shall have my horses, John shall have my cattle, and Sara shall have this house." He paused and looked directly at Henry and nodded. "Henry shall have my rifle. Care for it well, my son. I have no need for these things where I go. Do not let the people or my grandchildren grieve for me. Only you here, you send me to the happy land of the grandfathers. Do not be slow to take me there. My wives wait for me and I hunger for them." Slowly, with much effort, he pushed himself up, using the Yellow Boy for support; he handed the rifle to Henry and walked by himself the few steps to his bed by the fire. Redondo, Sara, and John helped him stretch out on the pallet in front of the fire. Sara covered him with a blanket, tears rolling down her cheeks as she gently smoothed his long gray hair from his face. He crossed his hands over his chest and said, "Adios mi amigos y ninos." He closed his eyes and was still for a while as they all watched the rhythmic rise and fall of his chest. Then, sighing deeply, he breathed his last, and was gathered to the grandfathers.

Roberta felt the tears drip off her chin on to her hands folded in her lap and a great aching hurt gather in her throat. She was shocked. She had seen many people die and had been heartbroken when it happened. She had never seen anyone die just because they heard an owl. Not eight hours ago she was sure Yellow Boy would live at least through the coming summer. Now he was gone. How could Henry know Yellow Boy would die as soon as he heard the owl? If she hadn't seen it with her own eyes, she wouldn't have believed it. She saw Sara, who had held both hands over her face to catch her sorrow, wipe her eyes and turn to her. "Will you help me prepare him, Roberta?"

"Of course," she said, her voice cracking.

"Redondo? John? Will you saddle the horses? His favorite is – was – the black and white pinto. If we leave before sun-up, we can be back before dark. Father Braun, you know it's a long, cold ride. Please stay here by the fire and keep warm until we return. I'm afraid the ride will make you sick and you too will die."

"Insignificant! I too am going up Sierra Blanca," the frail priest barked in a low voice.

Sara's call to action stirred her brothers out of their paralysis. They arose without a word, and, pulling on heavy coats, stepped out into the cold air, gently closing the door behind them as though not to wake their sleeping father. Henry, slow to regain his emotional equilibrium, sat down heavily by Father Braun. He was quiet in his sorrow for a time, then asked about the many slowly healing infirmities the Father had developed in a Japanese prisoner-of-war camp. He appeared to be worse since the last time Henry had last seen him several months before.

"I'm afraid I'm not getting my strength back as I should. Four years as a POW didn't do my constitution any good. I'd hoped to go to Korea and support the boys there, but it's not going to happen. The bishop says I must move to Phoenix soon where the climate is better. I know much work is needed there." He shifted his weight with a grimace and continued, "I don't want to leave my Apaches, but I must go. It is God's will."

"I understand, Father. You'll be badly missed here. Tell me about your aches and pains. Maybe I can give you some medicine that will help you heal or at least deaden the pain."

Father Braun stared off into space, looked at the women washing Yellow Boy's body and combing his hair, and then stared at the floor without saying anything for a long while. He didn't like to discuss himself or his medical condition. Finally, he sighed and began to talk as Henry made notes in a little spiral-bound notebook he kept in his bag. He watched as Roberta and Sara dressed Yellow Boy in his best flannel shirt, canvas pants, fancy vest, and the long black frock coat he often wore to town.

Sara found a piece of lightweight canvas Yellow Boy used to make a tent fly for shade during the summer months. Henry, finishing with his notes on Father Braun, helped them wrap Yellow Boy's body so they could tie him upright on his pinto. When the canvas was tied in place, they wrapped a fine blanket around him for the trip up Sierra Blanca.

John and Redondo stepped through the door, their shoulders hunched up around their necks and red-faced from the cold. Each carried a load of firewood and added it to the pile by the fireplace. John spoke so low Roberta strained to hear him as he and Redondo each put wood on the fire and warmed their hands. "The horses are tied in the barn, saddled and ready to ride. It took us forever to catch them. No one has ridden them since the leaves have fallen. Yellow Boy just didn't have the will or strength to catch them."

Sara stood up from wrapping Yellow Boy in his final blanket, and, with a little groan of relief, stretched her lower back. "He is ready," she said without a trace of emotion. "We should tie him on the pony upright for his last ride. Warm yourselves with coffee and eat the basket of bread I brought. Roberta and I will find some warm clothes."

In half an hour they had eaten, dressed for the long cold rides and were ready to go. Redondo chopped the back from an old straight-back slat chair and tied it to the paint's saddle. Then he, John, and Henry lifted Yellow Boy's body up and placed it in the saddle, tying him firmly against the chair back, and bracing his head up so he rode upright and with dignity. Henry stared at the paint for a moment. It looked remarkably like the one Yellow Boy owned when Rufus died.

The night was still black when they left the house. The horses slowly picked their way up the canyon trail that lead to the high forests and meadows of Sierra Blanca. John and Redondo knew the trail. They easily led Yellow Boy's horse, with the others following the trail switchbacks up the steep slopes, through the tall pines, and around patches of deep snow, toward a shelf on a high cliff where cairns marked the final beds of Yellow Boy's wives. The cold air felt brittle, ready to crack, and the stars were brilliant sparkling diamonds scattered on a black velvet sky. Roberta glanced at her watch as they started. It was at least an hour before the sun pushed the coming dawn into the cold day surrounding Sierra Blanca.

The sun broke over the mountains, spreading its dazzling cold light in purples and oranges against the fleeing shadows and a few high clouds. There was no sound save the clopping of the horses on hard ground and the soft swish they made passing over pine needles. A cloud of white vapor formed by their breath and that of the animals followed them along the faintly visible trail. Henry rode just behind Yellow Boy, prepared to catch him if the rig to keep him upright failed. Remembrances of their days together filled his mind. Days of hunting, days of fighting, days when Yellow Boy taught him the art of survival in a hostile land surrounded by hard, tough men, were chimeras before his eyes.

Yellow Boy managed to transcend white and Apache worlds, and be at home equally in each. He smoked cigars but could hunt with a bow. His accuracy with his Yellow Boy surpassed all but a very few Anglos or Mexicans. He could run all day through the desert, more than holding his own with any other Apache. He was truly a hard, tough man, a survivor in a land that rarely forgave mistakes. He could also be compassionate and caring for others, as he had been with Henry. He never beat his wives, always cared for them, and loved his children dearly. They passed a pool of water frozen smooth and black. Henry saw his reflection there caught in the cold morning light. He saw a man - half Mexican, half Anglo, all Apache. All Apache because Yellow Boy risked his life for him, formed his heart, and accepted him for what he was and came to be.

They reached the cairns of Yellow Boy's wives mid-morning. The cairns rested on a shelf at the end of a long meadow above a cliff that appeared like a tiny slice carved away from the side of the big mountain. Short pines surrounded the place for they were near the tree line. It was very cold. The wind came in fierce modulated groans that pounded against them then disappeared, only to return again and again. They dismounted, the women to find wood for a fire, the men to take Yellow Boy's body from his horse and lay him gently and straight in a rock crevice out of the wind, before unloading the picks and shovels they brought for their work.

Gathering sticks for a fire, Roberta looked out from the shelf and saw the world spread out far below her. She could see the basin with White Sands gleaming in the distance and the far mountains surrounding it. This was a good final resting place for a man who had ridden over that land without fear for so many years. Its image would lift his spirit as it traveled to the grandfathers.

Father Braun wrapped in a heavy blanket and too weak to help with the heavy work, shivered as he helped Roberta and Sara gather firewood. Close to where Yellow Boy rested, they made a place for the fire in the rocks and out of the wind. Father Braun warmed himself by the fire that soon leaped among the pine knots they gathered. Roberta was relieved to see him stop shivering as the flames grew.

Henry laid out the shape of the rectangle where he would dig in the hard shallow soil while John and Redondo gathered rocks for the cairn. He labored hard for an hour, chipping away at the frozen rocky soil as the pile of rocks grew. Soon he was out of his heavy leather coat and had his shirtsleeves rolled up with sweat dripping from his hairline. They all briefly stopped and took coffee offered by the women, and stood by the fire to keep warm as they drank it. Sara sat snuffling away the tears that wouldn't stop, and occasionally got up to gather more firewood with Roberta.

Redondo took over the digging from Henry, who began searching the area for more rocks with John. Redondo worked steadily, not making any sound of labor from his work nor stopping for rest. In a couple of hours the grave was ready, and, with great dignity, they gently lowered Yellow Boy into it. Henry kissed his cheek, and, covering his face with the canvas wrapped around the body, said, "Good-by, brother, walk proudly in the land of the grandfathers. Know that I, we all, will miss you."

Henry stepped up out of the shallow grave and walked to his saddle gear. He pulled out the fine tan leather scabbard holding Yellow Boy's rifle. He knelt by the grave and gently laid the weapon on top of the body, saying, "You shall not go to the land of the grandfathers without the symbol of your power my brother. It is mine to give now and it has come back to you as it should." Redondo and John watched with glittering eyes and nodded their approval of Henry's gesture.

Redondo, who had said nothing to anyone since he had walked in the door with Father Braun, lifted his hands toward the western sky and began singing a long prayer in a rich beautiful voice. Sara led the others as she took a handful of dirt and tossed it on the canvas and stepped aside. John, who tossed the last handful, took a shovel and began covering his father's body for its long rest.

It took over an hour to fill the grave and put the rocks in place. Redondo sang the entire time. When they were finished and stepped back from the cairn in a circle, he stopped singing and slowly lowered his arms. They all stood staring at the place Yellow Boy rested. Father Braun, who had worked with the others putting rocks in place, finally broke the silence. Looking at Henry, he said, "Speak your heart, my son, that we may be comforted."

Henry swallowed down the aching sorrow in his throat and looked at the solemn faces gathered around the pile of rocks that marked Yellow Boy's place in mother earth. He looked in the eyes of each of his brothers and his sister, the sad face of Father Braun, and, reaching over, took Roberta's hand and firmly clung to its warmth and life. Clouds floated in and out of the sun casting shadows that passed them by like ships on the sea, and the once fierce wind now softly shook the short pines on the ridge above them and those in the rolling canyon below, but let them be.

"Our father, our friend, and my brother knew this land. He was a part of its spirit. He knew the high places where eagles soared. He knew the hot, dry, pitiless places of lizards and snakes, where only the hard and the strong survive. He brought death to his enemies and life to his family. He found me in the desert sand buried under tumbleweeds caught in mesquite, and, with the help of a friend saved my life.

"He taught us to survive in this hard land and to be men of honor and courage. He lived in the worlds of the Apache, the Mexican, and the Anglos and walked as a man, unyielding to any other. His dust lies here between his wives, sisters he cared for and protected for years, even as they lived far apart, one in the little villages hidden high in the Sierra Madre and one in the tipis of the Mescalero here on Sierra Blanca. He was a man proud of his wives and his children. His pride shines in their lives today and will tomorrow. Our greatest monument and memory to him lies not in this small pile of rocks, but in how we live our lives, to walk upright without fear and with honor in the world around us.

"I am proud to be called his son, even though I am adopted. My brothers and sister who carry his blood have far greater claims on his life than I, but he knew us all and cared for us equally. We will all miss him much as he walks in the land of the grandfathers. I have spoken."

Father Braun took a little book from his pocket. "Shall I then speak a closing service for him from the Christian book?" He looked at each one and they each gave him a firm nod.

"Man born of woman is full of sorrows ..." he began, and spoke for fifteen minutes in the drifting shadows and rustling wind. High above them an eagle circled in long swinging loops. Henry heard its call and glanced up, the words of Father Braun briefly falling out of his consciousness. His mind formed the words, *Good-by, old friend; we will miss you.*

When they finished their farewell to Yellow Boy it was midafternoon. They warmed themselves by the fire and drank the last of the coffee. The men readied the horses. Soon the little group started the long cold ride back down the mountain.

Father Braun looked very weak. Henry was concerned he couldn't finish the trip back, but, each time he told him he didn't look well, the priest would almost shout, "Insignificant!" Henry offered to stop for a while, or even for the night, but the Father refused. The sun set before they reached the house, but the wind calmed, making the ride easier, and soon light from the house showed through the dark twilight. Redondo, John, and Henry unsaddled and rubbed down the horses while Sara and Roberta made a hot dinner. Father Braun was so weak he could hardly totter inside, and had to sit down by the fire while the others busied themselves.

With little conversation, they hungrily ate a meal of beans, venison steak cooked with red chilies, and hot black coffee. It wasn't long, however, before the good food revived their spirits as well as their bodies and they sat awhile sharing memories of the man who had just left them for the land of the grandfathers. They discussed how to best handle the ranch and keep their father alive in their hearts. Sara spoke the question that had been on her's, John's, and Redondo's minds.

"Henry? Now that Yellow Boy has gone to the grandfathers will you still come here? Will you still help us?"

Henry looked at them in hurt surprise. "Of course! I've not helped you because Yellow Boy adopted me, but because our people are my brothers. Blood does not change because one man leaves. Yes, I will remain as I have always been, to help you whenever I can."

Sara took his hand and squeezed it with a smile of relief. "It is good. Thank you, my brother. Now forgive me for asking, but my brothers and I know nothing of how Yellow Boy came to find you, or of your life before you came from the east as a doctor. Have we not lived as your family for many years? Tell us now and free our minds from their many questions about your childhood. They flit about like bees seeking flowers. Please tell us. We are your family."

Roberta saw them all lean forward to hear Henry's answer as she covered her mouth with her hand to hide her smile. Henry slumped back in his chair and stared a few long moments at the vigorous fire they used to warm the house. He said wearily, "All right. I'll tell only you the story and you must be silent to others about it when I do. I have been telling my story to Roberta since we left Las Cruces. She can tell you it is a long tale that will take several evenings around the fire to tell. Spring will come in a few weeks. Let us meet in this house then for a weekend, and I will tell you all there is to know. Will you wait until then?"

Sara smiled for the first time all day. "Of course. It is good to gather together again and share your story and remember our father in this place. We will wait. I ask only one more favor."

Henry smiled. "Of course, anything."

"Can you take us to our homes now? Our children must know that their grandfather has gone to the land of the grandfathers, and we must rest."

Henry squeezed her hand. "I saw Redondo's truck out by the road. I guessed it is out of gas?"

Redondo nodded. "Si, Henry. Father Braun was hard to find. We had to walk up the canyon to get here. We were lucky we were not up on Sierra Blanca!"

Father Braun smiled and barked, "Insignificant!"

Henry smiled. "I'll take you home. Get your coats. We'll leave now and I'll bring Redondo back with some gas. Roberta and I will rest here tonight and leave for Las Cruces early in the morning. I have many patients to see for the next few days. We will come when you need us. Just call my office or mi hacienda." He turned to Roberta. "The car will be full with the others. Do you mind waiting here by yourself while I take them home?"

Roberta shook her head. "No, not at all. You go on. I'll straighten up here while you drive everyone home. It's been a very long two days. We're all weary and need rest. Good night, everyone. I'll see you all again soon."

Sara hugged her and said in a whisper, "And you, my sister, you will be here when he comes again. Please?" Roberta gave her a squeeze and nodded, looking in her eyes.

Roberta hugged them all and wished them well as they began filing out the door. Henry was last and he whispered in her ear as he wrapped his arms around her, "Thank you. Get some rest. I'll be back in a little while."

She stood at the door as the Plymouth slowly rocked out of sight down the rough gravel road leading back to Route 70. When the headlights disappeared down the canyon, she turned and began straightening up the rooms in the old house. It seemed very empty, almost desolate, without Yellow Boy or Henry there to give it life.

Making up the beds in the two side bedrooms, she turned back the covers, then, staggering from fatigue, slumped wearily in the stuffed chair close by the fire to wait for Henry's return. The warmth and golden shadows cast by the fire quickly covered her in sleep as images of their long ride passed through her mind, soft whispers of a day she would never forget.

Jerking awake in confusion, her eyes found Henry's face looking at hers with concern as he gently shook her. "Are you all right? Just tired?"

Yawning and stretching, she nodded and pointed toward the back bedroom. "Yes, I'm okay – just a little tired. I fixed your bed there in the back bedroom. You look like you've been rode hard and put up wet. Please, sir, go get some rest and I'll take the other bed."

"Thanks. That's the best idea I've had all day." He grinned as they stumbled off to their beds for some much needed rest.

# 18

# OLIVER LEE

R oberta awoke to dazzling sunlight pounding on her eyelids and the sounds of Henry rummaging around in the big room. It felt late in the morning, probably near mid-day. Rolling over and propping up on one elbow she stretched to see the time on her watch lying on the night table. It was nearly twelve! She sat up with a start, pushing hair out of her eyes and trying to shake the fog out of her brain. The day was half gone! Why had Henry let her sleep? They could be seeing patients in Las Cruces by now if they had started at daylight.

She swung her feet on to the cold plank floor and, covered with goose bumps and shivering, walked to the chair where she'd folded her clothes. She clinched her teeth to keep them from chattering as she pulled on the pants and shirt she had worn the day before and staggered, only half-awake, into the big room. Henry was throwing wood in the firebox of the old iron cooking stove. He heard her door creak and looked over his shoulder as she walked out, holding her shirt together with one hand and her pants up and together with the other. Seeing her confusion and disarray, he flashed a big toothy grin.

"Good morning! Have a good sleep? Yellow Boy's hens cooperated so I thought I'd fix us a little coffee and a green chili omelet before we loaded up and hit the road. There's a bucket of hot water for your morning scrub on the stove."

She nodded, still disoriented and confused.

Henry clanked the stove firebox door shut with the side of his boot and lifted the full steaming bucket off the top of the stove. "Here, let me carry it in your bedroom so you can have some privacy." She stared at him dumbly as he stepped past her, careful not to spill any.

When he returned, she was still rooted to the same spot, her brain slowly beginning to engage and whir to life. "Why didn't you get me up at first light? We could be in Las Cruces by now!" She said in a tone of convivial exasperation.

"I know, but we hadn't slept in over twenty-four hours and we were physically and emotionally wrung out. We needed to sleep. Our patients in Las Cruces can wait one more day. I also think we need a little time together, just you and me. And, I want to finish my tale for you before I begin telling any of the others. Now go do your toilette, madam, and I'll whip us up some victuals."

When Roberta reappeared, fresh and ready for the day, Henry was dividing the omelet into two plates on the rough-hewn table. He motioned her over to sit down.

"Coffee with your lunch, señorita?"

"Si, muchas gracias, señor," she said brightly. Surprised to feel so rested and relaxed, she hadn't realized what a mental strain the past three days had been. "Thank you so much for that warm water, it was heavenly. That and letting me sleep were very thoughtful of you."

Henry smiled as he sat down at the table with her.

"Well, I have to look after my favorite nurse and best friend, now, don't I?"

She looked at his face with a mischievous grin and sparkling eyes. "How long have you been up?" she asked between mouthfuls of omelet and tortillas as she wolfed down her meal.

"Oh, I got up around eight o'clock. I washed some of the dirt out of my crannies, made a pot of coffee, and just sat here in this room reminiscing about the times I'd had with Yellow Boy."

His sad, serious look made her lay down her fork, and gently cover his hand with hers as she looked earnestly in his eyes. "I'm so sorry he's gone. I understand now how much he meant to you. It's just stunning how fast he went. There was nothing any of us could have done, most of all you."

He gave her hand a little squeeze and shrugged, letting his thoughts tumble out. "I'll miss him very much. But, you know, I'm not even sad. I'm glad, in a way, that he went as quickly as he did. He was too proud to lie around sick for a long time while his children labored futilely to save him. He didn't suffer much and he was ready. No, really, he wanted to go, back home, back to mother earth. I think he was bored with this life and wanted to go on to the happy land. His death marks the end of an era. We'll never see another like him. I'm feeling okay. I just thank God you came with me. Your being here and listening to me tell my long-buried secret has meant a lot to me."

"Me too. I'm honored you shared your secret with me. With Yellow Boy gone, I guess I'm the only other one that knows now, besides you. Will you tell John, Redondo, and Sara everything you've told me?"

He bowed his head for a moment. Looking at her with a sanguine smile, he nodded. "Yes, I gave my word. I'll just have to hope they'll honor my privacy, and I'm sure they will. They deserve to know everything they can about their father's history. Luckily for me, there were books written about mine. All they have is what other folks remember, and what is remembered is rarely, if ever, written down. The history of their lives is just scattered on the wind when their used-up bodies return to the land. Maybe that's the most meaningful record. I don't know. Plenty of time for philosophy later. Let's finish here and get on back to our other life."

"Yes, sir! We're running a little late, and, as they say in the movies, Pilgrim, we're burning daylight!"

They finished their meal buried in their thoughts and enjoying the intimate warmth they found just being together. Roberta washed the dishes as Henry checked the stock and did a few outside chores. The light filtering through the trees and the soft wind blowing up the canyon gave the day a gauzy, dreamlike quality. When Henry returned from the barn, they put the house in order, and loaded the few things they'd brought with them in the dust-covered Plymouth. Henry put out the fires in the stove and fireplace. He made a final check of the house while Roberta waited by the car, enjoying the light filtering through the tall, gently swaying pines. Closing the door behind him, he walked toward her before stopping and slowly turning, staring at the house, barn, and yard, burning one more look into his memory and telling its departed owner adios.

"It feels empty here without him, doesn't it?"

"Yes, it does. It's just not the same place anymore."

He nodded, and, without a word, opened the car door for her, walked around to his side, got in, and cranked the Plymouth smoothly to life. They rolled slowly through beams of sunlight and shadow down the rocky canyon road toward Route 70. Passing through the big trees that lined the highway to Mescalero, they didn't speak, wordlessly content with each other under the brilliant blue afternoon sky.

The road to Tularosa curved to the west just out of Mescalero and brought into view a smooth, dazzling streak of white shining in the distance – White Sands. It was like a great white lake shimmering in the distance. The view never failed to cause Henry's heart to open in gratitude to the Artist who'd made it, or to make Roberta marvel at its beauty glimmering in the distance.

"I've always loved that view. I'll bet I've seen it hundreds of times and it still thrills me like I'd just seen it for the first time," she said with a little sigh.

Henry nodded and smiled. "Yeah, that sight does that to a person. I remember the first time I saw it the morning Daddy and I were traveling over to La Luz from Doc Blazer's place. Seeing it always carries me back to the hardest time in my life, but I wouldn't miss seeing it every day, if I could, for anything in this world or the next."

She considered sliding over next to him, putting her arm around his shoulders, and hugging him. She hesitated, and then kept her seat, not wanting to do anything presumptuous based on the hints of their feelings for each other spoken over the past couple of days. Things spoken in the dark had a way of losing definition in the light of day.

The road dipped and briefly blocked White Sands from their view. Henry pushed his hat back on his head and looked at her. He started to speak, and pausing, seemed to change his mind. Finally, he said, "You ready to hear the rest of my story?"

"You know I am! While you were gone to get the others, Yellow Boy told me that you went through a lot while you were in Mexico and that a lady gave you the turquoise eagle you wear on your watch chain. Naturally, the mention of another woman has me thinking all kinds of things. So, come clean, Dr. Grace. I want to know it all."

"Well, slide on over here and keep me warm and I won't have to talk over the road noise."

She moved over next to him and thought, This is wonderful, but very indiscreet. Maybe a Las Cruces patient or neighbor will see us. She smiled and shook her head. I don't care how it looks!

"What happened as I grew to full manhood hidden down there in Mexico with Yellow Boy's people is a story I'll tell you another time. It's at least a three-day trip. I still have emotional scars from those days, from the people I knew and loved, and from some others we killed. It's hard for me to talk about, but I will, I promise."

"Then, I'll wait until you're ready to tell me. But, don't keep me in suspense about the rest of your story. When did you come back from Mexico?"

Henry fished around in his coat pocket and found his pipe. He handed it to her for their little ritual and mouthed the word, "Please." When she had a good coal going in its bowl, she handed it over to him just as he was cracking open the vent window. He took a couple of long meditative draws, slowly blowing the smoke out the vent window.

"I crossed back north of the Sierra Madre in the fall of 1906. I wasn't a kid anymore. Living with Yellow Boy's people had hardened me into an adult who thought coldly and logically about killing one's enemies, when to hide, when to fight, and when to run to protect loved ones. I left a woman I'd loved and her murderers buried in Mexico, and I guess, if the truth be known, a piece of me was buried there too.

"One day, about a month before I left, Yellow Boy told me that he was moving his second wife and part of her family to Mescalero to live with him and her sister, his first wife. He said he probably wouldn't come back to Mexico much anymore and asked what I wanted to do. I was welcome to stay with his people there, but his opinion was that I needed to return to my own land. It didn't take long for me to decide I'd come back too. I was long overdue to settle accounts with Oliver Lee, tell my mother I was alive after all those years, and find something worthwhile to do with the rest of my life.

"I decided I had to take care of Oliver Lee first, before anyone else learned I was alive. If he killed me, then at least my poor mother wouldn't lose the same son twice. On the ride out of the Sierra Madre with Yellow Boy and his wife and little son, John, I tried to think of all the angles I needed to consider in settling accounts with Oliver Lee. I knew he was so good with a long gun that I'd better get him with my first shot or he'd kill me. However, I desperately wanted to talk to him to find out how and why he'd had my father murdered. That meant I had to figure out how to catch and disarm him. It also meant I'd have to murder him in cold blood. By the time I was eighteen and had lived through some hard times in Mexico with Yellow Boy's people, that really wasn't a restraint. I knew that he often traveled across the Tula-rosa Basin by himself at night. That meant that I had to get mighty lucky to cross trails with him, or that I watch his every move from a distance and set up an ambush. In either case, I had to get the drop on him first before I could put fire on his scalp to get the truth, and, at best, mercy-kill him.

"I know all this sounds cold-bloodied, but I'd been living with people who neither gave or took quarter from an enemy. I had been thinking about how to take revenge on Oliver Lee ever since Yellow Boy and I had first crossed the river into Mexico. I blamed Lee for everything – killing my father, getting Rufus killed, the pain and misery I knew my mother had suffered, and all the other evil that had been visited on me. In my heart I swore he'd pay every hundredweight and penny-pound's worth of the debt he owed me, and that he'd suffer doing it. I'd learned some nasty tricks from the Apaches down in Mexico. He was going to be on the receiving end of some of them and beg to die before I killed him.

"I'd decided to stay at Rufus's place, or at least camp there if the shack was gone. I rode across river and up toward Las Cruces, but stayed off the road to avoid being seen. I didn't want to tempt fate by letting anyone see me before I was ready. I could have passed for a Mexican or an Indian, depending on how I dressed. Down in Mexico I'd stolen a fancy silver-trimmed saddle during a raid on a wealthy hacienda. I could easily have passed for a Mexican vaquero or even a pistolero, except I never wore spurs with that horse – didn't need to. I wore a big sombrero and carried an old single-action Model 1873 Army Colt in a double-loop holster. I knew how to use it too, although I still much preferred the punch and range of the Sharps I carried in the fancy saddle scabbard. And the horse I rode, lordy, I'd give just about every penny I own now if I still had that horse. The horse Rufus had bought for me, Midnight, which was like a family friend, had been shot out from under me during a raid on a miner's camp. The new horse was a jet-black Arabian stud that could run all day and out race any other horse on this side of the border. I found him at the same place I stole the saddle. He was unbroken when we took him. Yellow Boy taught me to gentle him down, then to train him without breaking his spirit. I called him Satanas after the black lord of the underworld.

"I worked my way up the Rio Grande until I was within a few miles of Las Cruces, then I cut cross-country and rode around behind Tortugas Mountain toward Rufus's place. It was getting late in the day and the sun was casting its gauzy light of reds, purples, and oranges everywhere against the mountains and the creosote bushes that covered the land between the river and the Organs. Like a lover's caress, the air was warm and soothing. It made you want to draw it in to your lungs as deep as you could and just float away. I could see the dark crack of the canyon slashed in the side of the Organs where I knew Rufus's shack was. I wished to my soul that he was there to meet me. As it was, with that beautiful sunset, I felt like I was getting a royal homecoming.

"I didn't know what to expect as I rode up the trail toward the shack we'd shared all those years. It was a relief to see the shack still standing in the dusty half-light as the sun disappeared. I dismounted and walked around it first. The way the paths had been kept clear and the general state of repair, it was obvious someone had been living there in the not-too-distant past. The windows had been replaced, bullet holes in the walls plugged, and there was no wind-blown brush on the porch. Even so, when I pushed the creaking door open I could see dust had collected all over everything. Buck must have used it for a line shack or maybe even rented it to some drifter. Whatever he had done, it had been kept in good shape all the years I'd been in Mexico and I was grateful. It didn't surprise me that the livestock were gone. No doubt Buck had sold them and was saving the money for Rufus. I unsaddled Satanas and stowed most of the gear in the house before I led him up the trail, deep into the canyon where Rufus taught me to shoot. It was pitch black dark going up there, but I knew every twist and bump on the trail as though I still walked it every day. I could barely make out the pile of rocks heaped against the canyon wall where Yellow Boy and I buried Rufus in the little mine he'd started. In the dim light of freshly-lighted stars, it looked untouched.

"After I rubbed Satanas down and watered and fed him, I dug a hole to make light hard to see from a little fire I made near the rock pile. It was hard to stay there. The place swarmed with memories and echoes from the past. I almost left. I still had every coin Rufus left me. I could have easily paid at a hotel and stayed in town, and I'm sure no one would have known me or cared how I looked. Still, I couldn't leave the canyon.

"I sat by the fire for a long time that night, sorting through all the possibilities I'd thought of to settle up with Oliver Lee. It was hard to focus because I kept seeing the ghosts of times past. Daddy and his death, Rufus and Yellow Boy helping me kill Stone and his riders, Rufus dying, and the satisfaction I felt when Yellow Boy brought me Red Tally's head. Just one more payback and I'd be done with the business that had changed my life forever. I went to sleep without deciding anything. When I woke up, I knew what I had to do.

"I decided that if I wanted to live a long life, and if I wanted to settle up with Oliver Lee, no one could associate me with him. I had to catch him on some long night ride or just ambush him at a long distance. I wanted to hear him admit he was responsible for those men killing Daddy before I washed my hands in his blood. All I had to do was catch him. As good a shot with a rifle as he was reputed to be, and as quick with a pistol as anybody half his age, I knew I had to be real careful when I took him on. I wasn't going to just shoot him and leave him for the buzzards and coyotes. I was going to be looking in his eyes when life's light went out of them. Living with Yellow Boy's people in the Sierra Madre taught me the value of patience – for hunting or for revenge. The only option for me then, was to watch Mr. Lee, learn his every move, and spring a trap on him when he least expected it. It might take a long time to get him. I didn't care. It'd be worth it.

"I had a little breakfast, saddled Satanas, and rode down trails I hadn't seen in four or five years – around the west side of the Organs, up over Baylor Pass, and down across the basin to the southern end of the Jarillas.

"I camped for a few days in the little canyon where I'd buried Tally's head and Rufus had died. I rode out toward Lee's place early every morning, hopeful of finding a spot off the eastern edge of the Jarillas where I might keep an eye on Lee's place and learn his habits without being seen. I found a place about a half mile from Lee's ranch house where I could stay in the shade of a big mesquite bush without being seen. I had an old pair of Army binoculars Rufus had used in his scouting days. My eyes felt like thay had half the desert poured in them from using those things so much as I watched the comings and goings at Lee's ranch house. It was dangerous business. I risked getting caught if one of Lee's cowboys came ambling by or if someone saw the glint from my long glasses. But, I had a clear view in all directions and no horse in the basin could catch me on Satanas, so I felt fairly safe.

"I stayed under that mesquite for three days watching Lee's place. He was something to watch, let me tell you. Every morning he was up working like a young buck by first light. He always wore a pistol, and worked his men right into the ground until the women in the house rang the dinner bell. If a man didn't do the job he wanted, he fired him right then. After lunch he took a little siesta out on the porch swing and the men sat or reclined in the shade of the big barn near the house.

"On the second day I saw a couple of Negro cowhands ride up to the ranch house for the noon meal and tie their horses to the corral fence. The horses were lathered up and looked wore down, but the fools didn't even give them water or loosen their cinches before they went into eat. I sat there gritting my teeth, just watching those animals mistreated like that made me wish I could give those men a rough lesson in how to treat horses. Lee was headed toward the ranch house with some of the other hands when he noticed the two horses. He pulled his hat down over his eyes, walked over to them, looked them over, and ran his hands over them. Next he pulled off their saddles and led them to water. The men with him just stood in a little group with their arms crossed over their chests, waiting. It was obvious they knew what was coming.

"After the horses finished drinking, Lee led them back and tied them to the corral fence. He turned, and, facing the house with both hands on his hips, he yelled something. I was too far away to hear anything distinct except the angry bellow of his voice. Those black cowhands were out the door and running toward Lee in nothing flat. I could tell he was yelling at them and pointing at the horses. He hauled off and swung a fist right into the middle of the face of one of the hands, knocking him out cold. The other one started to reach for his pistol, but old Lee grabbed his gun hand and smashed him in the head with his. He yelled something else at them, reached in his pocket, and threw some money on the ground as they started to get up, then walked past them toward the ranch house as if nothing had happened. The hands crawled to their knees and pulled themselves up by the corral fence and staggered over to saddle their horses. They managed to get mounted and trailed off toward Alamogordo slumped in their saddles. I had to smile. Old Lee had dished out some justice there, in my opinion.

"It was getting late on the same day Lee had beat those cowboys when a wagon pulled up to his porch. It carried a man and woman and four or five tow-topped young'uns who were playing and fighting like a litter of puppies. Lee came striding out of the house with a big smile on his face and yelling something that included the word neighbor. He was motioning for them to get down and come inside while he walked around behind the wagon and took those kids out of its bed by the double handful. They obviously loved him. The little girls hugged his neck and the boys were jumping up and down begging for something while Lee tilted his head back and laughed loud enough for me to hear it. Lee called for one of the hands to come take care of the wagon while he and the family went inside. Several hours later Lee and the man came out, smoking cigars, followed by the women and children. I could just make them out in the porch lantern light. They stood talking while the wagon was brought around. After it came Lee shook hands with the man, hugged the wife, and hefted the children into the wagon bed. When they were gone, he sat down on the porch step and finished his cigar in the pleasant cool air of the evening.

"That night, I recalled what I'd seen the past couple of days. Lee was a very hard worker, he was smart, he was kind to women and children and good to horses, and didn't tolerate anybody on his payroll who didn't live up to his standards. I was beginning to understand why most of the other ranchers were said to look to him for leadership. He had charisma. It was easy to see how he could even get others to kill for him.

"On the evening of the third day, rain clouds had been forming to the west and it was getting dark fast. I was about to put the binoculars away and get some rest when I saw Lee step out on the porch. He was cleaned up, wearing a business suit, and he was holding a gun holster. He slid the gun out of the holster and into his pants pocket. My heart started pounding. He must be getting ready for one of his night rides into town. A cowhand brought his horse from the barn. I could just make out the outlines of a rifle scabbard on the saddle rig. Lee hugged his wife, gave her a little kiss, and then mounted the horse, a big roan, and rode off into the retreating light.

"He might have been going to Alamogordo, Tularosa, or Las Cruces. I had to know which one. It still wasn't good dark, but I risked being seen as I saddled Satanas to find and follow his trail. I knew if he went to Las Cruces he'd ride north and just skirt the edge of the Jarillas, then ride near the same road Daddy and I took, this one we're on now, the day Stone and Tally killed Daddy.

"I gambled he was going to Las Cruces and that I could somehow find him if I watched for him from the northern edge of the Jarillas. I rode Satanas hard through the creosotes and mesquite to find a spot from which to watch Lee pass. I found a place and I wasn't there more than ten or fifteen minutes before Lee came winding through the creosotes, following no particular trail, and keeping a close eye on everything around him.

"After he passed, I mounted Satanas and tried to follow him at some distance. It was harder than I had imagined. On the way he stopped at a couple of cowboy campfires and had coffee while he talked to them about their cattle. He never did ride a clearly marked trail or road until he hit the road over St. Augustin Pass. When he got past Organ on the other side, he wandered off into the creosotes again, just generally following the road a quarter mile or so off to one side. He rode up to the Amador Hotel in Las Cruces at daybreak. He watered his horse before going inside, apparently to have breakfast. I didn't want to be seen, so I decided I'd ride out to the road to Organ and watch for him to come back.

"I waited and watched, but never saw him. After a week I gave up and rode back to watch for him at his ranch. When I returned to my mesquite bush hiding place, he was already back and working his cowhands hard. I felt like a fool. I was mystified, at first, as to how he got around me without being seen. Then I realized he must have gone to El Paso before returning home by way of the eastern side of the Franklin Mountains. It began to dawn on me that catching and killing Oliver Lee was going to be a lot harder than I thought.

"I watched Lee for over two months. It was nearing the end of fall and the weather was starting to get miserable. It was clear that I would never catch him down in the basin. The place would have to be some spot where he had to pass, a place where the chances of my catching him were high.

"I knew Yellow Boy was probably settled in at Mescalero with his wives by then, so I rode over to find him and ask him to help me. He and his family lived in a tipi back in the canyon where his house is now."

Roberta's brow furrowed. She was puzzled.

"I thought the government gave the Apaches housing. Since when did they live in tipis? The plains Indians lived in tipis. I thought the Apaches lived in grass and brush wickiups."

"Believe me, the government gave the Apaches no more than they had to in order for the Indians to get by. You're exactly right about the plains Indians living in tipis. The free Apaches usually did live in wickiups. But, the Mescaleros lived in the mountains and it gets too cold and uncomfortable to live in a grass hut when the snow is waist-deep. The Indians on the plains survived terrible winters in tipis. Those lodges can be quite comfortable when it's cold. I think it was only natural for the Mescaleros to use tipis up there in the mountains until the government finally came through with some lumber for housing. In any case, that's what Yellow Boy lived in on the reservation for several years. Down in Mexico where the winter's were bad in the high Sierra Madre, they even made little stone houses. Down where the winters weren't bad, they had wickiups, which were a lot harder to discover by Federales or vaqueros than any tipi.

"Well, I guess I'm learning all sorts of things I never knew before. Was Yellow Boy surprised to see you?"

Henry smiled. "No. He was glad to see me, but the first words out of his mouth were, *Did you kill Lee?* I just looked at the ground and shook my head. He was sitting by the doorway of his tipi having an after-dinner smoke when I found him. He motioned me inside and said, *There is still meat in the pot. Eat! Fill your belly then come and smoke with me. We will talk, Hombrecito.* Redondo was about eight or nine then and played outside while Yellow Boy watched him. John was less than a year old. When I stuck my head inside the tipi doorway I saw the round happy face of Yellow Boy's first wife, Juanita, feeding John and motioning me to come in. The second wife, her sister, Moon on the Water, was already dipping stew out of the pot into a plate and loading it with a side of fry bread for me. I was like a brother to them. So it didn't offend custom for me to sit and chat with them and leave Yellow Boy outside to enjoy the evening solitude while I ate. Moon on the Water told me that while she had been fearful of leaving Mexico, reservation life was a lot easier than always hiding and watching out for vaqueros or Federales in the Sierra Madre. Juanita was happy that Moon on the Water was there to help her, and that Yellow Boy stayed closer to their lodge now for much longer periods. I gave them a good belch when I finished and nodded approval of their good meal. They were all smiles.

"It was nearly dark when I went out to sit with Yellow Boy who had built up the fire. It was getting into early November and the nights were cold. He motioned me over to sit on his blanket beside him and handed me a cigar. We smoked in silence for a while, enjoying the night and each other's company.

"Finally, he asked, *So, Hombrecito, Oliver Lee still lives, eh? You have not killed him yet?*

"I could only shake my head and stare out into the darkness surrounding the tall pines. No, brother, I have not killed him. I have tried to watch and understand his tracks to Las Cruces, El Paso, and Alamogordo now for three moons. He is smart. He only takes trips to these towns during the day in the company of many, and only travels at night by himself. He is a strong leader. His cowboys and neighbors respect him.

*Why do you not use Shoots Today Kills Tomorrow and end it?*

"I will do that if there is no other way. But, I want to take him alive and make him tell me why he had my father killed and tried to kill me before I wash my hands in his blood and cook his brains over a hot fire while he still lives. I do not understand this man. He is a hard man, but he is fair. He will beat a man who does not care for his horse, and he is warm with muchachos. He is not afraid to fight an enemy face to face with his hands or his guns. The murder of my father was an act of a ruthless coward, one who will not stop to even murder small children. This man is no coward. He is hard. He is powerful. I do not understand how or why he caused this thing to my family. I want to know why. To do this I must catch him. He is a very dangerous bear to catch. I need your help and wisdom to do this my brother.

"Yellow Boy was silent for a long while after I spoke. The end of his rapidly disappearing cigar glowed brightly as he thought. I got up to put more wood on the fire. When I sat down again he said, *I will help you catch this bear, Hombrecito, but you must kill him. It is your duty to do this in a feud of blood.* I nodded I understood and agreed. It was what I wanted.

*You have hunted and watched him for three moons. How can this bear be taken?*

299

"I think the only way to take him is when he is alone at night on a piece of the trail he has to travel. Otherwise, we wait many months at any other place and he may never pass that way. We must watch his hacienda until we see he leaves one night and heads for Las Cruces. He always uses San Augustin Pass over the Organs to Las Cruces, and he goes two or three times in a moon. When we see him leave his ranch in the evening and start for Las Cruces, we will ride like the wind and get to the pass ahead of him. There is a set of big boulders to one side of the trail nearly at the top. The trail goes right by them. From the tops of boulder, you can rope him off his horse, I'll stay on the ground to get him as soon as he hits the dirt."

Yellow Boy grunted. "*Ummmph. You have thought about this mucho. Where will you take him after you have him?*

"I'll tie him over his horse and take him to the canyon where Rufus lies and this man made me live. There I will get the truth from him. Then he will die slowly and suffer much. I will burn his body there and scatter the ashes to the winds.

*You are taught well, Hombrecito. We will ride at first light. I want to see this place in San Augustin Pass at night and test how this plan of yours will work. You will have your enemy at your fire pretty quick now I think.*

"Gracias, uncle! Let us talk of other things now. Was the trip from the Rio Grande to Mescalero without trouble?"

*Si.* He spoke with a smile. I knew there was good story coming about that trip.

"We talked late into the night about his trip back and happenings on the reservation. When we finally lay down in the tipi, the women and boys were already sleeping. I don't think I took more than two breaths before I was snoring. It was still dark when Yellow Boy shook my boot. The women were already cooking a meal, and the aroma, there in the cold mountain air, was mouth-watering. I staggered outside to relieve myself and wash at the creek. In case you didn't discover it during the last three days, that water is cold! I saddled Satanas and tied my gear on tight. Yellow Boy had his pony and a packhorse ready. It was just turning gray in the eastern sky when he told his wives and Redondo good-by. He swung on to his pony as easily as a much younger man and waited while Juanita stepped forward proudly and handed him the Yellow Boy and wished him good hunting. He hadn't told them what we were going to hunt. If they spoke out of turn to other women on the reservation and word got back to the agent, soldiers wouldn't hesitate to come after him.

"We rode down toward Tularosa, swung wide of the town, and passed Alamogordo on the White Sands side before we swung back south toward the Jarillas. Yellow Boy knew a spot on the northeastern side of the Jarillas where we could camp unseen and watch for any passerby. That night we rode to the spot where I'd hidden to watch Lee. Yellow Boy eyed it closely and nodded his approval. It was hard to tell that man or animal had been near the spot and it had a good clear view of the ranch buildings.

"Yellow Boy nodded back toward the Jarillas. *Let us ride back to camp now, Hombrecito, as fast and with as little sound as we can. How long will it take us? Let us learn.* We sat off at a good fast trot, weaving through the creosotes and mesquites. I guessed it must have taken us about an hour for the night sky had not changed much.

"Yellow Boy asked only, *Was that faster than Lee rides in this direction?*

"I nodded.

"Yellow Boy said, *Bueno. Now we ride to your spot in San Augustin Pass.*

"That ride took us nearly four hours, including a couple of stops to rest the horses at water tanks. We rode, for the most part, on the main road. I knew that way we would make much better time than Lee, who stayed off the main road and out in the brush, even stopping to chat with cowboys at their fires.

"It must have been just a little after midnight when we got to the spot in San Augustin Pass I wanted to use. We first found a place to hide the horses. Yellow Boy went through every movement and event he thought might happen, from climbing up on the boulders to having me ride by so he could practice throwing loops over me. He never missed with that rope. He was as good with the lariat as any cowboy I ever saw. I never heard it coming, although, I was listening for it. The last throw he actually jerked me off Satanas to see how much pull it took, how much it stunned me, and what the horse did. I was surprised. I didn't have a clue what happened. By the time I had shaken the stars out of my head, Yellow Boy was standing there with the rifle pointed at my head. Satanas had trotted forward a few paces, stopped, and looked back in curiosity as to why his load suddenly got lighter.

"I got up and brushed myself off. Why'd you do that? I asked a little angry. I coulda broke my neck!

"Yellow Boy just laughed as he pulled the rope off me. *Try everything at least once, Hombrecito. There must be no surprises. It is a good plan so far. Now let us see if we can get to the canyon where you will kill him before the sun comes. Vamos!*

"It was nearly dawn when we rode by Rufus's shack and up the canyon. When we got to Rufus's burial spot, we unsaddled and rubbed the horses down, watered, and hobbled them so they could graze while we slept through the day on the ledge over looking the house. The next night as we rode back to the little camp in the Jarillas, Yellow Boy said the plan was good and should work, but that we needed to work out alternatives in case something went wrong. We talked about that for a long time and agreed that if all else failed I'd kill Lee with the Sharps at the first opportunity, and then head for Mexico.

"From the little camp in the Jarillas we got into a routine where one of us would leave well before first light to watch Lee's place from my mesquite bush. We'd watch all day and into the evening until we were sure that he wasn't traveling in our direction. About a week after we started, I was watching the place when he stepped out on the porch in his business suit and had his horse brought around. My heart was pounding and I was about leap on Satanas and rouse Yellow Boy when I saw Lee head south. He was going to El Paso! I silently cursed him, and then mounted anyway. My watch was over for that day.

"About two weeks after that, Yellow Boy took a turn watching the Lee place. The sun was just setting through high thick clouds behind the San Andreas Mountains, and a cold wind was blowing in short un-expected gusts. I was having a cup of coffee when Yellow Boy's paint popped through the large creosotes we camped behind. Yellow Boy's usually mellow expression was stern and his eyes were hard and nar-rowed in concentration.

*He comes!*

"I took a final swallow and kicked dirt on the fire. Excitement coursed through my body like an electric current and my hands were trembling. After checking Little David's and my pistol's loads, I sad-dled Satanas and swung into the saddle. We headed off into the coming darkness for the main road at a gallop. I figured we had at least half an hour on Lee, maybe more.

"The night was dark. The only light came from a half-moon shining as a dirty smudge of light through the thick clouds brought by the gust-ing wind. Once we reached the road, the traveling was easy. We set the horses into a steady trot that ate up the miles. We stopped twice to rest the horses and give them water, knowing that we were now far ahead of Lee. We didn't see a soul for the entire ride, or even distant fires from cowboys bedding down with their cattle for the night.

"It must have been close to midnight when we topped San Augustin Pass. It was cold and windy in the cut, just as I remembered it being ten years before when Daddy and I camped there. Without a word, Yellow Boy took his rifle and lariat, walked back down the trail to disappear in the darkness and climb up the boulder we'd picked earlier.

"I led the horses a couple of hundred yards off the trail so they'd be downwind and out of sound range of Lee's horse. I watered them, loosened their cinches, and hobbled them so they could graze. Returning to Yellow Boy's boulder, I tossed a pebble up into the darkness where I thought he was. Within seconds one from the top landed between my feet. He was ready.

"Crossing to the opposite side of the road, I drew my revolver and stretched out on the dirt close by a big century plant. We were ready. Time crawled. My patience was shorter than it should have been, every itch on my body begged for attention, but I dared not move. The man on the boulder had trained me better. My eyes strained without success to find Yellow Boy at the top of the boulder. He was invisible against the black sky. I pressed further down in the dirt trying to make myself just as hard to see. Getting cold and stiff as the minutes ticked by, I kept flexing my muscles, hoping I wouldn't be too slow when the time came. A thousand thoughts must have crossed my mind – the trip with Daddy, the nights we spent here in this pass, the years with Rufus and Yellow Boy, how best to torture Lee.

"I was getting drowsy and fighting sleep lying there in the dirt when I heard the crunch and clink of iron horseshoes against rocks on the trail. Instantly I was wide-awake feeling the rush and pounding drum of adrenaline filling my body. Slowly I turned my head and looked down the trail. It was too dark to see anything, although I could tell from the horse's pacing that he was coming closer. A dark shadow of man and horse passed within five feet of where I lay. I could have spit on his boots he was so close. Another fifteen or twenty feet up the trail and Yellow Boy would have him. I dug my toes into the dirt to get a good start, tensed and ready to spring.

"The horse stopped. It couldn't have been more than seven or eight feet from me. I swallowed hard and primed myself to jump behind a small boulder when the shooting started. I gritted my teeth in frustration. Somehow, he'd found us out. I could hear Lee fumbling in his clothes. There was a long pause, then a low *pop* and a flash of light as he lit a sulfur match against a thumbnail in his cupped hands. He never knew how close he came to getting a bullet in his head when he lit that match for a cigarette dangling from the corner of his mouth. He took a long draw and blew it out in to the air that had gotten cold and still.

"With a deep sigh, he creakily swung out of the saddle, stretched and yawned, adjusted his holster belt, and, in two steps, moved to the road side where I lay. He turned his back toward me and looked up through the pass notch while he fumbled with the buttons on his fly.

"My mind raced. Should I keep still? Should I risk him seeing me while he was urinating and hope that Yellow Boy could rope him before he killed me? His horse snorted nervously and jerked his head. He knew something wasn't right. Lee jerked the reins with his free hand and spoke in a calm, croaking voice. *Easy, boy, easy. The old man's just gotta pee is all.* Lee finally got his fly open and took another half step forward to do his business.

"I used every bit of Yellow Boy's training to rise soundless, a shadow floating off the ground, and stick the business end of my revolver hard just behind his ear as his flow started making a noisy splash against the rocks. He jumped, the splashing noise instantly stopping.

*Wa! What the devil!*

"Don't let me interrupt you, Mr. Lee. You just keep your hand off that revolver in your pocket or this'll be the last pee you ever take.

"Lee was a cool customer. He snorted in disgust and nodded as the splashing sound resumed. He had the bladder of a bull. I thought he'd never finish. Finally there was no more splashing sound.

"Put your hands up and keep 'em there until I tell you otherwise.

He nodded as his hands slowly went toward the stars. His horse was nervously jerking his head, pulling on the reins held tightly in Lee's raised hand, rolling his eyes at me trying to decide if he should run or stay. He calmed quickly when Yellow Boy's hand reached out of the darkness and jerked the reins out of Lee's hand while he rubbed around the horse's ears and spoke gently to him.

"*All right. What now? Stand here and freeze my pod off?* Lee sounded angry, but his level tone showed he was in full control of himself.

"Mr. Lee, there's a forty-five cocked behind your ear and a rifle pointed at your back. Just stay still a minute while I collect your hardware and you can button up.

I took his revolver out of its holster and stuck it in my belt. I felt his pants pocket for his other revolver, a .45 caliber Schofield with a short four inch barrel. Feeling the weapon brought back memories of Daddy's Schofield, which had a longer barrel. I worked to control myself, to keep from killing Lee on the spot.

*Be careful with those pistols, mister. There're full loads in both of 'em. Man never knows when he might need all his shots.*

"Don't worry, Mr. Lee. I'm real careful and real accurate when I handle guns. I wouldn't want any gun to kill you but mine. Button up with one hand, then keep'em both up.

"He fumbled with his fly for a few moments before slowly raising that hand up even with the other one. Yellow Boy stepped from the other side of the horse. He cocked his rifle and stuck the business end hard into Lee's back.

"There's a big bore rifle stuck in your back by a man who knows how to use it. You make the first wrong move and it'll splatter your guts all over this pass. Got it, Mr. Lee?

*Yeah. I got it plain. You sound like a kid. What'd you want with me, kid? I ain't carrying much dough. It's yours if you want to ride off now and leave me alone. Otherwise, you'll have to kill me. Ain't anybody ever stole or drew down on me and lived. I'll find you, and when I do –*

"Oh, shut up! Put your hands behind your back! I shouted. You already tried to kill me once, you son-of-a-bitch! I ain't afraid of you or anybody you own.

"He put his hands behind his back but showed no fear. I tied him off good and tight and Yellow Boy lowered his rifle. I was so relieved I could feel the muscles in my legs trembling. We'd gotten Lee without a shot being fired. Finally, I was going to settle the last item of business for my father's murder.

"I kicked his legs out from under him, and made him sit on the ground with Yellow Boy pointing the rifle at the center of his head. I walked down and got our horses. Then we set Lee on his mount and headed down the pass toward Organ."

19

# WISDOM

Roberta didn't know whether to laugh or cry. The image Henry painted of the highly respected rancher, politician, and deadly shot, Oliver Lee, caught while taking a pee in the middle of the night in San Augustin Pass and the way Henry was so serious in telling the tale tickled her imagination. She didn't doubt that Lee deserved the retribution Henry planned, but, she shuddered at the thought of how a brutal murder might have affected the direction of Henry's future life.

Henry looked at the turmoil written on her face.

"What's the matter?"

"Your taking Lee in the middle of a pee and being so serious while you're telling the tale. That old man, who everybody thought could walk on water, kidnapped at the top of the world in the middle of a pee by an eighteen year-old kid and a Mescalero. Henry that tale's a screamer. I'd pay money to be able to tell it to some of his biggest admirers just to shut them up, but I won't. I promised you I'd keep silent and I will. Yet, I can also imagine what might have happened if you had carried out the torture and murder you planned. Your life would have been much different than it was."

Henry nodded. "I've had a few grins over taking Lee myself. Even Yellow Boy thought it was a hoot when we reminisced about old times. But, you're right. What I did with Lee was a turning point in my life. Here, take the wheel for me, will you, while I knock the ashes out of this pipe."

They had passed through Alamogordo. The road pointed a straight black line through the browns and dull greens toward San Augustin Pass more than thirty miles away. She pushed against the seat to get closer to him, taking the wheel as he slowly released his grip. Cranking his window down, he thrust his arms into the cold wind and knocked out the old pipe's ashes against his palm. They were starting to feel the

306

chill as he cranked the window back up, and settled the pipe in his shirt pocket. The brilliant winter sun was dazzling, making them squint even at the dark places on the mountains.

"Wasn't it risky to take Lee down through Organ? I mean, suppose he yelled for help, or you met someone still awake who could testify they saw you or yell for help. Seems like it was much safer to go over to Rufus's place by Baylor Pass."

"Well, we thought about that, but it was getting late. By the time we picked our way over to Baylor Pass, then down to the road, it would have been getting daylight. The chances of early-rising ranch hands seeing us from a distance or running into us with Lee were high. Organ didn't have much nightlife to begin with. If nothing slowed us down, we'd be at Rufus's place before dawn.

"As it was, the only things that knew we went through Organ were a couple of barking dogs who gave us a salute, then went back to their beds. We saw no one on the ride to Rufus's place, and I believe no one saw us. Lee rode the entire distance without a word.

"It was close to dawn and pitch black far back in Rufus's canyon when we pulled Lee off his horse. We stopped where I'd camped when I came back from Mexico. I sat him down and tied his hands to a stake behind him, then tied his feet together with his legs straight out in front of him. We made a fire in the pit I had dug and put coffee on to boil. The night had been cold and windy. I was chilled to the core, and the fire's warmth, bringing life back to our numb bodies, sure felt good. Yellow Boy and I stood shoulder-to-shoulder warming our hands and staring across the fire at Lee as we waited for the coffee. Lee stared right back at us, unblinking, fearless. Yellow Boy's eyes were narrow slits and his mouth a taut straight line as he studied Lee. I stared at Lee without seeing him, turning alternatives over in my mind on how to get him to tell the truth before I took my revenge. Torture, lie to say I'd let him go only for the truth, not tell him who I was, tell him who I was and threaten to burn his place: fantasies all. I didn't have to pick a strategy. Lee, ever the leader, did it for me.

*Where'd you get the pup, Yellow Boy? He don't look like any of your kin.*

"Yellow Boy's eyes squinted across the firelight at Lee's face.

*You know me, Lee?*

*I know just about everbody in this here country, chief. We ain't been formally introduced, but I've heard enough tales about the marksmanship of a Mescalero cavalry scout with a Yellow Boy Henry to know who you are. Hope to shoot against you sometime so I can see just how good you are for myself.*

"*Señor that will never be,* Yellow Boy said slowly, shaking his head.

"Lee nodded. "*Maybe so, maybe not. You still ain't said who the pup is.*

"I couldn't speak, amazed at Lee's brass and lack of fear. I looked about for a stick to start beating him, a stick that would put pain and fear in his eyes, a stick to get rid of his brass. I wanted him to suffer – the sooner, the better. I saw a stick in the pile of wood for the fire and started to reach for it, but Yellow Boy put his hand on my shoulder. His powerful hand effortlessly held me still, telling me to be patient. Lee was not in control, we were. His death was sure and would be slow.

*Señor, I found este hombre. Si, señor, este hombre, under a mesquite bush many winters ago.* Yellow Boy's voice was warm and soothing like he was telling his children one of his people's stories. *That night he almost left us for the grandfathers, pero Rufus Pike help me keep him here. Señor, the day is now here for you to pay for putting him under the mesquite. The day is now here for you to pay for killing his padre, Señor Lee!*

"Lee's eyes narrowed. His lips puckered as though he was about to whistle but couldn't quite find the tone. Still, he showed no signs of fear.

"*What's your name boy?* He demanded.

"I stared at him, the hate making my blood hot and my lips slow to form words.

"Now I'm called Henry Grace. When Yellow Boy found me, my name was Fountain.

"Lee's sunburn-red brow raised high forming large leathery wrinkles as his eyes grew wide. *Good God Almighty! Everybody thought you were dead!*

"Well, I'm not. I've waited ten years to settle accounts with you. Today I'm gonna have my satisfaction.

Lee nodded but looked puzzled, even a little confused. *Well, son, if you want to settle accounts with me, since you already have made up your mind I did it, why didn't you just have your friend there pick me off at distance? You seem to know my whereabouts purty good.*

"I don't need Yellow Boy to put a bullet in you at any distance, Lee! I can do that with the old Sharps over there in my gear. I could have done it a thousand times in the last three months. I could have put a bullet in your heart while you had your afternoon siesta on your front porch. I don't miss either. Ask your friend Stone when you get to hell.

"Lee's eyes narrowed as he studied me closely.

"No, sir! We went to a lot of trouble to take you still breathing. I want to know the truth about my father's murder. I want to know why you'd murder a man over a few cows. I want to know how you set it up and how much you paid Stone and Tally to do it. I want to know how much you paid Tally after the murder. How much money were my life and my father's worth, you son-of-a-bitch!

"My voice was getting louder and louder. I was practically screaming at him when Yellow Boy gently squeezed my shoulder.

"He spoke under his breath, *Remember Hombrecito. Remember what Rufus tells you about nut-cutting time. Remember, my brother.*

"I nodded and stopped yelling. I remembered Rufus telling me to be cold and calculating. I stopped and got control, cold calculating control, of my rage. I lowered my voice to a hoarse whisper and spoke without emotion. Lee's jaw muscles rippled as he leaned as far forward as the stake would let him to listen.

"This is how it's going to be, Lee. You tell the truth and I'll just cut your throat. If I think you're lying, I'll tie your head over that fire. Your brain will do a slow boil until steam blows out your ears and your skull cracks. I'll make damn sure you don't die for a day or two while it happens either. Yellow Boy's people down in Mexico taught me all sorts of good tricks when it comes to cooking heads. Comprendé?

"Lee stared at my eyes and knew I wasn't bluffing. He believed he was going to die. He slowly nodded, keeping his eyes on mine.

*All right, son. I don't lie and I ain't never backed up for nobody. I'll tell you the truth. You deserve it, but you ain't gonna like it. Now does a condemned man get a cup of that coffee boiling on that there fire?*

"I sauntered over to Lee's saddle bags and dug around until I found his cup. Yellow Boy cut Lee's hands free of the stake and pushed him over on his side so he could drag his arms down under his legs and back to the front to hold the coffee cup. I came back and tossed Lee the cup. He caught it easily even with his hands tied. Yellow Boy found our cups and I lifted the steaming pot to pour a round.

"The sun was just beginning to drive away the predawn blackness. I was still cold and the coffee was good and hot. We'd done a hard night's work and were feeling pretty proud of ourselves. Yellow Boy and I slowly sipped the steaming hot coffee. Lee drank his in long swallows that must have burned all the way down.

*"That there ain't bad coffee, boys. How's about another cup?*

"He slowly slurped the next one. When he finished he smacked his lips, sat the cup beside him, and looked in my eyes as I squatted on the other side of the fire, studying his every move. Yellow Boy sat about half-way between us, and kept the Henry pointed at Lee's chest.

*So, Henry Fountain. This here is one for the books. You want the truth? You want the truth about something that happened ten years ago? You really want the truth?*

"Yeah, I really want the truth. I just hope for your sake you give it to me. If you do, your death will be quick. If you don't, the last thing you'll hear is yourself screaming and begging me to kill you.

*I got the message. Don't write me no book. Don't do me no favors either. Do what you gotta do. Only take my body back to the ranch for decent burial and so my family will know I ain't coming back. Will you do that?*

"Nope, your family's gonna suffer like mine. I'll bury you here so no animals will get your bones and I'll send your horse home if you tell me the truth. But you, you ain't going home. My Daddy never went home and neither have I. There is no home for the likes of you. I spit some coffee grounds to the side in disgust.

"Lee shrugged his shoulders, licked his lips, and stared at the narrow slits that were Yellow Boy's eyes, then back at mine.

*I reckon that'll have to do then, won't it?*

"Staring back at him, I nodded, and sarcastically mocking him, said I 'reckon' it will.

*Truth is, Henry Fountain, I didn't have a thing to do with what happened to you and your Daddy.*

"Damned liar! I instantly had a vision of Lee screaming for mercy with his head roasting over the fire. Stop lying and tell us the truth! Stop or you're gonna die a bad death."

*I ain't lying. Don't get me wrong. I didn't like your Daddy and he shore didn't like me. I was glad to hear the news somebody had finally given him what he'd been asking for all those years until I heard you were involved. Then I got kinda sick. I don't kill little kids. Your mama was right. I'd never have called him out if you'd been there.* Lee stared at the ground and shook his head. Then he looked straight back into my eyes, rock steady, never blinking or looking away.

*Your Daddy and me had our differences of opinion and were political enemies almost from the get-go. He was always sticking up for Mexicans and Indians. He used his reputation for representing peon farmers and your mother's family connections to win just about any election he wanted to win around here. It just wasn't fair the way he used those people who didn't have no land or cattle. They had nothing and contributed nothing to the range, but they had the same vote as any rancher who had ten thousand acres to work and twenty or thirty ranch hands to support. It just wasn't fair.*

*I had no use for him because of the way he used the law for his own political advancement. So, we ranchers, large and small, sometimes we had to play hard and rough. I admit that. I thought about calling him out and killing him several times. But, hell, he had a family. How many brothers and sisters do you have? Ten? Twelve? I just couldn't do it if he wasn't trying to kill me first. If I'd tried to kill him, I'd have taken him on face-to-face, not bushwhack him when a little kid was with him.* He stuck his chin out in pride. *You ask anybody that knows me. I'm of a mind that little ones need a chance to grow. They're the only folks around who're simple and to the point. They're the future. I ain't never hurt no kid for any reason.*

"I sat and eyed him, scratching my chin as I thought back over the past three months. I'd watched neighbors visit his ranch and the little ones crawled all over him as he played with them. I remembered how delighted he was to lift them up in his arms for a hug, two or three at a time.

"Is that why you got Stone to do it? You didn't want to be accused of murdering a kid?

*Listen to me. Listen! I already told you I had nothing to do with it. I didn't know it'd happened until Tally showed up at the ranch and wanted to know if I'd give him a thousand dollars for killing Albert Fountain. I asked him why. He said he'd just done it for Jack Stone. He figured since me and Fountain were enemies, it might be satisfying for me to sweeten the pot with a little extry.*

*I got mad. I got damn mad.* Lee's eyes narrowed. He spoke through gritted teeth and his jaw muscles rippled at the memory. *I knew everybody and his sister was going to think I'd done it. That killer had put me in a bad fix. I jerked Tally off his horse and beat the hell out of him. I punched him in the face and guts until my knuckles were bloody and my hands were hurtin' too bad to punch him anymore. His good eye was swollen nearly shut and there was blood all over his face and the front of his coat. I let him crawl over to the water tank and wash himself off. I told him I'd better not see him on any of my range again, and if somebody tried to bushwhack me he was the first one I'd come looking for. A couple of the hands helped him up on his horse, tied him on so he wouldn't fall off, and sent him off on a fast trot toward Tularosa.*

*Tally avoided me like the plague for the next few years. I heard he was going up into Colorado and Wyoming during the summers and coming back to the basin when it got cold. Nobody ever asked me about Tally shooting your Daddy and I never volunteered any information. It wasn't my business to tell the law anything. I figured they'd find it out for themselves, but they never even come close to thinking Stone and Tally did it. I lost track of Tally four or five years ago; he just seemed to disappear. I don't have any idea what happened to him, but I'd tell you if I knew, 'cause he shore as hell owes you some satisfaction.*

"I nodded. Not surprising you haven't seen him. Yellow Boy cut off his head. It's buried over in the Jarillas. Rest of him is in the sand somewhere between Dog Canyon and El Paso.

"Lee clinched his jaw, grimaced on one side of his face at the picture it must have made in his mind, and nodded. *Good riddance. Too bad that good-for-nothing Stone didn't loose his too. What happened to him?*

"My Sharps put a hole through him big enough to drive a buggy through. What bones the wolves and coyotes haven't eaten are scattered at the bottom of the canyon below the Eyebrow. That's what happened to him, I said in a menacing, low, matter-of-fact monotone.

"Lee grimaced again and nodded.

"What happened after Tally left? Did Stone come to meet with you and collect his money? How much did you promise him?

"Lee held up his head and stuck his chin out. His eyes got hard. *I'll tell you again, since it ain't sinking in and you've already been judge and jury for me, I had nothing to do with Stone and Tally killing your Daddy. After I sent Tally packing, I rode over to Wildy Well. I told the men over there what had happened. I wanted to let them know I had nothing to do with it and if they ever saw Tally on the ranch to kill him. They believed me and promised they would stand up for me when the law came. I was in deep trouble and I knew it. I knew I had to lay low for a while and figure out what to do. I knew the law would be pointing its finger at me sooner or later, probably sooner. When the men from the posse trying to track your killers came by Wildy Well and asked for help, I played dumb and refused. I wasn't about to be accused of leading them on a roadrunner-after-a-snake chase or trying to hide details from the trackers. I thought some more about what to do and finally saddled up and rode into Las Cruces to face my accusers.*

"I spat in disbelief. You're telling me Stone did it all on his own?

*Naw, I ain't telling you that, kid. There were others. Had to be. I'd bet even some of the members of that association your daddy worked for might have been involved. He might have had information that would make 'em look bad, and, worse, might cause 'em to be arrested.*

*Whoever put Stone up to it had a good pile of money to defend, and was willing to spend some to get any threat to it out of the way. Stone sure as hell didn't have any money. You can bet that he was paid off cheap too. He had his own tail to cover because your daddy was about to put him in prison. Your daddy probably had paper on me too, but I didn't care. My lawyer is old Albert Fall and I know he could have beaten any charge your daddy had. Stone wanted to do the killin', but he was afraid of your daddy. He knew your old man was better and smarter than he was any day of the week. He needed a first class, experienced killer to help him. Tally was the best around. He just couldn't afford him. So the only one that made any real money off your daddy's murder was Tally.*

"My mind was in turmoil. Lee's straight look in my eyes and a story that fit every detail I knew begged to be believed. Either Lee was the best liar in the country or he was telling the truth. I needed to think. I motioned to Yellow Boy to follow me down the path, out of Lee's hearing, but where we could still watch him. I yelled over to him, Lee, you make any kind of unexpected moves and Yellow Boy will put a couple of bullets in your knees. Got it?

*I'm sitting right here. No need to shoot.*

"I turned to Yellow Boy as he passively watched Lee, his eyes following Lee's every move and his rifle on full-cock. Do you think he's lying?

"Yellow Boy shrugged his shoulders, watching Lee like a hawk staring at a snake. *Maybe so, maybe not. My power is silent. You must decide, Hombrecito. What does your power say?*

"I too knew I was the one to decide. I will go listen in a wise place. Stay with him. Give him water when he asks for it. Kill him if he tries to run. I'll be back when I have peace with his words.

*Bueno, Hombrecito. I will watch. You listen. You come when you hear wisdom. I stay with Oliver Lee.*

"I knew he'd be there too. It didn't make any difference if it took an hour or a month, they'd be there when I returned.

"The Apaches believe that there are places containing wisdom. If you go there, sit quietly, watch and listen, wisdom will come to you. Your power will find it there. The porch on Rufus's shack had always been such a place for me. I sat down on the dust-covered step, leaned against a post, and tried to focus on the bright sun-lit valley below with red mountains in the distance. Moving black shadows were cast on the valley floor by floating clouds.

"For a long time my mind was blank. The sun felt warm and gracious on my face as I stared off into that big, hard country that stretched forever below me. I remembered the story Rufus told Daddy and me that Sunday afternoon as we sat and ate hot apple pie in Mrs. Darcy's place in Lincoln. You know, his tale about being careless and getting caught asleep by two Apaches? He thought Fast Hand was going to teach Caballo Negro how to torture him to death by cutting him so he'd suffer as he bled to death. Caballo Negro refused to cut him. He said he wanted strong enemies and that Rufus should come back later so they could have a respectable go at killing each other.

"Rufus told me that story several times. He always said the only reason he wasn't skinned alive or killed was because Caballo Negro wanted to be honored as a great warrior among the Apache. He knew he had to have worthy opponents – men that provided great victories – if stories were to be told about him around the fires and deep into the night. He could have killed Rufus easily. He'd caught him dead to rights, an intruder on land he claimed as his. Rufus was alive because Caballo Negro chose to let him live. Rufus was a walking dead man until Caballo Negro chose to give him back his life and release him from the pass he was given that day. Growing up, I thought that was an honorable thing to do. The fact that Rufus lived through the run to the Morales Place after they freed him kind of made him, ex post facto, a signatory to Caballo Negro's contract.

"The longer I thought about that story, the more I began to see that my situation with Lee was a lot like Caballo Negro's with Rufus. Lee's living or dying was up to me. Revenge was mine for the taking. I could make him suffer all I wanted. It was a debt I'd dreamed of paying for over ten years. But it wasn't a strong enemy I needed for stories around the fire. I needed satisfaction for my father's murder. Now I wasn't so sure I'd get the kind of satisfaction I wanted. What if Lee was telling the truth, and I killed him anyway? Oh, he probably deserved it. He said himself he'd wanted Daddy dead more than once. I needed a strong enemy, one that gave me satisfaction, not one that was weak, not one that made me doubt my honor if I killed him. There wasn't any satisfaction in that. There wouldn't be any rest at night in killing an innocent man, no peace at all would be in my dreams. If I let him live, his life was mine to take any time I wanted. If he was lying, he'd always be wondering if, somehow, I'd find the truth, and if I'd be coming back for him. The longer I waited, the older and weaker he'd get. If he did lie, even if I never touched him again, he'd live a life in hell waiting for me to come again, like a grim reaper out of the dark to snatch him and make him suffer as a weak old man.

"Those thoughts got fixed in my mind, and I felt better about where I knew my intuition wanted to take me. The day was long. The shadows swung slowly toward the east. I was thirsty and got up from the porch and walked over to the cattle tank where the spring continued to leave fresh water. I pushed my head down in its cold darkness and felt the fog in my brain start to disappear. I stayed buried there until my lungs began to burn. I jerked up, gasping for air, slung the water off my head like a dog shaking dry after a trip across the river, and drank from cupped hands several times before I wandered back to my seat on the porch.

"The day was beautiful. The sky had a kind of blue effervescence and hawks turned slowly high in the air, watching the valley floor, waiting for a rodent or snake to make its last mistake. Little puffs of clouds followed the upper wind currents, casting large shadows, black sailing ships that moved swiftly off down the valley toward El Paso. A big dust devil shaking mesquites and creosotes that lined the sandy road running down to Las Cruces from Organ tore across the distance toward Tortugas Mountain, and disappeared only to form again and again further down the valley. It occurred to me that my recent life in Mexico had been like that dust devil in the mesquite – a whirlwind in thorn trees. I had spilled a lot of blood down in Mexico. Blood for a cup of revenge. Blood for satisfaction. I still wakeup sometimes thinking about all the blood I made flow down in Mexico, all the men I killed, all the grief I caused, all the rage I felt."

Roberta strained to hear Henry's voice, a low whisper. His eyes seemed to loose focus. She shook his shoulder. "Henry! Henry! What are you talking about? I don't know anything about what you did in Mexico!"

He shook his head and the vision he was sinking into went away. "No, no you don't, and I'm glad. I need a little while longer to deal with it before I tell you, but I will, I promise."

She gave his shoulder a squeeze and nodded. He was silent in his thoughts for a while, before he said, "I guess sitting on that porch was the first realization of what I'd done and how much blood was on my hands. I had to stop spilling blood. I had to get my life under control rather than being driven from one promise of revenge to the next. I knew that there had to be more to life than making your enemies bleed. The longer I thought about it, the clearer it became that I couldn't kill Lee, unless I knew for a fact he was responsible for what happened to Daddy and me. His word that he didn't, and some gut instinct that said he wasn't lying, were all I had to make me believe that maybe he was innocent.

"I sat there on the porch watching the valley and listening to the wisdom there until the sun started burning a hole in the backside of the Floridas. Then I got up, dusted myself off, and started walking back up the path to where we'd camped.

"The fire was starting to cast shadows on the canyon walls in the dying sunlight high over head. Yellow Boy still sat where he'd been when I had left, the rifle still on full-cock. Lee was stretched out with his hat over his face and his hands tied to the stake behind his head. I nodded at Yellow Boy, and went over and cut Lee's hands free of the stake as I said, Wakeup Mr. Lee! We're gonna have us a little talk.

"He sat up as though jerked up by a tight spring, obviously not asleep, as I'd thought. He looked first at Yellow Boy's rifle, and saw it was still on full-cock. He looked at my face in the fading light and nodded. He must have seen something in my eyes that told him what was on my mind. He said, *Decided not to kill me, son?*

"I'm not going to kill you today, Mr. Lee. I'm tired of killing. I killed Stone and Tally. I know for a fact what they did. I don't know for a fact what you did. I was sitting down there on that shack porch all day, listening to the valley talk to me and remembering what Rufus and Yellow Boy taught me. See, Rufus told me a story about how Yellow Boy's father and uncle could have skinned him alive after they'd caught him sleeping. Yellow Boy's father was Caballo Negro and the Mescalero still tell tales about his bravery fighting strong enemies. They didn't kill Rufus because there was no honor in killing a weak enemy. They told him his life was theirs. They'd take it any time they wanted and be done with him. He was theirs until they chose differently. Rufus was so relieved to be spared when he thought for sure he was going to die, he always believed he was living on borrowed time. It was a matter of honor for Rufus. Caballo Negro always knew where Rufus lived and he knew Rufus would put up a good fight if he came for him.

"Lee nodded. *Rufus always was kinda crazy wasn't he, son?*

"He wasn't crazy. He just had his code. He was a man of honor. Every man has his code, doesn't he? I know you have yours. I reckon we all look a little crazy with our codes – you know, doing what we think is right. Caballo Negro wanted a strong enemy and he gave Rufus the chance to be one. Rufus could have left the country and never come back. He'd have been safe. But he wasn't afraid to live right where those Indians could come get him. He wasn't afraid of a fight to the death and neither were they. Respect for former enemies was what kept him alive.

*Whatever happened to old Rufus anyway? Buck Greer told me Rufus went down to Mexico to find some cattle and settle some business and he ain't been seen since.*

"I looked over his shoulder and nodded toward the canyon wall where a clump of mesquite hid the rocked-over entrance to the little mine where we'd buried Rufus.

"He's buried right over there. He got a little careless as Stone was dying. Stone managed to shoot him in the liver. There wasn't anything I could do except wait for him to die.

"Lee nodded. *All it takes in this country is one mistake kid. Looks to me like ole Rufus got by with a passel of them before they finally caught up with him. He was a good man. I liked him.*

"Yeah. He raised me. I owe him a lot and I'll never forget him.

"Lee nodded and studied my face across the fire.

"This is the way it's going to be Mr. Lee. There is only your word that you didn't pay Stone and Tally to kill my Daddy and maybe me unintentionally. Right now all I have for a fact is your word you didn't do it. Killing you when maybe you did or maybe you didn't do it isn't going to bring me any satisfaction. Like Caballo Negro, I need a strong enemy to find some satisfaction. I'm letting you go, but remember, sir: Your life is mine. Live where I know to come for you if I ever find you had even a whisper in the death of my Daddy. Don't run when I come, face me like a true warrior, a strong enemy. If anybody ever tries to murder Yellow Boy or me at distance, you'll be the first one I come looking for. If anyone of those reservation bureaucrats comes after Yellow Boy, I'll come after you. If I can't get close to you, one day you'll find a big hole in your chest and you'll never hear the gun that fired it.

"As for me, nobody knows I'm Henry Fountain. I want to keep it that way. My mother has suffered a long time. I don't know if she's ever gotten over it. I'll tell her I'm alive in my own good time. Don't you start no tales about me and what went on here. I ain't threatening you, Mr. Lee. I'm telling you for a fact the way it is and the way it's gonna be. Pray I never learn for a fact you were involved and keep your mouth shut about what went on here today. This ghost of Henry Fountain will fade away like a shadow never to return. Do you understand me?

"Lee sat and stared with eyes in a challenging squint. He was angry but he kept his emotions under control. I was offering him a chance out of all the terror I had planned for him. But, he'd always met danger and threats head-on. Now he had to walk away and trust what I was telling him was true – not just some way to tease him before I killed him. We stared at each other for a long time. I don't think Yellow Boy even blinked that whole time.

317

At last, Lee sighed, a long almost mournful sigh. Hunching his shoulders he looked away from me at his hands tied together in his lap, slowly shaking his head. When he looked at me again the challenge in his squint was gone.

*All right, Fountain. There ain't many men put the clamps on me and get away with it. You are your Daddy's son, that's for damn sure. Turn me loose and I'll keep my mouth shut. I'll not leave this country. Even if I did it, I wouldn't leave this country to run from you or anybody else. This here land is my home. If you want me, you'll know where to find me. But you ain't gonna come looking for me, cause there's nothing else for you to know. You done killed the men that killed your Daddy and I don't have any idee who paid 'em off. If I did, I'd get them myself for all the misery they brought on me. I ain't gonna shoot you or that Apache at a distance neither. You're taking a chance, and I'm givin' you my word it ain't the wrong gamble.*

"I must have eyed him for a couple of minutes after he said that. Then I took my knife, the one I was going to use to cut him in a thousand places, stepped around the fire pit and cut him free. Yellow Boy kept his rifle at full-cock and pointed at him, but he just crawled up on his knees and stood up kinda shaky as he dusted his pants off.

"He licked his lips and said in a hoarse whisper, *Water?*

"Yellow Boy tossed him a canteen. Lee uncorked it, drew it to his lips and turning his face to the sky drank three long swallows before he brought it down. *Sweet Maria that's good! You boys forgot to water me since coffee this morning.*

"We didn't forget. You didn't ask for it and we just thought we'd be wasting it offering it to a dead man. That's how close you came.

*I know. I know I was mighty close to leaving this here country a piece at a time.*

"I found his pocket revolver, flipped it open, dropped the shells out of it, and tossed it to him. He caught it with one hand, closed it, then flipped it open and spun the empty cylinder to be sure it was all right. When he looked up at me, I said to Yellow Boy, Let the hammer down on your rifle, uncle. He eased hammer down slowly. I tossed Lee a couple of cartridges.

"Load 'em up, Lee. If you're as good as I've heard, you might be able to kill both of us. It's your last chance to try, your last chance to prove my wisdom wrong.

"He shook his head. *No, son. I don't blame you for feeling the way you do. I'm innocent of all claims. The government's already tried to prove me guilty and failed. I ain't got no quarrel with you or your friend for what happened here today. Do I get my horse and gear back or do I have to walk or hitch a ride into Las Cruces?*

"We're not thieves. Take your horse and gear and get outta here. Don't ever come back unless you're ready to die.

"He nodded, and, without a word, turned to get his horse. He found him and brought him up to the fire pit, saddled him, tied his gear on board, and slowly mounted. He put two fingers to his hat in a little salute, then rode slowly down the trail toward the shack. I didn't have any regrets about letting him go."

# 20

# THE RETURN

**R**oberta saw the desert through new eyes. She rarely noticed the small ripple of stone called the Jarilla Mountains they had just passed. Now it stood out clearly, a place that figured prominently in Henry's life. The Jarillas were so obvious, yet seen so often as not to be noticeable to the frequent traveler. The great basin they were crossing swept south toward El Paso resting between the Organs, San Andres, and Sacramento Mountains. Compression of travel times from days to a couple of hours, and being shielded from the dust and heat, the bitter cold winter winds, and the unending ocean of creosote bushes and mesquite, made it difficult for her to imagine how hard and tough anyone was that survived in this great wilderness sixty years ago. Now she understood how huge and desolate it appeared to anyone riding through it on horseback and even more so if they were on foot.

The sun swung toward the west, bringing stark shadows to the Organs, and Roberta began seeing the edges of its cliffs shaded in bronze. Deep gashes in the stone-faced cliffs slowly appeared as the mountains crept toward them. There was no sound in the Plymouth save the smooth hum of the motor and the ragged whistle of wind whipping around the slightly open vent window. Henry leaned back in the seat, almost relaxed to the point of being too drowsy to drive. He breathed deeply, wiggled his toes, and flexed his leg muscles to stay awake. The reassuring warmth of Roberta's body next to his and the faint trace of her Cactus Flower perfume filled him with a peace and contentment he had not known for a long time.

Curiosity and a realization that the intimacy they shared on this trip were fast coming to a close made her ask in a soft voice, "Did you have any more contact with Lee after you let him go?"

Henry puffed his cheeks, blew the air out slowly and grinned. "Yeah, yeah, I did. I saw him about thirty years later. It must have been, hmmm, late 1940. One of his sons, I've forgotten which – I think it was Hop – stopped by the office and said the old man wasn't doing too well. He knew I was helping the Mescaleros on a fairly regular basis, and asked if I'd stop by the ranch and look the old man over my next trip in that direction. Of course, I said I would, and I did. I have to tell you curiosity was eating me up to find out if old Lee would recognize me after all those years. I stopped by his place a couple of weeks later. The day I nearly killed him, he was all cowboy sinew and muscle. Looking at him there in late 1940, he still seemed vigorous enough, but he was thin and dried up like an old yucca stalk. When his son told him who I was and why I was there, there appeared to be, for the briefest instant, a flicker of recognition in his eyes. It quickly vanished as he grew affable and charming. He invited me in for a cup of the strongest coffee I ever put in my body. He asked about my work with the Mescaleros and if I knew one named Yellow Boy."

Henry cut his eyes over to Roberta with a big grin. "Yellow Boy." She laughed and clapped her hands in sheer pleasure at the irony.

"I said I did and asked why. He shook his head and grinned. He said he'd shot against him and his old Yellow Boy Henry in a rifle match in El Paso in 1925. Now this is a direct quote. *That there Indian's the only man who ever made me look bad shootin'. Guess I musta been off a my feed that day.* Then he grins and winks at me. It was all I could do to keep from laughing out loud. I just bowed my head and mumbled something about Yellow Boy being a pretty good shot. I asked him if he wanted me to examine him. Shaking his head, he said, *The sand's about run out of this end of the glass, son. I know I'll be gone in a year or so. Just don't have the juice I used to. I'm not scared of dying either. It's been a great, hard ride. I ain't got no regrets.*

"We sat and talked ranching and local politics – as if you could separate the two – for an hour or so. He was an alert and fun conversationalist. It was easy to see why he had so many friends. I have to admit that I thought then, and I still think, I did the right thing not killing him when I had the opportunity. When I left, he told me to come back again and to mention to Yellow Boy I'd visited with him. I promised I'd speak to Yellow Boy that afternoon up on the reservation. The last image I have of him was of him leaning against a porch post giving me a casual wave good-by. I never saw him again. He passed away a few months later, in 1941, from a stroke. I was a little remorseful for not seeing him again before he died, but sick folks needed my time more than he did."

"So, do you still think, after all these years, he had nothing to do with Tally and Stone murdering your father?"

"I'll never know for sure. My gut instinct says he didn't. In any case, those days are long past now and I'm willing to cut his memory some slack. It's better to just let it be than have my guts in a constant squeeze over it."

The Rabbit Ears, mighty twin columns of towering stone sitting on top of the Organ's ridge line began to display sharp details as they caught rays from the lowering sun and the road started the long rise up toward San Augustin Pass. Roberta chewed on the inside of her lower lip, debating. Her heart finally got the best of her.

"May I ask you one more very personal question?"

His eyes stole a quick glance at her as he pushed for more gas to keep up their speed on the long climb to the top of the pass.

"For you, my life is now an open book. Ask what you will."

She paused, smoothing a wayward tendril of her shiny black hair with her right hand while she gave his forearm a comforting squeeze with the other.

"If you don't want to talk about this, it's all right. I won't be offended at all. It's just that, well, why didn't you ever tell your family you were alive?"

His face reflexively winced as though he had been slapped. He rubbed his tongue over his lips and hunched his shoulders trying to relax. They were half-way up the incline to the pass when he spoke.

"I did tell my mother, but I made her promise not to tell my brothers and sisters."

Roberta looked puzzled.

"When did you do that?"

"Oh, about a year after I let Lee go."

"Did she believe who you were and was she glad to see you?"

"She did and she was. But, I think initially she believed she was actually having some kind of hallucination – that I was some kind of spirit sent to relieve her suffering."

"Well, why didn't you want your brothers and sisters to know you were alive?"

"I know this sounds crazy, but I felt then, and, in some twisted way I feel now, that it was my fault Daddy was killed. I was supposed to be there to protect him and I failed. I was totally useless on the day Tally and Stone murdered him. I couldn't deal with facing my brothers and sisters feeling that way. I know I'm a coward for not dealing with it, but I just can't face them – even now. Henry Fountain is long dead except to you and it's better to let it stay that way."

Folding her arms and furrowing her brow, Roberta shook her head at him.

"You're right! That kind of thinking is crazy! You were only eight years old for heaven's sake! That you survived, and then made the men who killed your father pay with their lives when you were only fourteen is incredible! Promise me you'll tell your brothers and sisters you're alive. I'll do whatever I can to help you. Promise?"

She saw his jaw muscles rippling as he clinched his teeth, but he slowly nodded.

"Okay. I promise – someday I'll tell them. I promise," he said in a low whisper that she strained to hear against the road noise.

Roberta was tempted to press him for a no-weasel-word answer, thought better of it, and decided to be patient while Henry wrestled his demons into submission.

"Why did you finally decide to tell your mother you were alive after all those years of silence?"

Henry thought for a moment as he wiggled his head back and forth to stretch his neck muscles. He smiled at the memory Roberta had pushed to hear.

"Since the day I managed to escape Stone and Tally, I dreamed about telling her I was alive, and tried to imagine what it would be like when she saw me again. The year after we let Lee go, I stayed several months with Yellow Boy on the reservation. I rambled all over the basin and I spent a lot of time around Rufus's shack. I hauled the books out of the mine, and read most them again as I tried to decide what to do with my life. I spent hours sitting in front of the little mine where Rufus was buried, and days, maybe even weeks, sitting on the shack's porch steps waiting to hear some wisdom. It didn't come.

"Early one afternoon in late spring I was sitting on the porch watching a dust storm from Arizona come over the horizon. I could tell, even though it must have been fifty or sixty miles away, that it was going to be a hard blow. I remember I'd been thinking maybe I ought to go to college and study law. Then it came to me, just like somebody speaking directly in my ear. *When this blow is over, go see your mother.* Three days later the dust and wind were gone. The sky was a crystal blue, and the air had that crisp, springtime snap that makes you thank God you're alive.

"I saddled Satanas and rode down to Las Cruces. The people down in the valley and around town must have thought I was an Indian. The man who owned the livery stable insisted I pay him up front and the Amador Hotel clerk gave me a close going-over before he said he had a room and asked me to sign the register. I had a tub bath with hot water to clean up. The bath brought back a flood of memories of the tub I'd used in the house on Water Street during happier times, a tub I didn't want to use when I was eight.

"Smelling better and having a clean body, I took a walk down Main Street until I found a three-chair barbershop. There was only one barber there and he was sitting in one of the chairs reading the paper. The kindly old gentleman with snow-white hair, a perfectly trimmed beard, and twinkling blue eyes behind fine wire-framed glasses welcomed me inside. He just grinned and nodded when I told him I wanted the works and to trim my hair short. My hair then was nearly shoulder length and there was a wave in it where I'd worn a bandana, Apache-style, for years. The barber cut, trimmed, and shaved on my hair for the better part of an hour while keeping up a constant stream of chatter about several new contraptions I'd seen around town. He called them velocipedes. I'd seen several of those things up close earlier in the day, and often from a distance when I lived with Yellow Boy. I couldn't imagine why anyone would prefer some ugly, noisy, and smelly contraption to a beautiful quiet horse.

"I was shocked to see myself when the barber turned the chair around for me to look in his big mirror stretching the length of the shop. It wasn't an Indian's face that stared back at me. Rather, a dark-skinned young man, acceptable in just about any company, peered back at me. It's fine, I mumbled. He took his little whisk broom and stroked the stray hairs from around my collar, slapped a little lavender toilet water on the back of my neck where he'd used a straight razor, and whipped the cover apron off me with a flourish and snap. I gave him a dollar, which was about seventy-five cents more than he charged for a haircut and a shave. His grin made his blue eyes twinkle even more as I walked out. He called after me, *Don't let those velocipedes run you over, son! Come back anytime!*

"Rufus often told me about his trips to Las Cruces and buying supplies. He said a fellow could buy just about anything he ever needed in Lohman's store. I wandered around until I found it and bought myself a white shirt and studs, a simple black suit and tie, and a pair of good dress boots. I think I still have that suit hanging in a closet at home. I wore it so much the pants got shiny in the seat, but it served me well. The clerk who sold it to me said I looked fit to kill when I tried it on. I just hoped it would help me get a chance to talk to my mama.

"I went back to the hotel and tried to nap. I had it in mind that I'd try to visit Mama after dinner, when she was most likely without the company of my brothers and sisters. Sleep didn't come the whole afternoon. I lay there in the dark gloom of the room, playing different scenarios of our meeting over and over in my mind. About five o'clock, I gave up trying to nap, threw my feet on the floor and dressed in my new suit and boots.

"I walked over to the livery stable to get Satanas. The owner, who had made me pay up front and was down right scurrilous when I rode into the livery, flashed me a big grin and said, *Damn, kid! You clean up real nice. Going to see yore girl?*

"I said, *No, sir, just business. Is the Fountain place still over on Water Street?*

"The livery agent had a big wad of tobacco crammed in his jaw. He nodded as he took a strong chew and spat a long brown stream of juice that would have done Rufus proud.

*Shore is. 'Cept I think the only one living there now is Mrs. Fountain and her Mex housekeeper. Pore thang. She's a widder lady, you know. Husband and youngest child wuz kilt by Oliver Lee's crowd and the rest of her brood has their own places here 'bouts. Want me to saddle that swift black stud o' yorn?*

"Yes, sir! I'd appreciate it, I said, handing him a couple of dollars. I'll be back later this evening. Will that cover him through tomorrow for a good ration of grain and a rubdown when I get back?

"*Oh, it shore will, son,* his head bobbing so fast he almost choked on the wad in his cheek.

"I rode down Main Street to the Rancher's Restaurant and had myself a nice leisurely steak dinner. It was late twilight when I finally rode over to the house on Water Street. I stopped at the front gate, and, through the fading light I heard the voices and saw the outlines of two women sitting in wicker chairs on the front porch.

"I called out, Señora Fountain?

"There was a long pause. I could hear the two of them whispering back and forth.

"Finally she answered in a voice, old and silvered with culture. *Si? What is it you wish, señor?*

"My heart was pounding and my mouth so dry I could hardly make my tongue move. I managed to stammer, Señora Fountain, I must speak with you on a matter of great personal importance. May I come through your gate?

*You are alone, señor?*

"Si, Señora Fountain. I am alone and I must speak with you alone.

"Again there were whispers back and forth, one woman anxious, the other curious.

*I will receive you in my parlor, señor. Marta will make us tea. The night air is a little too cool, I think, for visiting outside. Please, come and be welcomed.* Their dark outlines arose and disappeared inside the house.

"I was trembling inside and out as I tied Satanas to the gatepost, pushed open the gate, and walked down the brick walkway to the porch. My knees were like water as I stepped on the porch. Lamps were being lighted in the front parlor and in the foyer. I knocked on the door and waited. Within two of my rushing breaths Marta opened it. She was in her fifties with a thin face, hawk-like eyes, and an arrogant tilt to her chin. She wasn't the friend I remembered handing the basket supper up to Daddy on the wagon all those years ago, and she scrutinized every detail of me from head to toe before she swung her arm toward the parlor. She said, *Aqui, señor. Por favor, sit down. Señora Fountain will come in a little while.*

"I could feel the blood pounding in my temples as I found a straight-backed chair facing the door. It sat near the chair she often used when I was small. I remembered this room well. It still had traces of her perfume and the flowers she freshened every day. I often had to sit up straight and unmoving on the sofa when guests came to visit. The memories were an irresistible flood. I didn't know whether to laugh, cry, sing, or howl. It was overwhelming to be in this house, in this room again, after so many years, so much living and dying between that moment and the last time I was there. Gradually, I relaxed, crossed my legs, and began to study each object in the room, trying to recall some memory I had of it. In a little while I heard a teakettle whistle in the back of the house and the rustle of skirts down the long hallway to the parlor.

"I turned to look at the doorway just as she appeared. My heart was pounding, about to jump out of my chest. She was more petite than I remembered, but moved with the same grace and poise I had known years before. I was shocked to see how gray she had become and how sad her eyes looked. She was dressed in black and wore a large cameo my father had given her.

"I stood and faced her. Not quite sure of the proper thing to do, I made a little bow. Her eyes studied my every detail as she smiled and said with a little twinkle in her eye, *We are not quite so formal as to require bows in this hacienda, señor.* She held out her hand for me to escort her to a chair. The soft translucent skin of her hand was warm and comforting. She led me toward her favorite chair, the one near where I had been sitting, and sat down gracefully. I stepped back to my chair and sat down. She studied my face and especially my eyes carefully. I thought I saw a momentary flicker of recognition in her eyes and that made my heart pound even harder than it already was.

"Marta walked through the doorway with a tray containing Prince Albert Rose cups, slices of pound cake on small plates, forks, and a teapot. She placed the tray on a table within easy reach of my mother. Eyeing me all the while, she asked, *Will that be all, señora?*

"*Si. Muy bien, Marta. Close the doors behind you as you leave, por favor.*

"Marta gave a little nod, and, making a presumptuous grand sweep out of the room, closed the double doors together behind her. I had the uncomfortable feeling she waited right outside the crack between the two doors, listening and waiting to see if she had to pounce on me to protect her mistress.

"My mother's kind, sad eyes studied me intently for a few more moments before she said with a slight smile and soft voice, *Señor, you are very young to have important personal business with an old widow lady. How can I help you? I have no land or cattle to sell. I have no jobs around this place. I have no unmarried daughters.*

"I stared at her and heard the blood pounding in my ears as I swallowed a couple of times, then I spoke in a rush as I struggled to hold back the tears, *Señora, you do have something of great interest to me. You have my blood.*

"She covered her mouth with a trembling hand and her big brown eyes grew wet as she stared at mine, knowing immediately what I meant. A soft, *Mi Dios! No! Can it be?* fell from her lips.

"I was out of the chair and kneeling on one knee in front of her as I took the hand in her lap. Tears were rolling down my cheeks.

"It's me, Mama. It's me, Henry. Oh, Mama, I'm so sorry I let Daddy die. I was sobbing. I couldn't help it, Mama. I couldn't help it. Can you forgive me? Please say you can forgive me for all the hurt I've caused you.

"She squeezed my hand and raised me off my knee as she stood and threw her arms around me, burying her face on my chest, her shoulders shaking as her tears made a big wet spot on my shirt. I hugged her back. We stood that way for a long time, not saying a word.

"Finally she took my hand and led me to sit beside her on the Queen Anne sofa. She wouldn't let go of my hand as she said in wonder looking at me, *Henry, is that really you, flesh and blood? You're not a ghost? Is it really you all grown up now? Dios in heaven! Is it really you?*

"Yes, Mama. It's really me. I'm truly your lost son, Henry.

*Where have you been all these years? Why have you waited so long to tell me you're not dead?*

"Where I've been is a long story. At first I didn't come back because my protectors and I were afraid the same men who killed Daddy might try to kill me and you. I've always felt responsible for not protecting Daddy and I just couldn't face you or my brothers and sisters because of it. I've settled all accounts with the men who murdered Daddy. I had to see you to tell you that my work there is done.

"*You've killed Oliver Lee?* she asked, her eyes wide with wonder, and her hand covering her mouth, opened in full surprise.

"No ma'am. I haven't killed Oliver Lee. I nearly did, but thought better of it. He swears he didn't have anything to do with it. I want to believe him, and I sure can't prove that he did. I won't murder a man in revenge if there's a reasonable chance he's innocent. I've killed those I know murdered Daddy because I was there. Mama, can you ever forgive me for not keeping Daddy alive?

*Oh Henry!* she said softly as she put her arm around my shoulders and hugged me again. *It was never, ever, your fault. I should never have sent a little boy out in that desert when I knew there was a chance your father would be attacked. It truly is my fault that I lost you both for so many years. I'm so sorry. Please, please forgive me for I've shed many tears of regret over it. Now I just thank God that He has allowed me to see you again before I die, all grown and handsome. Tell me everything, my son. You make an old woman's heart sing again with joy.*

"She wanted to know everything about the trip with Daddy and every detail about my life with Rufus and Yellow Boy. She made another pot of tea as we talked and we ate nearly all the pound cake. We talked until after ten. Hearing the rustle of Marta's skirts outside the door, I finally told her I needed to take my leave, take care of my horse, and let her get her rest. I felt emotionally drained and ready to collapse. She was still very excited, but it was obvious she was exhausted too. She begged me to stay at the house there with her, but I told her I had a room at the hotel and didn't want to get folks too curious about who I was. If Marta started talking about uninvited guests staying overnight, there would be all kinds of rumors and speculation.

"Mama wasn't happy with me staying in a hotel, but she decided that discretion was the better way at that point. I made her promise not to tell my brothers and sisters about me. I knew one of them or their spouse would let the cat out of the bag if they found out. Then there would be hell to pay with newspaper reporters, rumors, and gossip.

Mama said she had to see the place where Rufus had raised me and made me promise I would come back early the next morning to take her up there for a visit. I was reluctant to do that. She was not a young woman anymore. It was an all day trip to Rufus's place and back, and there was a good chance we might see a nosey neighbor or one of our relatives. Nevertheless I promised to be there at six and she promised to have a picnic basket ready to go. She hugged me for a long time and I could tell my shirt was getting wet again. She kissed me on the cheek and let me out the door.

"It was hard to sleep at all that night. My heart couldn't stop racing at the joy I felt in finding my mother again and her acceptance of me. I got up with the first glimmer of dawn. I dressed and walked down the street to a restaurant and had a big breakfast. It was going to be a long day.

"I rented a nice one-horse buggy rig at the livery after I had my fill of *huevos rancheros* and coffee. I drove over to the house on Water Street and tapped gently at the front door. In a few moments Marta's scowling face opened door. She didn't like me. Mama had led her to believe that I was trying to sell her some land and was taking her out to show it to her. Marta was convinced I was just trying to take advantage of an old lady. She planned to tell my brothers if Mama expressed the slightest interest in buying my land. She had no doubt my brothers knew how to take care of a scam artist.

"Mama appeared behind Marta. Smiling she said, *Buenos dias, señor. How good of you to come this morning so early. Marta, bring the gentleman our lunch basket while I get my hat and parasol.*

"Without a word, and with a deepening scowl Marta padded off down the hallway toward the kitchen. Mama smiled and winked at me, saying so Marta could hear her, *Un momento, señor.*

"Marta brought the picnic basket and a cold jug of water. Opening the door wide enough to place them in my hands, she mumbled something I didn't understand just as my mother appeared with a large floppy hat and her parasol. She frowned at what she'd heard, and, looking at Marta, shook her head as she walked through the doorway to take my arm for support as we started toward the buggy. She said gaily over her shoulder, *We should be back sometime late this afternoon. Don't worry my children about my whereabouts unless we're late.*

"*If you are late, señora, where shall I say you have gone?* Marta called plaintively.

"*Behind Tortugas Mountain,* Mama said merrily.

*"Pero, señora, that is a big country full of bandits and wild Indians,*
Marta whined. But, she knew there were no more Indians, except on the
reservations, and there were few bandits since Pat Garrett had been
sheriff.

*"Si, comprendo,* Mama called back to Marta as I helped her in the
buggy. I got in the buggy and started the horse off at a fast trot, leaving
Marta still scowling in the doorway.

"It was a beautiful bright morning, the air cool, and the sky ever
changing from dark to light blue. I swung south of town then back toward the east on a dusty road that wound around Tortugas Mountain
and out through the yucca, mesquite, and creosote bushes. The road
wiggled in and out of sight through the bushes like a long piece of ma-
nila rope stretching toward Dripping Springs Ranch and Rufus's
canyon. It was the same area I used to run in when Yellow Boy was
teaching me how to survive in the desert and training me to be strong. I
told Mama about those days. She couldn't believe that I could run
miles over this desert holding water in my mouth without swallowing
it, much less run such long distances when I was only ten.

"We talked about her life since Daddy's murder and how she had
worried her other sons would die trying to take revenge on Oliver Lee.
All her children had been worried she would go crazy with grief. She
said she still grieved for Daddy and would until she died. However, she
said that what almost drove her over the edge of sanity had been my
disappearance too, and how it had been her pushing Daddy to take me
with him that had lost me to her. The years had been hard for her, but
she had learned to deal with it and was still a firm believer in God's
mercy.

"The sun was half way to being straight overhead when I stopped
the rig in front of Rufus's shack. I helped Mama down from the buggy
as she stared, without speaking, at the patched porch once riddled with
bullets shot by Stone and Tally when they came for us that night so
many years ago. I gave the horse some oats and water, and then tied
him and the buggy in the shade behind the shack.

"When I came back around to the porch she stood on the step, looking out across the valley toward the Floridas.

"It's beautiful isn't it Mama?

*"Yes, my son, it is. How long were you here? Six years, I think you
said last night?* She took my elbow for support. *May I see inside?*

"Of course, Mama. Just remember this is just a place where an old
man and boy lived. Our housekeeping standards were nowhere near
yours or Marta's.

"She nodded and led me toward the door. I pulled the latch and pushed the door, creaking with age, slowly open. She stepped inside and paused, waiting for her eyes to adjust to the shadowy light from the dust-covered windows.

"Stepping over to the old wood cooking stove, she ran her fingers softly over the smooth surface where Rufus had cooked many a pot of beans and tortillas. She looked over the walls at the places where pots and clothes hung from nails, at the cots where we slept, and heard the creak of the floor as she walked slowly about, studying the simple room. The tall stack of books in the corner caught her eye. She went over to them and squinted in the dim light to read their titles.

*Have you read any of these books, my son?*

"Yes, ma'am. I've read all of them at least once, and some like *The Illiad* two or three times.

"She straightened up and smiled. *Rufus and your Indian friend taught you well. Your father would have liked these books and admired the physical strength your friends gave you. I have no regrets that you grew up here. No regrets at all, except I thought you were dead. Now, let us see the rest of the place. Where did Rufus teach you to shoot the big gun you talked about last night? Where are all the rocks you and Rufus moved to build a new house? Where is Rufus buried? Show it all to me.*

"She took my arm and I led her outside. The bright sunlight was dazzling. As we waited for our eyes to adjust to the light, I asked, Do you want to walk, or shall I get the buggy?

*Oh, no! I much prefer to walk.*

"She opened up her parasol to provide a little shade for us as we started up the canyon. I pointed out the big piles of rocks Rufus and I had gathered but never used for a new cabin and corral. There the stable, there the corral, there, just above us, the ledge where we'd hidden when Stone and his riders came looking for us. We walked slowly up the path, she holding my arm, and I explaining the significance of places along the way. When we came to the cairn in front of the little mine where Rufus was buried, she stopped and bowed her head, her lips moving in silent prayer while crossing herself.

"As we walked away from the cairn, I asked what she had said.

*Oh, I just thanked him for being so kind and generous to my son and for thinking of our welfare. I promised to light a candle for him when I attend mass, and I thanked God for all he has done for you through Rufus Pike. He was a good man, my son – a very good man, and I owe him much, perhaps more than you do.*

"We finally reached the place where Rufus taught me to shoot the Sharps. I pointed out the target locations for the distances we shot over and told her how difficult it was to find lines-of-sight in the canyon that were more than a few hundred yards long. She studied the places where targets had been, and marveled that any gun could be used to consistently shoot at and hit a target at those distances.

*You learned to hit those targets, targets I can barely see, with a big gun and when you were still a child?*

"Yes ma'am, I mumbled, embarrassed.

*That's remarkable – truly remarkable. I don't doubt you, but it is hard for me to believe that you did this. I'm in need of water and food. Come, let us go eat our lunch.*

"We strolled back down the path to the shack. I got the picnic basket and water jug from the buggy and we sat on the steps and spread the lunch between us in the shade of the porch. A cool breeze blew down the canyon, making us very comfortable, and the view was spectacular. The water was cool and refreshing and the burritos and fruit she brought easily filled my growling belly. We ate in silence as she gazed out across the valley.

"She said, *Ah me, Henry. I am so old and have seen so little. You are so young and seen so much. What will you do with the rest of your life?*

"I don't know. I've thought about going to college and perhaps studying the law to be an attorney like Daddy.

*Yes, I too think you should go to college. I will give you the money you need if you will go. But you can do better than the law, my son. You can learn to heal others and to make lives better. In my mind, you should study medicine. It is the right thing for you to do, for you have spilled much blood to make right your father's murder. God calls us all to atone for the guilt in our lives. Many of your blood sins will be forgiven if you are a physician, my son.*

"A physician? Her words were an epiphany. I'd often wished I'd had a physician's skills. The faces of those I might have saved had I been a physician swept before my eyes. There were many, and Rufus was at the top of the list. I spent many hours wondering and agonizing over how I might have saved him. I know now, I couldn't have saved him, but I resolved then, in front of my mother, and God, whoever or whatever he was, that as long as I drew breath, no one would suffer or die if I could help it. Her belief lighted a fire of desire in my soul for knowing and practicing medicine, and it has been there ever since."

The Plymouth hummed through St. Augustin Pass and rounded the curve at the top to start the long descent to the valley floor. Not more than a couple of miles down the road lay the little village of Organ. They could just make out the remnants of the Butterfield Stage road crossing Highway 70 stretched black and straight far below them. Off to the right, the bare Doña Ana Mountains sat stark and somber in the cold winter light. They were a sight they always looked forward to when they came back from Mescalero.

Roberta swung her arm around his shoulders and hugged him.

He grinned. "Easy, girl! You'll make me drive this machine right off the road!"

"So that was the beginning of Dr. Henry Grace? I always wondered how you came to be a doctor. It must have thrilled your mother when you told her that's what you wanted."

"Well, I just looked at her and said, I think that's a mighty fine idea. She didn't say a word, just smiled and nodded.

"It was past noon when we packed up the basket and started back to Las Cruces. It was hot and I didn't make the horse trot fast. We talked about whether we should tell my brothers and sisters I was alive. She agreed to let me decide when to tell them. We discussed college and medical school. She suggested I go back east for my education. She thought the best schools were there and told me she would pay for any university I chose to attend.

"I told her I thought I had enough money from what Rufus had left me. *Well,* she said, *let me know when you need money. Medical school is expensive!* I would rather have swept floors in an asylum than take money from her. Fortunately, less than half of Rufus's buried gold coins were enough to get me through.

"She insisted I move out of the hotel and come live with her until I left for college. I stayed in Jack's old bedroom. I heard her arguing with all my brothers and sisters about why she suddenly decided to take in a boarder. She certainly didn't need the money, and why this stranger of all people? It didn't help any when Marta told one of them that I had tried to sell her some land. The next day Albert was at my door, telling me in whispered threats that if I tried to swindle money out of his mother he would come looking for me with a loaded pistol. He looked so serious; I had to bite the inside of my lip to keep from laughing at him. I assured him that my intentions were honorable. I told him I just wanted to get some higher education before I left New Mexico, that his mother and I had become friends, and that she insisted I take a spare room she offered me. Albert frowned and stomped away with, *Just you remember what I said, Mr. Grace, or you'll be a dead man!*

"I learned how to use the library at New Mexico A&M and decided the best place for me to go to college and medical school was Stanford in Palo Alto, California. It was just getting back on its feet from the San Francisco earthquake and had joined forces with Cooper Medical School. I wrote the registrar there a letter and asked for admission requirements. It turned out it was a lot harder to get into medical school than I had expected. It helped if you had a college degree and had somebody say you were smart and a right fine fellow. So I decided I'd better go to college first, then to medical school. I wrote and asked when I could start in their college. They wrote back and asked to see my academic records and references, to determine my qualifications to associate with other fine young men at Stanford. I wrote and said I was a bush baby and didn't have any formal schooling. They wrote back and said there was just no chance of my success at their fine school."

Roberta nodded. She knew exactly the kind of brush-off he experienced. It had not been easy for her to get any medical training either. "Henry, it occurs to me that you had no more than a third-grade education when your father was killed and you disappeared. How on earth did you manage to go from the third grade to college without any education in between? I know you're a smart man, but you're not a genius!"

"Henry took his foot off the gas and slowed the Plymouth as they cruised through Organ, but when they were past the little village, he grinned and picked up speed to pass through the last twenty miles of desert before they reached Las Cruces and home. He grinned at Roberta's question.

"Pretty amazing fellow, eh? Actually, I was better educated than most of the fine young men who were being admitted to Stanford. Rufus had me read through his stack of classics before I was twelve years old. We talked about what they had to say nearly every night before I tried to shoot Stone and kicked over the anthill of trouble that got Rufus killed. After I let Oliver Lee go, I read them again and thought about what we'd discussed. Don't forget, too, that Rufus taught me enough arithmetic, algebra, geometry, and trigonometry to do surveying and to shoot the stars for navigating across the desert or the ocean. Except for composition skills, I'd say I was more than ready for college. I knew more than most of the seniors about to graduate.

"When it was clear Stanford didn't want me, my mother talked to some territorial politicians, old friends of my father, who knew Leland and Mrs. Stanford personally. She told them she wanted them to pull some strings for a bright young man she thought deserved to go to college. The next thing I knew I was on a train to San Francisco for a meeting with David Starr Jordon who was the Stanford chancellor.

"I met Dr. Jordon in his office on the campus where they were still rebuilding from the earthquake. We had a casual chat. He wanted to know how I came by my education. I told him I'd lived with an old desert rat who taught me the classics and the basics of surveying. We talked for a while, discussing philosophy, characters in *The Illiad*, and how accurate surveys needed to be. He asked my opinion about some of the classic ideas about ethics, politics, and leadership, right and wrong – the kinds of things I had discussed for hours with Rufus. To me it was just a casual conversation. You know, just a couple of men relaxing and shooting the bull. The interview was fun and easy and I kept waiting for the hard part. It never occurred to me that this talk was any kind of test. I must have spent an hour with Dr. Jordon when he turned to his desk and pulled out a sheet of stationery. With the fanciest fountain pen I'd ever seen, he wrote a note, signed it, folded the paper, and smiled as he handed it to me.

*It's been a pleasure chatting with you. Take this note down to the registrar and let me be the first to welcome you to Stanford, Mr. Grace! Your knowledge will represent our fine institution well and I'm sure you'll be successful. I expect to see you in convocation this Friday. Good luck!* And so I started my college education.

"I graduated from medical school in December 1915. I came back here to start a practive but got diverted by events beyond my control, like Pancho Villa's raid on Columbus. Those times are a tale for another day."

Roberta smiled. "I'll be waiting."

The road dipped down into the Mesilla Valley. They could see the first cluster of buildings on the outskirts of Las Cruces.

Roberta spoke softly from her heart. "Your life has been extraordinary. I could never have imagined all that's happened to you. Thank you for sharing it with me. As hard as it's going to be, I promise again that I'll never tell your story until you tell me I can."

"Thank you, dear lady . That means a lot to me. I thank you too for all you've helped me with this trip. I couldn't have gotten through it without your support. I have to say, that as blind and foolish as this may sound, this trip has been a revelation for me about the feelings I have for you, and have had for a long time."

She gave his shoulder a comforting squeeze. "I'm a mature woman, Henry. With me, you don't have to worry about things you said in the night coming back to haunt you during the day. I have strong feelings for you, but you don't have to make any commitments just because of things you said on this trip."

The look he gave her burned through her soul. They rode in silence for a couple of minutes. Without a word, he pulled off to the side of the road. He opened the door, got out, walked around to her side, and opened her door.

"Join me in the cold air of this beautiful afternoon." He said extending his hand to her. She was trembling inside as she took his hand and pulled herself out of the car. He led her to the front of the car and pointed across the desert toward a dark slash on the Organs to the south.

"That slash on the mountains is where I learned to be a man. My teachers taught me to always speak the truth and to never back up. I've deliberately killed some men and I've saved the lives of others. I've known many women and I never felt an attachment to any save my mother and one other, whose sudden death tore my heart out."

The wind swooping in swirls across the desert ruffled their hair. Roberta looked at him in surprise.

"Yes, she was part of my years in Mexico. I promise I'll tell you about them someday soon. After she died, I never gave a thought to marriage. I took my pleasure with all my lady friends, and then left them, never looking back. I'm sixty-four-years-old and have, in just the last three days, realized how incomplete a person I am without you. Here and now, in this cold wind with the mountains that raised me watching, I tell you from my heart I meant every word I spoke on this trip. I've lived most of my days already. The ones I have left I want to spend with you, on any terms you choose. Only...I beg you...don't send me away."

Roberta's eyes were wet as she turned, wrapped her arms around him, and laid her face against his shirt. She held him tight, like a drowning person tossed a life bouy, as she felt his arms enfold her. She whispered, but he heard her easily. "Hold me close, Henry Grace. Your days of being alone are done."

Printed in the United States
92681LV00003B/73/A

9 781595 260826